Spirit of the Straightedge

Spirit of the Straightedge

An Elsie Sanders Thriller

Babs Lakey

This is a work of fiction. Characters, places, and events are the products of the author's imagination or are used fictitiously. Any resemblance to real people, living or dead, companies, institutions, organizations, or incidents is entirely coincidental.

Copyright (c) 2001 by Barbara Lakey.
All rights reserved.
Printed in the United States of America

Over My Dead Body! Books
Post Office Box 1778
Auburn, Washington 98071-1778
www.overmydeadbody.com

Book cover design by Karen Lyster.

Library Of Congress Card Number:

ISBN 1-931616-00-0

Library of Congress Cataloging-in-Publication Data
Lakey, Babs, 1942-
Spirit of the Straightedge: An Elsie Sanders Thriller/Babs Lakey
   p. cm.
ISBN 1-931616-00-0 (alk. paper)
1. Adult child abuse victims --Fiction. 2. Revenge--Fiction I. Title.
  PS3612.A54 S65 2001
813'.6--dc21

To Lewis, my very tender man.

Thank You

Special thanks to Cherie Jung who has given me every writer's dream: a writer/publisher/producer/friend who believes in me and my books. This is only the beginning.

To my dear friend RC Hildebrandt who was there believing and prodding me forward from the start. Rosie said I was a writer until I believed it myself. Her editing wisdom is worth its weight in gold.

To my dear friend, Dawn Reno, whose advice always keeps me sane. And Ardy my Aussie great friend who helped me with *FUTURES* and thus gave me the gift of time to write, and Kiwi who made my image of the evil faceless woman shine in my mind and my many friends without whose love I couldn't have made it halfway here including my three pals from my writers group the "meet and eat." Including, Marcie Rendon who came into our motorcycle shop with my three manuscripts in her arms and face glowing, "I couldn't put them down, read them in two days, you're going to be famous." Ida Swearingen who saw to it that although she doesn't read this kind of book I did it right and got into that killer's head! And Ellen Hawley who came to our motorcycle shop's annual bike show to photograph me while I did a signing while thousands of bikers did burnouts and wheelies—noise and fumes rampant!

To my very special daughters—the very best thing life had to offer who make me prouder every day and fill my world with joy—Krissy, Jen, Trace. They helped me to believe my own words, "You can do anything." My children by marriage, Melissa and Christopher. My life has been so much better because of them.

To my glorious ten grandchildren who mean the world to me and absolutely may not read this book for at least thirty years.

To Momma who is watching over me and guiding me from above along with my brother Michael my personal Archangel. To my mom–in–law, the best of all moms, and my sisters and brothers through marriage whom I adore as they are just like their brother!

And to Lewis, my husband. The man who made my anger dissolve and became my best friend for life.

Prologue

I'm going to murder a man.

That fact has become my obsession, and obsession my master. This goal of mine controls my every waking thought and deed. It is a goal most women would never seriously consider, yet there is nothing I won't do to snare my prey.

Instinct told me that he would stay away from the restaurant where they met.

That same instinct helped me select my twelve–month–agenda. I'd waited one full year. I reasoned that he'd cower at the risk of returning sooner, but much longer and his vile appetite would seize his brain. He'd start to squirm, because although this wasn't the scene of the crime it was his pick–up–spot of choice and men were creatures of habit. He'd be back.

During that year I'd taken up a couple of habits of my own. My stark white walls were bare except for the calendar I'd tacked on the bedroom wall. Before bed I took a marker and blackened that day's square. If I closed my eyes I could flip through those pages of black blobs and count, seeing each one of them in my head. I'd never been a patient person, how could I be methodical now? Was someone, or some force from the other–side, nudging me—its will stronger than my own—along this path? I wanted to believe I was on a mission from above.

The months turned into seasons until my year in limbo passed. And when it passed I knew that I could begin the next phase of my plan.

Steel resolve, coupled with an air of expectation, joined me in my march into the Chit–Chat to apply for a waitress position on their morning shift. My best friend Lynn—inept words, she was more than a friend. Sister said it better—Lynn met the man I hunted when she worked on this restaurant's early shift.

In the beginning, that fact was about all I had.

I walked briskly through the restaurant door and "slap"—the scent of their house blend tea hit me hard. My knees buckled. That smell carried with it a heady collage of memories. I'd loved its spicy–sweet aroma from the first day Lynn brought it home. I hadn't used the tea or returned to our apartment since her murder.

I stood inside the door with my rubber knees and talked to myself. You'll gather some spine and work with that "homey" tea daily, I told myself. Either that, or give up this insane plan and go home, and have yourself a womanly weep.

That did it. My back straightened and the smell faded.

Determination got me hired on the spot.

Once working, I began to wait again. I changed the color of the marker I used to end my day; the new one was red.

Every single day I went to work expecting him, believing at the very core of me that he would come. I didn't have to imagine a monster behind every kind face.

And then one glorious afternoon, eight months and eight days after my first day on the job, months of wondering how many more "have–a–nice–days" were left inside my mannequin's smile, I bent over a just cleared table to wipe it clean and turned to see a man watching my behind. From out of the blue.

I looked into evil eyes and knew. Don't ask me how I knew. I knew. As luck or fate would have it, the hostess *brought him to my section. Yes, he'd done what I'd always known he would do. It was he who found <u>me</u>.*

The moment I'd waited for all these days, all these nights? It had arrived.

"You are a great undiscovered beauty," he flattered, as he extended his hand. His name, he said with a swagger, was Peter. The morning of her murder Lynn had told me his first name. I wanted to stun the beast poised slyly before me with a whispered, "But, I already <u>know</u> your name."

I pictured a tear streaked face, Lynn's face, as she talked about a man who wouldn't take "no" for an answer. This man. The fear from her voice rang in my ears.

I concentrated on keeping the corners of my mouth from turning up into a twisted mask of horror. Instead, I swiped my damp palms down the front of my starched white apron and with what I thought remarkable control, extended my hand to him.

I shook the cool, manicured hand of the devil.

Chapter One

I circled the block. On the second pass I drove past the house to the end of the street, parked at the curb, and got out. It was cold—the air heavy—the moon and stars blacked out by clouds preparing to dump a load of snow on the city. I looked over my shoulder toward the street. I'd chosen the car because of its lack of character; it was a perfect blend with the night.

Most of the neighborhood houses had lights on, shades up; made it easy to observe the people inside.

There was a chain link fence around their back yard and I stood by the gate. I watched a slight figure move through the house, check the door locks, then the windows. It was some dishy blonde—must be Lynn's roommate.

Lock 'em good, Babe.

I leaned into the shadows. It was a magnificent old house and it was strange to see a bare light bulb hang in what appeared to be the kitchen. The bulb gave the room a yellowish rooming–house–look that didn't fit the neighborhood. To watch her inside the house while I hid in the dark unnoticed, opinionating on their furnishings, thrilled me. I could do both women at once.

No. Stick to the plan. I'd never done two. And I had opening night jitters. At last I heard the front door close and roomie's footsteps clip, clip, away from the house.

I felt proud of my self–control. *If it's worth doing, it's worth doing it right*, squawked a parrot–like cliché. Was that from Joyce's book of rules–to–live–by? It was hard to think...my knees felt stiff...this powerful rush of adrenaline was a cloud over my blade sharp mind. I sucked in the cold air to clear my head and willed my pulse to slow.

I wore new shoes. The box they came in was snug as a bug under my arm. Inside the shoebox were several items, including leather straps. I'd considered using duct tape this time—but chucked the idea; there was nothing like leather. I loved the smell, loved the way it cut ridges in their skin when the twits twisted as they tried to wrench their way to freedom. Usually, that was first blood. First blood was best blood. I longed to watch it drip until it began its crawl over the sheets.

I wanted her sheets to be white. Lily white.

Sporadic fragments of savage past episodes flash—the flash is my mental strobe—making my temples hammer. I felt a quiver in my crotch. No, not yet. I must save Mr. Big–one for Miss Smart–mouth, the redheaded bitch.

Even in this euphoric state of mind I was clever, my senses heightened. I heard the thump of footsteps before I saw the figure in neon sweats. Someone was approaching fast—running towards me from down the alley—a late afternoon sprint for some health nut. Well, I'd anticipated even that. My free hand held a White Castle sack. I reached into the sack and forced the small burger into my dry mouth while I wandered away from the house, the fence, *and* the gate. *Um, um, good.* In an instant I'd transformed myself into a Mr. Any–guy, lumping around, stuffing his face. I almost laughed out loud at my cunning.

I smelled the onions before they touched my tongue. The moment of whimsey vanished, replaced by white-hot anger. Fireworks sparked behind my eyes. I took a breath to make the fury stop, to gain control. Control that froze the "fuck"—caged it in my throat. Instead of giving liberty to the oath I spat tiny chunks of onion on the sidewalk in disgust. It was the lesser sin, yet out of the corner of my eye I saw that the runner was now focused right on me. I felt his eyes and cursed myself. *That was a damn stupid move, you idiot prick.*

The fucker would want detailed knowledge of just who it was who littered *his* sidewalk. These people were clones. He was about to get a good look. With confidence I brought my shoulders back, my head up. I met his gaze with a howdy of a glad face that showed every tooth and made use of muscles never used.

I wished I could rewind my brain–film and see the bits of food leave the sidewalk and climb back over my lips. I'd called attention to myself and that was one of my golden not–to–do rules. Well, it wasn't my fault. I'd told that bitch behind the counter "no onions." No, I'd said, "no onions, *please*, Miss." Thinking as I said it—it would be a shame to ruin this breath. Want it *kissing* sweet. I should have checked and not trusted the twit. If you want it done right, you must do it yourself.

Walking again, chest no longer heaving, mind over matter. *Thank you for another of life's lessons, Joycie.*

I ate cold fries until the runner was out of sight, secure that his memory would give him a face full of teeth with no resemblance to me.

I flipped the bag at the trashcan in the alley and moved once again toward the back of the house. The streetlight glistened off of something in the gutter. Its glitter amused me. With another Grinch grin, I bent to inspect the refuse. An Old Style beer bottle. It looked far too sticky; my nose twitched at the thought of the filth that clung to it. Used condoms and other such memorabilia surrounded the brown glass.

Again, I forced myself to relax, to breathe, while I mulled. Could be a nice touch. Worth the effort.

I felt in my pocket. *Nothing there but my lucky pen.* I stuck it in the neck of the dark glass bottle, transferred the gutter–trinket to the inside of my shoebox and with reluctance tossed the pen at the trash. A shame, but the thought of using the pen to write ever again after it had touched such dung gave me the willies. I continued along the back walk, the gate

was now within my reach.
 I am a visitor.
 Time to visit.

I followed him that day, followed him to his office at the car dealership where he worked. His cashmere suit was evidence that Peter was more than a car salesman. Just what he did, I would discover soon enough. Driving slowly, I watched as he got out of his car and went inside. I felt a sharp pain in my chest—my heart strangulated in a fist of my own fear, my own knowledge of my plan, and what it would mean for me <u>and</u> for Peter. His name was an abomination, yet it handcuffed my mind. "Peter, Peter, Pumpkin Eater," my thoughts percolated. What lay ahead would mirror butter as it hits a sharp, hot knife— slip–smooth. . .silk–easy.
 Flowing blood.
 "This time it will be his blood." I said the words out loud as I tried to shove back images that strained to be set free of that frigid, manic room in my near–subconscious—the room where I housed horrific scenes from my past, as well as select previews of the future. Time to yank them from that skanky room and deal with the coming attractions.
 Alone in my car I realized the truth. It was now time for Peter to face the tomorrow his wretched soul had earned him. "Honey, I'm home," I whispered the words in a lame effort to mimic Mother Justice. While those words rolled over my lips I felt around in my purse for my one–hitter, put it to my nose and sniffed as hard as I could. I sighed, rotated the top, flipped the small bottle over, tapped more of the white powder in place, and stuck it in my other nostril. All with one hand. Modern ingenuity. You gotta love it. This habit was not as simple as the ritualistic marker. But I was careful. I would not let myself

get dependent. At the moment the cocaine calmed me; other times it did to my mind what the black marker did to the days on my calendar. A mind black–out. That was never one of its "advertised" side effects, but when you're a heavy user, it can do even that.

I drove up my driveway in a daze. Thick bile, the kind that real fear cooks, caked my throat. All these months I'd yearned to find him. Now, I knew where he worked. I had him! My skittering mind managed to focus on a slow, albeit clamorous, beat. All that while Peter stalked Lynn, had he seen me? I wasn't certain. If he had, it had been from a distance. No doubt he knew me only as Elsie, her roommate.

My movements were robotic. I put a pot of water on for tea and thought about the straight black wig I'd used to cover my blonde hair at the restaurant. Why had I bothered? It was uncomfortable, yet I'd thought it a necessary disguise. Believing I'd had to wear this fake hair, when I knew now that was not the case, was not a big thing in itself. But my success with this bastard meant that I must anticipate his every thought. My obsession with him had made me certain I knew him as completely as a talented lover's hands knew their subject's erogenous zones. The joke was on me! Why, he'd never have recognized me. His focus, his eyes, hadn't risen from my chest.

I stared at my reflection in the window over the kitchen sink. Perhaps this foolish disguise I'd rigged had helped make what I was about to do seem less than real. Was that it? I didn't or couldn't face my goal? Couldn't face his ultimate death at my hand? This past year had I only been pretending to be a character playing a role? Perhaps an actress in a dark classic Dostoevsky tragedy! Why I'd been playing at dress-up! Angry at my stupidity, I ripped the wig from my head and threw it.

The police investigation had failed to turn up the small-

est clue to the identity of Lynn's killer. I mentally discounted these many months—nearly twenty-two—that had gone by since the start of my plan. The fact that I'd found him this way, this easily, well, in my mind, it had to be our mutual destiny.

I watched myself in the window and leaned forward, resting my arms on the sink. My blonde hair was stuck to my head in matted clumps. I looked gaunt, a shell of my former self.

I was so angry. Furious. Why hadn't his hands felt slimy? I'd been so sure that they'd be puffy–soft and damp, that when I felt his hand today, his dry, cool, firm grip had shocked me.

The window image of me showed someone I could barely recognize. My eyes darted like a trapped animal. The tea ball fell from my trembling hand and hit the linoleum with a clatter that seemed loud in the silent room. I bent to retrieve it, my mind caught in the memory of his leer and the pressure of his loathsome hand on mine.

He was real, wasn't he? Flesh and blood like me? Those questions screamed inside my skull!

Suddenly I laughed. My roving eyes had hit on the wig as it lay motionless—it looked like a dead cat on my kitchen counter. Laughter was the release I needed and it wouldn't stop until tears blocked my view of the "dead-animal." I wiped the tears and looked back at myself in the window—the trapped image had faded, replaced by a woman with a heart of stone.

Sharpen your wits to a razor's edge, I told myself, or it'll be over. And over, with Peter, was dead.

I reaffirmed my strategy. This had to be my final day on the job.

I called the Chit–Chat and told them a story: I had to leave town; mother had taken ill. They were concerned. I *felt a twinge of guilt lying to people who cared. I tossed it off. Guilt was not a stranger.*

Everyone at the restaurant believed my name was Sally. When he returned, asking how to find me, and return he would, my identity would be protected. Of course he'd then forget me instantly—out of sight out of mind—and once again begin the search for his next undiscovered beauty.

If all went smoothly, I would be that beauty and his discovery of me would prove deadly.

Our futures were inevitable.

This was the moment I'd been waiting for, yet the actuality of what lay ahead crept over me with a chill that threatened to wither my spirit. I ignored it—telling myself that there could be no fear. Feverish, I began to hum the R–E–V–E–N–G–E song. That song gave me strength. It had been written for me and my butchered best friend on that terrible day she died. It had been written by friends, meant to add humor to our lives. Lynn didn't live to hear the words. What started as a cheerful joke was transformed into my personal dark anthem.

That night I slept without rest.

"Let it begin," I talked as I dreamed. I ran as fast as I could run all night while my plan nipped, then tore at my brain—a needle stuck in the groove of an old record album. Was I running after, or away from him?

My eyes opened. At last the sun was up. That terrifying first night had evolved into dawn. The secrets of the laciniated rabid room in my mind, had not just surfaced, but had taken over my consciousness.

It had begun.

To get a job at Bryan Mazda, where the monster works, will be a simple task. Still, I'll be cautious. I've not come

this far to be killed myself before his execution.
We'll work side by side. I shuddered.
Repulsive, but essential.
Now, it's not just an obsession, it's reality, and it's my reality.

I savored the details while I moved toward her house, including the night I'd first followed Lynn home.

I was sick of being respectful to the bitch. She got the point. My attitude that afternoon at the restaurant told the redhead how I felt. I'd made my decision. I was antsy to get on with it. Not like in the movies. I didn't *have* to do it. I'd proven that to myself. But once I'd made up my mind, why fuck around?

It was good humor—the way she fell for the bathroom routine that day at the Chit–Chat—I'd thought she was smarter. I went to the can and she snuck out. How could she think she'd given me the slip? I followed her home. Not only because I could. I wanted to check out her neighborhood.

Imagine my delight to discover she lived in fag heaven. "Those" people were so busy being girlie–polite, and out nice-ing one another they had no time to be suspicious of someone who looked this good. If they remembered anything, it would be my great ass.

So there you have it, I gloated, *Girls, and men who behave like girls. How harmonious.*

I walked around the block twice before taking a stroll up the alley. I'd run out without my jacket, not wanting to lose the trail. It was too cold to be without a jacket, but no one noticed; here fashion was more important than comfort. I got a kick out of catching the passers—by directly with my eyes. I wanted to say, "Hey, howdy–do. I'm a butcher—what do *you* do?"—my hand extended. *Probably not feasible.* But I gave them a good look all the same, and when they smiled invitingly, I'd nod. At least I knew my little secret. And, knowing what I was about to do made me start to swell. But no, a big hard–on now would not do. I felt smarter, in control of them. I could change my mind at any time—pick one of them instead of the redhead.

Fat chance. Ta–ha–ha, Red. Fat fucking chance.

...enough of memory lane. It would be easy. Dick–slick. She was like every woman I'd ever met.

Was.

Soon everything about her will be in terms of was, as in *used to be*. Christ, they were predictable. All tried to tell me what to do. I love to show them who is in charge. Me. It's me. I'm the one in charge.

This little redhead is a prick–tease–cunt.

I took one last glance down at my Reeboks, so new, so white.

Joycie always said, "Remember this, Peter, you can tell a man by the shoes he wears."

Right, Ma. You were always right. Check out these white fuckers. What do they tell you about the man, Ma?

The shoebox under my armpit felt damp. How was that possible? It was cold out. I could see my breath in the air. I tipped my head back and looked at the clouds. It could snow any second. I'd started to sweat. On such a cold day it made me feel good to sweat. Like I'd put in a hard, satisfying day at work.

Well, I was about to earn my daily bread. My heartbeat was rapid, no wonder I was dripping wet. Anticipation, they say, can be better than the actual event. That's often true, but not in this case.

"Here I come, Red," I said it softly, "ready or not."

Getting in was every bit as easy as I knew it would be. I'd stood back here often enough in the past week to be certain there'd be no surprises. Snip–slice and *in*. Whoopee! These withered old houses were not prepared for the likes of me.

Inside the back door was the kitchen. Once inside, straight

ahead across the room I saw a wide door; it went to what the redhead called the Ballroom. Told me all about the Ballroom when she was flirting at the start. Before she turned mean. I saw her piano from the doorway. This was indeed my Shangrila! There were two more doors. The one toward the right was her bedroom, the one to the left, the den. Good of her to have given me the "mental–blueprint" tour.

Their mutt was easy, too. A few scratches behind his ear and you were family—he was ready to follow you anywhere. "Pretty boy," I cooed in his ear. Mutt–butt followed me right into the den. A few pats, scratches, and tickles and he's content to lie back, settling down on the plush carpet for a short snooze. I closed the door and walked through the quiet house back to the kitchen.

Easy.

I pulled out a chair and sat at the kitchen table, tossed the shoebox on top of some spilled sugar. Something familiar here. My eyes roamed the things that made the place theirs. Could this *be* more perfect? Plenty of time. Time to sit, to feel the people who lived in this house. I took it all in—breathed it in.

What was that spicy scent? Tea and muffins? Ahha! Smelled like the restaurant. That was it! So fucking cozy, so small–townish, grandmother's house homey. I smiled and hated them all the more. Where were the signs of their swinging–single lifestyle? Too bad the roommate, the blonde, wasn't home. That'd be something. A double. My confidence was back—full force.

I frowned. The side of my hand felt sticky. I inspected the clean white flesh, then the table's Formica top. Must have been water from that sweet tea mixed with these grains of sugar. Careless. And irritating. I wasn't in the mood to wash. The sound of water running through the pipes could alert the sleeping bitch. I pushed the chair back and stood, grabbed my box, and thought, I'll wash my hand all the same.

I'll use blood instead of water.

"Little Red will lose her head," I sing–songed in a whisper. I turned the doorknob and was rewarded with a chill of fear. What if she had awakened, and had been lying in wait to attack her intruder! That possibility, however unlikely, accelerated my pulse. It felt like the descent on a roller coaster ride as I opened her bedroom door. It was a rush that made the hair on my body stand and salute. Each pore was alive and ready for action.

The light in her room was dim with only a small nap–light on the dresser for illumination.

I closed the door behind me and moved quietly to where I could see that the redhead was sound asleep. I stood beside the bed looking at skin pale as cream—splattered with freckles. A true redhead—that was obvious. Soon those emerald green eyes would flash fire. Oooh, I wanted to see that fire. This night the emotion behind them would not be anger, but fear. I savored the thought of her fear. I could smell the heat. It made me salivate.

She moaned and tossed her arm over the pillow. On her side now, I could see her breasts rise and fall with each breath. The knowledge that I was about to stop that movement forever set my own blood to boil. One glance at the veins in my forearms bulging with the heat of desire made me feel what I'd seen all my life in those movies when two destined–to–be–lovers meet—the heat of raw desire to possess another. It was worth anything to have this feeling overpower you.

How long could I stand here and watch her sleep until my thoughts penetrated her dreams and she awoke to scream?

An interesting experiment, but not practical at the moment.

It *was* time.

I moved fast, placed the shoebox on the right side of the bed. I undressed, except for my black socks, folded my clothes and placed them in a neat pile on the wine velvet chair that sat next to the bathroom door. I returned to take in one last glimpse of her swelled, heaving breasts. My body trembled with desire and I climbed on the bed and straddled her, one knee on each side of her form. She moaned and said what sounded like *Charlie*. The new boyfriend? Whatever. She'd soon be awake, but for now she was lost in dreamland, I could see it. I flicked the box cover to the floor with one finger and took out the knife. It was six inches long, with a tiny butterfly on the flat of the blade. The curves along the edge gave it a nasty, mean look. Similar curves in the handle made it fit my hand like a glove.

Comfortable and evil all in one small tool.

I was prepared to pounce in an instant and yet mesmerized by the soft moan deep in her throat that made what I began to rub on the outside of her thigh hard as a stone. *Oh, God, this is good.*

My breath came harder, faster.

Suddenly, without warning, her eyes flew open wide. Their hot green sea went from alarm to dread, then horror. I saw her mouth open just as the scream began and her body gave a violent twist to unseat me from this, my throne. Ah, but I had the advantage, thanks to Ralph, my old boy scout trooper who taught me everything about preparedness. I fell on her with all of my weight and pinned her arms back over her head. My knife looked like a bad way to die and I made sure she saw it clearly. Saw it and felt its sharp blade. I dusted the edge with blood from her throat. That got her full attention.

"P-p-p-et-er." That one word was a sentence that took her years of what remained of her lifetime to expel.

"Ah, my dove. I'm flattered. You remember my name, but stuttering is so unattractive. Try to speak clearly, would you?" I moved fast. Our first intimate act must be perfect and I was already close to coming. "In a moment I'm going to let go of your wrists."

I saw a flicker of hope, along with my own reflection, dance across her eyes. She nodded with those eyes without moving her head down against the blade.

"Do as I say and I won't hurt you, Red–dove."

Her arms were free of restraints but not at all free.

With one hand I yanked her head back, my fist filled with copper hair; with the other I held my knife to her throat. She did not move a muscle.

"Be still. Listen. I'd never hurt you, would I? You know how crazy I am about you, don't you? Or do you think I'm just crazy?"

Her skin glistened. Perspiration evoked by fear drooled from every pore. I buried my face in the side of her silken hair. It was damp. I caught a drift of lavender and rosemary. I felt her lower body tense under me. I asked again. "You don't think I'm crazy, do you?"

Lynn tried to answer with her eyes; they rolled from left to right and left to right and left to right. She was saying. . .no.

Oh sweet god, the power.

"Turn to your stomach. Stretch your arms to the bed posts." My voice was deep and filled with the strength I felt. The bitch moved as if in slow motion. This would never do. I was ready to fuck. It had to be soon.

"Do it." I boomed my command.

She shrunk as if my hot breath had seared her face. Then, just as her body went limp, she flung herself, one frenzied jerk. Her eyes were maniacal with desperation, arms swimming to bring her body upward, her mouth open in a snarl attempted to bite my hand that held the knife.

The fury of years of being pushed around by the world exploded inside me. I gave one hard punch to her jaw, heard the crunch of bones snapping. My fingers went around her throat and I cut the knife into the lobe of her freckled ear and sliced it off, just as her right hand raked my arm on its way to attack Mr. Big.

"Do it now or I'll kill that mutt!" I screamed as I rolled forward, saving my swollen appendage from her "fondling" nails. "Cut its throat. Right here." My breath punched in and out of my chest and I fought to keep from finishing her, fought to regain my self-control. "Here." I spit the words; my frenzy made my saliva bubble on her face. "I'll kill him right next to you on the bed, while you watch."

I wrenched her head back further and pressed on the knife till red drops ran like rain down her neck to the pale yellow sheets. I was angry. She'd forced me to do something I thought would never happen. I took great pride in the fact that I'd never done it. Hit a woman.

And I wanted white sheets. Fucking white sheets. Was that so much to ask?

"Pul-ee-eee-ase!" It was a wish of longing—a sigh for one last tomorrow.

"How would you like that?" The words came out a hissing rasp caught in my throat. My throat was dry, yet my mouth seemed wet with my own drool. I needed to fuck, not talk. Later we could talk. "After mutt–butt bleeds to death, we'll have our party with him right here on the bed, dead."

She sucked in air—a reverse scream of horror—and I knew I'd hit on the right button. Her face was soaked. It was her passionate desire to escape mating with my passionate desire to make her mine.

Sweat and spit.

I put my face down on the bed beside hers to demonstrate my lack of fear for her measly efforts to overpower me and spoke a few inches from her lips. "Want me to get doggie? Or do you understand?"

Her big wet eyes told me that yes, indeed, she understood.

Communication can be so simple.

Chapter Two

Elsie's body was wet with sweat. The sweat of fear. Her damp legs pushed her covers to the floor. She tried to "come–to," to come out of her dream, but it held her tight. And then she began to spin and fall, and. . .she could see that she was much smaller. Was she a *child*? There, above her on her ceiling was a child on a movie screen. *Was* it her? It looked like her. It had to be her. That child. . .that child who was *herself*. . .was in torment.

Her muffled whimpers turned into loud, terrifying screams. Tears overflowed her eyes, matting her fine blonde hair. She gasped for breath, her heart pounding, feet thrashing so hard her blanket flew to the floor. She kept running, trying desperately to escape. Fireworks of colors exploded around her; Crayon colors like the ones she loved to make pictures with, were blindingly bright. She was falling. "Oooooh! Momma, Momma!" she cried. It was going to get her—closer and closer, frothing, grabbing at her. The rosy fur that covered her small feet was dripping with a red slime.

She wasn't going to make it! Something snatched her with a terrible force, lifting her, and a blast of cold air hit her face; she sucked it in. Her eyes flew wide. She smelled tobacco and beer. Struggling to focus in the dark, she began to realize that the fiery monster had been a dream; she was in her Daddy's arms.

She heard her Momma's voice—but the voice was a whisper—as though she herself were afraid. "Eddie, come back to bed. Eddie, please, you know you need your sleep."

Didn't Momma hear *her*?

She felt a furry tickle that gave her goosebumps. Daddy was cramming those gummy rabbit slippers onto her feet! The slippers she'd once loved now turned to monsters in her dreams. They appeared to be bunnies, but she knew they had a mean side. "No, Daddy. . .Pl*eee*ase, Daddy!" Her lip quivered.

He didn't stop; he yanked her outside.

His body was rigid with anger; he slammed her against the cold concrete driveway. She could see the veins on his temple stand out as he leaned over her. "You will learn that there are no monsters out here," he said, his hot spit spraying her face, "and if there are, you'll learn to shut your goddamn trap. Don't you *ever* wake me again. Six years—you're too old for this shit."

The look in his eyes, first wild with anger, was replaced with an evil glint. "I'll teach you. I want you to walk *all the way around* the outside of this house," he was beginning to sneer like a monster himself, "and after that, if the monsters haven't bitten off your legs so you *can't walk*, maybe I'll let you inside. I bet you'll be able to keep your damn mouth shut then." His face loomed over her. "Get your ass up and get moving!"

She watched him turn his back and stomp inside. He slammed the door with such force her chattering teeth clenched tight. Ordinarily quick and athletic, she rose slowly, heart thudding. The night was pitch black. She trembled. Did he mean for her to go *alone*?

The wind tugged and tore at the few leaves that held stubbornly to their branches. Elsie could feel the cold burn her bare arms and legs. She glanced toward the house. In the dark she saw shadows that she knew were monsters that waited to grab her. She hesitated. Should she try to sneak back inside? The curtains moved. Daddy watched from the kitchen window. He frightened her as much as what lay behind the shadows. The clouds shifted; a sliver of moon lit his face—*his eyes glossy with a reddish hue*—sliding downward until it settled on sneering lips. Chills raced up and down her spine. Her feet seemed to be frozen in place on the concrete beneath them; rocks that scattered the drive had left her knee skinned and bleeding. Fear gripped her by the ankles.

She jerked, moving as if he'd given her a boot in the butt, as he called it, onto the lawn. The tall grass rubbed its frozen fingers against her feet and legs. Involuntarily she yelled again, "Momma?"

The answer was the wind as it twisted through the yard. It whispered, "Come little girl, step into these shadows." Its whisper changed to a howl, then to laughter which became a screeching wail. Her arms squeezed her body tight; she tried to make herself smaller, invisible. The wind shifted. Moonlight hit her flaming pink feet making them blaze. They were on fire! Run, she told herself, get away!

Elsie ran into the crying wind. Icy air filled her lungs.

Rose bushes reached out to claw her pink arms and willow branches hung down to whoosh against her cheeks. The bloody rabbits clutched at her feet, moonlight slashed through the treetops. She whirled while the wind spun her around; its icy bogeyman grabbed at her legs.

She slipped on the wet grass and pitched forward, fell with a splat and lay moaning. No matter how fast she ran she could never get away from these monsters. They were attached to her feet. Hopeless with exhaustion she lay shaking. Minutes passed. At last she dared peek through her hair and saw the kitchen door. She'd made it.

She brushed away dirt and bits of gravel, wiped her wet face and runny nose, and limped to the back stoop.

Her pint–sized shoulders shook. She crept timidly inside. There were no lights on in the house and the dark felt spooky, but she was relieved to be safe. Daddy and Momma were in bed. She moved on tiptoes, fearful of waking them. Once inside her room, she sighed, barely noticing her scraped knee was cut. Blood trickled down her leg landing on the bunny head. The fear she'd just felt was replaced with something else. She tore the slippers from her frozen feet and threw them at her closet door with all of her might.

Moonlight streamed through her window; the white glow sizzled over the scissors that lay on her dresser. Her eyes, watching that silver flicker and dance, blazed with anger. The furnace blower came on, making her jump; hot air felt like tiny needle pricks on her frozen skin. Her cold red fingers slowly picked up the scissors and attacked the unfriendly fur. Clumps of pink landed on her toes and floated in the air around her. The gleaming button eyes gave her a hideous glare as she snipped and watched them fall to the floor. The slippers had been an Easter present filled with rainbow colored jellybeans. Carefully, she replaced the scissors, and with suspicion eyed the animals. They did not resemble bunny–monsters now. Still, she stuffed them in the very back of her closet.

For a time, she leaned against the closet door, and then pushed her child–sized chair under the knob to make sure they would not come out again.

Their hippity–hoppity days were over.

Later, as she tried to sleep, she prayed that Baby Jesus would keep her from crying out in her dreams and make her the good girl Daddy would love. She would not scream again, she thought. She'd not let that sound slip out her mouth. Daddy must not be disturbed.

Elsie tossed and turned in her bed. Her dreams flashed

from today to long ago and back again.

If finding him had been easy, it was only because every day that passed I felt more as if I were the death goddess in training—the apprentice. My days were fairly normal, yet my nights were filled with madness. I was a raging animal caught up in a feeding frenzy—then, a sick child/woman—shivering and vomiting with the reality of what I was doing. I picked up men just for the practice, to know I could. With each setting sun came the dark, a black void that was a twin to the state of my soul, with that darkness came dreams of the past:

She moaned, "No!" She hugged her pillow to her breast and cried into it, trying to crawl out of this cave she was in, yet fearful of what was outside in wait for her. The movie began again and while she watched, her eyes clenched inside the hand of the devil, she whispered, *"this is a dream, only a dream,"* and then felt it, as the child that was herself returned to the woman that was herself and she heard the laughing voice of the devil say, *"It's a dream all right. A dream of what really happened, wanna see, it again, Elsie? Come, see it one more time with me."* And now she knew what played inside her brain, what filled her soul, what screamed and suffocated her whole being with pain. But she knew she was too late to save her friend. Her terror encased heart roared, *"Lynn!"*

Time to bind the bitch's wrists. I sniffed at the leather after tying her to the posts—my knee in the center of her shoulders—leaving her just enough slack to move her body under me the way I liked. Did the leather smell of other women's sweat and blood or was it my memory that brought those old scents back? No matter. Either way the smell was there for me.

I rolled a small Girlie sock, one that belonged to my oldest daughter, stuffed it in her mouth, and then whipped the roll of duct tape around her head. I didn't want to put too much in her mouth, but enough to keep our fun from annoying the neighbors. These old homes had such nice thick walls. Much of my enjoyment was in being able to hear her attempt to scream. What point would there be in this ritual of domination if I could not hear her complete and abject terror? I kept the tape from covering her ears, so she could hear me and because of the blood. An ear that is cut bleeds profusely. I took that bit of information and filed it for future pleasures.

"Bleed, baby, bleed." I noticed how the shiny mucus–like liquid spread—a slow fire under her head.

Secured and helpless, my little carrot–top now had a halo. Carrot–top to Beet–top!

Getting there *is* half the fun.

I began to explain to her how she was going to suffer wretchedly and how she would struggle (it was her nature, she couldn't help herself). "I just want you to know that with every buck of your butt, every twist of your body, I get harder—that's what makes me want to keep going until I've fucked you to death."

"Literally."

I could barely wait.

I grabbed her buttocks and spread them, guiding my stiffness with one hand. I was in position, ready to enter her lair. With one exquisite thrust, I plunged deep and hard. My mind was a deep purple mass hit with intermittent electric explosions. I burst immediately to the sound of her wail behind the tape.

It was worth the wait—she was virgin there.

I pulled it in and out, painfully slow—ready to come again—I could think of nothing but coming again. She thrashed and bucked. "Hold still, you fucking bitch woman," I rasped, knowing it would throw her into frenzy. I rammed harder, as hard as I could—wanting to stab her

SPIRIT OF THE STRAIGHTEDGE

to death with myself. So damn good. It was hard to stop.

But why stop? I picked up the knife again; the cold smooth feel of the handle drove me once again to the edge. Just as I spurted inside her ass, I stabbed the knife somewhere in and saw blood fly against my chest. My mouth and throat were parched; I swallowed for liquid and air. I'd begun to slip and slide in something wet. The blood was thick around her head; she choked and spit to breathe. What was she trying to say?

"iiiirrrrl!"

I bent closer to hear what she said and to see the fear in her eyes. Fear, that would make Mr. Big ready to ride again. Instead of fear I saw contempt! It seemed as if she was trying to spit at me, spit the word. Was she calling me a girl? I could feel my nuts shrink back and crawl up my ass. The room began to swirl around me as blood rushed back to my head. I felt hot. I felt fear.

"Girl?" I asked in disbelief. *"Did you say, girl?"* I must know.

Her head nodded frantically up and down. Yes! She said it without fear of me! I scrambled to grab the knife I'd dropped beside her breast, slipping on the wet sheets and her wet behind. The sight of that would have made me hard just minutes ago. But now, I needed more.

I took the knife and cut her flesh.

Soon I was an artist, making ribbons of her back. I felt myself return to the previous splendor.

Splendor in the ass. I laughed out loud.

I'd never seen this much blood. I took a photo with my mind. Doing a mental rerun would make me like steel. Oh, the beauty of it. I didn't just get to do it once and then—over forever (as it was for Lynn, the bitch). I got to play my tape often in my mind. It was mine to keep. I owned the copyright. It belonged to me. Just as she did. The *girl section* had already been edited!

I'd never been hard as many times in one "session." The way she fought. What a tiger. She bucked and humped like a crazed animal, while I hung on, slipping and sliding to ecstasy. She tried with terrified desperation to escape. She can forget that. *I* am in control.

If only I'd remembered to bring the riding crop! I could whip her ass as she tried to buck me off! What a spitfire. Could I pick them, or what? The fact that she wasn't tied down too tight gave her just enough hope. I wanted her to be able to move. I'd left slack in the leather straps and, man, did she move. I could have continued, but instinct told me time was growing short. I'd saved the best for last. I took the beer bottle and stuck it inside that red curly bush. I punched the bottom of the bottle. Hard. It nearly disappeared inside her.

She stopped the frantic bucking.

No more fighting to get free. Her green eyes no longer blazed. Her days of telling a man what to do were over. That's all she wrote, Red–Baby. This was the way to control a woman like her.

Control. The word alone made me stiff. I was a machine. I wanted to get inside her white fanny again, but there was so much blood, I couldn't be sure of where to stick what. Hate to make a mistake and cut Mr. Big. I'd have to settle. I stood, in the position of dominance, legs straddling—one on either side of her motionless form—I gripped myself and shook off all over her backside. I knew I looked like a Greek god. Or Michelangelo's statue of David. This was my birthright as a man and it thrilled me to the core.

I turned and with a leap landed on the floor at the very head of her bed.

She was still as stone.

I remembered her heaving breasts and smiled. Leaning over I kissed her cheek and then smacked her lips wet with thickening blood. *"Sssssmack!"*

My right hand still held the knife. It was difficult to see through the red goo. "Got to boogie, Red–Babe, sorry, but I don't want to leave anything to chance." I took my thumb and swiped a smear of blood off to feel her chin bone. Quick then, with a flick of the wrist, I sliced her throat.

I jumped around to face the dresser mirror. My body was in the pounce position, arms held out, one hand held the knife. I was covered in blood; my sanguine lips blew myself a kiss. Time for a quick shower. Places to go, things to do. That was all right. My mind would always hold the tape of this grand event.

This will be the last time, I told myself, heading toward the bathroom door. I watched the thick footprints that followed me across the carpet.

I was too smart not to stop.

Prick–tease. I'd shown her.

Fucked.

To death.

I took a deep breath of the icy night air and stepped outside wearing my old gym shoes. Lynn's shoes (as they would forever be known to me) were carefully placed inside the shoebox. The fresh air was exhilarating on my scrubbed squeaky–clean skin. Puffs of air like smoke came out of my swollen lips and I reminisced of blowing cold air smoke rings as a child. The snow that had been forecast had not begun to fall. Was God on my side? It was great to be alive!

I drove straight to the storage shed behind my house. Inside, I saw a thick blanket of dirt and dust on the old trunk. It had been a long time since I'd touched it. The trunk was heavier than I remembered, and I cursed as I lifted it down. The room smelled like mold. If it weren't filled with such momentous items I would have been very upset by the dirt.

I stared in anticipation. My palms sweat. I could barely wait to feast my eyes on what lay inside. Memories. I allowed myself to come to the trunk on these occasions, never in–between, because what I was about to see made me want more. I practiced self–control. I relished the moment. I closed my eyes letting the feeling bathe me. It was then that I realized I'd forgotten my leather straps! My heart raced. . .then, slowed. They couldn't be traced to me. What did I care? This was my swan song.

I stooped to open the lid.

Dust mites flew out and I wheezed. There they were. Five pair of shoes. This made six.

"Here's one more for you, Joycie." I removed them from the box and set them inside—with care. If only the bitch were alive. I'd give both my nuts to show her this trunk. It'd been nearly two years since the last time I'd opened it. Two long years. I sucked in the musty air of canvas, leather, and blood that scented that old trunk. The dead bitches' blood caked on shoes that had danced on their graves, figuratively speaking. About to turn, I re-membered and stuck my hand in my pocket for the final souvenir from my evening of love. The small piece of flesh I held had an earring that dangled—a musical note. It would be fun to keep it out to play with, but no, I'm not that stupid.

I let the top bang shut, heaved the old treasure chest up to the rafter, went to the door and flipped off the light with a grin of satisfaction. Why stop now? Just because I'd let some leather straps slip my mind? Maybe I could do just one more if I waited long enough. And I was good at waiting. When the going gets tough, the tough get go-ing, or blowing maybe? They get themselves blown. Yes. The bitch would blow me right before her expiration date.

Hey Ma, baby needs a new pair of shoes.

The devil's laugh was a siren of glee. Elsie heard other voices, too. *"There is power in the blade,"* they chanted. *". . .power in the blade. Ride the blade, fly with the blade."* She turned and hugged her knees. She didn't watch. Yet she knew. This part she knew not because it was shown to her, but because she'd lived it, she'd been there.

Elsie hurried toward the house—shivering, anxious to feel that blast of heat from the furnace.

"I'm glad that we could have our little R-E-V-E-N-G-E," she sang. The closer she got to their house the faster she moved. At last her hand was on their front doorknob. She entered the living room and stood, listening to the silence. There was that feeling again. *Déjà vu.*

"Lynner." Her voice was unnatural, loud and cheerful. The large empty room that they jokingly called the ballroom echoed. She heard Pip scratch and wail at the den door. She hadn't put her dog in the den. Why would Lynn have shut Pip in there? Elsie stopped and listened to his whine. She blew out a breath of air and opened the door a crack. Pip leapt and almost knocked her over. Another time she'd have laughed and rolled with him on the floor but she felt strange.

She looked towards Lynn's bedroom door. Closed. The house quiet now that Pip had stopped. Except for that back screen door—it clattered and wailed.

Bang–*wang*, bang–*wang* with the wind.
Wait.
I locked that screen.

She opened the kitchen door that led to the back yard and saw the cut screen. "Pip," her voice was a monotone, "come here baby. Get now. Get on out there." She had to shove his butt to get him out the door. He turned to stare at her with big sad eyes. Why didn't he jump on the screen the way he usually did? Why the sudden manners?

The kitchen felt wrong, like a place without heart; she thought of a song line something like "a town without pity." She sat at the table. This cozy space of theirs didn't feel the same. It felt violated. Her eyes returned to Lynn's door.

"Lynn." She said the name again. Not loud.

The screen. Why was it cut?

Could Lynn have left the house, gone out with Charlie? Maybe then tried to get back inside for Charlie's forgotten car keys? No. Not and leave Pip locked in the den.

The teapot sat on the stove while the cups and saucers they'd used earlier in the day cluttered the sink.

I should clean up these dishes.

Through the doorway she could see the piano. It sat alone in the ballroom. Elsie felt alone. She thought of the music Lynn played everyday. Beethoven. The Rolling Stones. Buddy Guy, Muddy Waters, Charlie Parks. Miles Davis. Mozart. Hank Williams. That was one happy piano. It lived to throw a variety of musical impulses, sounds, and styles from its keyboard at anyone who'd listen. From Lynn's soul, to her fingers, to the keys, to your heart.

For some reason Elsie pictured a little white plastic radio that she'd had as a birthday gift. Daddy had smashed it against a wall one night.

She pushed herself up from the table and walked the few steps to Lynn's room.

Elsie rolled to her stomach and pounded the bed until, spent, she curled to one side and brought her knees up under her chin, a babe inside momma's womb. *Overhead voices chanted, it is all connected, it is all connected. .*

.all connected." The movie flashed overhead and she turned her head to see, unable to ignore the woman she knew was "her." Or Lynn. Lynn was gone but was still with her.

It was five hours before they were found.
Pip would not stop barking. That wasn't like him. One of the neighbors became concerned and called the police.
The police arrived to find the front door stood wide open. The first cop inside said later that the house felt like an abandoned tomb.

"His blood will fall like rain." Elsie opened her eyes for a second, still asleep but aware of a change. She rubbed her ear and the voices stopped. She stretched. Her position changed from one of unborn babe to a woman of strength. The damp that had covered her skin evaporated and although she still slept she felt the warmth of the sun on her body.

I carried the yolk–yellow wicker basket that I used for gathering flowers and herbs from my garden outside. Spring was in the air. I loved my garden; I had been working on it for two years. It was part of the plan—and more satisfying to me than most anything I did. I paused, breathing in the aroma of the fragrant flowers that soothed my spirit.

The herbs were doing well for so early in the season. Starting the seeds in my greenhouse window in early January was the secret. I cut a few sprigs of European Pennyroyal. Their minty aroma was irresistible. Knowing this herb could cause convulsions in humans, I always wore gloves and used great care.

I used Pennyroyal for a variety of things. It was a good mosquito repellent; it also made the garden wasps that were sometimes a bother decide to nest elsewhere. I was careful, not wishing to kill them; there's no room in my conscience for tiny yellow corpses.

Picking off dead blossoms here and there, I poked my way towards the back of the house, to the west side by the woods. This wooded area tenanted the most bewitching of all my collection of wild flowers: breathtaking, mysterious plants that thrived in dark, moist, decaying soil. The plant that drew me to the woods today—Atropha Belladonna—had juicy black berries that made it easy to spot. The plant was named after the goddess Atrophos. In Greek mythology, she was one of the three fates.

She who cuts the thread of life.

These purple–inky berries could be made into a juice that was every bit as sweet as I knew my revenge would be. They were spectacular to look at, but of more significance to me, if properly used, they could be deadly.

Standing in these woods gave me comfort. The very idea that this black, fertile earth would eventually devour us all filled me with wonder. This earth, this was my Mass now. My gloved hands overflowed with the plump velvet berries. I resisted the impulse to squeeze, and I considered the awe–inspiring goddess, Atrophos.

She took her duties as goddess seriously.

My mind tripped over the name—Elsie Atrophos. I was certainly not a goddess, but this particular one interested me very much. My Belladonna plants had been bearing fruit now for close to a year. The berries were a sedative, a narcotic, and an anodyne. In small doses they would stimulate—in larger, paralyze—larger still. . .I smiled.

When Lynn and I moved to Minneapolis, I'd studied herbs voraciously. Was that also fate? Regardless, it proved worthwhile. The ringing telephone interrupted my musings. I ran with the berry basket full and spilling over the sides into the kitchen—pulling off a sticky glove to pick up the receiver.

"Hello. . .yes, this is El." It was the Mazda dealership—not Peter—someone from the office.

"Certainly. . .yes, Monday would be a most convenient day for me to start."

"Oh, yes, thank you so much for calling." With the utmost care, I replaced the phone. Standing in the center of the room I stared at my still bare feet. . .fertile earth that each day devoured life from the woods, held fast to my feet.

I took another deep, cleansing breath.
I breathed in the energy of the earth, and with it, power.

Elsie let out a yelp. She'd slammed her foot against the bed stand. Wide–awake, she stood and for a second or two wondered where she was until she noticed that her hand held the telephone. Sleepwalking again. She dropped the phone in the cradle. Her dream had been vivid; it clung and left her with jelly–knees. It was more of a memory than a dream; it was real. Oh yes, it was real. She felt the power of the universe surge through her body and close its fist around her.

She *was* the goddess.

Chapter Three

Law stood six feet three inches tall with thick black hair that had begun to fade around the temples. At forty–five, he was okay with his broad physique, including love handles that were the result of gravity's summons.

Marilyn, his ex–wife, left one day and never returned. *Cut deep, cut quick.* He'd faced it and eventually recovered. What he found far more difficult to face was the way his forehead had grown. Plentiful and wavy hair had been his best feature. *Had.* This hair thing cut deeper each day. It made him look like his younger brother who'd lived with this problem for years. "Hey! You're gonna catch cold. Here wear my baseball cap." More often that not, when he looked at his mug during his morning shave, his smart-mouth sass boomeranged—splat! It hit him where he lived. Law had enjoyed giving the kid a ration of shit about it—seemed hell–*air*–eous. Luckily he hadn't seen much of family in the past decade; paybacks were hell. His sense of humor seemed to vanish when it was his turn to pay the tab.

He broke down this year when Walgreens had bifocals on special. That he didn't need them was another lie he told himself. He didn't! Only if he wanted to see. He kept a second pair hidden in his desk at work. Why the hell couldn't they make a menu with print big enough to read? He found himself eating at the same old places where he knew the menu by heart.

Even workouts were harder. He didn't do that as much as he used to, but enough so he could still roll the shirtsleeves to expose his upper arms when he was out in the hot sun. He knew those biceps would soon turn to flab if he didn't get back to work. The old Catch–22. He promised himself he'd find more time. Tomorrow. Who was it who said, "When I die, I don't want to be healthy, I want to be sick."— Rodney Dangerfield, or W. C. Fields? Made sense.

His name was Gerald Lawrence. *"Why give a kid two first names?"* he often wondered. Well, no matter if it made Ma happy. No one called him by his first name anyway. They called him Law. Short for Lawrence. And, in a way, it was because of his job.

He was a cop.

Law's blue eyes were surrounded by creases he'd had since he was a lad and barely noticed they were there. In those days people said he looked tired but now he figured it somehow worked to his advantage, softened the whole area so the blue was bluer. Sometimes women commented. One said his eyes were filled with yearning. Actually now and then, he felt a yearn. Like now, he'd been thinking about innocence. You might say he yearned for it.

Not much innocence going around these days. Didn't take any thought at all to remember when he'd last been struck. It was Elsie. Maybe four years back, maybe only three. . .in Kenwood. He could see her sitting there as if it were yesterday; the Twins' T-shirt she wore was soaked in blood. Her mouth was open to scream, but—she was mute that day. Wasn't likely that he'd ever forget her. Not the minutest detail.

Detective Gerald Lawrence thought back over the details. The case where he'd met Elsie, the young woman who'd had that aura of innocence. Met her and been unable to solve the murder of her friend Lynn, the redhead. He'd been on temporary assignment in the Kenwood district. One of the locals had been shot and they were combing the area with no real enthusiasm or hope of apprehending the assailant. As he remembered, it had been mid–November; he got picked for the assignment because he had a motorcycle and loved to ride. He'd been pissed that because of that love he'd had to take on what the precinct bigots called fag patrol. He knew the time of year, not because of his great memory, but because he was sent to the streets on his cow—Kawasaki KZ1000 shaft–drive. Damn near froze his nuts clean off.

The plan had been that on his cow he'd look "tough" and as a result many of the guys in the area—well known for its homosexual residents—would be pleased to let him pump them. Pleased to be pumped, the precinct goons smirked at him. No pun intended, they laughed. Any fool knew that was exactly what they intended. Law hated to listen to their bullshit worse than riding in the stone–cold. The bike wasn't what made him look tough. The cow was a rice burner. The "tough" part came from riding it in the dead of winter, in Minne–*freezing*–sota.

He missed Elsie. Been missing her for years, he guessed. He'd no idea what to expect that day he walked into the old mansion. Violent smells and colors assaulted his senses, and there she was, sitting on the bed in a pool of blood that seemed to rise like the tide as he watched. She looked small…smaller by the second and the blood was a risin' fast and furious. He remembered thinking, "damn, this kid's gonna disappear! She'll drown." She'd been caged in some freakin' time warp and the rapids of blood were about to carry her away!

Not a sound in the room—just that pooch barking in the back yard and the screen going *slam* with the rhythm of the wind.

Right then, he'd thought she had to be bleeding too, and he guessed in a way she was. But on the inside—in the heart area. They'd discovered soon enough where all the blood came from; it was from her best friend—from the redhead. Rusty–red patches blotched Elsie's skin, matted her hair. The only way he could help her was to get her the hell out. And that wasn't hard. She wouldn't be answering any questions for a while anyway.

The scene returned to him clearer than he desired:
"Vince!" Law shouted. "Get your fat ass in here and bring Sara with."

To Law's amazement, they both appeared. What do you know? Sometimes it worked—sometimes it didn't. He checked his watch. 1:15 AM. He could see that the one that was alive wasn't in any shape to go anywhere but the hospital. "Officer Tonetti, have Officer Mitchell help you remove this girl," Law nodded in Elsie's direction. "Take her to Hennepin General for observation."

"Sara," he continued, taking mental note that Officer Sara Mitchell was damn pale. "I noticed a purse on the kitchen table, see if it belongs to one of them. Maybe it has an ID so we can locate next of kin. I'll stop at the hospital later. Look in on her." Again he nodded toward Elsie, "When I'm finished here."

There was no indication Elsie heard them. She hadn't moved. She sat Indian–style on the bed; both hands held her friend's arm. As they started to move her she dropped that dead, blood–encrusted arm and covered her ears with her hands. It seemed strange at the time, but thinking back now, he remembered that when he'd asked her about it later that night at the hospital she'd said that the screams in her head were unbearable. But right then as his crew prepared to take her away she'd begun humming sporadically—a lifeless dull tone. She didn't seem capable of conversation. Law never learned what the tune was. It sounded sorta like an old Tammy Wynette ditty. What was that one? Where she spells? Moxnix.

To say the crime scene was brutal and bloody was to understate what the redhead must have endured.

The body bruises that were covered in blood were not discovered until the autopsy. Her skin was shredded—spaghetti style. Even then, he knew she'd been horribly beaten. The appearance of the body coupled with his own experience told Law that it was ejaculate that covered her backside including the back of that beautiful red hair. His eyes took in the physical restraints. Law thought about the killer. It would take a wild animal to do this. There were thick leather ties caked with blood, garish red duct tape across her mouth and around her head. Does he feel more man, less monster, when he's rendered someone helpless? Ringlets of red hair were matted with dried blood and globbed with semen. Grotesque.

How could any one get his jollies out of this? To torture someone much smaller and physically weaker. Familiar questions thundered through his mind. No answers though. One thing was certain—her death had not been quick and it had not been easy. The bloody footprints showed what the animal had done at the end of his deed. Pounced and posed his dripping body in front of the mirror to glimpse the horror with pride.

Law's eyes scanned the room. It was filled with piano music and posters. The eyes of Wolfgang Amadeus Mozart stared down on him. Those eyes held a look of sadness that seemed to see right inside Law's soul. Did *they* hold blame? Did they look at this detective and judge him for his weaknesses, or was it his imagination?

If only he could detect as Amadeus composed.

Law felt a burning in his gut and popped an antacid. Heartburn, the occupational disease. Cliché of all clichés. Often true, and not always from doughnuts and fast food as the public likes to believe. Sure, the lifestyle saw that they got plenty of that crap, but the real heartburn came from the stench of death.

Her purse lay on the dresser, its contents strewn about. He pushed through them with his fine point pen. Brown mascara rolled free and fell to the floor. He found her driver's license. Lynn Fahey. She was twenty. Red hair, green eyes, a smile that could light a large room. The photos inside were of her and the blonde. In one of them they looked to be about twelve. So they'd been friends for many years. Another antacid found its way to his mouth. He turned to leave with one last guilty glance at the great one's poster, vowing to himself and the green–eyed dolly, to find the animal that'd done this. Find him and then what? Put his faith in the system he worked for.

Flap, flap–wham.

The screen door kept it up, like he used to be able to do himself if memory served him, and it probably did not. A cheap joke at any rate. It made him think of the pooch. He went to the backyard, unable to ignore the animal's pitiful moans. "C'mon boy. Your girls can't see you tonight. C'mon home with me." Law bent to scratch its ears. This would be a long night for everyone. Except the redhead. She was at peace.

He couldn't get the other girl, Elsie, out of his mind. A pit stop at the hospital on his way home didn't help. They'd cleaned her up. Her face was the shade of some old cracked pottery dishes his mother used for special occasions. Bone white, Mom called them. They looked colorless to him and he'd always wondered why she had such regard for them. Have to remember to ask her that, you never know when the chance will come again. Elsie's hair was no longer matted with blood, but her eyes were crusted.

She looked innocent and vulnerable.

It was weeks later when that look began to change.

"Law! Hey! Wake the fuck up!"

Law opened his eyes to see the Lieutenant's two hundred and fifty pounds tower over the semi–dozing, day–dreaming body of his detective—him. Okay, he was busted. Thought crime. The department frowned on unauthorized thinking.

"Would it be too much trouble, *Detective*, for you to haul your ass and your intellect, should you possess one, over to my office? I want to be briefed on your progress on these 'bite-it' murders." He threw the paper he was carrying at

Law's desk and slammed out the door.

His aim's not what it once was, thought Law, as he bent to retrieve what had fallen at his feet. That put a smirk on his face that disappeared quickly as he realized how much further the distance to his feet was getting to be. "Aaarugh." With a grunt he picked it up.

"The *Nationwide Examiner* for crissakes." he said out loud, but talking to himself.

A headline on the front page caught his eye. He opened it, as it directed, to page six—then sat straighter. "Whoa."

There he was. Law faced himself in the paper. Looking for all the world as if he didn't have a care in the world. Great. Where did they get this shot of him? Well, wherever it was taken, maybe he should take a trip back. He looked almost pleasant. The headline was real cute:

LAW BITES IT!

The tabloids ate this shit right up. *Bite–it killings*. Now that the bite–it aspect had somehow leaked to the press the shit had hit. National press. Christ. He threw the paper. Not the time for reading this crap.

Every man in the city who relished being tied during sex, and there were more than you'd care to imagine, thought Law, at least more than he cared to imagine, well, they were all at risk. Although most of the calls to the station were anonymous, they (whoever "they" were) were putting big time pressure on the brass. And, shit gets passed in a down hill fashion, etcetera. Right now it was an avalanche of dung ready to plop on his head. Being buried in shit was not his idea of a good time. Hell, it was probably some of the brass that was the most worried.

Law fumed. You can just damn imagine, how pleased and proud he felt when they announced to the press that this bite–it case was being headed by yours truly, Detective Gerald Lawrence.

Proud enough that he could hand out cigars.

Law tossed down the paper and forced himself to be motile, he pressed his intercom to the bosses' office, "I don't know why you'd wonder if I still have my ass, sir," he said to the Lieutenant, sure that a few others were in the room yucking it up at his expense, "but let me ass*ure* you that I do. We'll both be right in."

The fleeting image of Elsie, fresh–faced, innocent and crushed by her friend's murder, crept into his mind.

Innocent?

Not anymore.

Chapter Four

I stepped from the shower, hands trembling. The memory of Lynn's murder besieged me. I felt ill. The water had not just washed the black garden soil away, but with it a layer of my body's thin veneer had also spun down the drain. Fear clenched my gut and twisted for dear life; it sapped my strength. The armor that corseted my soul did not yet protect; it resembled a glaze rather than armor. I sank back onto the chair—my eyes fluttered, closed, body slipped, shrunk down—as the child inside remembered:

By the time Elsie was born, life no longer seemed promising. Elsie was born to Ed and Sally Sanders in the summer of '58. After WW II, Ed went to barber school courtesy of Uncle Sam. A town with two colleges could always use another barber. They were going to cash in. At least that's what they thought when they moved to Northfield, a small Minnesota town.

Ed worked long hours at the barbershop trying to make enough to save for a house. It seemed to Sally that everyone they knew had their own house. She complained, so he worked more. That left her with the housework and the baby...dirty dishes, dirty diapers. During the war Sally had been one of the army base pin–up girls—long dark wavy hair and tight sweaters—she was a looker she was. She felt that her still beautiful fresh complexion, her extravagant cheekbones, entitled her to a more regal existence.

She used to laugh when Eddie talked about the job he

had lined up after barber school; he called it a clip joint. That made Sally laugh—made it exciting to them. But these days a barber's wife seemed meager to Sally. She turned to sulking and smoldering; Ed turned to drink. The more he drank the meaner he got. It worried Sally, but she didn't mention it. She was afraid of him. Could the booze be related to what he had gone through in the war? She tried to understand but didn't really know *what* she was trying to understand. Never for a minute did she consider that he worked night and day to save for the new house that she *had to have*, or that once they had that house he'd have to continue right on working every waking minute until he could afford to buy his own barber shop before he could even *begin* to make her happy.

Never did she consider that *this* was the reason why he drank. What she knew for sure was that the passion she'd felt for Eddie had been fleeting. She thought of leaving him. She thought of it often.

The Catholic Church would never approve of a divorce and Sally would not do anything that they Catholic Church did not sanction, so she stayed with Eddie.

They stayed together, and things got worse.

Elsie couldn't have friends over very often because of Daddy's migraines. He couldn't tolerate noise. But today was her golden birthday, she was ten years old. More important today was Tuesday. On Tuesday, "rain or shine, hell or high water," as Momma always said, Daddy played poker. The men took turns playing cards at one anothers' homes.

On hot summer nights, they'd sometimes play in the basement rec-room at Elsie's house. Curious, she'd sit outside curled up on a lounge on the deck to listen. They'd tell jokes and talk about things that she didn't understand—until bored, she'd fall asleep. The Tuesday nights Daddy was gone were the best. She and Momma would have a quiet dinner alone. Sometimes they even talked during those dinners. Elsie loved Tuesdays.

Today, her primary concern was in deciding what to wear. Her bed was covered with dresses, and holding one last dress against herself, she posed in front of her mirror. The final choice was a soft layered dress with simple lines and red rosebuds on the neckline that matched the ones on the cake Momma was making. She slipped out of the dress and hurried, knowing that soon the house would be filled with friends, and here she was, her crinolines not yet ironed.

Ready at last, she twirled across the room, lightheaded, giddy, imagining that this was how a movie star must feel. Cheeks flushed, hearing the sound of laughter, she ran out to find that a few friends had decorated the living room with crepe paper streamers and dozens of balloons.

At last, fourteen ten–year–old girls filled the room and the party had begun. They giggled, ate cake like small pigs, and told the kinds of stories young girls tell one other. What a wonderful party and, oh, what presents! One was a big surprise. It was a jewelry box the size of a shoebox; it smelled like a cedar chest and had a tiny gold padlock with a key. Elsie opened the box to find that it was jammed tight with packs of Juicy Fruit gum—her favorite.

This present was from Alvin, a boy who lived a few blocks down the street. Alvin followed a few steps behind her to school each morning but seldom spoke. He wore a black leather jacket and greased his hair back in a ducktail. Elsie thought he was cute. Everyone said he was fast. Elsie was not sure what fast meant, but she'd heard rumors and knew that it was not a desirable trait. The girls were shocked that he'd dared to give her any gift at all and decided that Elsie should take the gum to school the next day and pass out one pack to each person in class. Each person except Alvin.

Momma got a kick out of the idea. "That'll put him in his place," she said. Momma said he was from the wrong side of the tracks, to stay away from him.

He only lived down the street. There were no tracks.

Elsie's favorite present was a small white plastic radio that her grandma and grandpa sent her. She couldn't wait to take it to her room, and listen to it all alone. She would lie back on her bed, sing to the music and dream of the day she would be an actress. Becoming an actress was her favorite daydream because they had some things that Elsie wanted most—a job where make believe was real, and many friends who loved them.

As the noise grew louder Elsie went inside herself. She ran her fingers over the plastic dials. This radio was the best thing she'd ever owned. Her mind wandered to Alvin. How could she think of doing that trick with the Juicy Fruit® to someone so nice? He'd feel terrible. Still, if she didn't do what these girls wanted, would they ever like her? The girls were not really her friends. They didn't know her——the bad girl Daddy hated.

The sound of tires that squealed, spraying crushed rock against the house like shotgun pellets, came from out front. The noise brought Elsie back to her party. Then a car door slammed and she ran with the rest of the girls to the front picture window.

It was Daddy.

He staggered from the car and wove his way up the hill. The sight made her heart sink. But, it was Tuesday! She frowned. Why was he here on Tuesday?

His face was covered with a grimy stubble. That stubble made her remember that she hadn't seen him the night before. He must have been out all night. His clothes were soiled and wrinkled. He looked as if he'd puke any second and smelled like he already had. From one corner of his mouth hung a crumpled cigarette.

She prayed to herself, *Dear Lord, make Daddy go right to his room till my party's over—till my friends leave.* She didn't want him to get close enough to her guests so that they could smell him.

A collective gasp startled her and she opened her eyes just in time to see Daddy unzip his fly. The girls stood, jaws agape, eyes transfixed on the one–man–show.

This is why they call it a *picture window*, she thought.

Daddy reached in his pants, fumbled, and proceeded to give Elsie's classmates a picture to remember. Standing square in front of the window, feet wide apart to keep his balance, he began to urinate on the lawn. He was a marionette; his body limp, moved side to side, with no will of its own. Holding his thing in hand, he came close to laying himself out on the front lawn for the young girls to view. After an initial silence, her friends shrieked and giggled through the awkward moments that followed. What could any of them say?

Elsie's cheeks flushed blood red. Could they hear her heart scream? She ran from the room. Whispers, squeals, and nervous patter chased her down the hall. How would she be able to look anyone in the eye again? Every day of her life, every comment she couldn't *quite* hear, inside her she'd know it was about her and her drunk of a Daddy.

"C'mon Elsie...don't cry dear. Come back here, Elsie." Momma called after her, her voice more demanding and blaming with each word. "*Why* are you so sensitive? No one blames *you*. This isn't *your* fault."

Safe in her room she dove for her closet, curled up in the furthest corner with her familiar tattered blanket.

"Daddy doesn't mean to hurt *you*, honey." She heard Momma outside her bedroom door. "Don't be such a *silly*," Momma's tone was sharper. "Elsie, please. You'll ruin your party. I worked hard to make it nice. Besides, what do you think your friends will say to their *parents*? I have to live in this town, don't I now?"

Elsie hummed to herself and shut Momma out.

Her old stuff was in the closet. Even those chopped up,

eyeless slippers that once caused her to scream in the night. The shame she'd felt when she ran into the closet was replaced with a feeling of belonging. It was a comfort to be alone with something familiar to hold. And it was safe. She wished she could stay in the closet forever.

Momma wanted her to understand Daddy. If only she could! She'd tried for years to figure this mystery out. Her head hurt to think about it. If Daddy did not mean it, if it was not Daddy's fault, whose fault *was* it? Was God punishing Elsie? If He was, what had she done?

She wanted *answers* so she could make *changes*.

Elsie became aware from the silence in the house that her company had gone home. She remembered her new radio and wanted it. She opened the closet door, tiptoed from her room, and then stopped to listen at the top of the stairs. Her body trembled. She noticed that her runny nose had left disgusting globs on her party dress. She swiped at her face with her skirt, and then held her body very still, barely daring to breathe. The only noise came from Momma and Daddy. She crept down the stairs. *Creak!* The floorboards were like alarms.

If Daddy caught her sneaking. . .at last she reached the living room.

Both voices were loud and angry. *Crash!* That came from the direction of the kitchen. Was Daddy going to catch her?

There were sounds of a struggle.

"Let me go! You're worthless, you bastard!" Momma screamed. "Get your filthy hands away. You stink!"

He did stink. Elsie knew that was true. She heard her Daddy stumble and curse.

"I warn you Ed. Stay away. I'm sick of waiting for you to make something of your lousy life. I'd rather be dead than feel you touch me. Do you hear?" Momma's voice pierced the air. "I'm sick to death of everything about you!"

Elsie snatched her radio and rushed tripping over her own

feet up the stairs. She threw herself on her bed gasping for breath, still in her stained, damp party dress, and pulled the old patchwork quilt over her head. Her present was clutched in her hands.

What was Momma talking about?

What did she want Daddy to make?

Minutes passed; the house was still as death. Elsie wriggled toward the bed's edge by the wall and plugged her radio in. Turtle–like she pulled back under the safety of her quilt. She turned the knob on ever so low and immediately felt comfort from the warm red glow of the dial. Paul McCartney was singing, "Let me take you down, 'cause I'm going to Strawberry Fields. Nothing is real, nothing to get hung about." She loved this music; it took her away to another place. It was in that other place, her radio a few inches from her face and her quilt covering her head, that she fell asleep.

Elsie was in the midst of strawberry fields. She smelled the fragrant berries and enjoyed their sweet nectar. There was a glow on top of the hill. She floated over to the glow. It was a field of dazzling painted daisies and sunflowers. And suddenly she was lying in the midst of it all, the scent of strawberries filled the air. Wild flowers, every color she could imagine, surrounded her. The sun toasted her smiling cheeks. She played with the flowers and rolled laughing over the hill.

The blackout came without warning. Black and cold.

How could that be? The sun was a warm giant peach. Her hands. . .something was scraping her hands. . .hard. . .much too hard. She pulled them back, close to her. They hurt!

What *was* that deafening noise? Her eyes opened wide.

Daddy.

He'd come into her room, thrown back the quilt and found her asleep, her radio playing.

"Miserable fucking snot!" He spat at her. "Do you think I

work my ass off everyday of my fucking life, so you can play your radio when you're fucking asleep?" His eyes bulged and the veins in his temples pumped in and out. He tore the radio from her hands, reached into his pocket and pulled out the straightedge barber's razor he always carried. "I won't put up with it. You and your whore of a mother think I'm made of money. I'll not stand on my feet all day with my arms in the air, cutting the hair of every asshole in this damn town so you can lie here at night and waste electricity! Selfish goddamn brat!" As he swore and ranted drops of saliva dotted her face. She smelled like him now. Like cheap Thunderbird® wine. His beet–red face had quickly transformed itself into a sick pasty shade of gray.

He grabbed her, pulled her out of bed by her hair. "Stand. Stand with your arms in the air like I have to do all day, and we'll see how *you* like it." He pushed her hard against the wall and pulled her arms high.

Elsie blubbered. Her face was drenched–tears, snot, and his boozy saliva. He was so close she could smell his sweat. She stared at the stains on his once white athletic T-shirt. He opened his straightedge with a flip of one hand.

She was terrified!

He reached around her with his other hand, grabbed her radio cord and sliced at the plug.

Elsie watched it fall in slow motion, roll to the floor and stop, safe beneath her bed.

With loathing in his eyes, he tossed the radio at her pillow. "Play the *fugger* now." His slur was a growl. He fell into the door. It gave a loud snap from the full weight of his drunken body.

Struggling, he managed to open it.

Cursing, he staggered out.

A streamer of shimmering gold crepe paper followed him, attached to the bottom of his shoe. As the door crashed shut a yellow balloon from Elsie's side of the room, jumped with the blast of air from the swinging door. *Whoosh!* and *Whack!* It popped and she jumped.

Elsie's arms were still in the air. She brought them to her sides.

Weary to the bone, she moved toward her bed and climbed in wearing that same soggy dress. For a long time she lay with open eyes. There were no more tears to cry tonight.

Bitter, angry voices from outside her room droned on.

Was it her fault? Why did Daddy look at her with such hatred? *What* had she done?

She held her radio, the radio that would never play music again, close to her breast. As she began to fall asleep she thought about her Momma, her Daddy and God. Why didn't Momma ever come to help *her?* Momma must think she was getting what she deserved.

Elsie sat up straight on her bed. But, she *didn't* deserve this. Did she?

The nasty argument, the screaming profanity, was louder again. With every bit of energy she could muster she threw the radio at her bedroom door. The plastic shattered.

She lay back on her pillow, her shoulders stiff her jaw clenched. Body rigid, she tried to think, to find answers for this mess that was her life. Every morning she walked to church before school to go to six a.m. Mass so she could ask God to help her. Maybe He did not hear her prayers. *Should she ask the priest for help?* She tried to close her eyes; all she could see was that light as it glittered off the blade of Daddy's straight-edge.

She'd been afraid that her Daddy would use that blade on her.

Chapter Five

Peter leaned back and propped his feet on his magnificent oak desk. His gaze went straight to his new Ferragamos. How many men could afford Italian crocodile shoes like these? He wished there were a way he could find to work them into conversation. What good was it to be wearing fourteen hundred dollar shoes if no one knew what they were? It did give him some, however small, degree of pleasure to sit and gaze at them.

He inhaled. Ah. Smell that animal smell.

He admired crocodiles. They had a certain presence, didn't they? Hard, cold, and sleek. They had one hell of an attitude.

And, attitude rules.

He thought about the restaurant. That dark haired waitress had attitude. Too bad she'd disappeared. Fortunately, where women were concerned, there'd always be more. The same nature that had given us crocks had seen to a plentiful supply of women.

He grinned just as his reverie was suspended with the opening of the door.

She entered without knocking, closed his office door quietly behind her, and sat directly across the desk from him. Her back was to the office window, anyone passing would see the back of her head and shoulders, and, of course, him, looking at her.

In her hand was a white Styrofoam coffee cup. She reached over and placed it on the edge of his desk. He didn't care for the look or feel of Styrofoam and he was meticulous about order in his office. He was about to open his mouth in protest. Something about her manner made him hold his tongue. He remained silent. Did she look familiar? No. He'd have remembered a piece like this.

He had no idea what she was up to, but it took only moments for her to clarify her position. No audibles required. She uncrossed spectacular legs, spread them ever so slightly while her hand slipped beneath the skirt. Her legs parted enough to show him a whisper of black lace and although he knew her hand was there he felt more than saw it move.

If he could not quite see where she put her fingers he could easily imagine. Her ivory silk blouse stretched tight as she began to breathe faster. Such long delicate fingers with satin red nails! Her other hand twitched and inside he begged it to reach up and touch her now heaving chest. But it didn't. She held her body quite still and that must have been as hard as he was, judging from the look on her face and the tight little noises she was making.

Outside his office a steady stream of people wandered by, some waved to him. He tried to pretend they were having an animated discussion for the benefit of those passing by, but he could barely breathe. He was close to losing control. In his mind's eye, he played a tape. He pictured himself rise from his chair and seize her by those dainty wrists. He would slam her down on his enormous desk and give her what she so obviously needed. He brought himself back into focus just in time to see her finish her deed, pull down her skirt, and immediately regain her composure.

She stood, and with an ease that he found almost as erotic as her just completed show, she slipped around the desk to his side. The coffee cup was once again in her hand and she put those damp fingers to his lips, her red *nails glistened.*

She handed him the cup. She leaned in close. Her breath was hot. Her lips were oh, so, red. For the first time she spoke. "Take my cup with you into the john; think of me while you jack off into it for me, would you? The manager's meeting begins in five minutes: I've been asked to take notes. Well, I intend to sip your juice from this cup while you and the rest of the management sip your morning coffee. I have an allergy to caffeine, you see." Red lips parted slightly, "Just hand me that cup as you pass by."

He looked into her violet eyes with shock.

"When the meeting ends, if you can stand without embarrassing yourself and walk out, I will meet you here later tonight; I promise you'll think I'm Satchmo and you are my horn. But if you can't do that, then you will announce my new 'position' as your personal assistant. Oh, yes. How rude of me. My name is El. This is my first day on the job. The work here? It bores me."

Her body was a feast for his hungry eyes as they followed her sensual stroll to the door. Those hips moved him more than any symphony. As she began to close his door, she leaned back in, "Hey sport," she breathed, "I am so very pleased to meet you, and either way, I promise, we both win."

He sat with her cup in his hand, his brain not the only thing that throbbed, and tried to concentrate on ice–cold water, gallons of ice–cold water, splashing over his body. But his lips tasted sweeter than honey. Her taste and smell filled his senses.

He knew exactly what he was going to do. He stood.
Thank God he had his own private john.
Her cup was in his hand.
It had begun.

Chapter Six

Law was dying for a smoke. After a close buddy died of lung cancer Law decided to stop putting nails in his own coffin. The fact that he even considered sneaking a butt was just one indication of the extreme stress he was under with this case. Bite–it? Bite me. Well, he wanted to say that to *some*one. How can you even talk about a bite–it case without feeling like a joke? Anyhow, a smoke might help, but it was three years since he'd had so much as a puff.

How the "blank" do you find a woman when you have zilch to go on?

And, who the "blank" did they think he was? Houdini, for crissakes?

Law lived his personal life trying to achieve one goal after another. It was a game he played with himself. Often, a low stake mind game—but a game. Many of the goals involved self–improvement.

The latest was this determination he had to remove the word "fuck" from his vocabulary; he used it too much. It'd gotten to be a habit and he didn't like habits. Habits were a sign of weakness. He found "fuck" just slipped out when he didn't want it out. Or worse, when he *least* wanted it out, like when a kid was around. A kid who either looked up to him as a big tough cop or thought of him as nothing but a pig. Either way, not a good deal.

In Law's book, if it was out of control—which made it more than a habit—it was an addiction. He tried hard to come up with a brilliant substitute, one that might work, not only for him, but also for the rest of the world. Nothing came to mind.

So he used "blank" in place of "fuck." Even in his thoughts. No thought–crime for him. No siree. He figured sooner or later he'd get sick and tired of "blank" and come up with another word that did the trick. Right now he could only think of one word. And it wasn't *"blank."*

Thinking about this case reminded him of this amusing idea he'd had just before he drifted off to sleep last night. He'd run an ad in the personals.

WANTED, said the ad. *White woman, age 20 to 35. Blonde.* Oh, and *love of bondage is a must.*

So, Blondie, mused the detective, you get off tying your men, or you don't get off, as the case may be, well, then, you bite their little dicks. Maybe this ad, since it was pretend, could say, bite *off* their dick. Then, pop it into the ol' garbage disposal and grind, baby, grind.

Law considered that. Did everybody nowadays have a garbage disposal? *He didn't.*

Did she only agree, he wondered, to blank a guy after she checked to be sure he had a disposal?

Okay, if he looked on the sunny side, which he could seldom see reason to do, that was *good* news for him. He could relax. Law visualized the scene:

They'd meet in a smoky, hazy bar. Say the Spot Bar. He liked that place, and one of the murders was not all that far from it—just across the river to the Minneapolis side. So. He meets her at the Spot. They have a mite too much to drink, which at the Spot can be one or two drinks the way they pour. And like the gentleman he is he invites her back to his place. And she accepts! They do some face nibbling and are at long last inside and slam the door by falling back into it in a lusty embrace.

Now, by this time, he's hot and ready for what's to come, namely them, he hopes with all his heart and other portions of his anatomy. That's politically correct, right? They've been working up to it all night. Not to be insensitive or anything, but he's ready, and she seems fired up, herself. After some more passionate clinch and pinch she pulls away.

"Do you have a garbage disposal?" she asks breathlessly.

His head droops in shame.

"Oh." she says. "You don't?" She looks at her watch. "Hm, let's see here, fella. I just remembered a very important engagement. I must be going. But, listen, hey! I'll give you a call." And out she goes. Her scent lingers, driving him insane—a nice short trip, that trip to insanity.

She doesn't call. Do they ever? And he dies a lonely horrible death.

Well, nothing new there, same old shit. He never seemed to have exactly the right equipment to give the women he wanted what *they* wanted. But really, how to predict that they'd want a garbage disposal? You could hardly anticipate *that* need. Okay. So that one that got away was not his fault.

Yup, he'd pretty much wrung all the fun out of that fantasy.

In a serious vein his thoughts returned to Elsie.

They teach you when you're indoctrinated into the force not to get close. Just how the blank do you do that? Unless you want to turn into a blanking machine. Cold, precise, robotic. In a lot of ways, that *is* what they want. Machines. Your humanity made you vulnerable, let you make mistakes. For him there was no choice. If you had to be a machine to be a good cop—blank it.

Elsie. So yeah. He'd gotten involved. The reason he had regrets was not because of the department but because of her age. And her age was why it could never have worked. He'd always have felt like a dirty old man. In his heart he knew that was not the case. Why the blank, he wondered? Why did he keep rehashing this same tired shit—didn't his life have enough shit? Important and *new* shit, as a matter of fact.

Apparently not. But he'd always followed his thoughts as

if they were simple instincts and knew they were leading him somewhere for a reason. He just had to figure out what the reason was. Law believed in his instincts.

Back to Elsie. She'd been gone from his life for a long time.

Elsie had been real certain that she knew who murdered her friend Lynn. Lynn seemed real to him; he knew her because that was all Elsie talked about. She figured that if Law knew as much as he possibly could about Lynn, it would bring him closer to nailing her killer. She was so damn sure she knew who it was, but at the same time, no idea who it was. How much sense does that make? Made sense to Elsie.

Law knew he'd let her down. She'd had a name. Paul? Not Paul. No...Peter. It was Peter. Yup. That was it. That was all she had. The name Peter.

Her theory went something like this: Puke–face Peter came into the joint where Lynn worked all the time. And he had the hots for her, even though he was married and had two kids.

Really narrowed it down.

Elsie had the impression he had money, but no idea why she thought that he had money. In Northfield, where the girls came from and where everybody knows your business, that may have been something to go on, but not here in the twin cities with several million residents. And with so little to go on, he couldn't begin to find the prick. And Elsie knew that.

Elsie understood. Law knew she didn't blame him, but she never could accept it.

Also, Peter was a good looking man, she said.

Good looking by whose standards, Law had asked? Was he tall? How heavy? Light skinned or dark? Black, red, green, white, *what?*

Okay, she got the drift. She was sure he was white and tall, yet she had never seen him. And Lynn had not described him.

At the Chit–Chat, they didn't remember the guy, but it's a

big place. Without a photo to ID it would've been a long shot that anyone knew him. Lynn had not talked about him *at all* to anyone at work; she saved her secrets for Elsie.

Law was sure that the slime that did this had planned it. It made sense that the killer would see to it that no one noticed him. At least he'd be sure that he didn't stand out over any other guy. After all, she had to talk to customers. It was her job. No, this bastard had killed before and would kill again. Law knew it. He'd never told that to Elsie. This creep had enjoyed himself too much for it to be a one–time shot. He was a killer because he liked it and a smart one.

Law wanted the blanking bastard bad. He'd done the right things to catch him, too. He'd canvassed the neighborhood for any possible witnesses—had taken statement after meaningless statement. Forensics gave him the hoop. Sometimes there is nothing that can be done but wait for the next time. That's the part that will kill your soul. Wait for the next one. Know there will be a next one.

Lynn's murderer was as slippery and elusive as this new case, this blanking bite–it investigation.

Law slumped in his chair; the weight of life pulled on him, hard and heavy. His eyes felt as if they'd been dusted with filth and polished with sandpaper. *Wait for the next one. Know there will be a next one.*

Chapter Seven

My basket overflowed with the inky berries. I heard a few drop on the floor and knew I'd have to clean up before stains set. It was time to prepare for the next step of my plan. I considered how fast the poisonous Belladonna juice worked, but even more important, how it took such complete control of them.

It played them like a piano. Putting it that way made me laugh. How apropos.

At first, the men were happy they'd taken it. Each was macho, willing to try anything, "game" for any game. That first sip of the Belladonna wine started them on a journey that they insisted on taking and relaxed their predictable little minds. They felt light, as if they were floating, gliding as their brains turned to feather-down! And then their throats would begin to burn, their pupils dilate. They were thirsty, very thirsty. They called out for water. But their throats were so dry that their voices were hard to hear.

Can I be blamed for their impotent vocal chords?

Hardly.

Next came double vision.

At this stage they all mentioned my four huge tits. Funny how each one of them experienced much the same reaction to the juice. The double vision would make them giggle—grown tough-guy men! The expected giddiness was taking over. Very soon the fire that had been in their throat would have made its way to their stomachs and now this burn was serious. It was not discomfort, it was pain. And the liquid they'd consumed would find its way back up their esophagus and erupt, and sour vomit would belch—a loud bark, from their mouths.

As they continued to belch and spit vomit all over themselves, I would introduce myself as Atrophos the goddess.

Here, at this point, I would take my time to tell them why they'd been chosen and precisely what they could expect to happen. Then, lest they delude themselves that the word goddess could mean anything pleasant for them, I would lean over them, put this mouth they so desired on them, and bite.

Hard. I bit as hard as I could bite.

On the way to putting my mouth on them it was always the same. I'd see a glimmer of hope dash across their miserable eyes—that flicker would pass as soon as I bit down. I hated putting my mouth on such slime. Course I had my tricks to keep from actually touching their flesh. Oh the very thought of it!

Lucky for me the potion blurred their vision and I could first "blanket" them with a square of plastic wrap. Even then, it was difficult to get that close to something so vile. My lips "felt" their skin and I quivered all over wanting to bolt from the room in disgust.

But I kept my goal in the front of my brain, kept it there till it grew and pushed all else out of sight. I wanted the complete shock of this experience to overwhelm their feeble hearts.

And next they would then begin to hallucinate, and right before their convulsions began I'd turn and walk toward the kitchen. Over my shoulder, I'd say, "Was it as good for you sailor as it was for me?" I'd smile sweetly, "Be back in a jif!" They thought they knew what I was off to find—a sharp knife.

And so, for the twenty minutes or thereabouts left of

their despairing, suffering lives, I would sit at the kitchen table with the razor in my hand and wait, not wanting to watch, but needing to dispose of the "thing" that they all possessed, the thing that helped to make them such evil men.

What was that thing? Why, their weapon of choice, of course.

I never did tell any of them that they'd be dead before I sliced it off.

Give them something to think about while they waited to die.

That was justice. I mean, I had to think while I sat waiting.

"Memories are made of this." *Well, my memories gave me the courage to go right back to their side and slice that thing off, then, stuff it where it could never again harm any innocent. The garbage disposal. What an invention. I thought it appropriate that I used my special straightedged razor.*

Thinking back, I realize that the first one should have been the most difficult. Actually, I enjoyed it. I wasn't sure until right at the end that I could go through with it, but I pictured my best friend as she lay massacred, and then I thought of the others in my group—the group they put me in after I left the hospital—the victims of abuse group, and while the rage inside me grew like a violent storm—a huge boiling, swirling pot inside my gut, I stepped back from myself, as I'd learned to do so many years ago on the doctors examination table.

Rise above.

I watched the first man, Roger Dove, do what it turned out every one of them did. I told them what the purple liquid in the decanter I'd brought with me was. I told them it was a drug that would prolong ejaculation—an extremely dangerous drug. My disclaimer!

That was no lie! It did prolong ejaculation! Well it would have if they had only taken a very small amount as I always suggested that they do. But no, they all four knew better. Evil begets evil.

Thank you, dear Lord, for the construction plan you drafted for their brains. I could not stand to think that they would be "hard" for all eternity. And on this point, I was not certain I could trust in God anymore than I had learned to trust in the judicial system. So I made certain. I cut it off. Then, I tried to dispose of it. Unfortunately, no one had yet made a decent garbage disposal.

I pulled off my garden gloves and prepared to clean the succulent, black berries. My basket was so full that I could barely heft it up to the counter top, but the strength came to me.

Peter, Peter, Pumpkin Eater.

Cleaning the plump berries brought me back to childhood days; I remembered my work in the kitchen with Momma, cleaning ripe rosy strawberries from our garden for the homemade jams, and cutting up bushels of peaches and pears that we got from the market for canning every year. Putting up canned goods was a lot of work, but it was something Momma did with me and so I looked back on it fondly. But then we moved into the house of Momma's dreams. Time to can fruits and vegetables was gone and so was Momma. Oh, she didn't move away, but like a tree shedding leaves at the onslaught of winter, it was off with the old and on with the new. For me Momma was gone:

The year Elsie turned thirteen, her Dad bought out the owner of the barber shop. Jesse James Barber Shop became Ed's Barber Shop. Ed found two barbers to work and leased them chairs. The two colleges in town, and the short "heinie" styles of the era that had to be cut every few days made business flourish.

Ed and Sally built a rambler with a walkout basement; it sat on top of a hill surrounded by three acres. A creek twisted below and back into a wooded area that housed frequently explored caves. They named this creek (now their very own) Heath Creek. One of those caves was where Jesse was reported to have buried his gold. The gold was never found, but a lot of boys in Northfield got lucky under the pretense of let's–search–for–it.

While her parents were busy with plans for the house it seemed to Elsie that maybe they would now be a happy family. After all, she reasoned, a successful business, a new house, these were the things that Momma always said she wanted.

Meanwhile, Elsie still tried to understand why her Dad didn't like her. She asked Momma for advice, but her mother was distant these days; she didn't seem to want to talk about anything but herself.

"I don't understand why he's so mean to me, Momma."

"Look, Elsie. You just see to it that you do your part. Be good, be quiet, and try to understand that he works hard. He's tired. Your father doesn't mean to drink so much and I'm sure he doesn't *try* to hurt your feelings. You've always been too sensitive." Sally was on her way out. "I won't be home until right before dinner. Peel the potatoes and set the table." She stopped at the door. "Try doing what Daddy wants for a change, Elsie, and things will be fine, you'll see."

That was the problem. Elsie didn't know what Daddy wanted. She believed that she did just what he wanted. It took most of her time to figure out what that was and *things* were never fine. Time after time of failing to please him had proved to Elsie that they never would be fine.

One thing Sally could not do was teach her daughter to relate to men in a healthy way. Sally had problems of her own in that respect.

When Ed walked in the house for dinner every evening after work at 6:00 PM, it had better be a spread, enough for company. The company never came; they weren't invited. Elsie helped with the preparations. The family of three sat somber at the dinner table. The sounds that cut into their silence were of food being masticated and the scrape of silverware over the glass plates. It made Elsie want to scream.

"Please pass the chops."

"Thank you." or, in Daddy's case, a grunt.

The tension in the air was thick. You could cut *that* and eat it if the meat ran out. The silence continued while the dishes got washed because Ed was in the room. He read the evening paper before going to the bar.

Dinnertime continued to make Elsie sick long after she'd moved and left her parents home.

"Baby, that was great."

The sound of a voice startled me.

"What? I scare ya'?"

I turned my head on the pillow and saw the face that went with the voice. Oh. Him. Why do they always look so much different up close?

I remembered him now. Wished I could forget. How do you forget someone you've been following for days? Someone you thought you just had to have. What did they call it? Stalking. Well, if a guy did it, he was stalking, if a woman did it, what then?

"Hey Baby, didn't you hear? I said you were a great time."

The hand on my bare breast woke me fully. Okay, so I was a great time. And now I was supposed to say? Jeeze. What do these guys want me to do, hire a marching band to play. . .hell, what would a marching band play? I placed his hand somewhere that made me feel more comfortable—on his own breast—and got up to dress. No time for a shower with this one.

"Get me a soda while you're up, Babe. A workin' man

needs his fluids." His voice had a grin to it. A cocky, "ain't I the cat's ass, lady?" kind of grin.

He didn't get it.

Not only was I up, I was practically out.

By now I could get these slim jeans of mine over my hips, pull on a T-shirt and sandals and be out the door before most of them had the brains to figure out I wasn't going in their pigsty kitchen to fix them their well deserved breakfast–in–bed.

"Hey Babe."

This time the voice was showing signs of irritation so I did my best imitation of Billie Holiday croonin' "My Man," while I slipped into the can and laid out a quickie line of white powder and sniffed it off the sink. Just one would get me home for more. I heard him again as I made my exit from his apartment and skipped down the stairs to the street. Who knew what he'd said. Who cared? Yet, whomever he was, the pain, the rush to get away, or the just plain boredom, softened the barrier in my mind so that I could revisit the past. On the trek home, I thought some more of Elsie the child.

Elsie walked to Mass every morning before school. She did it out of habit now more than a belief that it would change her life. She was the only student who went to daily Mass and the Sisters were impressed. Right after Mass they would send her next door to the convent and Sister Florence fixed her breakfast, you couldn't eat before communion. Why would God care if you had breakfast in your stomach along with the small white host, she wondered? Maybe it had something to do with respect, or even control, she thought. She didn't understand why but she followed the rule. Elsie hated going with the Sister, whose kind face always beamed, to the back of the dark and dreary convent to the kitchen. Yet, this was considered to be a privilege—something only nuns got to do.

Elsie sat at the counter. Her stomach churned and that burned oil smell as the eggs fried hard as little rocks made her dizzy. Sister placed the eggs in front of her, and then watched her eat with a kind smile. Elsie wiped her mouth with her hankie often. She transferred the burned eggs into the hankie and then tucked it into her pocket. Later, she rushed to the lavatory to wash it out before it left grease spots on her dress. Elsie's weak stomach made her sick and Sister Florence made her nervous. She considered not going to Mass anymore. But how would she explain to the Sisters?

Then came *real* trouble. Sister Edith, her eighth-grade teacher at Rosary School, said the class should get their families to say the rosary after dinner at night. Every night for a week Elsie told herself that this would be the night she'd talk to her Daddy. She was trapped. Her procrastination meant that during the day at school when Sister asked for those who had not said the family rosary the night before to stand, she would have to walk up to the front of the class and explain. Alvin stood with her every time. She'd never considered lying about it but half the class did. Alvin probably would have, too. Why was he nice to her after what she'd done with his gum? She wanted to tell him she felt sorry about that, but what could she say—they made me do it?

It was thoughts about just what a wimp she'd been with Alvin that finally gave her enough courage to ask her Dad about the Rosary. They'd just had dinner and she cleaned up as she always did.

This time, after she'd washed the dishes she went into the living room. She and Daddy were never in the living room at the same time.

"D–D–Daddy." The word stuck in her throat.

He didn't lift his eyes from the paper.

"Dad," she said, louder this time. "Sister Edith said we should ask our families to say the rosary together after dinner." She waited a long time. "Would you?"

She watched the red crawl up his neck until his face turned blustery. He stood, threw the paper in her face, and then stormed, snorting and fuming, from the house.

Days later Momma talked to her and she was real mad. "Why did you have to ask him? If it was so all fired important you should have come to me."

Elsie stared at the floor. "But Mom, Sister Edith told me I had to ask Daddy."

"It makes your father angry to have Sister Edith try to tell him what to do in his own home. Next time, I don't care *what* Sister says, come to me. Things are bad enough. I don't need you to rock the boat. Your Dad works hard. He needs to be able to relax at home." With her eyes spitting fire, Sally left the room.

This is unfair, thought Elsie. She couldn't remember the last time her mom had stuck up for Daddy. Now that she worked for the priest the Church was all she talked about. This was about church, why wasn't Momma on her side?

Sally had taken the job that spring to help buy things for the house. Her "position" was important to her. She was secretary to the new priest at the parish rectory. Father Andrews made quite a stir with the parish women. He came from a wealthy family and was not only used to the finer things but had the air of a man of the world. He was vibrant and sleek–bodied. A somewhat irregular nose made him look like he might have once been a fighter and added to his appeal. His hair matched his black clerical robe while the white Roman–collar set off dark olive skin. Sally started to spend more time on how she looked and dressed. In fact, she ended up wearing most of what she earned. She got a new hairdo and spent hours in the sun, tanning. Elsie noticed that there was a spring to Momma's step that hadn't been noticeable for years.

Elsie had planned to talk to the old priest that had been at St. Dominic's. She'd been too timid, but Father Andrews was nicer. She decided to tell him about her family problems and ask his help.

Look what he'd done for Momma.

Then again, maybe it was extra sleep that was making Momma feel better. Right about that time was when Momma and Daddy moved into separate bedrooms. Daddy snored and it kept Momma awake.

Elsie was going to start her first year in Public School. She'd passed the exam for her drivers' license. Today was her appointment at the family doctor for the school physical.

Momma unlocked the car door. "Let me drive, Momma, please?" Elsie begged.

"I guess it's okay. You'll have to drop me at the rectory on the way. I've got work to catch up on."

"Oh." She'd thought that Momma was going with her to the doctor. But that was silly. "Momma?" Elsie had so much she wanted to talk to her about.

Momma didn't hear. She was busy brushing her hair, picking at her clothes for any sign of lint and chattering about herself. Sally pulled down the visor mirror and began to touch–up her lipstick. "Honey, do you think this shade looks good with my skin this tan? I bought it way last winter."

"You look beautiful, Momma. You always do. Momma, do you think..."

"Oh I just can't tell you how special it makes me feel—working for the church an' all. Father Andy's *such* a good man. I wish your Daddy could be more like him."

Momma babbled on excitedly as Elsie parked in front of the rectory.

Father was outside. He approached the car as her Mom swung shapely high–heeled legs to the curb. He held out his hand. "Here, let me help you, Mrs. Sanders."

He poked his head in the car window. "You are certainly one lucky missie, Elsie. I hope you appreciate what a wonderful mother you have here!" His eyes twinkled and he gave them both a wink.

Her mother beamed.

It was good to have Momma so happy. But Elsie needed advice and that would have to wait.

Chapter Eight

What was going on with me? I felt like two completely different people. Or rather, two non–people. I didn't want the men I picked up. They made me feel like filth. The men were only part of it. Nothing I did filled the hole or satiated the hunger. Sex. That was the last thing I wanted.
I wanted Lynn alive.

As Elsie waited for Dr. Jack, she thought about starting a new school. She was both nervous and excited. She wished she'd been able to talk to her Mom about these mysterious feelings on their ride today but Momma had talked non–stop about Father Andy and what a perfect man he was. There was no doubt Momma was intrigued by the priest, and you couldn't blame her, he was terribly handsome. And, of course, she loved working for the Church.

The nurse bustled in, gave Elsie a paper gown to change into. "You just lie down on the exam table when you're ready, Dearie. Doctor will be right in."

Elsie undressed and hastily put on the gown, hoping he wouldn't come in too soon and catch her half–dressed. How does the doctor know when you're ready, she wondered?

The room was chilly and the table even looked cold. It was covered with a white paper roll that came over the top— ready to be torn off and made fresh after each patient. She had the jitters, but lay back to wait.

At Rosary school, having someone see you naked was never a concern. The boys showered together in one big room.

Sisters would never have allowed such a thing for the girls. She knew it would be different at Northfield High.

The door opened and Dr. Jack appeared by her side. Elsie noticed a peculiar odor—like the scented oil in the bead shop on Water Street. It wasn't unpleasant, yet it seemed out of place in a doctor's office. He dimmed the light slightly, took a candle out of his white jacket pocket and lit it, then pulled the rolling chair over to the table beside her.

Why did he dim the light, she wondered?

Why the candle?

Dr. Jack was older than Daddy. His black–rimmed glasses were thick and his gray hair stringy. As he leaned closer to Elsie she got a whiff of his breath, like a dentist, she thought.

He took her hand in his. "My dear, I know how apprehensive you must be. I thought we'd have ourselves a chat before I begin the examination."

She recognized the odor now, it was cloves. He must be using some kind of breath spray, although it didn't camouflage the garlic from his lunch. He continued to speak but her mind strayed. She needed to talk to someone but she barely knew Dr. Jack. Why did he want to talk to her? As a backdrop to her thoughts his voice droned on about his wonderful wife and children, what a beautiful marital relationship they had, how active they all were in the church.

"We're so very fortunate to have found one another." He was speaking about himself and his wife. It sounded picture perfect and made Elsie feel envy for his children, and guilty that she felt that way. Envy was a sin. One of his daughters was a year behind Elsie in school and she'd been to their home. It was a mansion. The doctor was president of a Catholic organization called the Knights of Columbus. Elsie wasn't sure what they did, but other parishioners accepted them as a cut above the rest. All were men. All had money.

"You know, Elsie, my wonderful wife was a virgin when I married her; that is my wish for you. Many young boys will soon want to date you. I want you to have the strength to remain pure until you find that one special person you will marry—just as my dear wife did." He massaged Elsie's arm as he spoke, every so often the back of his hand would brush against the side of her breast.

She felt strange. This didn't seem right. Couldn't he feel it, too? Well, no. He must not be able to. It had to be her imagination, still. . . .`

Had he just said that she looked sweet and innocent? That her skin felt like silk? *Felt?* He *could* feel it then, could he? He was brushing against her breast! *Oh God.* What was he talking about? *What?* She couldn't be impolite!

His voice was distant once again, background music to her thoughts. She felt as if she'd left her body and floated just above them both, looking down to watch them while her mind pingpong'd.

He was an important man, a good man, and a friend of her parents; he played poker with her daddy every Tuesday. Her mind bounced, taking her to that summer night she'd listened to the poker–boys from outside the screen door.

Dr. Jack was laughing, the drinks made his face red and his words slurred. He said the perfect woman was a midget with a flat head to set your beer bottle on. Oh, and big ears. Big ears? Could that be it? The laughter from the men around the poker table was loud. And she could actually smell the smoke and booze in the air. What did he mean, she'd wondered?

What was he saying to her now? It was hard to concentrate! She blinked. He was gone! She heard his voice, but it was so soft she could barely make out the words he was saying. Where'd he go? She blinked again and saw him. He was no longer by her side; he'd moved to the foot of the table. His lab jacket was unbuttoned. . . . *Why. . .?* His words penetrated her thoughts.

"I'm going to show you what loving, married people do,

my dear. Then you will know it's worth the wait and want to remain immaculate for your husband."

Husband? She didn't have a husband! What did he mean, immaculate?

"This is important for you to understand, Elsie. It isn't going to hurt, my dear." he said. "Don't you be nervous. This will feel *good*."

Why, she wondered, was he spending so much time telling her not to be nervous and how good this was going to feel? *Why tell her what married people did?* Elsie felt dizzy. The room spun. She couldn't see his face clearly because he had dimmed the light even more. When did he do that? More important, why did he do it?

Then it was not Dr. Jack's voice that she heard but her daddy's. She had been walking out of her bedroom when he called to her from inside her parent's room. "Elsie! Come 'ere!" She'd opened the door a few inches and was shocked to see her momma's white breasts, her daddy's tanned hands around them, pinching them; she'd jumped and yelped in surprise. Then Elsie heard Daddy laugh, "Your ma's got some big ones!" as she slammed the door and ran.

The doctor was saying that he was going to put his fingers inside her now, and softly stroke her clitoris.

Is this what doctors did?

He was explaining what her clitoris was, and that soon she would have this wonderful tingly feeling.

Tingly? This was bizarre! What should she do?

She could see just the top of his balding head. Why he was talking with his head tipped down between her legs!

What was going on?

She felt trapped—like an animal.

He was doing this to help her. He must be.

"Doesn't that feel good, Elsie?" His voice was relaxed, a voice of reason.

It didn't feel like anything much. Certainly not good. She

was very uncomfortable and wished with all her might that he would stop. She made a noise, not knowing what to answer.

How could she make him stop?

Inside herself, she was up there, above them both, running back and forth over the top of the table. Panic had set in. She was afraid to say something, afraid to say nothing, afraid to hurt his feelings, afraid not to hurt his feelings. She couldn't breathe. She gasped for air!

He'd made such a big deal about how he was helping her, how good it was going to feel—she couldn't screech at him, *Get away from me!*

Could she?

And just then he stopped.

Oh, thank you, God, she thought.

But there he was again; he was coming around the table. He took her hand and placed it on something hard and hot. She tried to sit. He pushed her back. He put his tongue in her mouth. What was that smell?

What was he doing?

Elsie began to gag. And then slid from the table—and ran. Her paper gown was torn. It flew wide open. Her voice followed her out the door—unnaturally high pitched and quivering, "I have to go to the bathroom, Dr. Jack. Real bad." Quivering. Her voice was quivering, but it was still polite.

Oh no, she had to get away! She hadn't known what else to say.

She looked down and saw that she was almost naked and clutched the paper to her body. Her head swiveled round. Had anyone seen? She hurried. The bathroom was across the hall. Oh God, oh God, *oh God*.

She sat on the toilet stool for a long time with the taste of that thick onion tongue in her mouth. The room was all white and silver. And it was icy, shivering cold.

To Elsie, it was a wonderful room, a womb that she didn't want to leave. After what seemed like a long time there was a knock on the door. "Are you all right in there?" It was the nurse.

"I'll be right out."

When she came into the hall the door to the office was open, the lights turned bright, and the candle gone. Only the stink of that candle lingered in the air to let her know that it hadn't been her imagination. Later she would learn the scent was called musk, and for the rest of her life musk would make her nauseous.

The nurse said doctor had been called away, that she would give Elsie the immunizations required, take some blood, and then she could go home.

"Did Doctor have time to answer all your questions, Dearie?"

"What?" Elsie jerked away from the hand placed on her back and the nurse's eyebrows arched. Elsie looked around her. She was fully dressed and they were standing in the hall— a strip of white tape held a small cotton puff to her arm. So the nurse had already drawn blood.

"Ah, yes. Thank you. H–h–he did." Elsie left without looking the nurse in the eye. Because, thought Elsie, somehow that nurse with the suspicious arch to her brow, *knew*.

Outside she was about to climb into the car when she bolted to the alley and vomited. *What had just happened?* she wondered. *This* was a school physical? It couldn't be *right*, could it? Something was wrong with her, she told herself as she drove herself home. Everyone in town knew what a good, religious, family man Dr. Jack was, a man who loved his wife and children. *It could not be Dr. Jack that was wrong*.

She told no one about her high school physical.

Elsie was growing up not knowing who she was, or what she wanted from life. Except she knew she wanted to be loved. She knew that she tried hard to please her friends and family so that they would love her. Why was she impossible to love?

Elsie had grown to be a mirror. And, the story her face told as its image hit the mirror was not the same story reflected back out at her. Going in, it brimmed with longing and hope; on the return, it seethed with anger.

Chapter Nine

It had been a long, hard day. An unsettling day for a man like me.

I'm used to being in complete control of all that surrounds me. It was the stunt with the Styrofoam cup that did it. And, I'd be willing to bet some heavy cash the bitch knew it. She was real damn sure of herself.

I drove south on Hiawatha Avenue looking for our "designated" meeting place, the Falls Motel. My ego was bruised but I could comfort said ego with the knowledge that soon she'd beg me for it; they always did.

I'll be on top, and it'll be business as usual. Oh, I'd use her on occasion, when and if I wanted, then get rid of her—free my mind for important matters. A real man counts women, well, on a scale of one to ten, he doesn't count them.

I know myself and once I get what I want it's, "so long Sister, so long." I'm a hunter. I crave that thrill of anticipation that only a hunter knows. That's a feeling that can't be appeased by anything except trapping or killing your prey.

I chuckled out loud. Tonight I hunt. She is the prey.

I'd picked the Falls Motel for its reputation. It's a well-known, "rent–a–room–by–the–hour" joint that plays the raunchiest fuck–movies for your viewing pleasure while you do–the–dirty. What better way to put bitchface in her place?

Who's on first, blondie? Ha! I'm amused at the pros-

pect of teaching this one just who is in charge. That's the reason I play her game.

Assistant, my ass.

I remembered the morning meeting. She'd sat, holding that damn cup and sipped my cum! Picturing her was like a quick browse through Hustler; it made me hard. I felt the heat spread until my nuts were a pair of rocks.

Ahha! The bitch was waiting. That wild and wind-blown hair of hers matched the car she drove. It was wheat colored sun–bleached hair and the car, a white Mazda RX-7 T-top convertible.

Got to get me some of this.

She slid out of her parked car when she saw me drive up. The Falls Motel's neon lights blinked on and off. Just what one would expect from this tacky joint. I smiled and pulled up to her car.

In what seemed seconds I could feel the heat of her breath.

The would–be sorceress had come to my window. If she hadn't bent over to look in at me I'd have had to grab those tits that begged for attention and pull her in to me.

She dropped something feather light in my lap, then glanced down pointedly, one eyebrow arched. "I can tell you're happy to see me, sailor. I feel like some air; follow me in your car."

I wanted to stop her, tell her I wasn't taking her orders, but she went right on talking as if I had no say in the matter.

"I brought something to get you in the mood," she nodded toward my lap, her voice like tiny bells in the wind, "but I can see you're already in the mood." She turned away before the blood returned from my crotch to my brain so I could answer. I sat, dumbfounded. Her taillights blinked red in the night.

I slid my car into first gear, in hot pursuit, before I

remembered that she'd let something flutter into my lap. I felt around for it. Hmmm, silk. I put it to my face. Recognition hit me with a punch; these were the black, wisp-of-silk-lace panties she'd worn in my office this morning. I was positive. She'd come on these panties! I remembered the taste of her as I inhaled her scent. My tongue fished the crotch into my mouth and I sucked, mad for a taste of her.

Who gave a shit who was going to be on "top?" I put the pedal to the metal, not wanting to lose sight of her. This was the part that thrilled me most—the hunt.

Her brake lights flashed and she turned right, heading into a large apartment complex parking lot. Ah. This was her plan; it wasn't "air" she wanted after all. The bitch lives here!

Same old, same old.

First, they get you to their place—the lair. A glass of wine, candlelight, romantic music, and their web's complete. All carefully designed to get things up close and personal. That web's only purpose is to snare its prey! Clever bitch. I had a good laugh, because I was even more clever, wasn't I?

It surprised me that I felt flattered. And the realization that she was like every other woman I'd ever known took the "edge" off my hard-on.

My grin faded. Why was she parking in the back of the lot by the bushes and the big trash containers? Trash containers are unsightly; they should be locked in a special building, out of sight. Should be a law. I parked, sure of myself now that I knew the tramp's agenda, but irritated.

Why, little dove, I whispered under my breath, must we continue this game of cat and mouse in a parking lot when your bedroom, your nest, is so close at hand?

When I caught up to her she was leaning against the

rear of an army–green van. The moonlight spotlighted off her pale ivory blouse. It was the same color as her skin. Her blouse was stretched so tight I could see darker bumps protrude as though trying to break free of the thin silky material that held them prisoners. My God, she was a sight. My irritation vanished as I approached.

I reached for her, and slowly, teasingly, our mouths came together, not quite touching, breathing into one another. I could feel the heat flow from her. She was almost too hot to touch. I longed to thrust my tongue deep into her throat, in and out, in and out, but no. I wanted to hear baby beg for it first.

I felt her hands push me away and I stepped back to look. She stood, her legs wide apart, skirt hiked high. The light flashed across her dark red nails as they caressed her body while I stared.

"Hey sailor–boy," she said, "give me your finger, stick it right in here."

"Right there? Someone could see us." I looked over my shoulder.

"Right here, right now," she said.

I obeyed.

She was so wet, so hot, so satin slippery; I felt the world around me disappear. I felt slippery myself, as if I myself were about to slide off the edge. My brain was on hold. I was being driven by another part of my anatomy.

"Stick that finger in your mouth," she ordered. "Taste it."

Again, I obeyed.

Her breath seared my ear. "I want to feel you deep inside me."

"Let's go inside, baby, inside, to your place, now. Now! C'mon baby," I pleaded with her. I had to have this, but not out here!

She pulled away, brushed her skirt down with a stroke

of red nails, and looked directly at me. It seemed that her voice had turned cold and hard, but no, I must be mistaken. "Listen to me carefully," the beauty's voice bit through the night to me, "I do not live here. I came here for air, just like I told you."

The fire in her eyes made Mr. Big throb.

She continued, "And, I do not now, nor will I ever take any man to my place, never. You get it? Now, no one will see us," she spoke softer, assuring, playful even, "besides, I enjoy an element of risk with my air."

Once again she began to stroke herself. "Are you in?" she asked it with a slight smile. Her skirt was violet, same shade as her eyes; it was a textured silk wrap-around with a single button at the waist. With one hand she unbuttoned it. It fell to the ground with a swoosh that sent a twinge to my groin.

She stood, legs still wide apart; her black lace garter belt matched the panties matted in my pocket. My mouth watered, and I groaned. I tried to take in all that she presented with all of my senses. Her black nylons and garter belt contrasted sharply with creamy skin and a thick blonde bush. Lips like dripping cherries and matching nails that seemed to flick everywhere at once had me dizzy with desire. But what hit the hardest was the sudden smell of her, the musk of her. I lost my head and nearly threw her to the ground right then. In my mind I repeated like a mantra, Oh yeah baby, I'm in, I'm in, God, am I in.

She turned her back to me and bent over at the waist. Her tight silk blouse burst open at last. I saw flashes of blood–red nails, and knew she was playing with herself for my amusement. I watched as she came on her fingers. What an animal! I choked on my own breath.

And then I lost all control, unzipped my pants and grabbed her breasts with both hands. I couldn't have at her fast enough! I bent over her back. I could feel her hand guide me inside her—or was it inside her? It felt strange but I could not think clearly; of course it had to be inside her. I rammed it home, hard as I could, and then still harder. I felt I'd never get it in far enough. . .never enough. Her butt moved like a wild dog in heat. I was caught up in a white blinding frenzy. I shot inside her, "My God. My God," I cried out, as I gasped to catch my breath. My juice ran between her legs. I held myself inside her not willing to pull away.

"More. . .do it again. . .one more time." she said.

Her voice was low and barely audible as she told me all that she wanted me to do to her. I started up again, slow at first, then hard and fast. I could hear my balls slap against her.

"What?" . . .I asked. . .she was pulling away!

"Baby," I started to argue but she put her finger over my lips; then I heard voices too, they were close, very close.

"Hey man, it's easy for you, but what am I gonna tell my wife? She'll fry my ass!"

"My advice, you crack–head you, is to lie. Lie like a Persian rug. If you don't wanna lie, bring a shitload a flowers an' get out the kneepads."

The footsteps went toward the building and the voices grew faint.

They'd startled me but the scare was over. I looked for El. In those few seconds her skirt was smoothed down and buttoned, her tits covered in soft silk, and while I was deciding if I should zip it up or down, the little bitch turned and walked away from me!

"Thanks for the air, sailor–boy!" she called over her shoulder. . .and then. . .only the scent of her lingered in the air.

I stood there with pants that were wet in the crotch and no place to change them. I couldn't concentrate. One *thing was clear. I wanted this bitch woman and I wanted her my way.*

Next time, that's precisely how it would be.

Chapter Ten

I began to stalk the men a few months after Lynn's murder. Part of me trusted that Law would catch her killer, another part was beginning to learn that life was never that simple. Three times a week I met with the psychologist, Lorenzo. He talked about having me join a group he facilitated, but, according to him, I wasn't ready yet.

The thing I did with the men was just an effort to stop the pain.

I used them.

The first time it happened was an accident. I'd begun to take long walks. I told myself that exercise and a change of scenery could stop the screams that filled my head to the brim. Out in the world I felt intensely claustrophobic. It was as if these buildings, cars, and people were all closing in on me, their collective goal was to crush me to death.

One early evening I saw a man who reminded me of my girl–talks with Lynn. It made me wonder. I decided to find a man and give it a try, use him as a self–prescribed drug. It took me quite some time to find one that appeared tolerable, but I did it.

I followed him until he saw me. He did the rest. They all did. Getting rid of them afterwards was the only problem. I'd discovered that I didn't want to be with them any longer than it took to do it. I also discovered that if I went somewhere with them where they could get me right to bed, I could lie back while they pounded inside me, and

escape my brain, escape my pain.
Those spaces in time...they became my hideout.
Mostly I just thought about the old days. The good old days were seldom good, but at least Lynn was still alive:

"Wait till you hear this new record!" It was Elsie's best friend Lynn Fahey. She ran through the door to Elsie's bedroom squealing with delight and shoved the new Animals record in her face. "Put it on—put it on!" She flopped backward onto the bed.

Even lying on the bed she could not stop jittering. Since the moment she was freed of the constraints of her mother's womb at birth, she exuded so much energy you could get a whiplash looking at her! Her adrenal glands pumped like an oil well that had just struck the mother lode. Her short fiery hair was made to order for her personality.

Elsie watched Lynn bounce up and strut around her room to the strains of *"Sweet Little Sixteen."* She was doing a Mae West thing with her hand, pushing at her hair. "How do ya' like my new do?"

"You look fab–u–lous!" Elsie went over and put her arm around her. She admired the thick curls; her own was straight. They stood next to one another, wiggling to the music in front of the mirror. Lynn's chest was a smidge bigger, and she wore her skirts tighter. They were both knockouts.

Trying to control Lynn was a full time job. But her folks were terrific. Her dad was the best piano tuner around, her mom, the high school English teacher. They were liberals in a very conservative town. Elsie loved talking politics with them; it made her feel like part of their family. Watching her friend dance to the Animals and goose around the room, Elsie glowed; wherever Lynn was, life was interesting.

After burning off some excess energy, they got down to business. They spent much of their waking hours talking about boys and it was time to exchange secrets.

Lynn, the free spirit, rolled up her bobby-sock and pulled out two cigs. "Lynn!" Elsie pretended to be horrified. They were sixteen; at sixteen you had to do forbidden things.

Lynn's response to the horror was, "Oh, shit–damn, shit–damn." She lit up and blew her Pall Mall at Elsie.

Elsie was too serious to be that much of a free spirit. She did get down on the floor and pull out a fruit jar hidden there that held some of the Mogan David red wine that she'd swiped from her Dad's stash. She pulled it out and took a swig.

"Ahha!" Lynn hooted. "We're wicked women!"

On the topic of guys Lynn was Elsie's mentor, and Elsie was endlessly curious. In some ways Lynn was like one-of-the-fellas; they could be themselves with her. She'd been out with a few of them, done some first-base petting with one, but never the infamous "all-the-way" thing. Elsie was a different story. Around her they were awkward and tongue-tied, and that made Elsie certain none of them liked her.

Lynn blew smoke rings that floated around the room in various stages of form. She'd just made a disclosure about her and her boyfriend that sounded interesting to Elsie. Lynn took a deep drag just as Elsie asked her next question.

"But, what does it feel like to give a blowjob? What did you call it, head?" Elsie was always interested in how things felt. Right now, for instance, she was sipping some of good ol' Daddy's wine; she felt warm and kind of electric all over.

The redhead coughed, and gagged through the laughter, then yelled, "I'm choking here, but don't bother trying to save me! And, I don't have a *clue* how to describe it, kiddo. No *special* way."

"Why do you do it? Tell me that, then."

"That's easy–sleazy; 'cause he loves it! Frankie loves me totally when I blow him." Frankie being the love of Lynn's life.

"Okay, now, I wanna get this, right." Elsie started to slur her words although some percentage of it was pretending.

"You put it in your mouth and then you move up and down on it, like this?" she bobbed her head goose–like.

Lynn giggled. "Well, har–de–har–har! You need some practice, girlie." She raised dark reddish eyebrows. "Just kidding about the practice. Jimmy's not gonna get lucky with you. You knew I was joking there, right?"

Elsie ignored the Jimmy comments completely. "Um, I have an important question. Listen. Okay. What do you *do* with it? I mean, um, you don't swallow it?"

"Oh yeah, for sure they want you to, like, swallow every drop. I try to spit it out, but only if I can do it so he doesn't see me."

Elsie all of a sudden had a vision of Sister Florence standing by her side while she tried to spit those greasy eggs into her hankie.

Lynn continued, "I want Frankie to think that I want to swallow his ah, his stuff."

Picturing the eggs made Elsie want to barf. "But you *eat* it! Does it make you sick? What does it taste like? What's the flavor? Is it thin like, oh god, is it thick? Tell me!"

"Oh gosh girl. This is hard. But it doesn't make me sick. I think what it tastes like depends on what he's had to eat or drink. Hey! I got it! It tastes like snot. Really, that's it. Like *hot–snot*." Lynn caught the look on Elsie's face. "They say it has only 35 calories. It's not so bad as it sounds, really it–*snot*!"

They rolled on the floor, hugging, their cheeks wet with tears. "Bleah!" gasped Elsie, getting serious. "I don't get it. I wonder what they like about it. I bet I'd get dizzy and throw–up in their lap." She began to bob her head again to demonstrate.

"Well I don't have all the answers yet. I only did it twice, and only with Frankie, but he sure loved it."

Not in her wildest dreams could Elsie imagine ever doing "it," but she was glad she had Lynn to tell her stories. Maybe blowjobs were not that important to all guys. She hoped they weren't important to Jimmy.

Lynn stood and brushed herself off, "Hate to run, but I got to. Dad's on my case every second. The concert's only a week away and every time he looks at me he says to go practice. My butt's schmutt if I don't do good." She laughed, "I know he's right. How else will I have the fame that I'm one day destined to have? Practice, practice, practice. Good thing I play the piano, so it's only my fingers that get sore and worn out and not these fabulous lips! Don'tcha think, Els?" She gave her a shove, a one–two punch, and seemed to glide out the door. Elsie was left to ponder her good friend with what was left of her wine induced glow.

Elsie couldn't sleep that night. She kept thinking of Jimmy. She'd noticed him long ago, when he was short and kind of shy. She was attracted to *that* Jimmy, the way he used to be, the way she thought he still was. Now he stood six feet tall, hair a jungle of blonde waves, cheeks with dimples that peeked when he grinned. The looks were a bonus. When he passed her in the hall at school her heart almost stopped. He seemed shy, but he was easy to talk to. She liked that the most.

Tomorrow night was their Homecoming dance and Elsie was going to it with him. She couldn't wait. They'd been dating for a month; he hadn't kissed her yet, but she knew it would happen soon. She closed her eyes, took a deep breath and imagined he was with her. She fell asleep to dreams of his kisses.

Bam!

Elsie sprang straight up in her bed. Her eyes took a minute to adjust. The room was pitch black except for a crack in the shade where the light from the stoop outside had managed to wriggle in. Her eyes were drawn to that crack, her mind blank. She heard another crash and then it registered; she knew where she was. She shivered. What was that last noise?

If the light out back was on then Daddy had not yet come home from the bar. But then she recognized the familiar voices as they yelled and swore. She slumped back onto her pillow. There were sounds of flying furniture as it was thrown or just knocked over and crashed against the floor and the walls. She was about to turn over and pull the pillow around her ears to muffle the roar. This was nothing new. The voices got louder and, after a huge boom that had to be glass shattering, Momma screamed.

"You fucking bitch." The noise was deafening. . . "and then we'll see what your Church thinks of him, won't we?"

What was Daddy saying? It was about the priest, Father Andrews. He must have punched Momma as he said it, for there was another brawling crash.

Elsie was old enough to realize her Daddy was a drunk and that her Momma was far too happy working for the priest. She wished Momma had never gone to work for Father Andy; things at home had only gotten worse.

Tonight's parental thunderstorm wasn't going to stop on its own. She stumbled out of bed and went downstairs.

The living room was in shambles.

"You fucking, cock–sucking cunt." Daddy had Momma by the throat, choking and shaking her. "You can't do this to me!" He was a madman and he was trying to strangle her! Momma would suffocate!

Elsie shrieked at him to let her Momma go, but he was beyond hearing. Herself in a frenzy, she managed to push in between and separate them. Momma fell free to the floor and crawled to the stairway.

"You meddling little bitch!" Elsie had Daddy's complete attention. She felt a flash of sharp pain and just as she heard what sounded like a bone crack along with her own scream she felt another of Daddy's fists land hard. It forced the air from her lungs with a blast.

With one hand he grabbed a fistful of her hair while he

slapped her with the other. Her arms and legs were like useless rubber sticks as she tried to kick and hit at him. Desperate to get free, she used her nails as weapons and scratched what she could reach of him. Suddenly he let go and Elsie felt her back hit the counter. It had to be the booze getting to him; he looked woozy as he staggered.

Elsie shoved as hard as she could and broke into a run. And as she ran past the kitchen counter she seized a butcher knife. Still running, but now totally out of control, she aimed herself in the direction of the bathroom, the closest door she knew for certain had a lock.

He was right behind her.

She pushed the lock just in time, climbed on top of the vanity, and crouched as far into the corner as she could get. She cried and wheezed for breath, doubled over at the waist, clutching her painful ribs with one arm.

Angry fists beat on the door and she heard it crack. The knife slipped from her hand and fell with a clang into the sink below her. She cried harder and bent to pick it up, her hands wet and slippery with sweat, saliva and fear.

A trickle of blood, from when he hit and punched her, ran down her cheek like tears. She knew that any second the door would break and open. Her brain was fragmented. There were lucid moments of sanity when she felt ridiculous standing on the bathroom vanity with a knife in her hand, and moments of complete *insanity*, as she pictured Daddy bursting through the door as she leapt on top of him and plunged the knife into him. It played many times, rolling through her mind like a movie in painfully slow motion.

Her eyes flicked around the white bathroom walls and she felt they would close in on her, squeeze the life from her, and just as her heart beat more frantically than ever, she heard the silence outside the door. The pounding had stopped.

In the distant background was the doorbell's frantic repetitive ring, followed by footsteps thumping down the basement stairs. Probably Daddy. Yet she stayed on the vanity, unable to move, barely able to breathe, lest someone find her. Elsie heard and saw the door lock moving.

"Elsie!" The voice was a loud whisper but it was Momma. Momma had come to help her! And she looked worried. She helped Elsie down, pried the knife from her fist and washed the blood off her face, all without another word.

Then, "Look here, Elsie. Listen to me." Momma whispered. She explained that their next–door neighbor was waiting in the other room. She slipped Elsie's coat around her shoulders. "You be quiet, let me do all the talking."

The next few hours were a blur. Their neighbor drove them to the hospital emergency room. It was a quiet night in the ER; she was admitted right away.

"My daughter was sleepwalking and fell down the basement stairs, doctor." Sally's voice was loud enough for Elsie, and Mrs. Fink, the neighbor, to hear.

*Sleep*walking? Elsie watched a black ant crawl under one of the chairs and sit motionless. That ant probably thought that if it didn't move, it was invisible.

Elsie felt eyes on her back and turned to see Mrs. Fink behind her. The woman's eyes looked down at the floor.

Fell down the stairs? As usual, Momma was concerned with what people would think. Everyone except Elsie. She watched the ant and knew what it was like to feel invisible.

A kind nurse led her to the lab for an exam and some tests. The x–rays showed that she had two fractured ribs. "Broken ribs are painful but they'll heal by themselves." With that remark the nurse gave her a shot in her behind for pain and they were sent on their way home.

"Elsie's been walking in her sleep ever since she was four or five years old." Sally tried to talk to Mrs. Fink while she drove. The woman didn't answer. Did she know the truth? The rest of the ride was burdened with a heavy silence.

Back home, the clock on the kitchen wall said 2:40 AM.

Elsie was so sore she could barely walk. As she passed by Momma their eyes met. Neither spoke.

Alone in her room, Elsie sat by her painted pink vanity table. The paint was chipped and it was way too small for her now, but she loved it still. She remembered the Sunday she and Momma had painted it. Elsie'd ended up wearing more of the pale pink paint than she got on the vanity. Her eyes floated up, and like a ride in a time machine, the mirror shoved her into the present. Her eye was black and her jaw, swollen. Her scalp hurt. She used her hand mirror and tried to look at the crown of her head. Daddy had yanked her hair right out of her head! Where was the handful of hair that was missing from the back of her head? Was it on the living room floor?

Maybe she should get it to keep as a memento of the evening's festivities. She put her head in her hands. What had gotten into her? Was she going *mad?* It must be the shot they gave her in the hospital. Yet she couldn't get that hair out of her mind. Why didn't the doctors notice that so much of her hair was gone? Did they think that when she tumbled down the stairs, the stairs reached out and pulled out her hair? *Did they?*

She crawled painfully into her bed. Suddenly she remembered the dance. Oh no, could it be possible that the dance she had been waiting for was tonight? Only hours away? It seemed remote, a school dance. . .that was something other kids did, not her. Her face was a mess; worst of all, there was a huge bald spot on top of her head! There was no way to explain this to Jimmy.

He'd think she was a freak. And perhaps she was.

As she began to drift off, she thought of the earlier fight. What had Daddy said? It was about the priest. . .the priest and Momma. She would ask Momma tomorrow.

Momma. Why Momma? Why did you say that I fell? Was it to try to protect Daddy? Why protect him? I tried hard to protect you, Momma. Why didn't you return the favor? Did you have something to hide? My head hurt too much to think.

Inside the anger simmered.

Chapter Eleven

He tried to kiss me first and I turned my face into the pillow; oh good, the sheets smelled fresh. As was he—a fresh fish, a newbie. For some reason I found that thinking of him in the same vein as the sheets humored me.

So, fresh sheets, a plus point for him. The good thing about picking up a freshie, was that they were very excited and it was generally hard and fast. Or that was the plan. So many things to consider.

I hope he's a pounder, I thought. Some of them actually expected my participation. They were disappointed. And so was I. But most of them didn't care or notice.

And because there was something about their rhythmic thrusts that hypnotized me, took me away from today and back to yesterday, I found it was worth the risk. Please let this be a good one. This was a day when I needed that escape.

Today the risk was rewarded. He pounded. Goodie for me. And then he fell asleep as I sighed with relief.

Afterwards, I couldn't have told you the color of his hair, but for some reason, because he'd given me that trip home I'd craved I thought of him fondly. My brain once kick started couldn't forget the past. I kept returning to days of old. The movie reeled on as I strolled my way home:

Elsie appeared older and more sophisticated than sixteen. She'd inherited those high cheekbones from Sally and coupled with her deep violet eyes her face was almost too perfect but something saved her and made it interesting. Maybe it was her state of mind.

Momma had called school this morning while Elsie ate oatmeal at the kitchen table.

"Elsie took a bad fall last night, sometimes she's not too graceful!" Sally laughed. "Oh she'll be fine but she won't be able to make her morning classes." On Fridays she had an afternoon of study hall followed by gym—not hard classes to skip. Sally hung up the phone just as Elsie bolted for the bathroom and puked up her oatmeal. Funny how often she felt queasy.

An hour later she was picturing how Lynn nearly choked on her cig smoke when she'd pressured her for details on the taste of Frankie's come. Elsie's giggle was the laughter of a young child and it brought her out of her trance and back to her thoughts of the dance. She was going to go because she couldn't think of anyway out of it. The pain in her head made it difficult to concentrate. Before long Lynn called to find out where she was. Minutes after they talked, Lynn was at her door.

"We're saving the Ed and Sally talk till later, 'cause this'll be a great night for you, Els, an' they aren't part of it. We'll sure as hell get to them tomorrow though. C'mon let's make you into Cinderella—impossible as that may seem!"

Lynn did what she said she'd do, and did it without Elsie's help.

First she packed her face in ice till Elsie could barely feel she *had* a face, then after a hot shower started in on her hair.

Lynn cracked her gum—a habit that annoyed Lynn's parents. Elsie thought it was cute and, well, snappy, like Lynn herself was snappy.

"You know," Lynn stepped back to admire her work. "Now that we've hosed you off you don't look half bad. Hmm.

Who'd a thunk it." *Snap!—that gum again!* "These cuts and bruises give you kind of a mysterious, devil–or–angel aura. Heh–heh!" Lynn had arranged tiny roses in Elsie's hair to cover the bald spot.

Elsie never wore much makeup. For one thing she didn't know how to apply it and, as Lynn would say, minimize her "defects." They experimented on the black eye. By late afternoon they were both howling with the glee of the moment.

"Listen to me, kiddo. This is your big chance with Jimbo. There'll be no more, *what's a kiss feel like, Lynner*, from you—or that's my bet, any*hoo*." Lynn kissed the top of her head. "Not that you're gonna do anything *big*, but a kiss'd be okay. Regardless of what I think about Jimmy boy–o, he's bound to be a good kisser." Lynn's voice went into her Mae West imitation, "Rumor has it he's had plenty of practice, little chick*adee*." They both laughed at Mae and then with a more sober tone, Lynn added, "Yeah, I'd watch him if I were you."

Elsie frowned. Lynn had dipped into her motherly mode.

"Don't give me that look. One kiss'll be okay—that's one thing less for me to describe to you. We'll compare notes!" Lynn gave her friend's cheek a soft pinch. "Well, not to worry. You can handle him. Tonight might get us beyond the what–does–his–tongue–feel–like–in–your–mouth talks and on to juicier things! Okeedokee, let's make those lips desirable."

"Did you forget that we already branched out from the kiss talks?" Elsie laughed. Lynn ignored her and pretended that she needed her to keep her lips together. Elsie knew she was lucky to have a friend like Lynn. "Okay, pal–o–mine. Get out now. I love ya, Lynner, but I can do my *own* lips. And look how late it is. Shake it outta here, or you won't be ready yourself. And hey, I feel much better."

"Ah, but here's the difference between us, Els," Lynn got her things and started out the door. "I'm a *natural beauty*. Doesn't take *me* hours to get ready!"

Elsie noticed a pensive expression on Lynn's face as the

door closed. Her voice said one thing, her eyes another. *Probably my imagination*, thought Elsie. As she waited for Jimmy to pick her up she knew that the night would have to be pretty special to be better than the preparations for it had been.

Elsie heard Jimmy's car in the driveway and checked for a preview of him out her bedroom window. He had on a white wool blazer with a red rose stuck in the lapel. He approached her house with a comfortable cocky gait. The remnants of last summer's tan made his skin appear polished, and his blond sun-bleached hair had streaks of white.

She opened the door right as the doorbell rang, took his arm, and ushered him down the steps. He'd been ready to meet her parents but his manner didn't betray his surprise.

Pain from her fractures made her grimace, yet she was happy now that they were together. She slid into the car and he turned to give her a wrist corsage of burgundy roses and white baby's–breath. "You look sensational, Elsie, but, man. I mean, what happened?"

Her eyes darted between the house and the corsage. "Mind if we just drive awhile?" He was easy to talk to and she wanted to tell him about things a lot more fun than this, but it had to be done. He started the drive toward the dance at the school gym while she let her story unfold. She told him how hard her Daddy worked and that sometimes he needed a drink to relax after a long day. Sometimes one drink would turn into many. Momma could not understand so they'd argue. She held back the part about Momma and the priest. She wasn't *that* sure about it.

Around this time they passed the high school. Derek and the Dominos's, *"Why does love have to be so sad?"* drifted in the open window. Clapton's music jumbled with other thoughts and brought tears to her eyes.

Jimmy patted her hand and drove past the school. He headed north. "Let's drive out to the bluffs, Elsie."

Elsie hadn't been there but she heard comments about it often. By the time Jimmy turned off the main road they were no longer talking. The wind and steady hum from the tires filled the car. The bumpy dirt road that led to the bluffs was overgrown with trees and wild bushes; the branches swept both sides of the car at once.

Elsie sat straight, alert.

All the greenery that surrounded them appeared black in the dark and blacked out the stars; it looked like they were driving fast through a dark tunnel. The car lights were the only lights. Jimmy drove real fast, as if he knew the road well. For a minute Elsie felt anxious. But suddenly they came to a clearing and the whole scene changed. All around them were tall rocky hills that in the moonlight glowed white—this was what the kids called the bluffs.

Jimmy parked and sprinted around to open her door. "C'mon, Elsie." He took her hand and pulled.

"Oooh." Elsie explained about her broken bones.

There was evidence of a multitude of previous bonfires; some were "fenced" by logs. It was romantic and secluded.

Elsie was drained from all the talking she'd done on their drive. She was glad when Jimmy got comfortable on the ground at her feet, leaned his back against the log she sat on and told her some surprising things.

"The fact that Ed's a drunk is no news flash for me," said Jimmy. "In fact," he said, "I'm pretty damn sure you're one of the last in town to know." Jimmy went on to tell her about how his own Dad was almost as bad; nearly every night his Mom sent Jimmy to Big Al's, either to drive Dad home, or wrestle his paycheck away before he drank it up. So Jimmy'd had plenty of opportunity to watch Ed in action. He'd watched him do more than drink with the local barflies. There was a bloated bleached blonde that Ed spent lots of quality time with. Jimmy called her BBB, knowing she was too dumb, or high, to catch on. She probably thought he stuttered and thought her name was Bea. Her place was about a block from the bar; he saw them stumble in that direction often after last call. He knew what a mean drunk Ed was; it wasn't a pretty sight.

Stars blinked like fireflies around a sliver of moon in a clear sky. There was an autumn chill tonight. Jimmy put his arm around her shoulder. A slight breeze caught an occasional leaf as it danced a slow dance with the air currents and fluttered to the ground. It also brought them an aroma of someone burning leaves and toasting marshmallows.

"Can't you just taste those marshmallows, nearly burnt on the outside and oozing and sweet on the inside?" said Jimmy.

Elsie smiled. This was a peaceful place to be. She was glad they were here instead of the gym and she felt comfortable with Jimmy.

He talked to her about his Ma and Dad. Jimmy didn't seem to mind talking about their personal lives. He told her his Dad worked at Tiny's Smoke Shop. It was just down the street from the barber shop. His Dad and Ed were friends. His Mom cleaned for Tiny's and Perman's, the clothing store on Main Street.

"Yeah, Ma has to go clean their slop at night after store hours when everyone else in town is settling in at home, or going off to the bar like some we know, right Elsie?" Jimmy's Dad was a happy–go–lucky drunk. Not bad when you compared him to Ed, but, all the same, a drunk. Because of him his Mom had to go out to work at night, and they never had enough money to make ends meet, much less any extras.

Jimmy understood and that gave Elsie the courage to tell him some of her secrets. Like about the time she found the dirty magazines Daddy had hidden in the garage. She had burned them. She did it for him. But Daddy didn't believe that. From what the Sisters at Rosary School taught her, she knew he was going to hell for looking at those pictures, and she wanted to save him.

"It's true the pictures horrified me, but I really did burn them to save *him*." Elsie was embarrassed to talk about it, but she did. She told him how when he found out they were missing he went on a rampage from the devil himself to find out what happened. Momma asked her if she'd seen them, she told Momma, and Momma told Daddy. He didn't speak or look at her for a month. Later, Momma chewed her out. She said the magazines weren't bad because he looked at the pictures as if they were works of art. Daddy was a dilettante, she said, and told Elsie to look up the word.

"Which is just what I did," said Elsie. "I wanted to understand. The dictionary said: *A lover of art, yet not a serious lover of art*. Well, I told that to Momma and she said I should be sure not to tell anyone about what I'd found." Elsie sighed. "Momma said it was no one's business, especially not the Sisters'. Anyway, because they were works of art, it wasn't a sin," said Elsie. "They didn't look like works of art to me. Do you think they were, Jimmy?"

Jimmy agreed that they were probably not. "Hey, are you pulling my leg?" he asked.

"No!"

"Oh, well maybe it's that Catholic stuff that makes the difference."

She frowned and didn't answer. *What did the Catholic Church have to do with it,* she wondered.

Watching her confusion, he laughed, "You let me know if it happens again. I'll be happy to check out any future art."

Elsie decided Jimmy was joking, trying to cheer her up. At least *he* didn't think she was silly to get rid of those magazines. She could feel his eyes on her. What was that about?

"You scare kinda easy, girlie." Jimmy laughed. "On the dark road, right before we got here, you were scared, weren't you?" When she nodded, he went on. "What else scares you?"

"Well, my Daddy's razor strap from the barber shop is

scary. It's an old strap, the one he keeps at home. He uses it to beat me when he's real mad. It's thick, two strips of leather—a double–strap," she held her finger about four inches apart. "This wide. Barbers sharpen their straightedge razors on them. It makes black and blue marks all over my legs and," she looked down, "you know, everywhere back there. It leaves red welts."

Jimmy put a finger over her lips to stop her. "That's enough."

He went to his car, turned on the radio, then held out his hand. Elsie went to his arms and he danced her around the clearing.

"Tonight you're mine completely, you give your love so sweetly, tonight, tonight, the stars are in your eyes, but will you love me tomorrow," sang Jimmy.

She could feel his warm breath in her ear, humming their favorite song from the oldies' station. This was the most romantic night of her life. For once she had something to tell Lynn. She gazed at him with adoration.

"You're beautiful, Elsie," he said.

And then he kissed her.

Chapter Twelve

Pete sat in his office and tried hard to concentrate on what his service manager was saying; the guy was a bore. There was a tap on his door and she walked in.

"Excuse me, sir," she said, "I need a quick signature from you on these papers." He took the pen she handed him and signed the papers without bothering to read them, then extended the papers and pen back toward her.

"I do need these papers but you keep the pen, sir," she said, "I believe it belongs to you." She turned and just as he realized how hot the room had gotten, she was gone.

"That's some assistant you've got yourself, Pete!"

"Yes, ah," he cleared his throat. "She's very efficient." Without thinking he put the end of the pen she had given him into his mouth. What a nasty habit. It used to drive his mother nuts. It crossed his mind what a short trip that was for his ma, and the corners of his mouth began to rise and then—My God. It was El. Her taste, her smell! On—the—pen.

What was it Stan was saying? Something like, efficient isn't all she is I'd be willing to bet.

You don't know the half of it, Stan–the–man. If only he could share his secret with someone like Stan.

"Okay. Right. Ah, look, uh. . ." Peter's face was a blank which matched his mind. He'd forgotten the man's name! He was in a state of panic! "Oh, Stan." He said his name a little too loud, as relief flooded over him. "Yes, well, Stan, could we continue this later today? I just re-

membered something urgent I've got to take care of, Stan. Right away."

"Hey, sure buddy." Stan stood, "after all, you are the boss." He left the office, but his face was puzzled. Not only was Peter the boss, but he'd been ragging on Stan to go over the service figures and they'd had this meeting scheduled for over a week. Something with that woman...

Pete sat alone and sucked the pen. He could not believe he was doing this. It was as if she had cast a spell on him—on him! A spell that he could not shake if he wanted to. She hung, a heavy drape over his brain. He sucked every bit of her off of the pen. He wanted more and he wanted it now.

There she was—outside the office window watching him. Her little yellow Carmex jar in her hand. He saw her bright red nail dip into the jar then rub across her plump full lips. She gave him a slight knowing smile.

She walked in without so much as a knock. "We never got to finish what we started last night, did we?" she asked. "So when I arrived here this morning, I went into the john with my pen. I thought about sucking you, while I pushed that pen in and out of me, faster and faster. When I pictured how rock hard you got last night I came all over the pen. More than once." She gave him a hard look. "I thought you might like to participate in this little rivet in my mind so I brought you the pen...so glad to see you enjoy it." Her tongue flicked over her red lips and before his body would allow his voice to speak, she vanished.

He sat, because he could not stand and thought, "What am I going to fucking do with this bitch?" He picked up his phone and buzzed her extension. "I'm taking you to lunch," he said, "be out front in five minutes."

That should be time enough for his hard–on to subside.

"Well, certainly, sir," she said, "but are you sure you're

'up' for lunch?" she chuckled.

He tried to clear his mind for a few minutes, but all he could think about was how he was about to show the bitch how 'up' he was. Finally, he thought, fuck it. He put on his coat though the day was quite warm and walked out to meet her.

Chapter Thirteen

"Since we know so friggin' little about our mystery woman," the Lieutenant's steely pouched eyes parlayed with each of them individually as he spoke, "we must concentrate on what we know about her *victims*. Maybe we'll be able to get to the crux of this enigmatic woman by studying the gentlemen she favors with her big–bite." His voice was heavy with sarcasm and he *bit* at each word. When the Lieutenant spoke of we—he did not include himself. He meant everyone *but* himself.

Or in this case he primarily meant Law.

"Well, Detective Lawrence, may I invite you, now that you've decided to favor us with your presence, to begin by filling in Officers Tonetti and Mitchell, and yes, even myself, with what you know about the background of these gentlemen, our four victims."

Invite as in invitation? Law stood. He knew an order when he heard one. A building did not have to fall on his head. "For a start," he began, "none of the victims are gentlemen—just so we're clear on that."

No comments.

"Well, let's get right to it then. Victim, I use the term loosely, number one: male Caucasian, age 31, Name, Roger Dove, married ten years. Had two children, one's a girl, ten, one a boy. . .ah, eight. Here we have a recent mug shot from the file on him, 5'11" tall, reddish, wavy hair. . .usually wore a mustache and down–to–the–jaw–bone sideburns. Reported to be a firearms expert. The man loved all guns. I gather he fancied himself some sort of a cowboy—hence the strange facial hair. He wore cowboy boots and often carried a six–gun on his person. Colt 45. Extremely high IQ—181 it says here. He had a job, off and on, at the Wonder Bread warehouse. Some kind of a flunky job for a schmuck whose so blanking smart."

"Blanking?" Tonetti made the inquiry.

"Yeah, you get the idea, I'm sure. Please, continue to stuff your face while I finish here. . .warehouse. Yeah. Nothing wrong with working in a warehouse; my old man worked in one most of his life. But this creep has serious delusions of grandeur. His hobbies? Molesting and assaulting children—not your typical guy. He's a known pedophile—been through Minnesota corrections, was never corrected. In and out five *blanking* times. A repeat–repeater. The last time was four years ago; he served thirteen months of a four year sentence. Hard to feel real sorry for Mr. Dove. He had many good years left in him, using his 'six-gun' to rape and ravage."

Mitchell grabbed Dove's mug shot and whatever other photos were in the file. "What say we call him phallic–boy for future expediency. I'd say he led a rather sedentary life from the look of him—looks plumpish, bloated—wide in the beam. Not much of a cowboy, more like the doughboy."

It was funny but you could tell that no one felt like laughing.

"Yeah. Must've ate more than his share of Twinkies to get an ass like that. Oh. Reminds me." Law's face was hard, "His last victim was a twelve–year–old girl. He worked part time at her school—volunt*eer* work. The parents said he was such a nice, polite man. Only complaint the school heard was that he always brought the kids chocolates—parents these days don't want their kids smarfing down that shit."

"My, my, not that blank? We can say the shit word, can we?" purred Mitchell, batting her big baby–blues at him.

"Get off my ass. I'm going for some self–improvement here—more than I can say for you." Although for the life of him he couldn't think of what she'd need to improve. She was a blue eyed brunette with bounce—willowy, yet stacked like the proverbial brick house. And long legs.

"Well, watch what you say about chocolate." Mitchell snapped.

That made them laugh.

Back to business. "Now, let's us—meaning of course *you*—go back and talk to the wife and kids again. I don't think he had any friends. But hey, maybe the NRA knew him. Tonetti, you and Mitchell check that out and check the local gun shops—see if somebody there can give us a new angle. Who knows—could be somebody saw him with blondie. For what it's worth, I got the distinct impression his wife and kids are not all that sorry he's gone."

"Oh what a shocker!" Mitchell put her hand over her breast and they looked at her hand. "Well, I swear," her voice was mock dismay. "You're *all* pervs."

"Back to business. The wife and kids were not sorry. Fine."

"What? Just because they threw a huge bash, and stayed drunk for a week after the planting?" Tonetti thought he had a sense of humor and everyone needed a turn at frivolity during *this* meeting. He finished, "Some families have a different slant on how a funeral should be handled, is all."

"I remember talking to the little girl right after he was killed. She was so nervous and shy. Reminded me of a bird." It was big blue eyes talking again, and not smiling now, those eyes were fogging over. "But once I got her used to the idea that he wasn't coming back to hurt her she told me how he always got so angry with them. She said she and her brother Joey could never use the front door. And that one time, when she had to pee real bad—she said pee–pee—she ran in the front door so she wouldn't have an accident. He got mad; he took the broom and beat her two–week old kitten. He tied it up first—what a sport—in her room, then whacked at it with the broom while he yelled at her about how bad she was to have used the front door. Then he left the kitty with her to die while she watched."

Tonetti checked his notes, "Here it is. I talked to the boy. He was afraid of his Dad. He mentioned the cat deal. Also said that Dove, AKA phallic–boy," he winked at Mitchell, "sat around the house in his boxer shorts, and picture this, he'd have a six–gun shooter stuck in the waistband of his undies."

"Too bad he never had an accident and shot off his phallus with his phallic." Sometimes Tonetti *was* funny.

A few seconds of dead air was followed by the Lieutenant's voice. They'd almost forgotten he was in the room. "I know what you miserable excuses for police 'persons' are thinking," he barked. Some days it was harder than others to sound tough. He made up for real emotion with volume. "You are thinking that with all the crimes going on out there why should you people waste your precious damn time trying to find out who did the people of this state a favor by offing this asshole–lowlife. *Why*?" Volume up another notch, "because I say so. You got me?"

"You are mistaken sir, we were not thinking. We know we're not allowed to think without a direct order, sir." They all knew that the boss's bark was worse than his bite.

"Alrighty. Let's just continue, shall we," smirked Law. "Let's do number two."

Mitchell. "Do–doo?"

Tonetti. " Right here in our pants?"

Law gave them a look that said shut the blank up. "Okay. This one was a Roman Catholic priest. Another bad boy. He was an ex–priest when he got what he deserved." The lieutenant favored them all with a surly look. "38–year–old male Caucasian. 5'9", brown thin hair—mostly around the edges. He was getting bald."

"Hey, she saved him from the indignity of total baldness." Mitchell knew that Law had a hair thing; why miss a golden opportunity to get him where he lived?

"Okay smartass, I will not say the obvious, about how everybody likes a little ass. Again, number two, and spare me the bathroom humor this time, Ralph Barker, formerly *Father Barker*. He was married, has two sons, excuse me, *had* two sons, ages five and six. He had a history of abusing young boys."

Multiple groans. Something cops have much more opportunity to hear than multiple orgasms, mused Law, and continued. "The Church had complaints about this one for years—basically they prayed with him over his 'problem' and covered it for him."

More groans.

"Then occasionally they'd transfer him so he'd have a fresh group of boys to molest. He left the church six or seven years ago to marry a use–to–be nun."

"Got into a nun's habit, did he? What a lucky lady." They stared in slack–jawed disbelief. Was that really the Lieutenant who'd just said that?

Mitchell was first to recover, "Do we know if he abused his own kids?"

"I don't see if that aspect was checked out, not sure what it'd tell us, or if they'd talk to us, but let's check it—ASAP. It seems safe to assume that could be the reason why he married, to have his own little toys. If nothing else, maybe we can turn the kids over to social services for some help. Sara, that one's yours."

Tonetti interrupted, "At the risk of offending you, Lieutenant, the garbage disposal was not that bad a place for this dick's dick."

Law looked at his watch. "If we don't speed it up—I'll soon be sick to death of you."

"Oooh, let's have a closed casket for your funeral—then we don't have to see your grumpy mug again." That from Mitchell.

The Lieutenant cleared his throat. His rather ample body was getting tired of these small chairs; movement would soon be required.

"On to number three. Again, Caucasian male. Age 45. He's the runt of the litter, 5'4". Black hair, gray at the temples, but yes, Sara, before you ask, it was all there. This story has a different twist. His wife of twenty–eight years—must have been high school sweethearts. Anyway, she gets the news that she has breast cancer, has to have 'em removed. We can assume he was a breast man 'cause he chooses that time to inform her he's leaving her for his nineteen–year–old secretary."

"It's all in the timing, they say." Mitchell took off her high heel and began rubbing her silk covered toes. With her legs it was a welcome diversion.

"He sounds *special*, but what's his crime?" Tonetti asks.

"Let's see. He'd been planning this for about three months before her actual operation. Has all of the assets transferred to this young chick's name—seems the wife trusted him completely—nothing owned jointly. Now, here she is—very ill, he's about to leave her with zip. She has no family of her own alive, but they have one daughter."

"Oooh, I bet she's proud of Dada."

"It gets much worse. The daughter's fifteen, and she's in very expensive therapy. The therapist comes to the hospital to visit the woman to tell her Daddy has been having intercourse with his daughter." Law looked down for a minute, his face sagged. He took a drink of his coffee to cover his need not to talk or risk laying his emotions out on the table.

Tonetti covered for him, "By intercourse, I sincerely hope you mean that they were verbally expressing ideas to one another?"

Law took a deep breath. "Intercourse—since she was ten years old. The daughter's pregnant. Fortunately, they had life insurance and were still legally married when he died. He hadn't thought to change the beneficiary yet, so when he was murdered the woman and her daughter got half a mil."

"Yea! Bite–Woman!" clap, clap, clap.

"The rest of his estate is tied up in a civil suit, but they'll eventually get it back from the bimbo. They'll need it. From this report—they didn't get all her cancer."

"Maybe she'll have a chance to get well now that cannibal–dad is dead. State of mind being as important as it is," said Sara softly. Pensive now, "What about the baby?"

"She's around a year old. And lucky not to have gramps in the picture."

Sara continued to look morose. "Well, at least now the baby has a chance, and maybe the daughter can get the right help. Anybody check into a copycat on this one? Seems the wife and daughter had one hell of a motive. Excuse me, Law, a *blank* of a motive; don't want you to think I'm not as pure as you."

"You're as pure as I am hairy. Neither one will last forever." He shuffled through his file folder. "Nope, appears legit—no copy–cat here. We got her teeth marks; remember—those garbage disposals just don't cut it."

"Now there's an idea," Vince seemed excited, "if we could come up with a good garbage disposal—one that actually chews up the garbage instead of plugging the sink—we'd be rich. Then we could quit the department an' not have to deal with *human* garbage."

Law ignored him. His patience was wearing thin. "This copycat idea of Sara's reminds me of another point I was going to mention. People! This does not leave this room. Any leaks, you'll answer to me." He gave them his no–blanking–around glare.

"We'd take the firing squad before leaking, sir."

Law's granite look. "No toilet jokes."

No one moved. Satisfied that he had their attention, he continued, "Okay. The bite–it blonde doesn't actually bite off their dicks. She gnaws once—that's where we get her teeth marks—then finishes the job with what appears to be something like a surgeon's scalpel, or a barber's straightedge. The one bite? Don't get me wrong—it's a good hard one. We held back this information for a reason; we don't want it to come out until we're ready. Got it?" Heads nod. "Okay. Now we come to number four."

The mood had turned too serious for Tonetti; he ran his fingers through his dark curls. "I got this idea, boss—let's us award her a new set of false teeth in case she wears hers out—and be done with this entire thing. Let her have at these bastards."

"Well, Vince, I'd expect that from Sara, but we guys got to stick together when it comes to our dicks. Doesn't this bite–it notion make your balls shrink right up your ass? Got to draw the line." He looked at his notes. "Okay back to number four, maybe I'd have to agree. Number four, male Caucasian. Age 36. 6'2". Hmmm. She's found a way to handle the big boys. He was a high school gym teacher. Man, are they stokin' the fires down below for this turd. He had what he termed a 'safe' house for teens at his domicile. Neighbors confirmed seeing kids go in and out all day. But no adults. It was a place where, among other things, kids could gather and smoke dope. Dope that he conveniently sold them."

"Oh, I think I love this guy. Does he have a brother maybe?" Sara feigning heavy breathing.

"I don't believe you'd want any of his relatives. Mitchell, let me continue, would you?" Law was getting testy. "The last hurrah for this asshole—name was Richard Pluck—well, seems Richard got carried away with a sixteen–year–old girl. Kept her tied in his basement for two weeks. Gagged most all the time; if her classmates were upstairs doping they wouldn't know she was on the premises. Don't believe I have to draw you a picture of her two–week stay. It's been sixteen months now; she still has the mind of an eight–year–old child. Doctors say she may stay that way the rest of her life. It's a safer place for her to be. A child's mind doesn't process evil the way an adult's can. *Tweedle–dee–dee, tweedle–dee–dum.* I might go back to being a child myself before we're done with this blanking shit."

No smart quips—the mood in the room was heavy.

The Lieutenant chose this time to begin one of his famous coughing jags—and left the room. Whenever he'd heard more than enough he developed a tubercular hack.

Law showed his strain, too. "We believe he may have committed similar crimes in three other states using aliases; the computer picked up his MO, but there was never enough evidence to put the asshole away. He'd lose his job, move to another state, change his name, start in again. Generally, the state gave him severance pay, too. Made it easy. He was out on bail—awaiting trial when our bite–woman got him."

"Yea!" cheered Mitchell and Tonetti in unison.

Law checked his watch again. "I have to hit the streets. I need fresh air—maybe walk off the slime." His face was haggard, shoulders bent. "Sara, why don't you and Vince check the school administrators again? We'll reconvene tomorrow at 8 a.m. Bring your reports on those gun shops with you."

"Yep, will do sir." They watched him drag his butt from the room. No more jokes today.

Chapter Fourteen

Driving to Lorenzo's office I knew I was in for something I had no desire to do. I was nervous. I didn't need this. I knew I didn't need it. Life was bad enough without dwelling on the worst of it. Would he want to know everything about me? I pushed at the side of my hair, looping it behind my ear—a nervous habit. Even I knew it was a nervous habit. I didn't need any shrink to tell me that. I glanced in the rearview mirror—my teeth were clamped tight on my lower lip. My jaw throbbed. Okay Elsie, relax.

His office was on LaSalle Avenue. The neighborhood seemed okay—not too ritzy—might as well get it over with. I checked my watch again—ten minutes before I was expected. It'd be rude to break the appointment this late. I'd try it just this once. I'd made some promises.

When I got there, it was Lorenzo that made me comfortable. He was a large velvet brown teddy bear, paunch and all. And so friendly. His skin reminded me of chocolate-kisses, and his gnarly hair had gone gray. I liked him instantly—he inspired trust. I found out that he thought a lot like Lynn. Funny how I compared everything I liked or disliked about a person to Lynn. He was frank and open, straight to the heart of things. No bullshit—no frills. No more daydreaming about snowflakes like I'd done after her death. I could just see myself lying in the hospital hiding my eyes—my heart and soul, too—behind my arm. None of that crap now, at least not for awhile. His office was not richly furnished, in fact it was poorly furnished.

The chairs were uncomfortable, the walls a streaky drab brown—to match the rugless floors. I felt right at home. Lorenzo had an old–time Victrola and played the blues non–stop. Robert Johnson, Charlie Parks, Muddy Waters and others I didn't recognize. It was a reminder of Lynn playing piano and although I'd been avoiding music in my life this was somehow a comfort .

I was cajoled into visiting with Lorenzo daily. He promised that soon I'd be ready to participate in a group he headed. That was the therapy I needed; support from others in this group would help me grow strong. That's how he put it to me.

I noticed that though he charged me for an hour I was often there much longer. He charged according to what patients said they could afford—simply taking them at their word. Lorenzo listened to me for days—getting my life's background: I talked about home and I talked about Lynn.

"Why not come out and ask her, Elsie. I mean, *is* she balling this priest, Father–what's–his–name, or isn't she?" Lynn was not Catholic. "It's a *totally* simple question, right? Am I right? Look at me, damn it."

"Oh, hey, don't do this. You know very well I can't talk to Mother that way. She'd lay down and *die* if I said anything remotely close to that. I can't even ask her what her feelings are for Father Andrews, much less ask her about the *other* thing."

"Okay sure. Okay, I get it." The red–head's eyes flashed. "It's fine for the entire town to be in heat with gossip about this whole sordid affair, and they have been for over two goddamn years, but heaven forbid that we bother sensitive Sally with any of the gory details. Let's be sure we don't let her in on the secret that what she's doing on the side might be the cause of the slightest pain for her daughter."

Lynn fumed. "While we're at it, why not chat about how we're going to put a stop to the way dear old Daddy Ed treats you like his personal punching bag, for crissakes. And where is Sally when you're getting your hair pulled out? I mean it El...Listen to me, damnit! Is this shit going to go on forever? Is it?"

These questions were rhetorical. They had this same talk often. Elsie knew that Lynn didn't require an answer. There were no answers.

Still, Lynn went on. "I'll tell you what should be done with Ed; what should be done to any man like him. In the dead of the night somebody should appear, or sneak up on them. Like a *spirit* maybe. Sneak in and snip their dicks right off. What do you think? That would slow the old dick–heads down."

At another time they'd have roared with laughter at those words, not today. They both understood that Lynn was overstating the solution, but overstating it at least let them both feel some power. "I can't stand it, Els; you're in the middle of a nightmare here, and half the time you blame yourself."

This conversation seemed to be happening more than usual lately. Elsie was about to turn eighteen in a few days, and Lynn wanted her to move in, live at her home. The Faheys all wanted her and more than anything in the world she wanted to go. If she did what would happen to Momma?

Lynn seemed to think Sally was looking out for herself just fine. Sometimes she said maybe it was Sally and what she called "that–father–guy" that made Ed crazy. Elsie knew better. He'd been crazy long before Father Andrews came along. Lynn didn't care who had caused what as long as Elsie got the hell out.

Elsie kept the visits she'd had with Father Andrews to herself.

Lynn would go ballistic if she knew about that.

Elsie had been desperate when she finally went to the

rectory to visit him. She'd been sure the Father would try to help her. She was careful not to mention the rumors about the priest and her Mom. She talked to him about how her dad seemed to *have* to drink—like he was obsessed with it, and how her parents always seemed to find something to fight about, and then when they fought how she'd be scared for Momma and try to protect her and somehow it would end up with Elsie getting beat up.

"What I really want to know, Father, is when this happens, well, if I should call the police."

"No. Not the police, my child."

"But I'm scared. I'm afraid of what he's going to do to me or to Momma."

"It won't help to call in the police, Elsie. He'll probably take it out on your mother if you do that. And it will only make him drink more and get more violent. All you can do is pray to the Lord that your Daddy will get better, pray for God's help and that God will help you try to understand."

Elsie thought about what Father Andy had said. For a long time she could actually hear his soft voice telling her not to cause more problems for her mother. The more she thought about it the more it bothered her.

Something didn't compute. It was like hearing little–sir–echo spout her mother's words. She was getting old enough to realize that sometimes adults just try to cover their own behinds. Could that apply to god–like adults like Father Andy? What if more people found out about this affair with Father and Momma? Would they think he was a bad man?

Maybe the stuff about covering your behind applied *especially* to Father Andy. He had a great deal to lose.

She didn't like thinking these thoughts. That was what kept her going back for one more talk. The hope that he would change his advice. Father Andy's advice bothered her as much as the fights and the beatings. At least in a fight you didn't have to wonder what was going on, it hit you smack in the face.

There was something about this ordeal with Momma and the priest that came at you sideways.

If it made her feel the way it did, what did it do to Daddy?

Elsie still had the bad dreams. But rather than bunny monsters chasing after her she chased someone and was never quite able to reach them. Although she'd come close it was almost...almost...never could she make the connection she desperately needed to make. She'd wake up feeling frustrated and vaguely angry. She felt anger at the smallest things and wondered what was going on with her? Where did this anger come from? And what was it that she wanted so much and could never seem to get? So much, she dreamed of it constantly? She felt as if there was a fog, a mist over her brain, and that made it hard to think.

Even though thinking was hard, she'd figured out why her Daddy did not love her and probably never would. She'd decided that when he looked at her he saw Sally and all that he'd lost in life with the one woman he'd loved. Elsie was just a reminder to Daddy of Momma! She still wanted to please him, tried everything she could think of to please him, but she didn't really expect that she could, and it was not as important to her as it used to be. After all, she had Jimmy; he was what mattered now. He was all she needed.

Tonight they were going to their special place to celebrate her upcoming birthday. Since that first kiss the bluffs had become their place. Every minute they could spare they were there making plans for their future. Elsie told him all her dreams. It wasn't as easy for Jimmy to talk to Elsie about his dreams, but she believed that they were true soul mates.

Jimmy was not going to turn out like his Dad. His plan was to go on to college, although his grades had fallen out of scholarship range and paying the tuition could be a problem. Their plan was to get married next Christmas, then Elsie would work while Jimmy was in school. As soon as he graduated from college, they'd start their family. That was the part of the plan Elsie was in a hurry to get to. She wanted to be surrounded by a dozen happy kids. She would give them so much love and Jimmy would be a perfect father. They'd have the kind of family she could only dream about.

As she dressed for their evening date she glanced at her face in the mirror. There was a hint of pink to her cheeks that she knew came from thoughts of Jimmy. Her dress hugged her body above the waist, and below, falling away from her in soft folds, the violet color matched her eyes. She was seldom this careful with her preparations but tonight she wanted to look impressive. She never tired of thinking about how much she loved him, and how perfect their lives together would be.

Elsie snuggled close to him on the ride to the bluffs.

Jimmy smiled at her as he spread out a blanket and they lay beneath *their* bluffs. The air smelled of pine mixed with the sweet clover that covered nearby hills. Gusts of wind parted the curtains of leaves to expose nature's romantic backdrop. Overhead was one giant pearl of a moon surrounded by bits of fire that danced the dance of love. "The stars are beautiful," said Elsie.

Jimmy brought out the bottle of wine he'd brought. "C'mon birthday girl of mine, you're what's beautiful."

"Jimmy, you're the sweetest."

He set out two wineglasses—telling her how he'd swiped them the night before from Big Al's. "What do those drunks need wineglasses for anyway?" Jimmy asked. "Most of Big Al's customers prefer to drink their wine in extra–large tumblers, or straight outta the bottle."

She protested, but then took a sip and giggled, picturing her Daddy drinking wine from this small glass. Jimmy was right. It would never happen.

They toasted their first kiss. Pouring more wine, they watched a shooting star, and toasted the star! This night was magic.

Jimmy busied himself nuzzling soft slow kisses all over her face and neck, and then because of the wine and the night or because she was now eighteen, Elsie was the one who wanted longer, licking kisses, and soon Jimmy was on top of her.

A voice in her head told her that this could be wrong, even dangerous. But it felt good. How could something that felt this good be wrong? He took both of her hands in his and held them pinned to the ground over her head. He kissed her ears, her eyes and finally he kissed her mouth like she knew no one had ever been kissed. He kissed with so much love and tenderness that she felt her willpower dissolve. For once in her life it felt good not to have to feel strong, to feel his power and to give herself over to his power.

Because tonight he did have the power over her.

Many nights in the past Jimmy had begged and Elsie had remained strong but that would never happen again. His begging days were over. She was his.

She opened herself to him, trusting him completely. He would always be there for her. When she felt him come inside her, she knew she had never been this happy, or felt so close to anyone. This had to be much more than what other people experienced or they would always stay together. She felt sorry for all of those people and wished they could find someone to love them the way Jimmy loved her. Elsie had been waiting eighteen years to feel the way she felt at this moment. If only her parents could feel like this!

As they pulled into her driveway later that night each lost in their own thoughts, Elsie felt a spidery chill slide fast over her body; goose bumps poked out on her arms, as if there were tiny, minute creatures trapped inside—desperate to get free. That chill came from something in the house, she was sure of it. To Elsie, the house looked dark and dismal, with an eerie almost mysterious aura surrounding it.

They kissed goodnight but the magic of the evening had disappeared.

"Elsie. Hey, baby, what's up?"

She got out of the car not really looking at Jimmy—gave him a quick glance and, "I'm fine. Nite, Jimmy," her voice trailed.

She brushed her feelings aside. This was silly, she was just apprehensive. Maybe Daddy was watching them, lurking right inside the door and *that* was what she sensed. She stared at the house.

If he took one look at her he'd know exactly what she'd been doing.

She'd forgotten Jimmy's words as she walked up the front steps to the stoop. Something held her back, she felt vulnerable and exposed. A neighborhood dog barked and she winced; this feeling of dread kept her hand at her side; she tried again to raise it to the doorknob, but it didn't want to budge.

Then she remembered Jimmy.

She forced herself to look over her shoulder and give him a wave and a half–hearted smile.

Her hand drifted from her wave to the door. At last, she turned the knob and pulled it open. The living room was black; she stepped over the threshold, entered and was smacked with stale air—that aroma of beer and cigarettes hung in the room. Nothing about this room felt right, nothing familiar. She stopped inside the door to listen. This was a habit, something she'd done for years when she entered the house. The odd feeling grew stronger. She sniffed. Besides the booze and smoke there was another smell. Copper? It wasn't familiar.

As her eyes grew accustomed to the dark, she began to slowly move around the room. Quietly, she slipped out of her shoes, and crossed the hardwood floor; she stumbled over what sounded like glass. Something spun. Empty beer bottles?

She found her shoes, and put them on. She heard what had to be glass crunch as she walked. So it was a broken bottle.

Thud!

My god! She jumped at the sound, trembling. She was about to panic and run. For the first time, she noticed a strip of light wink at her from under the door that led to the den. That's where the noise had come from!

Someone was in the den! Her entire body trembled, she continued her slow motion movements and followed in the direction of the thud.

She stopped—she could hear her own breath and it sounded as loud as a scream in this deathly still house! She was dizzy, the room closing in. . .she grabbed the back of a chair.

Okay. Think it out. What was that noise? There must be a rational explanation. Something fell over. *By itself?* Well, it had sounded like dead weight. Sure, that was it. Where were Momma and Daddy? Asleep, she hoped. This was no reason to wake them, especially not in her disheveled condition. And what if they'd had a fight? What if Daddy was drunk? She moved again, going steadily toward the den, put her hand on the knob, then gave it a sharp push.

The whine of the door hinge added it's own eerie notes to her fright.

The small light from the table hit her like a blaze—a wash of fire that blinded her. Elsie stared through the blaze and saw red on red on red. . . .

Click–click. Her eyes snapped photographs for the album in her brain. A brain that bled, impaled, pierced by the scene in the den.

The lens focused and captured each photograph of shattered and violated flesh and bone. Click–click, the camera snapped the blood, the bile, the parts of a human skull. Fresh blood ran, cockroaches in flight, down the walls. Red drip, drip–dripped from the ceiling.

Elsie put every ounce of her being into a fortress of concentration. Inside she crumbled and screamed. She didn't think to check to see if someone waited behind her, someone still in the house, waiting to kill again.

The camera inside her was stuck on this one shot:

His big toe was caught in the trigger gizmo part of the shotgun, but the barrel had fallen to the floor, probably with a *thud*. Was that what she'd heard? There was one brown shoe and one white sock lying neatly beside him on the floor.

They were soaked red–brown.

"What do you call that trigger gizmo, trigger gizmo..." Her words repeated like falling dominos.

Pieces of flesh—a face?—parts of bones, *flash*. The picture registered. This headless form with one naked white foot was Daddy. *Her Daddy.*

The top of his head was gone, but it was Daddy.

The arena around her had been visited by a futuristic painter. The splattered red was copious, covering three walls and the ceiling. The ceiling had become a faucet in need of repair...drip, drip...splat; droplets did their faint Morse-code dance on top of her head.

The silence was horrifying; her lips hung, frozen open. There was no release for the scream that pressed at her every pore with its need to assault.

Inside her head that scream invaded and besieged her mind, its appetite so voracious as to drive her into raving rabid madness. But no sound escaped her twisted lips. Elsie blinked. Her mind was back.

She saw that Daddy's white sock had a gaping hole in the toe. She would buy him new socks, poor Daddy, his sock had a huge hole.

And then it came to her.

Now, for certain, forevermore, she would never please her Daddy.

In the background the phone rang. It rang for minutes at a

time and then stopped, only to begin again.

Lynn hung up the phone and slumped back in the over stuffed chair, her legs up over the arm. Why wasn't Elsie answering the phone? She had to be home by now and she'd promised she'd call. They had lots to talk about! Lynn wanted that report on Jimmy. She wanted to know just how he really behaved himself. She tried to call a few more times, looked at the late hour, and checked to see that the folks were in bed. They were. She grabbed a sweater and the car keys and snuck out.

Elsie's house looked, well, heck, thought Lynn, it looked *empty*! Oh man this was too weird. She ran up the walk and around the house to rap on Elsie's window, kept going and rapped on all the windows until she'd gone full circle. She rang the bell and yelled out, *"Elsie! It's Lynner! Lemme in!"*

Lynn stood back and looked for a few minutes. Only that one dim light, but nothing moved anywhere. The lights at the Fink's house next door went on and Mrs. Fink came outside in her bathrobe just as Lynn ran over to meet her. "Call the cops," she said. Mrs. Fink was pale, she turned back inside and you could see her hurry to the phone.

Jimmy was concerned about the way she'd behaved. All the way home he'd felt unsettled. Something was up with Elsie. He was sure of it. He'd gone right to his room and grabbed the phone. He'd get to the bottom of this. The ringing annoyed him, but although he tried many times, there was no answer. He was stumped. Why didn't the noise wake her folks? And, she'd looked so strange standing at her door. Something had to have been going on. What did she know that he didn't?

Maybe it was Ed. Could she have seen him standing watch inside the window and been afraid to say one word to Jimmy?

What if he'd found out what they'd done? But how could he?

It was this kind of paranoia that drove him to go back to her house. But when he got there, there was a squad car, lights flashing and every light in the neighborhood was on. Then he spotted Lynn's car. What was *she* doing here? Had Ed done something? My God, had he followed them? Jimmy put nothing past Ed. One thing was for sure, *something was wrong*.

Northfield had two police cars and the second one arrived with siren and tires squealing just as Jimmy got out of his car. Streams of white, swirls of red, in a place that moments before had been dark and still made it seem as if the circus had just come to town.

The police went right inside ignoring Jimmy. He followed them up to the house and when he was stopped at the door he told the cop who he was and that he'd just come home from a date with Elsie.

He heard a voice from around the corner call out, "Send the kid in if he knows her."

Jimmy was stunned. *If he knows her?* "Is Elsie okay, sir?"

"You mean is she alive?"

"Well, I guess."

"She's alive."

Jimmy heard the crunch of broken glass under his feet. Jimmy followed behind the last of the officers and gasped when he looked into the room. The cop lowered his voice, "Walk over there and if she'll look at you, try to talk, if not, just come back out of the room. Got it?"

Jimmy nodded. He looked at Elsie. She stood beside the headless body of her Daddy, wrapped in a moist veil of red. One hand lay on his arm, covering part of a tattoo that said Mom, surrounded with a heart; the other held a white sock. Lynn was on the floor beside her, with her head leaned against Elsie's leg and her arms around it, her eyes closed, talking softly, "Lynner's here, Lynner loves you."

Jimmy felt faint and hung his head, only to see that there were chunks of flesh under his shoe. "Ugh!" He puked into his cap as the officer took his arm and steered him from the room.

"Oh god, ohmygod," became Jimmy's chant. "I know Ed real well. I don't understand. How could this have happened? And it happened while Elsie and me...oh, *God*."

Jimmy asked the cop about the shotgun that hung from Ed's bare toe.

"You sure you want to know this?"

Jimmy nodded, yes.

"Your arms aren't long enough to pull the trigger of a shotgun when it's all the way inside your mouth. You put the barrel in, then pull the trigger with your toe, otherwise the power of the blast can make your grip slip; you could be left alive with no brain." The cop was grim–faced. "Using your toe is insurance that it'll be done right."

"How much do you think Ed drank...I mean, to be able to do it?" asked Jimmy.

The officer looked at him for a minute. "That in there?" the cop nodded toward the room. "That's not just drink. Despair and rage mixed with the booze. That'd be my guess."

Jimmy went back to the living room. His stomach was beginning to settle down, when they discovered Sally's mutilated body. Elsie had already been taken away. The cop's words, about despair and rage, rang in Jimmy's ears. He knew Ed was an angry drunk, but this? He didn't get this. Rage, for what? He wanted to ask that cop, but didn't dare.

The priest was called to give last rites to what might have survived of their souls. None of the cops talked to Father Andrews. Jimmy hung around and watched and listened and learned.

After the funerals, the Chief of Police called Elsie and

stopped by to see her. He gave her the letters which Ed had written right before the murder/suicide. He told her they had been left in the car. The police had found the letters about the same time they discovered the bodies.

The suicide notes told how Sally was having an affair with Father Andrews. Elsie knew that. Evidently, so did the police. The Chief didn't call him *Father* Andrews, just Andrews. Elsie felt more anger toward Father Andy than she could ever remember feeling. She couldn't get out of her mind how many times she'd gone to see him, to talk about her Momma and Daddy, to ask for his help. For God's help. He never told her to tell the doctor, or the police, or anyone when she got beat. *Try to understand*, he would say. Give it over to God.

Oh, she understood. Completely.

And what she understood was that he'd tried his sacred best to protect *himself* from the scandal that would come out along with the news of this affair. He'd helped ruin her family and it was too late now to save any of them.

After the Chief left, Elsie picked up the phone and dialed the rectory. Father's private number. He answered it himself as she knew he would. "I called to tell you how little I think of you, Father Andy. You have destroyed my faith in you and your God, forever."

She hung up on his answer.

The letters said that Ed had planned to kill the entire family. *Elsie just didn't make it home on time.*

She knew that she should have been home to take care of Momma. Maybe Daddy would have been happy and Momma wouldn't have had to sleep with that *priest* if she had been a better daughter.

In her dreams now, she came home ten minutes sooner. One less kiss. Elsie was in a place complete and total despair takes you.

She was in hell.

Chapter Fifteen

She sat out front in her white Mazda waiting for me. The top was up, and I wondered why, on a day like today.

That question was answered in seconds.

I opened the door to get in and voilà, her bra and panties were a cozy twosome on the bucket seat I was about to cradle my ass in. I had to grab them or sit on them; I chose the former. The fabric alone was sensual. Lace can be scratchy—especially the cheap stuff. This was made with silk so soft it felt as if it would melt in your hand. It occurred to me right then that this was not silk from a silkworm but the silken threads woven by a spider for its lair.

She laughed. A musical sound and yet it made me want to squeeze her throat till her face turned purple, a color that would match her eyes.

I felt like Lot's wife—I couldn't pull my own eyes away. What would I turn into if I did, or then again, if I didn't? This woman muddied my brain so I couldn't think straight. I wanted her too much. Way too much for it to be healthy for me. And although she didn't know it, it was certainly not healthy for her.

Her blouse was open almost to the waist, giving me an eyeful of that magnificent body. Her skirt was pushed high on her thigh; I saw blonde wisps. Did I imagine it, or did she smell like a bitch in heat?

A trucker drove alongside us and honked as he blew her a kiss.

She sighed, "So many hard pricks, so little time." She

gave him a wave with a laugh and sped away.

"There's a motel three blocks north on the right," I commanded, "go there." I rubbed the panties and thought of where they'd just been. What was she wearing now? I knew the answer.

She looked over at me as her red nail flicked one of her nipples, making it stand and beg to be noticed. I noticed. "Motels are for romance. . .for lovers," she answered. She pulled into an Amoco station and parked around the side, and before I knew what was happening she'd opened her door and walked to my window.

She leaned in, her tits poke–me–in–the–face, close. "It's not romance I want." She put two red dipped fingers between her legs, and then waved them tauntingly under my nose. "I'm going to the john. If you want what I want, wait one minute—then follow. Oh, by the way," she said as she walked away, "isn't it a bit warm for that jacket?"

Bitch. Fucking bitch. She was going to get her way once again and I knew it.

I waited. One minute seemed like thirty. I should have been thinking about nothing but what a bitch she was, that and how could she force me, me!, to go inside that filthy restroom. It was a gas station! I should have thought about all of that and more, about how soon I could get even. I hated the way she could control me, yet here I was counting the seconds before I could ram it to her. And, in a way, I liked the way she made me feel.

No one had dared do this before her.

She opened the door when I knocked, "Are you the service manager? 'Cause if you are, come on in. I need service."

God, she makes me crazy.

The scene that followed was not tender. We tore at one another. With no self–control and no inhibitions. We *rolled and bucked back and forth over the cold, hard and dirty floor of that gas station restroom.*

She pulled away. She seethed, she boiled with something that was projected as anger in the extreme, although I knew that it couldn't be anger—merely heat for me. She had to feel what I felt.

She got herself up on top of the toilet, legs wide apart, and dripping. "Come here, and lick it off my pussy."

"My pussy, you mean?" *I wanted her to acknowledge her true feelings and my upper hand.*

"No. I mean mine. Now lick."

I licked. It was a picnic. Whatever made her hard inside made me harder still. I wanted to push my entire head up inside her. I rubbed my head, my hair, my face, everywhere I could between her legs. As my tongue flicked over her she told me what she was going to do the next time we met.

"Next time, Pete," *her voice was a caress,* "it will be in bed, like I know you want it. I'll tie you to the bedposts while you lie on your stomach. I'll suck and lick and nibble until you're so hard, that when I finally let you inside me you just might stab me to death."

Bang, Bang! The noise came from fists pounding on the restroom door. We'd locked it, thank God.

"Hey, anybody still alive in there?"

Her last words had gone off like a gun in my head. Did she say, stab her to death?

The beating on the door continued; someone wanted in.

We did the best we could to pull ourselves together in a hurry. We were both covered with her "glaze."

She took her ever–present jar of Carmex—threw it in her handbag, and out the door we went. . .there was a line of about a dozen people. I could feel my face redden as we passed them. On the other hand, she didn't seem to notice they were there. Mr. Big was still standing tall, and we both smelled like we'd spent a week at the Mustang Ranch. She drove past the station pumps and turned onto the street with not even a look toward me. It was all I could do to keep from asking when I'd see her again.

I hurried to my car when we got to the office and headed straight for the club. I needed a steam, followed by a cold shower. And I needed to think about this witchy woman.

Her day was coming. Sure as my dick would live to get hard another day, she was going to get what she had coming to her. And soon. It had to be damn soon. Meanwhile, this was all mighty entertaining. Yes, it was.

I sat in the lobby for a moment to gather my thoughts before heading toward the locker rooms. There was a newspaper lying on the table beside me. Idly I glanced, then picked it up to read an article that caught my eye.

The Minneapolis Star and Tribune had made this story front page news.

My eyes skimmed the first few columns, then they had my interest. I read every word of the last part of the story:

Minneapolis police have released reports on four murders in the past nine–month period. These murders appear to have been done by the same person or persons. Complete details are not available at this time. Police have few clues with regard to the suspect's identity. They are looking for a Caucasian woman, 5'4" to 5'8" tall, approximately 110 to 118 pounds, age 25 to 35. The victims have been Caucasian males between the ages of 30 and 45. All have been married with one or more children. These men were found tied, arms and legs spread–eagled to a four–poster bed. All four were nude. They were mutilated in a way that police have not disclosed. Additional information may be forthcoming later this week. Police ask your help in locating this woman for questioning.

She may have some interest in, or knowledge of, herbal medicine. She may work in the area as a hair stylist, or in a barber shop, or some aspect of the medical profession. Police urge caution for men of the listed age group when meeting with any woman they do not know well for the purpose of having sex. Show caution if any form of bondage is suggested by the other party. Please call the Minneapolis Police hot line and report any unusual incident. You will not be asked to reveal your identity. Police Chief Dargis, when asked if the fact that all four of the victims have criminal records that involve repeated rape, murders, and child molestations, could mean that we have a vigilante woman on the streets, declined comment.

"Well, well, well," I mused aloud. So this tying scene wasn't all her own imagination. She must have read the Star and Tribune article earlier today. I might have known. Too bad, but, there is more than one way to look at it. If she was getting her "lines" from the newspapers, maybe she was controllable after all.

I headed for the steam room feeling amused and relieved. I was now most anxious to participate in her little drama. In fact, I'd written a few scenes myself—scenes that would greatly surprise even a tramp like her. And my inspiration did not come from the newspapers.

Ah, well, let "romance" take its natural course. No rush. Not anymore. Now that I know where the bitch is coming from. Why deprive myself? The lady is one hell of an exciting lay.

Chapter Sixteen

Lorenzo listened to me, his body still, his face solemn, then he did what I'd never imagined a therapist would do—he let me listen and he began to talk. On TV they ask questions and wait for you to answer. Lorenzo told me things that had never occurred to me. Without him they never would have. Not until after years of frustration. He told me:

I didn't have to love my Daddy. I didn't have to love Momma either. I hadn't asked to be born, had I? It wasn't that I chose them and made a rotten choice—I hadn't chosen at all. Life was a roulette wheel. As a baby, you didn't get to spin your own wheel. You were stuck with the spin life gave you. Of course, my parents had that same roulette wheel. They had their own problems with where the dice rolled. But, and this was the new concept for me, that was not my fault.

Lorenzo was on a roll.

Where their dice rolled was not my fault.

Not only didn't I ask for what fate had laid on me but it was okay to be upset about it. In fact, Lorenzo said, it was healthy to be angry and whether I realized it or not, I was angry. He gave me the Minnesota Multiphasic test—my anger shot off the top of the chart. There was no denying the fury I felt.

"*Aren't you angry that your Daddy never gave you the smallest sign of his love?*" *he asked.* "*What would it have cost him? If he didn't feel it, he could have faked it, couldn't he?*"

I guessed he could have.

Lorenzo evidently didn't think that my story of how Daddy had worn an ugly pink shirt I'd bought him for a present once was proof enough of love. He sneered at the thought that it was. When he talked his massive body lumbered back and forth. The rage he projected spit out along with the fire in his eyes, and when he stopped, because he'd made his point, parts of his large body continued to roll and wave.

"How about your Momma? Aren't you angry that she didn't protect you? Why did she tell you to put your Daddy's needs first?" Droplets of sweat flew from his brow in all directions as he paced.

"Your Momma, Elsie, listen here! Your Momma was busy screwing the priest instead of dealing with her failing marriage in whatever way she could even if that meant getting out of it—dealing with it, instead of hiding from it. Aren't you angry that Father Andy who should have been trying to help an abused young girl was instead busy balling the child's mother and trying to cover his own ass?

"And now, your best friend has been savagely murdered by some psycho–whacko man who may never pay for what he's done?

"What about the fact that good old Dad planned to kill you too! It isn't fair. . .is it?

"Well, Elsie, is it fair?" Lorenzo demanded an answer, "Is it?"

"No. I don't think it's fair," I whispered.

"You'd better believe it's not. And that's a fact, Elsie. A fact. Nothing can be done about it. We're going to help you to learn to deal with that fact. First thing you'll learn is to get angry on the outside instead of holding it sealed in your gut. That's what will make you sick. Do you understand?"

I nodded, and pushed back the hair from my face, twisting it around my ear.

"You can't begin to forgive—not that you should be concerned with that now, but you can not begin—until you get that anger out."

Made sense.

"Why let it have this power over your life? You're going to get it out in the open; it will fly away on its own."

Fly on its own. Let it out in the open. I thought back to all the things I kept sealed inside my gut from years back:

The murder/suicide was the hot topic of conversation around town.

"I waited years to get you to 'do–it', now no one's interested in hearing about that." After a few beers one night, Jimmy confessed to Elsie how disappointed it made him. "All they can talk about is how lucky I am." He took a drink and mimicked, "You're damn lucky Elsie didn't come home any earlier. I try and tell 'em that with what I was doin' to you, you weren't likely to leave early."

Why he's pouting, he's jealous! Elsie thought to herself.

"An' another thing I want you to know. You're beginning to get on my nerves. You cling. You're too needy."

Maybe it was the beer talking.

"Are you saying you don't want to be with me anymore, Jimmy?"

"Hell no, I put in my time, paid my dues. You got plenty of cash. Let's see a justice–of–the–peace and get married. We can do it this weekend. Time *you* started to pay dues to me."

"Jimmy!" Elsie threw her arms around him. She knew he'd been teasing her all along. He wanted to marry her!

Chapter Seventeen

Elsie and Jimmy had been married a year. She kept what had happened to her parents locked in her mind. She had Jimmy. She thanked God for him. He was all she needed.

For their first Christmas Jimmy gave Elsie an adorable black–and–white beagle puppy. "You're so smart, Jimmy, you knew what I needed, even before I did." She named her puppy Pip, after one of her favorite Dickens' characters in *Great Expectations*.

As it turned out, Jimmy had a few expectations of his own.

Now that they were married she missed the romance, particularly all the kisses.

"You're a fab kisser, Jimmy!"

Not that they didn't kiss, but never like before, under the bluffs. Jimmy explained to her how unreasonable she was to expect that from him. She was sure he must be right. He always was.

What Jimmy *did* want, was a blowjob.

For some unfathomable reason Elsie could not make herself do that one thing. The more obsessed he became, the more stubborn she found herself. She wanted to make Jimmy happy more than anything, so why couldn't she do this? Why be such a stick–in–the–mud? Although that whole idea of lapping up hot *snot* had not appealed to her from the very beginning days when Lynn talked about it with her.

Lynn would know how she felt.

Lynn understood all. Elsie should have called her sooner, she thought as she picked up the phone to talk to her friend but she felt funny. She knew Lynn didn't think much of Jimmy. She was afraid to ask why. 'Cause with Lynn, if she asked she would surely be told, and maybe she wouldn't want to hear the answer. She told herself that Lynn's feelings were all because of the way she and Jimmy'd eloped without telling anyone.

The way that Jimmy wanted to have sex now, without getting her turned on, was harder than she ever imagined. Elsie didn't want to admit that maybe he wasn't perfect.

And these days she had things besides sex on her mind.

Daddy and Momma might be shoved to the back of her brain, but at night when she closed her eyes they came out of their hideaway and wreaked havoc; images flooded out, blood red images, doing the *cha-cha-cha*.

What she needed was time. She begged Jimmy to give her the time to get over this. She was getting sick to her stomach often lately, even throwing up in the mornings. Maybe she was pregnant. That was a laugh.

Lynn was on the way over to drive her to the doctor right now. She'd insisted that Elsie find out what was going on. It was most likely nerves, but whatever, they'd soon have the chance to talk and get these problems figured out.

Elsie saw that fireball head as the car drove up and she ran out eagerly.

In ways she was closer to Lynn than Jimmy. It was hard to accept that she and Jimmy never got beyond the stage they were at on that passionate night at the bluffs, never moved on to the next level of intimacy.

With Lynn she was open; with Jimmy there was a barrier.

Elsie was never sure he loved and accepted her. Accepted, that's what she never felt with him, accepted.

Lynn grinned, like the imp she was, as Elsie hugged her hello. That was not what Elsie had expected. She'd heard earlier today, in the way only a small town spreads gossip, that Lynn had given Frankie the boot. Elsie couldn't wait to get the details but she didn't want to push.

As they drove Elsie managed to beat around the bush awhile before finally coming out with her problem about sex and Jimmy.

"Do you come?" Lynn, as always, got right to the heart of the matter.

"What?"

"You heard me. Stop choking. Does he bring you to orgasm? Do, you, come?"

Elsie studied her shoes. "Oh. I don't know."

"Bull, Els. Even I know that you know. We talked about master–diddlie–bating years ago. I know that *you* know. So? What's the answer?"

"Not really."

Lynn gave her most incredulous look. "What does that mean? A little, tiny come, or what?"

Elsie was almost in tears, and now she started to giggle at the same time. "Man, the things you say. It means I don't know what I feel. I mean, I know I don't come. But I don't know why. I'm afraid there's something wrong with me. I know it can't be Jimmy's fault."

"So, he's a good lover then?"

"Of course! Well, I'm sure he is. It's just that things were so different before. He would kiss me, and I'd melt...like dissolve. You know? I could feel his power. I'd get lost in him."

Lynn looked as if she was about to puke and Elsie stopped. "Yeah, okay I get it, go on, go on!"

"We talked all the time and I felt like we were so close. Now, he's busy with school. We hardly even hold hands before he grabs for me in bed. I try to pretend I'm asleep, because otherwise he begs, *"please, baby please, blow me,"* over and over. I hate that begging. I think it makes me think less of him. Anyway, I can't make myself do it!"

Since Lynn seemed, for once in her life, to be speechless,

Elsie went on. "Lynn, you've got to help me. I feel like I'm going crazy! What I need from a man, I thought I was getting from him; now I find that I'm not getting what I thought I needed at all. Maybe I don't even *know* what I need. The things he wants from me don't seem to be the same things he used to want, and they aren't the same things I thought he wanted. It's the very same way I used to feel about Dad. I go round and round in my head, and all I get is a headache."

Elsie rustled in her purse. "Oh, I found something the other day when I was going through some papers in my old vanity. I wrote it to you years ago. I guess I put it away and never gave it to you. It's in my purse here someplace."

"Frankie acted the same as Jimbo, Els. That's the biggest reason why I got rid of him. I want to be a concert pianist. I mean, there is more to life than his dick, however nice it *was*, and he could not get that fact through his hard head. Either hard head," she laughed.

"Do you miss him so much that it, like, you know, *aches?*" Elsie was so glad that Lynn brought up the subject of Frankie.

"Nah, not that much yet. I don't think we were right together, you know? As long as I did what he wanted me to do and *thought* what he wanted me to think, things went rolling right along. But you know me. Dad's told me what to think and do for too damn many years, bless his heart." Lynn was not as liberal as her Pop. "I'm not letting some man do the same thing just 'cause I like what's between his legs. I'm told they all have similar equipment. Now, if I find one where I like what's between his ears, then it's more plausible. I want some time to do things my way. Frankie's history."

Elsie nodded in agreement, "Here. I found that note; listen. 'A relationship with a person of the opposite sex (male) is in many ways like a bottle of aspirin. Allow me to explain; say you have a bottle of aspirin—the more you like your person—the bigger the bottle. You get a headache, you take an aspirin. You get a really big headache, you take more than one. Before you know it, the bottle is gone. You can't stand the headaches anymore, so you go out and buy a new bottle of aspirin. Such is the way of life...by Elsie'. The title is, *My Thought*. Well, what do you thinka, My Thought?"

They giggled. And, as always when they talked and laughed they felt better.

"Well, har–de–har–har! I think it's high time I went out and got me a new bottle of aspirin is what I think. Let's make it the colossal–size this time." Lynn was always ready for what she called real life. "Look, Els, you know I'm not all that nuts about Jim. I can't hide my true feelings from you, but if he's what makes you happy let's talk more about it. I know we can figure out something. Now go on; you're gonna to be late for your appointment. I'll be waitin' in the lobby. You go see what your doc has to say."

Elsie had been sure to make her clinic appointment for Dr. Jack's day off. She pretended he didn't exist.

Lynn watched her friend walk away. She knew how important they were to one another. Elsie needed love and approval. Lynn understood why. But it made her such a wimp with men. How could she make her realize the love and approval she really needed had to come *from* herself *to* herself? Lynn had already tried telling Elsie how she saw the world through fashionable, albeit naive, rose–colored–glasses, but Els didn't have a clue what she was trying to say. She wore the rose glasses and saw strawberry fields! How in hell did someone who'd had Elsie's life see things that way? Maybe the "glasses" kept her from becoming a screaming meemy; her reality was too harsh to deal with.

Well, anyhoo, Lynn thought, *I'm gonna protect her, and teach her things about life, love, and most of all, men and sex.*

Lynn worked in town at the Malt O' Meal plant. As she left work one night last week she'd seen Jimmy sniffing like a hound around one of the girls from work. This girl was fast. A kind of, "it ain't pretty bein' easy" girl, in the literal sense. Lynn knew she'd have to tell Elsie.

Speak of the devil.

"Yeah, what's up?" judging from the look on Elsie's face, the news would be big.

Elsie beamed, put both hands on her stomach, then flapped her eyelashes.

"You're lookin' like a goon there, girlfriend." Lynn joked. Then the significance of Elise's gesture hit her. "We're gonna' have a baby?"

Elsie nodded. "You're going to be a godmother!" They jumped, spun one another in a circle with arms outstretched. Suddenly they were two young girls at play.

Elsie stopped. She looked concerned. "What's Jimmy going to say?"

"Why, he's going to be thrilled. Just like we are!"

"Oh, you don't understand. We agreed not to start our family for awhile. He wants me to keep working. It's important to him to stay in school."

"Hey, you've got enough money to have three babies!"

Elsie shook her head. "Never enough. He doesn't want to be poor like his dad. Oh god, he's going to think I planned this, and I didn't. I want him to be happy. Do you think there's a chance he'll understand?"

"Whoa there, girl. Sit. Relax. Everything'll be okay. I'm sure Jimmy will be fine. He knows how much you want a baby. Look, I'll help you. We can arrange our schedules so I can baby–sit when you're at work. How can he object to that? Jeeze, you got your *own* money." She put her arms around Elsie, hugging tight. "Are you okay? C'mon, let's go. You'll feel better after you talk this over with Jimmy. I'll come with you. We'll make sure he understands."

"No. I don't think you have to come with, just drop me off. It'll be like you say. He'll understand. But let's meet for lunch tomorrow. Then, we'll go look at baby stuff. I do have enough money. Jimmy doesn't have to worry. But we think of it as *our* money, now."

Lynn bit her tongue. "I'll get you from work. We'll eat on the run, an' go find out where they keep the pink and blues. If it's a girl you have to name her after her Auntie Lynn!"

Lynn told her later how worried she'd really been that night.

She tried to practice her piano, but Elsie was on her mind. She wished they could have gotten back to the sex, love, life, men, talk. Elsie had to stop letting the men in her life push her around. It was almost as if she wore a huge sign on her back, "I'm wounded. Hurt me, and I'll love you anyway." It was enough to make a person want to shake some sense into her.

Lynn had tried to stay out of the way, to give things half a chance for Elsie and Jim. She knew herself. Knew she'd never be able to keep her big mouth shut. She cared too much for Elsie. Seeing him after work that night, sniffing around Rena, the bitch, well, it made her realize how much Elsie needed her. She should have tried to do something before this.

Jimmy was nothing but a wart on the asshole of life. *Our* money? He did not deserve Elsie, and she sure as hell didn't deserve him. She'd never get the kind of guy she deserved if she didn't first get a new attitude. Attitude, with a capital A.

Her fingers stumbled over the piano keys. *Shit*. She could play lots better than this. . .it was a surprise that Pops didn't come in to remark on that fact. Probably because it was so bad he was embarrassed for her. She was making stupid mistakes, couldn't begin to concentrate. What bothered her most was the thought that maybe her *biggest* mistake didn't have anything to do with playing the piano. It was leaving Els alone tonight. Alone, but with Jimbo.

Well, her mind was for sure not on piano. Should she go over and try to talk to Elsie?

Maybe she'd first give her a call.

While Lynn fretted, Elsie waited.

Jimmy should have been home from school hours ago. True, he didn't expect her home this early. The longer Elsie waited, the more excited she became. By now, she'd gone over it a hundred times in her mind. He would be just as happy as she. Things happen for a reason, don't they? Pip curled beside her in the antique olive–hued chair, so she told Pip her good news. He wagged his tail and nuzzled her lap, then licked her face.

If Elsie was excited so was Pip.

After what seemed an eternity she heard Jimmy's car. She ran to the door, and when it opened threw her arms around his neck. The beer on his breath was acrid, not what she wanted at this moment. And it happened often lately, too often, but he *was* under a lot of stress. To hear the stories he told some of his professors were real creeps. Still, sometimes, like tonight, she thought she smelled perfume mixed in with the booze. Once she asked him about it—in a teasing way—he was furious. She'd never forget his cutting words.

"You're as crazy as your old man. Why couldn't you have taken after your ma? Just my luck! You're a nut when you could have been a round–heels instead!"

Elsie worried something was very wrong with her thought processes, because she would say something to Jimmy she thought was okay to say, and he'd go nutso. It'd been that same way with Daddy. She never could figure out why they got angry. This must be something others instinctively knew. She felt as if a major piece of the puzzle was missing from her brain.

Tonight Jimmy didn't stop to chat. He pushed her aside and headed straight for the shower before she could get a word in to tell him her news.

Elsie could barely contain her joy as she waited. "Jimmy?" Would he ever get out of the shower? She knocked on the bathroom door so that he could hear her over the running water.

"Will you leave me the fuck alone?" He screamed. "What does a man have to do to get some peace?"

At long last he walked out, still drying his hair. The thick red towel had been a wedding present from Lynn. He's so good looking, Elsie gazed with admiration, the baby will be beautiful. "Jimmy, don't you want to know what the doctor said today?" she bubbled, choosing to ignore his bad temper. It was odd, but he appeared to be dressed to go out.

"Look, Madam *Nagme*, I've had a hard day. Why don't you stop playing your games and tell me whatever it is you want to tell me? You're going to do it anyway, and I'm in no mood for your little quiz."

She paused, a lump formed, coating her throat. Why was he glaring at her? She was nervous now, her natural high left her hanging and she was about to slam back down to earth. She must have done something to make him mad and he didn't even know about the doctor yet. She felt dizzy. "Well," her voice was tentative, "here's the thing, Jimmy, *you* are going to be a Daddy."

The hush roared through the room.

"That's what the doctor said," she stammered, "isn't it fantastic?"

His eyes shot through her. "*How*. How did this happen?"

She giggled, nervous. "You know."

"Elsie, will you grow the fuck up! Get a fucking grip. You know that's not what I meant. We had a plan. We were going to wait to have us a bunch of brats. Wait, until I finished school. We had an agreement. What happened to that?"

"Nothing happened to that, Jimmy. Don't be mad. I can work while I'm pregnant and Lynn's going to help me take care of the baby. You won't have to worry. You won't have to quit school, I promise."

"You promise!" He brushed his fingers through his drying

hair and picked up his jacket. "What did your friend Lynn have to do with this? What does *she* care what I'll have to put up with? You'll have to quit your job eventually. Even if you don't, where will I study? Did you think of that? With some screaming brat here, I won't be able to study in my own home. I'm not going to let you ruin my life this way. No wonder your Dad drank the way he did. He was right about you all along. I'm sick of your selfish attitude about every damn thing."

He was moving toward the door while he ranted.

Elsie ran after him, hysterical. "Jimmy, listen! I didn't plan this. You can call the doctor if you don't believe me. I always use my diaphragm. It was an accident. He said things like this just happen. You know how much I want a baby, maybe it will help me get over, you know, *things*." She clung to his arm as he tried to go down the front steps.

"Jimmy, do you still love me?" she cried. Those words echoed around her and she felt ashamed, but she knew she'd say them again. She needed Jimmy.

He turned to her. "I'm so damn sick of your always asking if I love you. I'm here, aren't I? That ought to be good enough for you." As he spoke he gave her a rough shove, "Get off a' me!"

She stumbled on the step and fell.

He glared. Disgust evident in his face. In his best imitation of her voice, he leaned over, his face right in her face, "*Do you love me, Jimmy? Do you love me, Jimmy?*" he whined.

He gave her a hard toe in the stomach for good measure. Maybe that would take care of the kid. He left her that way, sobbing, lying on the cement driveway.

"Christ!" he yelled again, as he squealed the tires.

Faintly, in the background, Elsie heard the ring of the phone, but she couldn't make herself get up to answer it.

Chapter Eighteen

The days flew by.
One day I asked Lorenzo what he thought about a joke someone told me that morning at the Tom Thumb. I was offended, but I didn't know how to handle it. I wanted to know what he would have said.

"What's the joke?" he grumbled.

Embarrassed, I said, "What's the Harlem High School cheer?"

His eyebrow arched.

"Watermelon, Barbecue, Cadillac car, we're not as dumb as you think we is."

His poker face changed for a mere millisecond, his jowls began to pinch then relaxed blank once again. Instead of an answer, he gave me an assignment.

"Make new lines for the joke," he said. "Lines that might offend other groups of people. The next time we met, we'll read them, and talk about it." Then he said I was ready now to begin my days with the 'group.' He added that he would give them all the same assignment.

The group? I knew I wasn't ready. I didn't feel ready to get attached to any more people. Thinking about talking to people made me think of the men.

They wanted to talk too. First sweat all over me, then talk. As soon as they discovered that I didn't wish to talk, they had to. I thought of Lynn's words when she was upset about Dad. "I'll tell you what should be done with Ed; what should be done to any man like him. In the dead of the night, somebody should appear, or sneak up on them.

Like a spirit maybe. Sneak in and snip their dicks right off. What do you think? That would slow the old dickheads down."

Well, lately, all thoughts of the men made me remember those days when my friend Lynn was still here to help me:

Elsie calmed herself.

Jimmy was right, she shouldn't have gotten pregnant. It was her responsibility. She knew how important school was to him. How could she have done this to him? And she did hang on him like an albatross. She would change.

She could feel the wet between her legs and saw that it was blood.

"Dear God, don't let me lose this baby," she prayed, and then felt guilty. First, because she didn't talk to God anymore unless like this, she wanted something, and second, she knew that Jimmy wanted precisely what she was praying to not have happen.

He couldn't have his way this time. She had to find him fast, apologize, then they'd go to the doctor together. The doctor could tell him that it wasn't her fault. Although, she could see now how Jimmy could feel that she'd let him down.

She drove the streets of Northfield, her mind going like a siren, and the car tires squealing right along with her siren.

He couldn't vanish into thin air. Where could he be?

They were in love, she reasoned, he'd be anxious to see her, too. Thinking of their love made her remember. Their place. That's where he *had* to be.

The short drive was like a climb up a mountain—how could she survive until she touched his face again? There at last, she parked her car down the road, she'd walk in and surprise him. He was here. She could feel his presence.

How romantic that he'd come to their special place to think over their problems. He was sweet. *She* was the inconsiderate one.

But, was he right? *Was she crazy like Daddy?*
Whatever she was, she'd make this up to him.

As she got closer she heard the music. Jimmy's stereo, and it was playing their favorite oldies station. Oh, thank you God. She felt faint, but she hurried, the need to feel his arms around her was even stronger than her need for survival.

He must be sorry too that they'd argued. That's why he was here at their bluffs, their place, playing their music.

She heard voices. The radio?

Maybe. . .there was music in the background.

She barely breathed as she felt a trickle of liquid dribble down between her legs; they would have to hurry to the doctor, or even the hospital.

Elsie parted the leaves to see into the open clearing beneath the bluffs. Spread out on the ground was the blanket Jimmy kept in the trunk of his car. It was the red plaid stadium blanket she'd given him for his birthday, the one they used to make love on.

Moonlight put a radiant halo around the bodies that lay on the blanket and painted their flesh with white neon. The wind played too; it choreographed the event. The neon white flicked and flashed with the rustle of the leaves. So gaudy, shrieking, harsh, and heartless was the flame of light that it burned her eyes.

Jimmy lay on his back, his legs spread wide. As if they were staked out. Between his legs, "she" was on her hands and knees. Her breasts teased, back and forth they went brushing against his cock. Her mouth came down closer, lapping, teasing too, and then devoured him. The woman seemed to enjoy what she was doing immensely. Elsie was reminded of Lynn and the goose–like lessons of bygone years.

"Was it hard. . ." The laughing voice took time out to talk between slurps and smacks, and it sounded vaguely familiar, "to get away from her?"

"Baby, it's always hard." They both laughed at the old lovers joke and he continued, "Hey, after that afternoon delight that you gave me I was determined to get away from her and be with you tonight. I planned it all out on the way home. As it turned out I needn't have bothered. I went right to the shower. Had to scrub the evidence of our afternoon *tête à tête* down the drain. Then, I was gonna lead her into a fight so I could storm out. Well, it was easy. She had to have her little clingon gabfest; you know how she gets on my nerves. But she's the one with the cash cow, I gotta be careful. She kept asking if I loved her. God, I'm sick of her need for constant reassurance." His hands grabbed the she–devil's head; evidently the time for conversation about his wife was over.

Elsie had never seen Jimmy in such a state. She stood entranced, as if she were watching a film, listening to him fuck talk his "friend."

"God baby, oh, my God. . .suck. . .hard baby. Suck it. . .hard. You're my whore, my slut!" He held her head and he fucked her face like a possessed, wild man. He couldn't get enough of her.

Elsie turned and walked away.

She'd had bloodstains on her clothes and on her body.

Jimmy had just put his own mark, his personal stain, on her soul.

She didn't cry a tear as she considered what she would do.

She would go to Lynn's. This wasn't all that bad, she thought. She'd seen worse. Standing in pools of Daddy's blood had been bad. Losing Jimmy was nothing!

She leaned her head out the window and gulped in the fresh night air. On this street you could catch a hint of pine needles if you breathed deeply. How could the God that scented these pine needles have also. . .oh, well, no, she had to stop this thinking. She had her baby. God made the baby, too.

Lynn had been crazy with worry, dialing Elsie's number for hours. It made her think of the night Ed and Sally died.

She was pacing the floor when she saw the car pull up and ran out to it. Right off she knew something brutal had happened, "Elsie, there's blood on your hands, on your shirt." Lynn put her arms around Elsie and nearly carried her up the stairs to the house.

She had no idea how long Elsie had been bleeding, but it was obvious, Lynn said later, that the baby was aborting. Lynn got the blankets, pillows, and soothing hot tea—she made her friend as comfortable as she could. She didn't question Elsie, and she didn't lecture, she listened.

Before they went to sleep, Lynn looked at her friend's white face—bleached by the moonlight in the clearing, thought Lynn. She said only one thing, "Els, what kind of a Daddy do you think Jimmy'd be? Would you want him for *your* Daddy?"

They both knew the answer.

Had her dear baby somehow known what it would face out in the world?

Was it better that she didn't have to put a sweet innocent through it?

The next day she filed for a divorce and she never looked back.

Elsie was looking forward, she searched for something she needed desperately to find.

The idea of a group frightened me. Lorenzo would be there to give me confidence, but I was still timid. In group I'd have to open myself. I wasn't sure that I could. It was kind of easy to turn Lorenzo's attention to other things—like the jokes. But could I do that in the group, or would I be forced to really come out?

I didn't want to come out.

I'd been out.

Then I remembered something Lynn had said, "Con-

quer it and make it yours." Wasn't that it?

And Lorenzo'd said not to let it have power over you.
Get it out in the open—get rid of it.

I would find a way to take charge of my life. That would be my goal. It had worked in the past. I remembered how Lynn had proved to me how well it could work. I smiled that day. The first real smile since Lynn's death.

Revenge.

I thought about the word, and knew that somehow, someday, I would make it happen. All I needed to do was to keep going, and be ready. I'd find a way to do that; the reward would be worth whatever the effort.

R-E-V-E-N-G-E. I hummed the tune. It wasn't as much revenge that I was after as it was justice. Justice. The same amount of letters. J-U-S-T-I-C-E. It fit. It fit the song.

I felt strong.

Even thoughts of my lost baby were more tolerable when I thought of justice and our song:

The weather reflected Elsie's mood. For three solid weeks it rained. Meanwhile, she sold the house and barber shop. There wasn't much to argue about with Jim. He had the BJ queen to take care of his basic needs.

It was painful for Elsie to go through the stuff in the garage—her Dad's stuff—but it had to be done. Lynn and Elsie were having a talk about leaving Northfield for good when they discovered some papers in an old metal ammo box.

"Els. Look at this." Lynn pointed. The box was in a beat up beer cooler, along with a half full bottle of Thunderbird wine. "Ed musta forgot this was here, or the wine would have been history." Lynn tried to lighten the mood. "I bet he's had this ammo box since the war."

"Gosh. *Look* at this, Lynner! Daddy must have had these

insurance policies since before the war—maybe from when his father died. I wonder if he was hiding them from Momma?" Elsie was stunned. Because the house and business mortgages had death insurance Elsie already had more money than she needed. This was a bonus she hadn't counted on.

Elsie and Lynn knew it really was time to get out of town.

After arduous conversations with Lynn's parents, they decided to move to Minneapolis. They both knew that the only reason they were allowed to go was the consensus that Elsie needed to get away. They'd take freedom whatever way they could get it.

By the time they were ready to leave, Elsie had her old puke green Rambler stuffed to the gills with things they couldn't bear to leave behind. The sun came out, an omen they were sure, to wish them well. The hour ride to Minneapolis was the start of their new lives. The car radio blared, cranked to the highest volume, for the first time in Elsie's life. It was making a statement for her. This was living.

"Yahoo! Should I feel bad that I feel this good?" she asked, yelling and laughing, over the top of Lynyrd Skynyrd's song. Here her parents were recently dead and Jimmy might as well have been dead, and she was happy.

"Hell, no!" The answer pulsed with the tunes.

The wind in her hair, the sun on her face, and Lynyrd singing "'Cause I'm free as a bird, now, How 'bout you? And this bird they'll never change. . .and this bird you cannot change. . .and this bird you cannot change." The song was new, called *Freebird*. They were free birds.

Damn, thought Elsie. She would soon be twenty and this was the first time she'd ever thought the word damn.

They were two hicks from the farm that made it to the big city. First they bought a newspaper to see what was for rent; the rental section was as big as the entire *Northfield News*. Names of streets meant nothing. They were two mice wandering in a maze. Stiff and thirsty, they stopped at a coffee shop to regroup. They took the paper with them to look over those ads again.

Lynn poked Elsie with her elbow. "Look," she hissed. "See who's waiting table?"

It was Alvin.

Alvin, who didn't come from a decent family, had been chased out of Northfield years ago by all the decent church-going folks who didn't think he was good enough for *their* kids to associate with. He'd come to the big city to hide from gossipmongers, because his Dad was a drunk who couldn't hold a job and his Mom a vulgar floozy.

Imagine that.

Elsie stopped at the cash register on their way in and bought six packages of Juicy Fruit gum.

He came over to the table with two glasses of water, menus, and a big smile. "What can I do for you, ladies?" he grinned.

Elsie was so excited herself that she didn't even wait to say hello. She blurted out what was most on her mind, "Alvin, I want you to know I've never forgotten your gift." Elsie looked him in the eye as she handed him the packets and felt strangely dizzy.

He accepted them, but took a step back. "Okay. Thanks."

The coffee shop was slow, so, at their request, he joined them for tea. They caught one another up on enough events that Elsie's divorce was out in the open, then got down to the business of where the two women would live.

Alvin was so familiar with the area he told them in minutes where he thought they'd be most comfortable. He circled addresses in the paper and drew a map of directions so they could find their way around an area called Kenwood. It was close to Lake of the Isles where they could bicycle or go on long walks. Many of the homes were old mansions now converted into rental units.

Elsie watched his hand and forearm as he drew the lakes, the streets, and listened to his voice talk about long walks. His skin had always appeared tan even in the winter, and what she'd seen of his body was covered with soft hair. She'd always found him attractive, and found that while he talked, her mind had drifted to thoughts of what might have been.

"Elsie?" said Alvin. Both he and Lynn were looking at her.

The place was beginning to fill up once again. "I've got to get back to work." Alvin stood. He took a matchbook from the table, wrote down his phone number and address and reached for Elsie's hand.

Elsie felt a tickle in her abdomen at the same time she felt the matches pressed into her palm.

"It's been great seeing you." His eyes were on Elsie only. "I'd like to see you again. Call me if you need help getting settled or help with anything, or," he laughed and looked at both of them, "well, just call me."

Elsie tried to be discrete but couldn't pull her eyes from him.

"What are you thinking, Els? Yes or no?"

"Shush!" Lynn's whisper had been too loud for Elsie's comfort.

They heard Alvin's friends and coworkers at the coffee shop call him Skip. He'd mentioned that he worked several part time jobs, hence the name; he skipped around. One of the jobs was at a co-op called the Wedge. Elsie thought, as they walked out, that she'd pay the Wedge a visit once they were settled.

With Skip's directions it was much easier to navigate. In no time at all they found a great apartment. It was in Kenwood and he was right about the area, they loved it. It was an artistic community of imaginative and friendly people.

Initially, they were unaware that many of their neighbors were gay. And, as no one seemed to mind that they were straight, they fit right in. Sexuality was not something openly talked about in Northfield. If there was a gay community there, it'd been hidden.

In Kenwood the people didn't hide, they lived.

Elsie and Lynn were happy and felt safe. They'd found a home.

Lynn searched and found a job in Lake Street Square; the Square was a hip place to shop and hang. The job was at The Chit–Chat Café which was located in the Square and served health food—another new concept for them. After the small town atmosphere of Northfield, Minneapolis was very different. It was time, and the young women were ready, to see what the rest of the world was up to.

Lynn worked as a hostess and every day brought home something new. The first was the spicy tea the Chit–Chat served as its house blend. Just to have a pot of this aromatic concoction brewing gave their apartment a homey touch both craved. They didn't have to drink it to enjoy it, just simmer some on the stove and let the spices filter throughout the rooms.

Elsie spent her days making the place feel more like home. It was fun to shop for small insignificant things. She'd always given whatever money she earned to Momma to help out. Later, when she and Jimmy were married, he took over the pocketbook.

Her first purchase was the Lynyrd Skynyrd album with *Freebird*—the song that had became their song of hope for the future. They were restricted by nothing but themselves, their vivid imaginations and unlimited energies.

Their apartment was on the bottom of three floors. The huge house was classic 19th century architecture with enormous plush rooms. Lynn called it swank.

The thick, mauve carpet was so luxurious it made you want to run through it barefoot. Because of the size, they didn't attempt to fill the living room; they named it the "ballroom" and left it bare. They concentrated their efforts on making the kitchen, bedrooms and gigantic bath cozy. The ballroom would have to wait.

Elsie avoided job hunting. She *had* money, she rationalized. And, she needed time to figure out what was going on inside her. Sometimes, she felt explosive—a time bomb waiting to ignite and blow. Other times, she felt invisible. Those times she wanted to scream, "I'm right here!"

But Elsie didn't scream.

She burned to know who she really was. These reflective days seemed to her to be the happiest of her life, yet an elusive sadness followed her like a shadow.

Chapter Nineteen

Today, Elsie loved life.

She'd spent hours studying, drinking in, the many books she'd purchased at the Wedge. These were books on herbs, natural health, holistic healing and, best of all, on *spirit*. She found it fascinating. While she studied, she did piles of laundry, even that gave her satisfaction today. She felt free, content.

She was making homemade soup that was to–die–for. Perhaps she'd name it that, to–die–for soup. Lynn would soon be home to enjoy it with her.

Right now, thanks to her homey little efforts, their house smelled like the–house–from–heaven. She'd already done her time in the–house–from–hell. This was better. She felt proud of her accomplishments today. To–die–for soup in the house–from–heaven. She'd done some writing in the journal she'd started, too. For today, she was living the Henry David Thoreau lifestyle, or close enough.

Deep inside she knew she was pushing back the demons that were trying to surface and spoil her mood. Those demons enjoyed unnerving her. They whispered, "Elsie, Elsie, think of *this*, Elsie."

They meant for her to remember this: *things–are–going–too–good–so–when–is–the–ax–going–to–fall?* She pushed them back, out of sight, out of mind. Momma used to say that to her. When? She strained to remember.

Who cares? she thought. I'm not thinking about Momma either. She returned to reading about the herbs that captivated her. There was a process here that she could appreciate—*the planting, growing, harvesting of the herbs, and then the healing.*

She was going to start a garden of her own.

The front door slammed. "Baby, it is *bleak* out there! Don't I just love this Minnesota frigid hell?" It was Lynn—cold, wet and shivering, "What is that smell? God, I'm starved."

"Lucky for you, here I am slaving over a hot stove, lucky for *you*! I made turkey soup with every veggie you can imagine, plus beans, and lentils, and barley. And, those tiny egg dumplings Momma used to make on Tuesdays when Daddy was out doing poker–and–what–all. Also, it has a few new herbs I've discovered, *seeecret* stuff. I'm calling it to–die–for soup. Go dry up."

They both laughed. "You mean off."

Elsie ignored her. "You can eat while we talk. We *need* to talk, plus, I've got good news. Good news for you."

Lynn shivered her way into the other room. Their warm home, coupled with the smells of hot dinner cooking, would shake the offensive chilled–to–the–bone feeling that was part of living in Minnesota. In Minnesota, one day could be a glorious fall day, and on the next, a killer winter would be sayin' "howdy."

By the time Lynn came back into the kitchen, Elsie was taking dark crusted bread out of the oven.

"Have I mentioned that someday you'll make someone a great wife? You know a wife is something everyone deserves to have—not just guys."

Elsie was setting her a place at the table. "Well, har–*de*–har–har to you! Sit. Eat. I walked to the Wedge today. Got stuff to make great dill bread. What a place...saw Skip too." She mumbled that last part, not wanting to get into a discussion about him, yet wanting exactly that.

But it passed over Lynn's hungry head. "I'm happy you went there, Els, but when are you going to start *really* going out, you know, to meet people, maybe even a *guy*?"

"Like getting back on the horse when you're bucked, or in my case, fucked off, is that what you're tryin' to say?"

"I'm not suggesting you fall in love, just find someone to play a little slap–and–tickle with. I know the last thing you want is some horny toad hanging around, but you could move slow, hm?"

Elsie smiled, waiting.

"Hey. Did you say you saw Skip? How'd that go?"

"Look, let me talk for once—you eat. I've got stuff on my mind. By the time I'm done, you'll be done eating, an' there'll be plenty of time leftover for you to nag."

"Tee–hee. Yeah, okay, go on, but don't think I don't know it when you're evading an issue," Lynn's red head nodded, her mouth crammed, "God, Els, this is such fabulous soup. It's unfuckinreal."

Elsie handed her friend a paper towel. "You're making a mess and I just cleaned, and it's to–die–for, not unfuckinreal soup."

"Okay, first things first. Your Ma called, and they're going to haul your piano all the way up here! She says it's taking up too much room. What a sweetie. I told them if you could get off work this coming Sunday, I'd make a dinner for all of us. Imagine this! A grand piano for our ballroom!"

Lynn nodded, grinning while she ate, soup dripping down her chin. "Pass me more bread, will ya, sweetie?"

"I miss hearing you play. And your Dad, I talked to him, too. Well, he seems to think that having the piano *here* will keep you out of trouble, give you something to do with your time, other than hang out on the streets and bars like you do now." Elsie laughed out loud at that pretended misconception.

"Bull, he just knows how much I miss it. He doesn't want me to have to ask him for his help. I sure lucked out when I got my Ma and Pop, didn't I?"

Elsie agreed. "And how did they get a bratty kid like you?"

"Luck a' the draw. Anyhoo, I'll call 'em tonight. Sunday'll work fine. I can get off. The store manager thinks I'm hot." She returned her attention to dinner. "You're giving me that look, Els. What's on your mind? More bread. I'm inhaling it. Why *do* only men get wives? You would make the *best* wife. A shame to waste wives on men."

Elsie frowned. She wanted to get serious and sometimes that was hard with Lynn. "Well," she studied her feet, "You know I'm trying to sort things out. I've been thinking about Jimmy. Hey! Don't look at me like that! I just don't want to make the same mistake again. It seems that some of the ways I screwed up with him, were like *déjà vu* with my dad."

She took in an awkward gulp, "Well, what I'm wondering is. . .you'll say *exactly* what you think, right?"

"You know I will! Out with it!"

Elsie blew out the air and talked fast, not sure she wanted to know the answer. "Do you think Jimmy would have gone out with that *person* if I'd given him a blowjob when he wanted? I mean, is that what it was about? Do you think I'd be home, my baby still alive, if I'd done that?" Elsie never talked about the baby anymore.

Lynn put down her spoon and pushed aside the dishes. "I've been wondering when you were going to start thinking that the Jimmy–deal was your fault. I knew you were *thinking* it, but I wondered when it would surface."

"What I think, Els, now, you listen to me good, is this— Jimmy's slime. You blame things on yourself; it's the most annoying damn thing. Sure he had problems in his life and blah, blah, blah. He has responsibility for what he does or doesn't do. Sure, if you'd sucked him, he'd have been in heaven for awhile. Probably kissed your ass, and you'd have been delirious. . .two little love–fucking–birds. Then there would've been something else that he just *had* to have. He was a baby about it, wasn't he? I mean, did he or did he not beg and whine?"

Elsie glumly nodded, playing splash–splash with the spoon in her soup.

"If he loved you, if he was capable of any damn human feeling, he would've had some patience. The primary virtue. Cut out that shit with the spoon and *listen?*"

Elsie stopped splashing and lifted her quivering chin.

"He would have cared about how *you* felt. He never would've expected you to do something you weren't ready to do. You think you're odd for not wanting to blow a guy who hardly kisses you? Why the fuck didn't he have *you* at the bluffs that night? If you weren't always right there to handle his every need, and I have a hard time even imagining that scenario, what does he think God gave him two perfectly good hands for?"

Lynn's face was flushed and she got up. You could just see that she needed to move. "Well, I'm sorry, this shit really gets me going, but that's what I think, Elsie, and there's something else. Why don't you get some revenge? Revenge can lighten the soul. And as I see it, your soul could use some frivolity."

"What do you mean, revenge?"

"Oh, get that worried look off your puss. I don't mean revenge where you have to *see* him, or god forbid, hurt him. I mean the kind of revenge that only you know about. How about a little game of do–for–others–what–you–wouldn't–do–for–him. Just for starters."

"I don't get it."

"Of course you don't, blondie. Your heart is pure. Listen. Remember the time he was going out with the boys, and you didn't want to stay alone that night? It was, um, maybe two months after your folks died. You were having those horrendous nightmares. Any*hoo*, he wasn't about to stay home, so, like the good–little–woman, you made him those great burgers before he went out. The Gainesburger hamburgers that you made out of Pip's dog food, remember?"

"Yes!" Elsie squealed.

"You were so excited that night! I remember we talked on the phone for an hour. I couldn't believe you'd thought of such a devious thing all on your own, much less *did* it. And he never found out about it, did he?"

Elsie's tears made her cheeks and nose shine. Just thinking about it set her off; it was almost funnier now. "They were California burgers with the works, just like he liked them. He raved about how great they were." Here was a memory she'd enjoy forever!

"But did he *know* what you'd done?"

"Nope. Never figured it out. In fact, he asked me to make them again! Asked what I'd done to make them so great."

"See?"

"I told him it was my secret ingredient. I don't think I could have duplicated it. I just tried so hard to cover up the taste of the dog food that I made them extra good."

Lynn sat down at the table and buttered another hunk of dill bread. A blob of butter landed on the floor. She blushed. "Okay! I'm a slob!"

Elsie was already wiping it up. "You know, it did make me feel a lot better for some reason." She sounded wistful. "Once he ate the burgers, I didn't care if he left. I *wanted* him to have a ball. I knew I'd enjoy myself that night."

"See? I rest my case."

"I don't see how that little episode of fun applies here. I'm sure not doing any cooking for Jimmy now. Wait. I'm making a list of things that are good in my life. . .let me write that down before I forget it." She grabbed her journal and wrote as she said the words. "am no longer cooking for Jimmy. Yeah."

"Oooh, this is cool." said Lynn. "I feel like a teacher. Okay, let's go back to what Jimbo wanted. A blowjob." She emphasized *blow*. "Giving a guy a blowjob—a nice fella that you like, I must add—is something you'd enjoy, Els. I know you, and I know what you like. Trust me on this. And if you do it and you like it and the guy likes it, you'll feel like you felt with the Gainesburgers."

"Why are *you* so sure I'll like it? I don't think so."

"Well, should the opportunity arise, just give it a go. You'll see why."

"Oh sure, should I maybe go up to some goon on the street an' say, *would it be okay if I blow you, mister?*" Elsie flapped her eyes and they both hooted.

"Hardly. You know very well that is nothing like what I mean."

"Oh, I know. Well, what if I, as you say, have the opportunity and the, *sort* of, desire, and I don't do it right and they don't like it? Then it will be Jimmy who gets his revenge on me."

"Okay, Els, listen to me. Picture this huge penal colony. Close your eyes and picture it! Now, all of the 'penals' in the colony are locked up, right? You are going to set one of them free, release him, so to speak. Think of it just that way!"

"So, here's the plan. Tomorrow, go to the Wedge, only this time you buy bananas!. . .and then, we'll have class, like right *here*, in the kitchen.

"Blowjobs 101!" She hooted and slapped her knees. "Upon successful completion of the course, we get you a date with a likely suspect. You may have to date a bunch. Get it? Banana, bunch, huh? Well, it may take some doing to find one you like enough for this experiment, so we'd better get started. Okay?"

Elsie groaned. "Okay."

"And don't forget to take a peek at Skip while you're picking out those bananas. Any*hoo*, kiddo, if it happens, you'll no longer have this hanging over your head, like there's something you just can't do. *Conquer it and make it yours.* Who always said that? Me? Besides, inside, you'll know you did it great for someone else, not for Jimbo! Get it?"

Elsie grinned. She thought about Alvin. Skip. He'd looked good today. His jeans were worn and tight. He'd been unloading crates of produce. His black curls were damp and he smelled, well, male and so clean. Was *that* what got her thinking about Jimmy?

Lynn was right. Elsie felt tons better right now. She went to the back door to let Pip inside. A rush of the cold air rode into the warmth of the kitchen on his back. The smell of soup and hot bread mixed with the warm feelings the girls exuded were too much for Pip. He jumped around the room, first chasing his tail, then knocking Elsie over on the carpet with him. He licked her face and finally stood on top of her stomach, looking from one of them to the other, tail wagging. They laughed with him.

Elsie lay back on the carpet and crossed her arms behind her head, completely relaxed. She looked toward the kitchen table. "So, Lynn. Enough about me. What's going on with you? Something's in the air. I want to know what it is."

It was Lynn doing the twitching now. She looked uncomfortable.

"Is it a guy?" Elsie tried to look her in the eye. "Have you been releasing someone from the penal colony and not telling me?"

Not even a smile.

"It *is* a guy! I can't believe you're being this evasive. Bring him around so I can meet him."

Lynn's eyes darted like a fly after fruit.

"Jeeze, Lynner, if this were a court of law, I'd have to say, guilty as charged—based on the suspect's demeanor." Elsie kicked at Lynn's chair with her foot. "Give."

"How did you know?" Lynn kicked her back, teasing, "It's spooky the way you figure me out. Well, I want you to meet him, at least I did, now I don't."

My god, *she sounds like me*, Elsie thought.

"I have to forget him, Elsie. I didn't tell you, because it

happened so fast, and something didn't seem right. I was trying to figure it out. I was attracted and then not. God, I might as well say it. The jerkoff's married."

Elsie frowned.

"I can't believe this is happening, Els. His name's Peter. You've got to help me stay strong. Well, I guess I don't need help now. I feel like a goose. He started coming into the restaurant my second day on the job. He stops in on his way to work. We talked as if we'd always known one another. I mean, he loves Mozart and Beethoven, for crissake!"

Elsie was still stuck on the part about his being married.

"The only difference I could see then, was politics. He's a heavy duty Republican. That should have told me, but it didn't. Well, kept getting more and more anxious for him to stop in. Then one day, he said he wanted to show me his new car. I walked with him outside. We were talking as we walked, and he kissed me. Just like that. Grabbed me and kissed me."

She ran her fingers through her hair and slumped back in her chair. "I was going to talk to you about him that night, but whatever didn't feel right I couldn't put into words. I wasn't sure what to say. Then, maybe a week ago, he came in and said he had something to tell me. That was it. He told me he was married, has two kids! He went on about his wife not understanding his needs but I was through listening with the word married."

Lynn took in the look on her friend's face. "Els, he only kissed me that one time, I swear. I mean how did he get from Ludwig van, to *his* needs, so fast? Well, now, he's like obsessed with me. The only way not to see him would be if I quit my job. He wants me, and he knows that I *did* want him, so he won't take no for an answer! I'm not giving in. But, he's making my life hell."

"Does he come in a lot?"

"He comes by, like I said, in the morning on his way to work, whenever he doesn't have an early meeting. At least a few times a week." Lynn started to cry.

Lynn cry? Elsie sat up.

"Lately, he's been coming in everyday, Els. He's trying to break me down—I've become a challenge."

Elsie went over and put her arms around her friend. Pip sensed there was a problem and tried to help too by licking Lynn's hands.

"Men can be hard to understand," said Elsie.

"Well, I can usually understand them just fine. I understand what Peter's after, and it ain't pretty. There's just something weird about him."

"What do you mean?"

Lynn shook her head, "Oh, it's my overworked imagination. Let's forget him for now. Okay?"

She believed in Lynn's instincts. And a guy who could make Lynn cry was a first. Elsie wanted to know much more.

Chapter Twenty

All the material things I could ever want or need, were with me in this house. Even the colors were my favorites—ivory on ivory—accented with mirrors, brass, and glass. The largest of the rooms, the living area, was a feast of plants and books.

In recent years I'd grown more afraid of the dark so here in my haven light was everywhere. There were spacious windows, skylights, an abundance of candles and a collection of rare and beautiful floor lamps. These days I did more and more cocaine and though I tried to cut back on the amount of cocaine I seemed to be doing more rather than less. I would take care of that in due time. Anyway, the coke went well with champagne so I kept it stocked in the wet bar. I loved music and allowed myself to have a great and wonderful large white custom made stereo. I no longer wondered why I wanted white enough to pay so much to have it made. The fabrics were silk and an imported cashmere that felt better than silk and they too were ivory. There were fresh and silk wildflowers in wild exotic colors and plants everywhere.

If your greatest love is books coupled with plants, what, I wondered, does that say about you as a person? Most of the things that I loved to touch, smell, see or do, were right here. And there was no one to tell me that I was extravagant, lazy, silly, or what–the–fuck.

In many ways having no predetermined rules made what I was doing easier. I'd never learned to have boundaries with regard to other people—now I was forced to make them up as I went along.

It was as I wanted it to be, and although I never felt happiness, I felt satisfied; at least I felt I would soon be satisfied.

I would be satisfied or it would be over. Well, either way it would be over and it made very little difference to me which way it ended. Or so I thought.

The books were important. They were what helped me live as a fugitive from my real life—from the reality I would or could not face.

But now I was forced into a "face off."

I needed these things for comfort, to help me escape from the world. The little box of ivory powder that sat on my glass coffee table was a great help in that escape. I looked out through the glass at the garden I loved. I realized that the best part was that here I felt as if I belonged. The only other time I'd felt this "connected" was a few years ago, in what seemed now a previous lifetime.

I tried not to think about that lifetime. Well, it's true what they say, you know? You can run, but you can't hide:

Lynn came home from work furious. "Els, we gotta talk."

"What?" Elsie knew it was big because Lynn was generally easy going and happy and because she had these blotches on her skin—red blotches, that meant her insides were trying to get out the venom.

"Well, I hadn't had the pleasure of creepo's company for days. It lulled me. I started to believe that he'd given up—moved to an *easier* target." She'd been much stronger after she finally unburdened herself and told Elsie about Pete.

Elsie set a cup of tea in front of Lynn and began preparations for a snack. "I'm listening." They'd always used food and tea to calm and assure one another.

"I was talking, joking around with a few of my regulars and I can't explain this. As if something reached out and touched me everywhere but yet didn't touch me at all. God it was awful!"

Elsie could see that Lynn's body was shaking. She tried to stir sugar into the tea and the cup rattled. Elsie reached over and stirred it for her, not talking, not pushing, but listening.

"I felt this evil presence. I knew it was Pete before I turned. And, sure enough! Picture the devil and he appears. I seated him. I mean, that *is* my job and I sure don't want to lose it. I put his coffee in front of him. Took every speck of self–control not to fling it in his face, but I learned my lessons on basic urge restraint at a young age. Thanks, Pops."

Lynn took a sip of tea and smiled her thanks to Elsie. It was good to have one another to count on. Lynn's voice oozed sarcasm. "Okay, here's what he says, *'So baby, I got a joke for you. Wait'll you hear this one.'* And right here he really leers at me. Then he says, *'You know why men in the city like women?'*"

"You *must* be kidding!" Elsie was already horrified.

"As if I could give a shit what*ever* he had to tell me!" said Lynn.

"And?"

"*'No?'* says this flunky creepo when I don't answer him, *'Well,'* he says, giving me the punch line, *'it's because there's no sheep!'*"

Lynn's green eyes flashed as Elsie gasped and knew that this was the way her friend had behaved when this Peter person told his stupidassed joke.

"I tried hard not to get upset because it seemed to turn him on in some sick way." Lynn took a chocolate coconut cookie from Elsie and continued her story.

"*'Come, my little dove,'* he says to me, *'you're off soon, I'll walk you home.'*"

"I said, 'Look here Peter, my boyfriend picks me up after work, and, I'm not your dove.'"

"Good for you." Elsie was angry. "Where does the puke get off calling you his damn dove?"

"It's not the usual thing for him to come in that late in my shift, Els. He's never done that before."

Elsie's eyes got wild. "No? Well what did he say next?"

"'Oh, yeah, *sure*, your boyfriend.' He said it like he didn't believe I had one. But, luckily, he went to the bathroom, and I saw my chance to escape. While he was in there I ran out the door. I jogged all the way home."

"I hope he takes the hint, Lynner, but maybe you better get another job."

"Yeah. I think so too. All the way home I kept looking over my shoulder. Man, he just gives me the creeps! As soon as he found out I wasn't going to fall for his song–and–dance routine, he changed. And it was a dramatic change, too. The way he behaves now? This is the real him."

"What worries me," said Elsie, "is how he changed completely, and so fast."

"Yeah. And today, that crappy joke? It was *bait*. He was trying to get me. What a nutcase."

"Have you thought about calling his wife?" Elsie bit her tongue, sorry as soon as the words came out.

Lynn grew silent. A tear rolled down her cheek.

Chapter Twenty–One

"It's integrity. That's what he has. Not a lot of razzma*tazz* about Charlie, but you know you can trust him with the key to your house *and* your heart."

Lynn's boyfriend Charlie wasn't make believe like Peter had intimated, he was the real thing. Charlie owned a gas station a few blocks from where Lynn worked. He'd been pumping gas for her since they came to town. There was something about this soft–voiced, average looking guy, with a trace of grease always somewhere on his person that appealed to Lynn. He called her Red. Lynn liked that, too.

"What?" Elsie decided she'd better pay attention. Something big was happening here. And, as often happens with love it's unobtrusive until it sneaks up with its big whamo, the big bang.

"I'm trying to tell you that this is *serious*." Lynn brushed her copper curls, getting ready for her big date, and grinned.

Elsie giggled. *This was exciting!*

Lynn giggled, too. "He's intelligent. That's a must. But he's such a teddy, so vulnerable, and sweet, and kind." Her green eyes were damp with emotion.

"Why, Lynner, you're gushing and all googooy!"

"Well, I guess." Both of them roared at the same time! Lynn bubbled on, "He never seems to get caught up in the bullshit of life, you know, Els? Like living for his career. Tell me what *you* think of him." Charlie had become a fixture lately. Elsie'd had plenty of exposure to enable her to form an opinion.

"Well, okay. I'll tell you. He can be spontaneous. Look at

how he completely changed his weekend plans just because you got the time off. I love that in a man! Men like to pretend they're spontaneous, but in my limited experience they really aren't."

"You're right. About your limited experience, I mean. *Har-de-har-har!* What else?" Lynn gave Elsie an elbow poke while she brushed tiny white Pip hair off her burgundy sweater.

"Oh. I know! Instead of being so concerned about stuff that has no real meaning, things like, are they more successful than their friends? Do they make more money than their friends? Do they have a better–looking woman than their blah, blah, blah? That's a real doozie, that one. Not, of *course*, that you are not better looking than any of his friends' girlfriends! But, to continue. Charlie is serious about his business, but it's not a symbol of who he is, he's more concerned about treating people right than getting rich and he's *really* serious about you. That's just *some* of what I like about him."

The doorbell interrupted their talk and Elsie grinned to herself as she watched the two lovebirds walk to the car. They had a big evening planned and were going to top it off by staying at the downtown Hilton. Elsie thought Charlie was going to propose. And he was made to order for her friend.

She thought about their conversation. Charlie did worry about his thinning hair, that was about it. His one vice. His gorgeous personality made him a hunk. Maybe she had been too hard on the male majority. Women had their own peccadilloes, but Elsie had spent her life concerned with men. You focus on what you know. And who was she to say, could be that their problems today went back to the cave–man days. Men'd had to be concerned with their family's livelihood since the dawn of time; now that they could relax, they couldn't relax. There were plenty of good men out there. Lynn's Pop was a perfect example.

Was it time for Elsie to change her perspective? Life was good these days. Now, with Charlie in the picture, it was even better.

Elsie had plans for the evening, too. She sat in the ballroom at the piano and thought.

The Sunday Lynn's folks came up with the piano was the closest to a night with a family she'd had in her life. She would remember it always. She'd cooked rolled roast, made fresh asparagus, twice–baked potatoes, and cherry pie. Mom and Pop Fahey loved the food, the apartment, and the neighborhood. The size of the ballroom impressed them because the acoustics were what a concert pianist deserved.

Every few minutes, she heard Pip's yip from the back yard; he wanted to remind her he was out there.

The best thing Jimmy'd done for her was to get Pip. She'd come a long way since Jimmy. At first, she didn't think she could stand to go on. That was because of her baby. She'd kept her feelings about her parents hidden. She could remember the day her Momma made Daddy move his stuff to the rec–room in the basement. That was to be his new living quarters. She made him do his own cooking and laundry too. He lived like a stranger in his own home. Elsie knew things were going to get worse and threw herself into Jimmy and love.

She remembered asking, "Momma, why don't you get a divorce and leave Daddy?"

Momma sat at the kitchen table painting her nails. The red enamel glistened. She looked at her daughter with hard eyes. "Damn right I'll leave him. Just as soon as the Bishop gives us his special dispensation. Father Andy thinks it would be best to wait for that."

Elsie sat without comment until her mother asked what she'd been asking every night for months. "Hon. You can get dinner, can't you? I've so much work to do at the rectory. I think I'll have you drop me there. Andy, ah, Father Andy, will run me home later."

It was relaxing to sit at the piano in the silent house. Even when the old memories returned, like today. She was healing, getting better.

The wind had begun to take the leaves covering the ground for a ride. *The leaf dance.* Doin' the leaf dance, hummed Elsie, contented. Pip yipped again. Elsie blew him a kiss through the window. If he got cold he'd have to stay in his dog house for a couple of hours.

Weeks ago she'd decided to try to rekindle her friendship with Alvin. Skip was what she called him now. She saw him often at the Wedge. There was a definite attraction. So far they'd avoided the life–in–Northfield topic. But they loved to talk.

It'd started with a conversation one afternoon about herbs. Skip's body was firm, his hair and eyes had that healthy shine. It put a lump in her throat every time she saw his taut muscles flex. Elsie asked him what could help her regain her old energy. She'd read about herbs for energy but there were too many to pick from. Skip explained his theory. She found herself drawn to him as he talked. She must be attracted to the teacher type. She continued to find more questions for him to answer.

"Lynn always catches such bad colds. I want to help her strengthen her immune system." She wondered if it was obvious to him what her *real* interest was.

"Here's what you need. Be great for you both." Skip held a bottle of Echinacea. "The Sioux Indians used it for blood poisoning and snake–bite, called it purple coneflower."

"I like that name." And, she liked the way his damp T-shirt clung to his back when he turned to take the bottle off the shelf.

"Just the ticket for Lynn, it's a blood purifier."

It worked, too, thought Elsie; Lynn had never been so healthy.

Skip's variety of interests made their talks all the more fun. He seemed to understand that she wasn't looking for a *relationship.* There was a good possibility he'd be moving to the West Coast for at least a year; it was unlikely that he was much of a love threat. He couldn't take the time a good relationship required either. Skip was an actor and musician currently working at The Improv, a Second City type comedy club where they wrote their own comedy sketches. He wrote guitar music, too.

One day, out of the blue they wondered if they might be good for one another on occasion. How had it come up in conversation? She couldn't think how.

But, tonight was the occasion. That could be why she couldn't think so well.

Could he be the perfect man for Elsie? Unlike what Lynn used to say, perfect man was not an oxymoron. And, if things went according to plan she could be pretty perfect for him too.

First, there was that little matter of revenge on Jimmy.

What if that should backfire on me, she thought.

It was Skip's affection she craved! She knew how needy she was. And not for sex. Just hanging around him had been good for her. She felt urges she'd never known she could feel. They had nothing to do with the need to be possessed that she'd had when she was with Jimmy. Neediness was not attractive and she was determined to dump that characteristic.

And, she sure didn't need someone who had power over her. She wanted her *own* power. She wanted to be like her friend, Lynn.

The leaves continued their dance. She sighed. What an awesome sight. "What would you say if you could talk to me?"

Maybe they'd talk about patience. *Things that were worthwhile take time and patience.* "Is that what you'd tell me?"

It was just before dusk and Elsie was laughing for talking

out loud to the trees when Skip knocked on her door.

Elsie wore jeans and a sweatshirt. She had a certain no–frills femininity and she knew he was a no–frills kind of guy. When he walked through the door he was already laughing. She loved his laugh. It was Pip that got him going. Out in the yard Pip leapt and barked like a fool. Each time he jumped he came up a little higher, trying to see in the window.

She looked Skip over good. Your basic jeans, faded pale blue—tight, yet not too, covered the lower part of his six–foot frame. Then, a darker–blue Italian v–neck textured–cotton sweater matched his eyes and set off black curls that smelled of a minty shampoo. Loafers without socks? It was kinda cold for that. She had an urge to warm his feet. Is that why he did it? As he moved past her she nervously flipped her hair with one hand.

"Umm, you smell sweet," Skip said.

"So do you."

He carried a bottle of wine in his hand and extended it toward her.

"Want a glass before we go to dinner?"

She agreed. Food was far from her mind.

They sat in the two bean bag chairs that were in one corner of the ballroom.

"I feel like a dog myself sitting here all comfy, drinking wine with you, while Pip is outside freezing his little hairy butt off." The dog's barking had increased as soon as they sat down and he could no longer see the tops of their heads. "Can't we let him in for a visit?"

Elsie knew that Pip was fine. Pleased that Skip was concerned about her dog, "You remembered his name," she said opening the door prepared to be knocked over backwards.

"You talk about him every time I see you."

Instead of knocking her over Pip looked sheepish, he knew things were fine and he was just vying for her attention.

They felt better letting him in for awhile and it calmed him, too. By the time they put him back outside he was mellow once again.

They continued to sip wine and talk like the old friends they would have been if he'd not been from the wrong side of the tracks!

They didn't talk as much about old times as new. It can be hard to think of the future when there's so much to remind us of the past, thought Elsie. Having a friend who was interested in today was great fun.

"So, ah, Els, what's the deal with this room? No furniture. Except these chairs and that piano."

"You noticed that, did you? It's last on our agenda of rooms to fix. We call it the ballroom." Elsie could feel his eyes already loving her.

Their chemistry made the room quiver with electricity.

Laughing, Skip stood. "It seems a shame to sit this far apart in a room with a name like that." And with that, he came over to share her chair.

The warmth from him drew her. He was the white line down a highway and she followed that line wherever it led. Skip was too much to resist. Plus, she didn't want to resist. They kissed. Until kisses were not enough.

Elsie got up, believing that space between them might clear her head. She put on her favorite music, dinner forgotten. It was getting dark, but there were no drapes in the ballroom. The beautiful bay windows, some of them with stained glass, let the stars wisp in. The only artificial light available for the room was a big antique chandelier that hovered over the piano. Elsie moved in that direction and then stopped. The wind kept their evenings "illumination–from–the–heavens" in a flux that shimmered through the room, to transform it into a magical arena.

Suddenly the music changed. It took Elsie on a trip back

to her days as a young girl. She was on the hill midst the *Strawberry Fields*, only this time she was enveloped in Skip's arms. Her mind reeled her back and forth from that hill to their bodies. She revealed her innocence to him with unintelligible whispers that were tender words of love. This was not frantic lovemaking it was gentle; *they flew with the angels until they became one.*

As Elsie became more and more enthralled with Skip's body her desire shifted. She wanted to spread them both out in a field of fresh berries. Was it the wine? She could smell the sweet fragrance. She moved on top of him and took control. First, she kissed him, then, down, down she went, smelling the red berries...nibbling them, until at last she was *there*. She could taste bananas and smiled inside as she put her mouth on him.

Skip moaned, his body recalibrated under her mouth. The gala festivity had begun. His body was the main feature on the evening's menu.

Elsie was filled with love feelings for this man who was so pleased with every little flick of her tongue. She moved her lips on him and responded to his movements, to the heat she could feel building in his body, fast, then slow. She sucked harder, softer, harder, softer, until at last he held her face lovingly with both hands while he burst with rapid jerks, again and again, inside her throat. He brought his face to her head—she still held him inside her mouth. Neither of them would let go as he pressed his mouth to her forehead and she felt his hot breath spread over her face and down her body.

My god, she thought, *this feeling*—it was like nothing Elsie'd ever felt. It was not what she'd imagined. It was as if *she* were in control! As she sucked and licked up every drop of him, he stroked her face and talked sweet words of love that she could barely hear; her mind raced with her pulse and she felt herself come.

She lay on top of him.

Lynn had been right.

It was incredible to feel him get harder, feel his body quiver, hear him moan, and then to feel that fluid hot in her throat.

And almost as good as the sucking itself, was the tender way he stroked her now, as if she were made of velvet and gold. Oh she *liked* this.

That one was for you, Jimmy.
The rest will be all mine.

They fell asleep like that, Elsie's head on Skip's chest, his hands on her face, combing her hair with his fingers, on the ballroom floor, midst the smell of strawberries, bananas and love.

At the first signs of dawn the sun kissed the stained glass windows above them and Skip kissed her good morning, then he rolled on top of her and filled her with himself.

Elsie's memories of the night before were so strong that when he came she felt as if he were inside her mouth, too! He was with her in the ultimate connection of body and soul and she came again. This was the second time she'd experienced orgasm with anyone but herself.

She pushed up from their nest on the floor, stretched her ivory body in front of him without shame and pranced bare as a babe, without a thought of seduction, into the kitchen.

"Is that all? I mean, you run off! No after–play? What am I just another pretty face? Is that it?" he teased.

She returned, smacking from a bowl of strawberries and sliced bananas, "Umm, good." The perfect food. *Well, almost.* She fed him, while she told him stories. Stories about Jimmy, the Gainesburger event, what Lynn had said to do and why she'd bought so many bananas at the co–op.

"And," she said as she sucked in a juicy berry that had slipped and fallen on his hard, furry stomach, watching what it did to other parts of his anatomy, "revenge is *way* sweet."

"Bam!"

"Wa. . .?" Elsie couldn't seem to pull herself out of her dream. But finally the insistent pounding on the door woke her. It was hours later. She'd fallen asleep as soon as Skip left for work and must have been too deeply asleep to hear the doorbell. She stumbled to grab her purple terry robe, then opened the door as soon as she saw who it was.

"I'm brain dead. Forgot my key *again*, sorry!" Lynn rushed in with Pip in one arm, and Charlie on the other.

"Give us a kiss, lover boy," she dropped Pip, and grabbed Charlie's head. "Go on home—but, call me later, hunbun," she yelled after him as he ran down the stairs. "Or, sooner!"

Elsie watched Charlie run to the car, his face seemed to glow. Was that possible? "Charlie looks. . .I don't know, relaxed, I guess. Ouch!" Pip jumped like a wild dog all over Elsie. Then, he ran in circles, jumped over the bean bags, happy to be inside with his family.

Lynn's spirits were equally as good. "I'm in love, Els! I'm in love, for the first time in my life! Charlie's the man for me!" Her eyes shone.

They both talked at once.

I made my plans with the hot wench for Thursday night—big plans. On Thursday nights wifie plays bridge with her college chums. Because they imbibe, ever so slightly, the wife must stay over night with the "girls," as she calls them. Bunch of withering hens is the term I use when I mention or think of them, which is seldom. Bottom line—my bitch, the sainted mother of my adorable children, won't be around to check up on me, or to see that I'm home by her imaginary curfew.

I wonder if El knows I'm married. Funny she hasn't asked. Not that it matters. But, it's odd. They always ask. Of course she works with me so I bet she's asked someone at work. So she can play it cool. Make me think she's disinterested.

I drive by the Amoco Station on my way to work every day. It makes Mr. Big stand up and take notice. Just the thought of our "date" Thursday makes me crazy. I have to have it my way, and have it soon. What a hot bitch this one is. Thursday night will be the night I get her out of my system. Have her the way I want to have her then be done with her. I'll be able to get on with other things—back on track. She'll cry for mercy before this is over.

It's embarrassing to have a woman so in control. Even if it's only in her feeble mind.

Control is my game—my domain.

I hate thinking that she even thinks she's in control. Yet here I am—in the midst of what should be a busy day and all I can concentrate on is how to find a way, any way, to have her before Thursday. I know when I'm getting ready to beg. Even the word beg makes me ashamed. If I feel shame, the bitch will pay. There has to be a way to get this over with. But I don't want it over, I want it to go on and on. Whatever happens, whenever it happens, she will pay.

God, there she is. I see her now, through my office window. Smiling ever so slightly at me. She knows. The bitch knows! And she knows that I know it. My face is so hot that it burns! I can feel the color creep, spreading to cover me like a dark red glove. The color of blood. Her blood. I want to wash myself in her blood.

Enough. I'm going to lose control right here.

I can't let this happen. There must be something in these papers on my desk. I feign interest in them. But then, I'm drawn back to the window, to the sight of her. I glance just in time to see her reach for her jar of Carmex and head for the john; she never goes anywhere without that small jar. I don't see the need; her lips seem plenty soft. If only it could make them more yielding.

As I thought about her lips yielding, my office door opened and she entered, closing it behind her.

She leaned her back against the door. She brought up her red leather skirt—how could she get it to move that easily when it was skin tight? Easy—her body was made of silk. Did the gasp that I heard come from me? Her panties were already off. So that was why she went to the john, to take off her undies for me!

God. Mr. Big was steel and I could feel myself about to shoot. I reached under my desk—grabbed my balls with both hands and pinched them so hard I damn near cried. Better that than the alternative, to come in my pants like a sixteen–year–old.

Was that a smile on her lips?. . .no, my imagination.

My camel hair jacket hung behind the door. She turned her back to me, her skirt still bunched around her waist, what a sight, and reached for my jacket pocket. In her hand was something red; she shook it out and I could see her satin panties. She slid them into my pocket, turned slowly, as if on a pivot, to face me, and with a hip–wiggle easily shook down her skirt.

"I wanted you to have a little something to play with later while you think about what I told you we'd be doing on Thursday, Sailor–boy."

That voice was a caress that lingered in the air after she'd straightened herself and was gone. Her voice. . .her smell. . .

I could barely contain my desire to get these hands on those panties. I rushed to the door, pulled them from my coat pocket; they were slippery and slightly damp—the crotch milky–moist. I went directly to my bathroom where I covered my face in them, inhaled and sucked the red satin while I hurried to get my pants unbuckled in time. I barely had to touch Mr. Big before he fired at will. . .a splat hit my crocodile shoe. I'd lost control of my senses, but instead of putting up a fight, I gave myself over to it, sat on the toilet seat and sucked every bit of her from the satin.

I thought of what I would do to her Thursday; things she definitely did not have listed on her dance card.

"We'll see whose fucking sailor–boy I am."

Thoughts of Thursday's exercise in power made me hard again and slower this time, I moved my hand on Mr. Big, and favored myself to a trip back in time. I went through all we'd done in that filthy restroom, until I felt the familiar, uncontrollable jerks that preceded expulsion of the evil inside me.

"Look at these sheets!" I heard Ma's voice as if she were here in the can with me, "You filthy boy, this is evil!" She would push my face in the sticky mucus as if I were a dog who'd crapped on her rug. "Lick it up, Peter!"

She'd been dead for over a year and yet she wouldn't leave me alone! Often I talked out loud to her. Like now. "I know it's evil, Ma, but at least I get it out—get rid of it. I don't leave it inside my body to grow like a cancer."

I sat on the toilet and looked at my new and now newly soiled, shoes. I felt beaten rather than satiated. And then I laughed out loud. I had decided. I would not clean these crocodile shoes; they were beyond salvation. I'd never be able to look at them without the instant replay of this moment, and her control over me, haunting me. She won't be another ghost of Ma. I will wear them one final time— when that time arrives, that small splotch of my body's fluid will be insignificant.

They will be washed with blood. A wash that will remain forever.

Permanent. Indelible.

I stood, buckled my belt. And felt much better.

BABS LAKEY

In control.
Crocodile shoes would be a fitting sacrifice.

Chapter Twenty–Two

Elsie answered the phone, "Hello." She heard nothing but felt the presence of someone on the line. "Hello?"

Click. The dial tone gave its steady drone. She replaced the receiver.

It rang again.

"Hey, Red, get it!" Elsie yelled. "Soon's they hear my voice they click off. I can feel my blood pressure rise. It's a secret admirer, a pervert or kids playing with the phone. Whatever it is, I've had it."

Lynn ran to snatch it, as her hand touched the receiver, it went mute. "Next time," she said, "I'll be our official receptionist," she added in her sugar–won't–melt voice. Then, she mimed, "Hell*ooo*, Fahey and Sanders here, penal colony release experts." She rubbed her hair with a thick mauve towel. The color was made to go with her red hair. "By the way, Els, before I forget, this rinse you made for me is the best ever. What's in it? Smells *witchy*; makes me feel as if I could cast a spell or two of my own." She giggled. "Ooooooh! I *did* cast a big one on Charlie! What's in it? Secret stuff, forbidden to mere mortals?"

"I think your *witchy*–ness has more to do with the you–and–Charlie chemistry, than any secret powers held captive in my hair rinse." Elsie went to the pantry, and opened a cupboard door. "But, come on. I'll show you."

Lynn raised her freckled button nose at the bottles that lined the shelves and sniffed while she used her fingers to air dry her short curls. There were dozens of different sized bottles, all carefully labeled in Elsie's hand. Elsie had already explained that she was never to touch those marked with an X. Lynn inspected the jars of dried weeds, bark and peculiar twisted roots.

"Don't you think they look neato?"

Lynn thought about her food. Elsie *did* cook all their meals. "It looks weird. I mean, don't get me wrong, but this stuff's bizarre."

Elsie gave an evil laugh, "Yeah. That's one of the things I like most. Don't forget, I was raised on weird."

"Don't remind me."

"Hey. These're just herbs—stuff I've read about." She paused, "Maybe next year I'll grow my own. I bet the landlord would let me have a small garden out back."

Lynn raised an eyebrow. "You have a multifaceted personality, Els. That's my polite way to say you're nuts. Nutty, but nice."

"Ta–ha." They both laughed. "This time, I get to be the teacher; what a switch. Shall we begin with the rinse?"

Lynn began by dancing around the pantry, singing, *"Teach me tonight, yeah, yeah, yeah."*

"Tales–of–the–night will come later." Elsie cleared her throat, her face serious in an attempt to impress. "First, lavender flowers. Lavender was used by the Romans to fumigate; it'll keep bacteria and bad bugs away. And, it's s'posed to help one keep one's chastity! I figured, what could it hurt?"

"Too late, too late, it was a very important date. . .cha, cha, cha." Lynn didn't want to be this serious. "Way too late, I'm pleased to report!"

Elsie smiled and ignored her; she had reports of her own she was anxious to get to. "Next, Madam Red, is rosemary. Rosemary means *fond of the sea*; you know how you love water. It's your special herb. It will bring you luck and do away with evil spirits or bad dreams—though I don't think you have those. I don't want you to have any, either."

"Aw, that's sweet."

"Almost forgot; rosemary will prevent premature baldness. You can share it with Charlie."

"Elsie! You witch, you! Wait till I tell him that; he thinks you're so innocent. No. Better not tell him. He's self–conscious of those few wisps on top; it might hurt him."

"I've noticed it bothers him and this could help. You don't have to tell him what it's for; it's a hair rinse. Hey, if Charlie goes completely bald he'll be even more adorable. Now, where was I before you so rudely interrupted and insulted me? Ah, I remember. Quassia chips—this tree bark stuff," she held the jar in front of Lynn's face and shook it.

"Looks just like tree bark."

"Some slave from the West Indies used this to make a secret remedy for bad, deteriorating fevers—a big problem in those days. If he'd have been a white man instead of a slave this discovery would have made him rich. Anyhow, it's used today for dandruff an' itchy scalp."

"You really worked all this out."

"Told you I did. Now, the red poppy flowers. I used a lot of those for you—just for color, you'll be relieved to know."

"Sounds like it came right from a cosmetic company."

"Umm, well, it didn't, it came from me! Ha! Just so you don't think I'm *too* normal, some Indian tribes considered the red poppy so poisonous that only witch doctors could use it. It was probably that tidbit of folklore that drew me to it."

The phone's ring interrupted.

"I'll get it; it's probably Charlie. He loves me so much he's already lonesome." She picked up the phone, "Lynn here."

Her face fell. "Look, don't call me again. I don't want to talk to you."

Elsie stopped to listen to the conversation. . .this wasn't Charlie.

"No. I've already said no. Don't you get it?"

"I won't meet you anywhere! Not ever. And, while we're

at it, stop coming into my work."

"Prick tease? What do you mean? Are you *nuts*? I never led you on for a minute!"

"Listen here. Carefully. No. . .*stop that*. Stop *now!*. . .listen to me, you creep. . .yes, I said *creep*. I'm not hot for you, as you put it. You're a moron. I'm seeing someone I really care about. You're not fit to be in the same room with him. Even if there was no one special in my life, you'd still be a moron. God knows why I had any interest in you but we all make mistakes, and that was *before* I knew you had a wife and family, before I knew the real you. I've met a *real* man."

Elsie noticed that Lynn's skin was damp.

"What. . .you'll *what*?"

"*No, you* listen. There's no way I'll change my mind. Buzz off, creepo."

"*What?*"

"Hey, you call again, and I call the cops, and then, *your wife*!"

Lynn slammed the receiver. "*Damn* him, Elsie." A tear rolled down one pale cheek. "Gives me the creeps. I can't think what I ever saw in him—even that first day! God Els, how did I get into this!"

Elsie continued to go through the motions of getting their tea, while trying to console, "You know you only liked him when he was pretending to be someone other than who he is. *What a loser!* Man, you look white as a ghost. He's not worth it. You need rest."

Lynn looked nauseous. "I'm afraid of him, Els. He says *terrible* things to me. He sounds more like a nutcase all the time. And why me? He's good looking. I never told you this, but he's much better looking than Charlie—don't ever tell that to my sweet Charlie—this creep's a nothing! If Peter did get me in the sack he wouldn't want me again. He has to have me 'cause he can't. Does that make sense?"

Elsie nodded listlessly. She had that feeling she'd not been able to shake. What made it return?

"He changed. It's hard to explain. You know how in the movies when you see a psycho, they are obsessed with one thing?"

Elsie nodded again, her stomach ached.

"For Peter, I'm that *thing*."

"Does he know where you live?"

"He got my number, didn't he? I sure as hell didn't give it to him. I didn't think he knew my last name. And, that's another thing, he keeps saying he'll have me one way or another. That frightens me. *One way or another*. Then he says. . .I wish I could remember exactly, oh this sounds so stupid, but it's about *his shoes*, something weird. It's like, "Aren't my shoes good enough for a high class chick?" That's not quite it. I don't know. Who could think of me as high class?"

"Oh, Hunbun. You are *the* classiest of dames." The tea was steeping, as usual the aroma soothed. "Wait. What was that about shoes?"

"Oh, Els, It's probably not important," Lynn sighed. "For weeks I gave him this "my–date–book–is–full" routine. You know, trying not to *hurt* him. We women feel like we have to protect a guy's feelings even if we'd rather just tell him to scram. Got to be polite. I thought he'd give up. In retrospect, it was the wrong thing to do. But it's instinctive. We've been taught to be polite for too damn long. It made him more persistent, Elsie. Some people only want what they can't have. Am I right?" She laughed. "Or am I right?" The tea was doing its job relaxing her, or maybe it was Pip curled on the floor beneath her chair. He licked her feet and that soothed her, too.

"The thing is Elsie, he acts so strange!"

"What if it's *not an act?*"

Chapter Twenty-Three

"All right students. We will now hear from our number one student in *BlowJobs 101*, Elsie Sanders please come up to the front of the class and tell us how this class helped you perform your duties in the real world."

"Well, I'm happy to see that you're not going to let that scum bag ruin your day off. I know you don't believe all men are like that."

"Nah. We've just been hitting more than our share. The tides'll turn. Look at Charlie, my dream guy, and Pops, my other dream guy."

"Ahhh, speaking of dream guys. I hate to change the subject, but..."

"Change it? Ah, Ms. BJ Jr., I think I just *did* change it!"

"Well, har–de–har–har, Ms. BJ Sr. Okay. Before you say I told you so, I want to say it! Lynner, you told me so!"

"You did do it then. You really did, didn't you?"

Elsie turned red. "Um, yeah. I did. With Skip."

"Oh, with Skip! Well, roll me over in the clover, I'd a never guessed it was with Skip!"

Elsie had a dreamy look on her face and ignored the ribbing. "Man. I never would've dreamed—and I'd never have tried it without your mentoring."

"Hey, don't you dare kiss me with those lips!" Lynn held her hand, palm out as if to ward her off.

Elsie was excited. "It was the ultimate—in my limited sexual repertoire." Her voice dropped. "I don't want to like someone this much right now—you know what I mean."

"Yeah, well, you'll see him some more. I know you. At

heart we're both kinda kinky and slutty." Lynn stopped. Elsie looked stunned. "I'm *teasing* you!" She gave her an elbow jab. "Hey, maybe we should start our own club. *The sluts from hell!* What do ya think, Els?"

Elsie laughed at that. "Hey, we're *good* girls!"

"Good, true. But we've been having fun *talking* about wild sex since, well, forever. You know what they say about the heart of a whore? Well, maybe we're whores at heart! Ha! Aw, c'mon, tell me the juicy stuff, will ya? Hey, juicy stuff, Juicy Fruit. Get it?" Lynn elbowed her again. "Forget the *he's so fine* crapola, you can come back to that later. I wanna hear about the banana trick.

"Talk, banana girl, talk!"

Actually, Elsie couldn't wait to talk. It was Lynn that gave her the inspiration. "Well, I planned it like you said, but we didn't even make it to dinner. Sorry, teach, I forgot most of my class lessons. Maybe it was the wine, or the music, but all of a sudden there he was in the chair with me..."

"Wait a minute, what chair? There's no...oh! You mean the *bean–bag*? You were in the *ballroom*? This is so fine!"

"The ballroom." Elsie nodded. "Anyway, we were just kissing. Oh, is he a good kisser. And then *Strawberry Fields* started to play."

"You're kidding! Did you plan that?"

"Not exactly, it just..." Elsie shrugged, "ah, it happened. Oh, you know what they say about the importance of timing."

"Oooh." Lynn was fifteen again. "I've waited a long time to be on this end of one of these conversations!"

"*You've* waited? What about me? So, my head was spinning."

"Get to the real stuff."

"I'm doing this *my* way. Just like I did with the Skipper! Okay, I started to nibble on him and Lynn! I could actually smell and taste strawberries! I mean *really* I did, Lynn! By the time I got..."

"*Down!*"

They giggled like small girls.

". . .to the main course, so to speak."

"My dear girl, speaking has nothing to do with this!"

Elsie ignored her. "I was in another world. I could smell banana! Clear as if there'd been a banana tree over us! I swear it to you. If it'd been anyone but Skip I'd have burst out laughing and spoiled the moment."

Lynn beat her fists on top of her thighs like a drum—a habit whenever she was excited.

"But, how did you know? How'd you know how I'd feel?"

"Elsie, I just know you. I knew you'd get into it."

"*Your mind's bent!* Don't get me wrong. I mean that in a good way—a nice bent.

"One thing I figured you'd like is that *you'd* be in control for once in your life. This is *not* the sort of thing that people generally write love songs about. *Strawberries and bananas, fields and romance, all because of a blowjob!* You, my kooky friend, are one of a kind."

They sat sipping tea in comfortable silence. It didn't take much to make them happy. The earlier tension had vanished. "You don't want to hear about how wonderful he is?"

"I already know that you're loving him or you'd never have gone through with that experiment of ours!" Lynn's shoulders slumped with contentment and fatigue. "I'm bushed, Els. Tell me about the love later, okay with you?" When Elsie smiled in agreement, she continued. "Think I'll take a nap. What're you gonna do today?"

"That was my other news."

"So? Tell."

"You know I'd like to work at the Improv. Skip thinks he can get me a job! Just doing sets, but who knows what might come."

"Besides him, you mean?"

"Huh?" Elsie had that look.
"Never mind. It skimmed over your blonde head."
"Hey you—I get it. Look, I'd love to sit here with you and be insulted but I've got to run."
"So run, already." Lynn yawned.
"I'm dying for you guys to get to know one another. I know you didn't have much to do with Skip back home. Hey! Let's double date!"

Lynn nodded, and Elsie looked at her watch. "I've got this interview in twenty minutes."

On her way to change, she gave Lynn a bear hug from behind. "Thanks for being here. I love ya, Red." She started towards her room. "By the way, this *was* far more satisfying than the Gainesburger event."

Lynn stood, stretched with her arms in the air and smiling waved her fingers to Elsie to get going.

"I guess this makes us the first two official members of the *sluts from hell* group, huh?" Elsie didn't want this talk to end.

"Okay by me." Lynn's back was turned; she walked into her bedroom. "We'll be a revenge group. So, har–de. . ."

"Har–har." Elsie finished Lynn's infamous saying.

It was an idea preposterous enough to make them both laugh.

Elsie tried to hurry and still dress with care. She wanted to make a good impression which wouldn't happen if she was late. She took one last look in the mirror. For some reason her feet did not want to take her out the door. She walked haphazardly around the apartment checking the locks on the doors and even the windows. She looked in Lynn's room—dear Red was fast asleep.

What felt very much like a premonition of danger wouldn't leave Elsie at rest.

Should she cancel?

Voices inside her head argued, *"listen to what I'm trying to say,"* or, *"you paranoid fool."*

At last she put it off to pre–interview jitters. Or maybe she was getting lazy, looking for an excuse to stay home and hibernate, winter *was* almost here. That last one was a hard sell. Maybe yesterday, but not now, not after Skip. She closed the front door after herself and locked it securely.

It felt as if someone were watching her every move. The feeling leeched to her. Could someone be watching? She looked—no one in sight—not a sound but the wind playing in the bushes and dashing throughout the eaves of the old house.

She grumbled at herself, "Are you beginning to *believe* you're a witch, endowed with supernatural powers, girl?"

I slipped into my ivory silk dressing gown, poured a glass of champagne, and began chopping the rocks into a fine powder. It amused me that the drug was ivory, my color.

There were so many details to go over.

Thursday was only three days away.

I leaned my head close to the glass table and sniffed a huge line. "Thank you, God," I said aloud and shrugged, "you haven't been around much, but at least you had the decency to create drugs. For my money you could have better spent the time perfecting your design for certain kinds of people. But, thanks anyway."

Not that the drugs were much fun anymore. Were they ever? I don't remember. At least they do the job—numb my senses. That's worth almost anything.

I shuddered. How could I bear to have that pig touch me again?

How?

Thursday it would all be worth it. I told myself I didn't mind the things I had to do with my body just to bait the trap.

Because, what am I?

I am no one. I am not important.

What I'm doing, my purpose, is all that matters.

The trap. That's what is important, not me.

I went to the kitchen to rinse out my Carmex jar, then took the Old Home plain yogurt from the fridge and refilled the small container, then placed the little "prop" in my purse.

It would not do to leave home without that.

He expected me to be wet for him. Wet because of him. The one thing I could not fake—I found the yogurt to be an excellent substitute. It wouldn't do to fake orgasm and be dry as a prune. He was smart enough to notice. I fancied myself an actress of sorts, at least I'd spent my lifetime day dreaming of becoming one. Well, I had my golden opportunity now. I had to continuously remind myself to keep focused on my end goal.

I enjoyed thinking of it as the end.

Still, it made my skin crawl to have him touch me, to even think of having him touch me.

Every time he did I wanted to whisper "gotcha." But had I? Not until the end—his end. Until that day, it was him that got me. He was the winner of this little game.

Until the game was over.

My chance was coming. I could not wait to let him know what a colossal hoax it was every time I pretended to have another orgasm! I looked over at the jar of Carmex filled with my yogurt "come."

And he believed he was such a stud!

I felt whimsical, almost childlike, remembering our last "encounter."

I made him nearly shoot in his pants without having once touched me. What a coup!

His lack of self–control was no surprise, but I found myself disgusted all the same. I did another line, then sat back to go over my plan. This was not a game played for small stakes. I knew that my remaining days were

few in number.
Few, but oh so satisfying in the end.

Chapter Twenty-Four

Lorenzo was about to make a point.

I was serious when I asked his opinion of the Harlem High School joke, but intentional or not I was also trying to divert attention from myself. He was determined to show me how well that tactic worked. He had the entire group doing what he'd asked me to do: take the joke and fit it to another group of people—discover how *that* makes you feel.

Always back to feelings.

Today's music, there to help us think about how race fit in with our personal problems, was a background of blues to go with our blues—Robert Johnson, *Me And The Devil Blues*. "You may bury my body, whoo, down by the highway side. . .So my old evil spirit can get a Greyhound bus and ride. . . ."

Watermelon, barbecue, Cadillac car.

Nobody in my group thought the joke was funny in the first place, they barely got the joke. After much discussion we decided it would be difficult for any of us to speak up and say that the joke was *not* funny, 'specially if it was someone who intimidated us that told the joke.

This joke of mine had turned into an uncomfortable exercise. The truth reared its ugly head, the only group of people we enjoy making fun of is men. Over thirty–year–old white males were not popular here. We tried other people in the slot, but nobody laughed. The joke wasn't funny.

Finally, I made a suggestion. "How's this? Belching White–Boy High School Cheer. *Budweiser, tank-top, Chevrolet truck.*"

"*Varoooom*," mimicked Tony.

The shy group twittered.

"What about this?" asked Lorenzo—the therapist sat back with his shoes on his desk. They showed holes worn clear through the soles. "What do you call one dead lawyer at the bottom of a river?"

No answer. Puzzled faces.

"One hell of a good start." I said that. And then, "but that's *old*."

Small giggles.

Lorenzo said how hard it was to get this group riled on the outside. "Try using another group of people for lawyer."

Nothing.

"Come on, try it, we'll go around the room."

No one wanted to start.

"Okay, I will do it myself," barked Lorenzo. "What do you call one dead black boy at the bottom of the river?"

No one laughed. But we got the idea. Jew, Polack, woman—all took their turn at the bottom of our river. None of it worked for anyone in *this* room. No humor there.

I said, "May as well stick with the white man."

Spurts of nervous laughter answered me.

Lorenzo's poundage seemed to rise like bread dough shot in fast forward. He was upright and beginning to pace, his body labored to keep up with his mind. "*Now* we know what you all think. You have various degrees of hostility, not without reason, but so what? Listen to me closely, fellow humans. Listen as I tell you: *You are all wrong!* We have two separate issues. First. Humor is based on some degree of truth. If you laugh at a joke that puts down an entire group of people, you show your inner feelings. Second. How can you hate a *group of people*, because someone, or even many, from that group have hurt you?"

We studied the floor. Lorenzo was the one who asked us to do this exercise. *Why is he yelling?*

His eyes read each one of us. His voice boomed, "All of you. Listen up. *Your behavior is racist*."

We were horrified. None of us met Lorenzo's eye. I flipped at the side of my hair with a pencil.

"I want you to each make a list of the white men that you know, have known, or know of, that are *real* people, good men. This list? It better be long. There are a lot of them. "No form of racism or hatred will help make you well. But, it *will* keep you sick! I'm not saying you've no right to be angry at the bastards. But it's easy to hate. Yes, it is. Well, sad as it may be the easy way will not make us well and it sure as hell won't make us strong."

The room was so quiet you could have heard a spider weave.

"Don't worry about things that are out of your control. And, remember," he said, "only *our* inner values are within our complete and total control."

For now, the group was my life.

It was comforting to be a part of something that resembled a family. I loved Lorenzo—as we all did. He made us think about things—not only past pain, but important things that concerned the entire world around us, the world we had to learn to live in once again. The diversion gave us time to heal.

I could tell that he liked me. He laughed aloud when I apologized for not knowing black history. "But then," I said, "I don't know any women's history either. *What if we could rewrite history, now, today, pretend we are all important? As if everybody matters. What about that?*"

Lorenzo seemed, at times, to be taken aback by things I said. Like that time. He just shook his head. As if there were no answers.

He told me quietly one day that although I was intelligent and personable, one aspect of my personality was under–developed. "Honey girl, you know plenty about others, you know how they feel—far better than yourself." And, he told me that I cared more about others than about me. In group it was a snap when the others dealt with their problems. Not that I found it easy to hear their pain; they'd all been physically and/or sexually, abused/raped, but I got so much out of giving them comfort.

If they turned the talk to me, that was the other side of the glass. A glass that was painted black; no discernible entry. I didn't have the answers to their questions. I was used to doing, saying, even thinking, whatever people around me expected or wanted. How could I know what I thought? I didn't even know that I *should* know what I thought. I missed Lynn. Startled, I realized that part of my pain came from the fact that Lynn *had always been able to read my mind*. She'd known me for so long she knew my thoughts and had no problem verbalizing them.

What did I want, the group asked?

"To be loved. To be happy."

Okay, they asked, *what will make you feel loved and happy?*

What? Did they mean it was up to me to find my own happiness?

Yep. Exactly. That's it. Where could I begin? I'd spent my life trying to make everyone else happy so they would like me and show me the love I thought I needed. That was how it'd always been.

My own endless circle.

The days spent on the other seven people in the group were much more satisfying. This was familiar ground. I knew instinctively how to care for others, give them love, empathy, even protect them. They said I was co–dependent. That didn't sound so bad. It felt good to help someone else. . .and so, I learned that I loved to protect those I cared about. To protect them made *me* happy. So be it.

That little fact was about to change my life.

Chapter Twenty–Five

No man had ever been to this home, and none would ever be welcome. Well, that wasn't entirely accurate. I'd love to have Tony here—but it wouldn't be in his best interest.

So, no man. That was a good rule. The very idea that you could live a pleasant life with no man. Imagine that.

Oh, yes, my second rule was good, too.

Never suck cock. Bite–it.

My closest friend in the group was Tony—only first names were used in group. We had an immediate connection. Tony was nineteen, and he was gay. Like me he'd never grown up because he'd never been allowed to be a child. He'd been sexually abused by a Roman Catholic priest. It began right after he turned nine and continued until the priest left the church to marry. Tony was twelve at the time. The priest didn't just get a wife when he married, he also got two sons of his own, ages five and six. Was it possible that the Father married just to have his own small boys to abuse? Tony was worried about what might happen to these kids. No one from his church seemed to care.

The Catholic Church taught that any form of sex without the Sacrament of Holy Matrimony was a mortal sin. Same–sex sex was always a mortal sin. Why, then, when one of their own priests did this *thing* to a child, did those in charge look the other way and just pray over it? They pretended it had not happened.

"Father Barker was always understanding," Tony said,

"so easy to talk to. He made you feel like anything you did was okay with God. He did things with us that our own Dads were too busy to do because they had to go to work. Father had all day to spend, and he thought we were important enough to find extra time for us. He took me under his wing—said I was special. We went camping, just us. Sometimes one or two other boys would come, too. At night we'd all lay our sleeping bags by the campfire.

Father's was always next to mine. I *felt* special.

As the others fell asleep he'd rub my back. And later, he'd whisper to me to turn over and face him. I can still feel his hot breath in my ear. At first he'd just rub my chest and talk to me, but after awhile he'd rub further down. And eventually..."

His hands spread over his face to hide as much of it as he could hide, "I'm so ashamed!" He cried. His shoulders shook with his sobs, "I remember how much I hated his hands. They were smooth as silk, and white, white as the keys on a new piano."

I started when he said that word—*piano*.

"His fingers were real long. They were terrible hands. I used to have nightmares about his hands. They would stroke me everywhere—like velvet sliding over me—only, in my dream they were dipped in something. It was a liquid, a goo, that flowed over my skin, until I would blink and when my eyes opened the goo had turned into maggots—slimy maggoty-worms that were red, filled with blood, plump with blood. It was awful, because as much as I hated it there was some part of me that wanted it. And that small part, that made *me* as bad as him."

As I listened to Tony, I felt fortunate that Dr. Jack had not been able to take me camping. I also felt hatred for Father Barker. Right at this very minute he could be touching one of his own boys, or someone else's. His blubbery body up against even one boy was one too many.

I picked up the tiny gold metal straw and opened the small box of ivory powder. Ivory, the same shade as the silk and the walls that surrounded me. This, a pleasant life? Who was I kidding?

The powder I sniffed was fast becoming my true love.

I inhaled two lines of what I liked to believe was happy dust, from the glass table and let my head fall back into the down sofa with my eyes closed, hoping to forget, but only remembering more.

Tony had to get over his feelings of guilt. I wanted to teach him the R-E-V-E-N-G-E song. It would cheer him.

"Listen, Tony." I knew he needed to think of something else for a few minutes. "Let me tell you a story." We got comfortable and I continued:

"The snow had begun to fall earlier that evening. I tipped my face toward big wet flakes and caught some on my tongue. Have you ever done that?"

He nodded, he had.

"I'd been gone nearly two and a half hours and couldn't wait to get home. You ever get to feeling like you'll burst open if you don't get where you're going to see the person you want to see?"

Tony smiled. Sure. He'd been there.

"I wore Skip's Walkman-type headphones and sang along with the cassette he'd just given me as I walked. *". . .but if you love him you'll forgive him. . .*hmmhmmhmm."

I knew I looked goofy. I didn't care. I wanted to share this life I was beginning, this surge of happiness, with my very best ever friend. With Lynn. As I walked along singing I also planned what I'd cook for dinner while Lynn and I talked about Skip and Charlie and life.

"*Stand by your man.*" I belted those words at the top of my lungs. It was the first time I'd heard Tammy Wynette.

"*Give him two arms to cling to. . .*"

"Well, you get the idea. My mind wouldn't keep still, Tony. It was chaotic—scenes of the future, for Lynn and me, were a kaleidoscope rolling on my mind–film. First, I'd gotten the job at the Improv and that was great. I knew Lynn would be proud. Then, Skip. The very sight of him gave me erotic thoughts. I mean, *thoughts of sex, not just love*, for me that was a first. While we were at the Improv earlier I'd caught myself kind a mooning over his body.

"But, he'd just gotten a fabulous offer from a theatre in San Francisco. He asked if I'd consider moving out there for a year or so. Well, he said, we don't have to *live* together right away. Skip knew I'd be afraid of that. 'Elsie,' he said, 'couldn't you talk to Lynn and see if you could both come out?'"

"Did you think that might happen?" Tony hung on every word.

"No. I don't think I considered it a possibility. I mean, what about Charlie? I knew no one would want to move except me and I wasn't sure about *me* if it meant leaving Lynn. A year would go by fast. It'd be okay to slow things down, give me the chance to find out what I wanted before getting all caught up in Skip.

"Well, anyway, the *best* thing was this skit they wrote.

"Skip wrote a song for me and Lynn. He played it at the Improv while the entire cast sang. As soon as I heard it I remember saying, "Lynn will just *die*! This is so cool!"

"I had the lyrics written. I pulled them out of my pocket and looked them over. The music was on the tape, playing on the headphones. I couldn't help but sing out loud. It was like having my own personal choir practice so that I could perform for Lynn when I got home. I wanted to wake her up from her nap with my serenade. The lyrics were to be sung to the music from the D-I-V-O-R-C-E song where you spell out the words. I sang and hummed along with the singers once more to get into the proper serenading mood. Then went right into the one they'd written for us. They called it R-E-V-E-N-G-E.

"The paper I carried was soggy with snow flakes. I'll sing part of the song for you, Tony!"

"R-E-V-E-N-G-E What we're hiding from him—he'll never see, yet the thought of it, makes us double up with glee! Our R-E-V-E-N-G-E became final today, me and my honey, S-K-I-P, paid a visit to Strawberry Way. Doin' for him what I'd never done for that B-O-Y, was a B-A-double L for me. I'm sure glad that we could have our little R-E-V-E-N-G-E."

"I wondered how a few words could make me feel so damn good! I knew Lynner would go *ball*istic when she heard it. Our new theme song!"

Tony was excited to know my secret song and happy to think of something besides his Father Barker.

These thoughts of Tony and all that had been done to him made me want to cry.

Then I remembered something Lynn had said. "Conquer it and make it yours." Wasn't that it?

And Lorenzo'd said not to let it have power over you. Get it out in the open—get rid of it.

I would find a way to take charge of my life. That would be my goal. It had worked in the past. I remembered how Lynn had proved to me how well it could work. I smiled that day. The first real smile since Lynn's death.

Revenge.

I thought about the word, and knew that somehow, someday, I would make it happen. All I needed to do was to keep going, and be ready. I'd find a way to do that; the reward would be worth whatever the effort. Even thoughts of my lost baby were more tolerable when I thought of justice and our song: R-E-V-E-N-G-E. I hummed the tune. It wasn't as much revenge that I was

after as it was justice. Justice. The same amount of letters.
    J-U-S-T-I-C-E.
    It fit. It fit the song.
    I felt strong.

Chapter Twenty-Six

How could I attract a man who coveted small boys? A man who got off on using children?

I'd have to look very young. That was not a problem, I had that kind of face. But I had to cut my hair short. It was hard to pay for a haircut after having it free from Dad all my life. I guess it wasn't all that free from Dad, either.

So, the plan was that I'd look very young and look up to him, be impressed with him. Impressed? That was the absolute worst. Although I'd had years of practice at doing that very thing, it was hard to force it with the vile Barker. Because I was no longer a naive young woman.

In the end—the end for Barker—it was easier than I'd thought. Tony was right about the former priest's hands, they gave me the willies. I knew what he'd done with them. I remember looking, thinking, "these putrid hands touched Tony." Only Barker and God knew how many others. He took Tony's trust in a man of the cloth and used it against him. I had no pity for him. No sorrow for his Almighty soul. I knew the devil would be waiting for this one. Standing at the gates of hell with a pitchfork in his hand waiting to spear the hard metal picks into Barkers cellulite ass and toss him into the flames for an eternity.

While Barker blubbered and cried to be saved I sat in the kitchen of the small apartment I'd rented for a week.

A week—for him to have his weak moment.

I knew it would be plenty of time. These sick moments

had been guiding him, leading him by his dick throughout his repugnant evil life. It was a blessing when he gasped his last disgusting breath of life. I wore tight rubber gloves. I sliced off his dick.

I had no gloves to cover my mouth when I bit these bastards, nothing except a slight film of clear plastic wrap. Lucky for me I'd seen a show about magic. Fire Eating was part of it.

Fire Eating. Who'd have guessed?

It was a special that was on TV when I was still in the hospital after Lynn's murder. At the time it was like background music but some of it stayed with me and gave me ideas later. I was glad of that.

Fire Eaters coat their mouths.

I could hardly do that, at least not so that my lips wouldn't have to touch their skin, but these men were drugged and I could easily cover their pricks with something. Even doing it the way I did, it gave me the creeps. Creeps or not, I did it. It was my path to mental health.

I was grateful to Tony for helping me realize this was the way.

I remembered that first night:

Our group had a New Year's Eve party. We needed one another on celebratory days. I was in a festive energetic mood while I dressed for the party. That enthusiasm nudged me into a decision to drag out the bicycle that I'd put away for the winter. There wasn't much snow which was an oddity for Minnesota in January. Besides, it wasn't far and the sun was out.

The ride over was fun, the party just okay. None of us hung back when it was time to go. Outside it had turned cold and dark. I was sorry I had been so impulsive. As I was getting up the courage to hop on my bike Tony came out.

He saw me start to maneuver my bicycle on the icy sidewalk and took pity on me. "Hey Chickie! Have we met? You have a familiar look."

"Cheep cheep," I nodded.

His grin was inviting. "C'mon, I'll drive you *and* your wheels home." He picked up the bike. It was heavy for his small frame, but he made it look easy and threw it in the bed of his mini-pickup.

"No need to ask me twice. Thanks, Tony. I wasn't looking forward to freezing my rear off."

I eyed his lithe sinewy body as I climbed inside. He must work out. I knew he was self–conscious about his size. Fragile of body and spirit. That's how he seemed to me. Tony had tried to commit suicide a few months ago, which was what got him into the group. I wanted to talk to him about what made him want to do that to himself. It was another of our connections.

"I have a new apartment." That was clumsy. Still for some reason I was nervous.

"I have a new pencil." Smart ass. I liked that about him and I think he knew it.

I ignored his attempt. "It's on Bryant Avenue, wanna see it?"

"Sure. I'll check out your etchings." He raised an eyebrow.

Conversation on the ride over was light. As we rode the elevator to my apartment on the seventh floor we studied one another knowing there was the potential, here, for a serious visit.

"I've only been here two weeks, so it's not much to see."

Suicide, a subject of importance, loomed over us as I unlocked my door. "It's an efficiency. Real small." I opened the door standing back to allow him to enter.

"Where's your dog? I distinctly remember your tales of a *rascal* dog." Tony made nervous chatter, too.

"Pip. His name's Pip. He's staying with the cop who's trying to find Lynn's murderer. I miss Pip. No animals allowed here," I sighed. *Why not go for it? Truth, that is.* "The real reason is, I'm having trouble taking care of myself. But I'm looking for a house right now. This is a temporary arrangement. Law, that's the cop, offered to keep Pip to help me out. I miss him but I'll have him with me soon."

Tony paced the small room—then flounced into an old beanbag chair. He noticed my frown. "What'd I do?"

"Oh, nothing!" The chair was one of the few things I'd kept from my life with Lynn. "Really."

He fiddled with the ring on his pinkie finger. "Elsie. Um, I hope you won't be offended, but I'm a teeny tense. We both know what we want to talk about, don't we? As if we don't get enough of this baring–our–souls–shit in group. So. Mind if I do a line first—to get my motor revved to speed?"

"Line?" My face was vacant.

He seemed surprised, amused even.

"Yeah, you know...blow, sniff, candy? *Cocaine.*"

I stared.

"Hey, it's no different than having a glass of wine. You *do* drink, don't you?"

I nodded.

"It's made from the leaves of a South American shrub." I smiled.

"They used to put it in Coca–Cola, Elsie. I mean, Freud did it all the time! It expands your consciousness...at the same time it numbs your feelings."

Ding! *Sold*. Sold to the blonde with the silly grin on her face.

He could tell the *numb the feelings* was what sold me. "It makes you feel as if you can do anything. Want to try? C'mon. We should serve it at group in cereal sized bowls."

"Did you say it's an herb?" I could talk again.

Tony nodded, then spoke as he chopped, "You have a

glass table and everything, how conv*eee*nient!" He emptied the small square of paper that held the drug out on top of her table, chopped, then formed the powder into ten good-sized lines. He handed me a straw. It looked like a plastic straw from a fast-food place that he'd cut short. "Here, do one up each side."

I wondered what Lorenzo would say. *It was from a plant, how bad could it be?* I looked at the plastic straw.

"Nothin' but the best for us, baby." Tony was trying his best to get me to relax. Since I didn't move, he took the straw from me. "Like this," he bent over to demonstrate.

I took the straw and followed his example. I felt a rush. Flushed, excited, energized. "Hey, Tony, I like this." And, it was forbidden—all the better! "This is a blast." Fun wasn't something I'd had much of in recent times. I missed the naughty things Lynn and I used to *talk* about doing.

"Hey." I wanted to change my mood. I took his hand, "Let me show you around, Sport!" I walked him to each of the four corners of the room, and for some unfathomable reason this made us laugh. It was funny. Wasn't it? I poured white wine. Why not have wine *and* cocaine?

"Well, Tone buddy, I s'pose you know what I want you to tell me. I want to know why. Who made you want to do that to yourself? Were you trying to punish someone?"

Tony's large haunted eyes accentuated his young boy appearance. He looked painfully vulnerable. Those eyes seared through me, then dropped to the table. He did another line.

I thought perhaps he needed me to divulge something first, so I told him what I'd never told anyone—about my school physical with Dr. Jack. Afterward, I said, "I've an idea how it happened with the priest, Tone, or how it made you feel. Was that why you tried to kill yourself?"

Tony flinched and shook his head. "Oh no, I didn't want to off myself for any reason like that."

Funny how the people who do their best to die don't want to call it suicide.

"It was the traffic ticket."

"*What?*"

"I, ah, well, okay, let's see. I'd just started school at the U of M. It was around Thanksgiving. I was driving home from class one evening. I looked in my rear view mirror and noticed the red light flashing. I thought I'd die right then and there. I could *not* get a ticket! I was terrified.

Anyway, the officer was nice enough, and I noticed that he had an outstanding tush, so *that* calmed me down. Thinking about it, I mean.

Then, I heard his voice saying that I was going 45 in a 30 MPH zone. I swear I didn't realize it.

Well, he wrote the ticket. He leaned in my window. He was handing me the ticket when he stopped. I noticed that he smelled like alcohol and cigarettes. The cigs were a turn off for me. I don't like to kiss an ashtray.

The cop said, "Maybe if you blew me. . ."

Well, I was shocked. I thought, you mean to say he *knows* with just a *look* at me?

"Thank you officer, but *I'd rather just fan you*," I said. 'Course that was a mistake.

He didn't crack a smile, just handed me the bloomin' ticket."

We did another line and filled our wine glasses.

I kept quiet. I didn't want Tony to stop the story, wanted him to get it all out.

"I came home with the ticket in my hand, sat at my kitchen table for awhile, not thinking of anything much. I'd done nothing *but* think for the past eighteen years, you know?"

Boy, did I know.

Tony squirmed. "What I remember most was that I didn't want to have to ask dear old Dad for the cash and I had *no* money. Zip. And since I couldn't afford to pay the ticket, eventually I'd *have* to call him. Daddy calls me his little fag–boy. So, I'd call, and then have to listen to his fag–boy routine."

I watched this transformation come over Tony while he talked. At the start of this tale he'd looked like a frightened deer; right now his face was empty.

"Well, I shuffled through my stuff and found these pills I'd been given when I couldn't sleep; they were years old. I'd kept them for a rainy day. We sat at the kitchen table, my darling pills and me, and I poured us a big glass of soda. I took the pills a few at a time 'till they were gone." Tony played with his ring, turning it around and around on his pinkie finger. The finger was red but he didn't seem to notice. His eyes came to life. "Don't you know what I'm saying, Elsie? Haven't you been there? Been where you just couldn't face one more day, one more second? Even if you'd faced it all of your life, everyday, this one last time was not going to happen?"

I knew it was hard for him to look at me so I walked behind him. I combed his hair with my fingers in an effort to soothe his inner child—Lorenzo taught us about our inner child.

"I wanted to be sure I had lots of ice in my glass. I remember that. I like a lot of ice. Profound, huh? That's what was on my mind in what I believed were my last moments of life. . . .

". . .*would the ice last?*"

Although I couldn't see his face, I knew this conversation was a roller coaster ride for Tony. He was hyped, filled with emotion, when he told about Father Barker, but as he talked about his attempt to kill himself the sound of his voice went monotone; he could've been talking about the constant rainy weather.

"I know." He suddenly perked up. "Here's something I remember. It was like I was in a corner, a cage. All my options were gone. I wasn't upset. But I knew this was all that was left for me."

"Why didn't you call a friend?" It had been on the tip of my tongue. I finally let it out.

"What I think we can learn from suicide," Tony said, "is not *why* a person *does* it. The lesson is that if we reach out to others suicide won't happen. Sounds simple—it's not. Not at all."

Why is he ignoring my question, I wondered.

Tony sighed. Hearing my unspoken thought. "I didn't call a friend, because then *I wouldn't have been able to do it.* And I *wanted* it so damn bad. That cop knew what he knew about me in an instant—just as Father Barker knew. That was the worst thing about Father Barker, Elsie. I enjoyed it. I didn't think I wanted it but I *came*. Don't you see? I had nightmares about it but I *must* have enjoyed it. How else could I have had an orgasm? I was ashamed. My whole life's been about shame. I hated his hands on me. Hated it even more when he made me put my hands on him, but still, I came! How did that happen, Elsie? I had to have liked it. I had to take part of the blame."

Tony's voice was a scream as he spit those last words. Then a pall spread over him and I thought he would cry, but instead he leaned to the table and sniffed another line. Then another.

Tony raised his eyes—they were shadowed—a picture out of focus taken at the wrong f-stop.

I hugged him, kissed him on the lips—a loud smack. There was so much to say, but I had to ask, "Tony, if you didn't have any money, how'd you get the drugs?"

"Oh, I didn't do drugs *then*. Oh no. My first time turned on by the powder was by a guy who, coincidentally, also turned *me* on. He was a nurse I met while I was on the nut ward. That was *after* the suicide attempt. This nurse and I. . .we had a short affair." Tony laughed.

I was relieved to hear the sound of his laughter.

"He had a *really* short affair—which is why our affair was so short. Get it?"

On purpose, just for fun, I hung out my vacant sign. "Remember, I'm blonde." Lynn always did the blonde jokes. I'd picked up the habit and thought I might like to pass it on to Tony. He went for it.

"Oh, exc*uuuuu*se me! His dick was barely a mouthful. Get it now, sweets?"

He'd returned to his usual light banter, and even though I wanted to keep his spirits up I had to tell him what I felt about his abuse. "Tony, what could make a man do what that priest did to you? He'd have to know the only reason you'd do what he asked would be that you looked up to him, trusted him. How could this man–of–God betray a helpless child? I can't accept it, Tony. *It should not go unpunished.*"

"Who cares *why* these perverts do what they do, Elsie? Why should we try to understand?"

I fluffed with his dark curls. "You're *so* smart. And, you're right, why pay them any attention? They aren't worth a fart."

We giggled. Oh, I *liked* him! This was the beginning of a beautiful friendship. One I hoped would never end. Tony started to hum a few bars of R-E-V-E-N-G-E.

"Listen, why don't I tell you the rest of that story? There's more to it than just the revenge song I taught you. You'll dig it!" I got up. "First, more wine."

"And another line?"

"Wine and cocaine." Made sense to me. "Okay. First, Gainesburgers, then Strawberry Fields—that part will amuse you." Tony was adorable. We talked long into the night. And as we talked, I began to understand some things about myself, about what happens to children who are abused by those they trust. How could Tony reach out to another human being without fear—even for conversation? He'd lost his power, lost all control over his life. That power was inside himself and it was trapped. No way to move forward; no way to move back.

A trapped animal will gnaw off its leg. But what does a human do?

I thought about the ticket and the cop. Did Tony seriously think that ticket was something to die for?

The cop's words, *"Maybe if you blew me"* curdled my insides. I trembled with anger and for a second I thought of Dr. Jack.

It was the loss of power. If you felt strong and powerful—you didn't feel shame when a cop spoke that way to you. *You got mad.* That cop was the one who should feel shame. The speeding ticket was just one more drop plunked into the bucket of Tony's life. It had overflowed; it was out of his control.

I made myself a promise. I would help him regain his power.

First—we'd free his spirit—make him a freebird, like I'd been. I'd been guilty of knowing others' feelings better than my own. Hadn't the group told me that? Well I knew what my feelings were now. I damned well knew.

I sat on the floor yoga style; my back propped against the sofa—the glass coffee table positioned directly in front of me. With one hand I flipped at the baby fine hair that always seemed to hang in my face, with the other I held a razor with which I carefully chopped the small pile of ivory rocks. My complexion, usually pale, felt flushed with anticipation. I sighed, felt my shoulders rise, then drop low.

Soon it will be over.

It helped me unwind to sit like this and prepare my cocaine stash for the day. Always be prepared. A good motto, although I was no Scout. Thinking of that made me grin, but sadly. My how life changes us. I laid out a couple of long lines, then did one immediately. "Ahhhhhhh." My shoulders heaved again.

Gratification.

Nothing like a snort. Why did people call this snorting? That sounded rude, and there was nothing rude about sniffing a pile of cool blow. Interesting that I liked to call it blow. Symbolic even. "I think I'll give myself a little blow." I laughed out loud, then sobered. The mood change was instantaneous. Enough fun and frivolity. It was time to decide what to do with Petie–boy. Let's get it on.

On to the final fillet.

It amused me to think of it that way. The final fillet. Sounds like the last dance from an opera. In a way, it was. I knew I was hovering on the edge with him, and a dangerous edge it was. The cutting edge. Perhaps I would be the one filleted. The end of a tragic opera.

By now, Peter had to be trying hard to find out where I lived. I'd been careful, but careful enough? Who knew. I'd given personnel at work a PO Box for my address—no one noticed at the time, but he was crafty enough to eventually find me. . .and figure it out, PO Box or not. After all, I'd found him. I did have one distinct advantage—I had a brain. His was between his legs. And that made him a potentially easy mark. I had to keep his mind in turmoil, leave him no time to think, and I'd been too elusive lately.

What to do to keep his mind in a spin?

The thought of his hands on me made it easy to forget my goal.

My eyes drifted across the room and rested on the piano. The piano.

The keys moved. . .and I heard, "R-E-V-E-N-G-E." Enough cocaine and I would see my friend's hands glide over those piano keys and the music would crowd other thoughts from my head. Not now!

I had to concentrate on Peter.

Peter was a stain on my soul. He'd taken lives, one very

particular life; now I would take his. His mark was on me. I tried to shake that awareness of him. I took the tiny silver straw—bent to the table and sniffed—then sighed and tried once again to concentrate.

The key to his lock was to keep him thinking with his cock. I thought about the gas station restroom. That episode was so odious that I could never tolerate it again. At the time I knew that it had to be done if the trap were to be set, and I did it, but never again.

I was smart! I could do this! I could keep him in control. I could. Think, damn it!

Two more days. . .and then it came to me. Of course!

I took the phone and dialed his office—I blinked and gave my head a shake to clear it—the phone rang and rang. *"Be there. Be there, you creep."* I held on, waiting. . .foot tapping. *"You've got to be there."*

"Hello." Bingo!

And it was him! "Howdy, Sailor–boy—wanna do it on the phone?"

"What?"

"I said, do you. . ."

"I heard what you said." He interrupted. "Where are you?" His voice was snarly—as if he spoke through bared teeth.

Tsk–tsk. Never get laid that way, Sailor–boy! "Where I can lie back and touch myself while I think of all the things I want you to do to me, and all the things you've done. . .now, find my pen, Sailor–boy. Oh! are you alone?" *The mention of the pen got him. His voice changed.*

"I'm alone—everyone's gone home, and the building's locked tight as a virgin's twat. How'd you know I'd be here?"

"I have ESP where you're concerned, Sailor-boy—only instead of my mind, I get my inspiration you–know–where. Tonight, it sent me a signal I could not ignore—all I did was follow the signal; it led right to you."

"Tell me what you're doing—exactly." he demanded.

"Ooooooh, honey," *I gave a fake moan.*
"Tell me!"
"You're sure you won't think less of me if I tell you what I'm really doing?" I demurred.
"Tell me, baby. I won't think less of you. . .C'mon, tell me."

He can hardly think less of me than he already does. What am I to him but a woman? The way he spells woman is c-u-n-t. "Do you still have the pen I gave you?"

"It's in my mouth. I can taste you on it." he said.

"Oooooh God," I dredged up a moan for him. "Well, do you remember yesterday, when I was in your office—what I was doing?"

"You tell me." he said.

"I had my red leather skirt pulled up around my waist—remember when I turned to put my satin panties in your coat pocket, the coat you had hanging on the back of your door, do you remember what I looked like from behind?" I paused, I could hear him breathing harder already.

"Ummmhmm."

He remembers, I thought. A picture is worth a blah, blah, blah.

"Wait," he rasped, "tell me what you're wearing right now."

I could hear him smack away on that damn pen. "Remember those black lace panties you sucked? I didn't wash them, your saliva is still on them. It's as if your mouth were right here next to me."

Could he possibly believe this shit? "I have them pulled high on both sides of my hips so they're stretched tight over me, and I can feel the satin rub against me. . .I'm pulling up on the sides and moving my ass in circles. . .again and again, while I come on them."

I paused to stifle a yawn. "It excites me to remember that these panties were in your mouth. . .they're soaking wet—

and my tits are hanging free as two lovebirds. I'm bending over the sofa and rubbing them over the velvet...god...ohmygod." I yelled into the phone. I wonder if I could do this and read the newspaper, too? A girl had to keep up on her reading. The funnies would be appropriate.

"*God, I want to fuck you. I want to fuck you hard in that gorgeous ass.*"

Yes. He saw the picture...nice and clear. Well, in your dreams, Sailor-boy. "Ohhhhhh, Sailor–boy, slow down. And baby, would I ever love to have you do that! Get your hand off that big, juicy cock! I'm not finished with you yet. I want to tell you what else I'm doing."

"What. What?"

Don't have a stroke, man, I can't really see through the phone. "I'm defrosting this big hard sausage that was in my freezer." I felt myself being led by my nose and this stupid game over to my glass table. I did another huge line—slid my finger over the residue and rubbed the powder on my gums...meanwhile, I could hear him gasp.

Man, he was predictable...and so unimaginative. "I'm on my hands and knees...my knees feel too weak to stand...my ass is in the air...I can't hold still...ohgodoh, if only you were inside me." *I could hear his moans and groans of ecstasy—and as I did another quick line I knew he was shooting his wad all over himself.*

Messy bad boy.

He could barely catch his breath—the man needed to get some regular exercise. It would never do for him have a heart attack and croak before Thursday.

"Oh, sailor, was it as good for you as it was for me?"

"Tell me where you are, damn you. I'm coming over right now!"

"Bye–bye, sailor. You sure know how to show a girl a good–time!"

"Wait! I told you to wait!"

Peter sat alone, the phone in one hand—himself in the other—a look of complete disbelief on his face. One sound echoed in his brain. Click.

Click.

The dial tone was a siren inside his head, "She's got the power! That bitch has the power!"

Chapter Twenty–Seven

Something was up. I knew it had to do with me and that I wasn't going to like it.

I've always been able to "feel" things that were about to happen and when I walked into group that wintry day I was hugging myself. The temperature *was* freezing but the hug was body–language protection. I'd used up all of my "get–out–of–conflict–in–group–free" cards. The faces of those gathered were friendly, but timid. What was Lorenzo up to?

The second I saw her, I knew. *Georgia Fairbanks*. She was a crisis volunteer I'd met at the hospital. My mind raced. Lorenzo has brought her here to try to motivate me, to crack, what he likes to call my "veneer." I knew what he was trying to do, but even still, I was thrilled to see her.

"Georgia!" I ran into her open arms and we hugged. We'd only spent a few hours together yet we'd made that special connection. The sight of her took me back. I'd been lying in the hospital bed, still as death. I heard her voice before I saw her face because I was hiding and unwilling to let the world inside. A voice straight from heaven—that was Gee. She was whatever you needed her to be. I don't remember talking much myself, or maybe I did, but it was Gee's guidance that pulled me back from hell.

I slipped out of my coat still holding Georgia's hand.

"Elsie, you look wonderful, my friend." Her soothing, lilting tones trilled throughout Lorenzo's room. There was a collective sigh of relief from my group, and Lorenzo's round face showed how white and brown can compliment one another as his seldom seen teeth were displayed in a magnificent fashion.

She kept by my side and tugged me down to the well-worn sofa.

It hit me square. The reason for her visit was about to begin. No small talk, no jokes to analyze, no *nothing*. This was it.

I was boxed in fear. Claustrophobic. Heat prickled over me in a flash. I had to stay and face this. Besides, I couldn't easily escape and I *did* want to hear her voice again, absorb the comfort of her soul as it enveloped me *just as it had more than a year ago*.

I knew what was going to happen, why she was here, and within seconds my shoulders shook, my body heaved with the kind of sobs that give you hiccups. It was instantaneous, that breakdown of tears and it made me remember that she'd done this same thing to me before. What was it about Georgia?

"Tell us, dear," came the voice of the angel within her. Her hand stroked my hair, tears stored inside me exploded. The room was silent. Except for me. She hugged me and then I poured out my guts:

"I don't remember much of anything until later— in the hospital. The police found me with Lynn's bod...with Lynn. And took me there. The hospital room was cold. I was uncomfortable. I wanted to be uncomfortable, or worse. That in itself gave me comfort."

Georgia pushed hair from Elsie's eyes.

"Someone had cleaned my clothes. And that bothered me. It was the way they were positioned—neatly folded on the window ledge. The sight of my once bloody clothing made me think of when Dad died. Dad died. It sounds so clean. And quiet. Well, after Dad shot himself. *Blew off his head.* They'd had some woman who didn't know us come in to clean the room. I'd gone there alone, to look around, I guess. I found two pieces of Daddy's head in the corner on the floor. They were small pieces no more than an inch or two long.

What did I do with those pieces of Daddy? Where are they? Did I put them in the trash? I can't remember; not for the life of me. The room smelled of pine disinfectant and other, unspeakable things. Anyway, her cleaning didn't do the job. Not that it was her fault. I don't mean *that*. The walls and the ceiling had to be painted three times before the blood all disappeared. Lynn helped me paint. I think of that blood sometimes. It is still there, underneath all that paint. I mean, it is, isn't it?"

Elsie looked at her friends. Would they understand what she was trying to say? "So I already knew," she went on and got louder with every word until she was nearly screaming at them, "I knew how hard it was to get blood out of stuff. I didn't want to check my clothes to see how good a job they'd done. I wanted someone to come and take the damn things out and burn them!"

The group listened, horrified, to what Elsie had kept locked inside for so long. This was her story, what they'd been waiting to hear.

"The room Momma died in was okay except for the carpet. We got new carpet because of the smell. I never stayed in the house again, even so, things had to be done before I could put it on the market for sale. Without Lynn to help me, what would I have done?"

"But, Elsie. It's Lynn's *body* that is gone. Her spirit lives on in your heart, does it not?" Georgia's round face held beautiful almond eyes that shone with the spirit she spoke of. Her tone was a musical sedative for all.

I nodded. Of course Lynn's spirit lived in me.

"Go on darling."

I sighed. I was resigned. I could do this. I would get it out, get it over with, give them what they wanted. I did wonder why they seemed to have to know these things about me. Would the memories fade because we talked? I continued dry eyed, "With Lynner gone, I missed my parents. Oh, not *them*, but what I wished they would've been. It seemed unfair that when I thought of them, I thought of them together. He was worse, wasn't he? *Yet I blamed them equally.* I wonder why. Maybe Momma let me down because I expected more from her. And Father Andy. Now *there* was someone to blame."

Lorenzo's head bobbed in agreement. I knew he'd have liked to take my last sentence and fly with it—I'd have enjoyed that, too. I could feel Georgia's hand on my arm; she was sending me her calm—from one spirit to another.

"I sat for a long time by the hospital window watching snowflakes crunch against the glass. I could see my reflection. The bed lamp glowed behind me and made my form appear phosphorescent.

I followed my imagination one foot further, and there I was, outside, as transparent as the snowflakes. I studied their shapes. Crystal and lace. At that moment it was difficult to comprehend so much beauty. I looked in on myself, too. Funny the things you focus on when you can't even recall the day of the week."

"Your spirit displayed those things to you for a reason."

I heard Georgia's voice, but I wasn't eager to let the words come inside and reach me. I continued, thinking to myself, *okay, if you're so smart, answer this:*

"How could the same creator who spawned the monstrosity that slaughtered Lynn be responsible for those snowflakes?"

I looked at Tony. He understood.

"Well, that thought consumed me all that day. I sat frozen and stared through the glass pane. I don't know how long I sat without movement until, at last, I felt a tear roll down my face and before I knew it my sniffles turned into a wail. My eyes searched for a tissue and I saw that next to my pile of clothes on the ledge was a glass filled with flowers. I hadn't even seen the flowers earlier, all I could think of was Lynn's blood on the clothes. I'd forgotten. That cop, Law, the detective, he'd brought them for me the night before."

Georgia frowned at the mention of the detective, and I felt her grip tighten slightly on my arm. I looked at her and thought, she must know Law.

"He brought me painted daisies and baby's–breath. Along with the snowflakes, they almost made it worthwhile to be alive one–more–minute. Did the cop know, I wondered that night, that the flowers were what I needed? Did he know why? I wanted very badly to think that he knew."

"He knew, dear." Georgia's voice was so soft I could barely hear it.

"When he came to visit I'd been lying in bed, arms crossed over my eyes. My arms didn't want to move. I didn't want anything to enter my field of vision. The sound of his voice brought me back from wherever I'd been hiding. Talking to him was important. It was the most important thing in the world. I tried hard, but I was jammed up inside. I tried to remember everything Lynn had ever said about that Peter creepo, because in my gut I was certain it had to be him. And something important just seemed to linger at the edge of my mind. I couldn't shove it forward to a conscious level. Law said don't push; he said, if it's in there it'll come out. I was grateful that he understood. He said it would come when I least expected it, when I was thinking of other stuff. He said he'd return until I remembered.

"So I went back to the snowflakes and I guess he left. It wasn't cold enough for the snowflakes to stay—they melted seconds after they stuck to the window. Exquisite, yet gone in an instant."

I could barely get the words out, "They were like crystal butterflies, melting against the glass."

Why in the world was I sobbing about what was essentially flakes of water?

Tony hurried over to kiss my cheek and Lorenzo cleared his throat. His way of telling the group to leave me alone so I could continue. Tony sat back down.

"There were other things besides beauty that my mind couldn't comprehend. I'd started to realize that there was plenty of evil in the world that had nothing to do with me. Not everyone encountered it, but it lived. Just as surely as Lynn's spirit lived in me, the spirit of evil lived in the monsters who did its bidding."

I looked into Georgia's kind eyes. "Explain, Gee, why this dark spirit is allowed to exist? Or tell me how it selects its victims?"

Georgia's lips parted to answer as Lorenzo spoke, "You are getting off track, little bird. Let's not try to understand the world in one hour. Continue." His presence commanded obedience and respect.

Even Gee settled back; she'd looked uncomfortable, had she been?

"Okay. Where was I? At the hospital. I thought a lot about Dad. I tried to think of anything he'd done to show me his love. All I could remember was the pink and black shirt. The thought started me crying again." *I'd told Lorenzo about the shirt, but not the others.*

"It was long before he died. I was maybe ten. It was his birthday and I'd saved my money. I wanted to get something that would, I dunno, make him love me, I guess. It was the first time I'd bought him a present on my own. Well, this shirt was a vivid pink with black trim around the pockets. I realize now that it was pretty ugly. But he wore it. That's why I cried. He wore the shirt. Did that mean he loved me? And why did I think about him at all when I'd just lost the one person I knew loved me completely? I had questions—not answers."

"You have us. We love you with no strings." Tony said.

"Yes." I smiled to let him know how I felt about them. "Well, then Charlie showed. He'd aged overnight. His body appeared bent as he approached. You never know where a visit with evil will take you. But it will be far and it will be fast. *Charlie'd had the devil smack in his face.*" I stopped to take a sip of tea and searched their faces to see if they thought that was a dumb thing to say. It didn't seem like they did. At least, no one laughed. I went on.

"Charlie sat beside me on the bed. We hugged and cried. For Lynn and for ourselves. Charlie stopped crying first. "I've just come from Northfield. The police took me along to help tell Lynn's folks. I stayed the night with them. They're kind, civilized people, how can they understand this? I'm taking a few weeks off work to help them," he shrugged, "however I can."

Elsie stopped. *Why did she have to do this?*

"I knew that would be good for the Faheys *and* Charlie. Lynn's dad had a bad heart. Her parents were taking the news as you might expect. As though their lives were over. Maybe Charlie could help them get their lives back. He had come back to Minneapolis to see me and to pick up some of his stuff.

"Charlie, please help me get out of here. I hate to ask, but I need someone to tell the doctors I'm okay. I don't want to be 'observed' any longer; I'm too tired to talk." Out came the tears again. "Where's Pip? I can't go back to that place. Oh Charlie, where's Skip? He's not with you, is he?"

"Charlie held me closer. 'It's all settled, Els. I ran into Skip at the police station. That detective Law, had us in for questioning. Skip and I got most of your things as soon as the cops said we could. We got the basics—whatever wasn't germane to the investigation. It'll get you by for now.' He brushed back my hair. 'We got your stuff and took it to Skip's. He's in the middle of packing himself—for his big break, and feeling lousy about it. He's talked about not going. You two will figure that out. Anyway, if he does go, he'll be here for a few more days. You can stay at his place up to six weeks after he's gone. He's paid the rent and can't get out of his lease. So, what do you say? Oh, and Law has your Pip. I'm surprised he didn't tell you."

"He did. Last night. I'd forgotten." With all that Charlie had on his mind he was worried about me. What could I say? "I love you," I kissed his cheek, "I know how dearly Lynn loved you, too."

"Red was the greatest thing that ever happened to me, Elsie. I don't know what I'm going to do without her. I didn't know her for long—some things are supposed to be. I'm way too serious and she made me laugh and I felt like I was funny 'cause I made her laugh. She showed me what it's like to have a mind of your own. I've always done what I was expected to do.

"She was a rebel. Right?" He laughed.

"There're times when what your own self tells you to do is much more right for you than what others say. I didn't appreciate that. She taught me that the things I did that were different were the things that made me interesting to her. That's one of the reasons I'm going to stay with her Ma and Pop. To be closer to her."

"Oh Charlie, she did the same for me. I was a damn robot. Programmed to do what others wanted. Her Ma and Pop are free thinkers; they'll be good for you, Charlie. You'll help one another."

He smiled. "Get your shit together, and let's get outta here."

"Wait. Question. Would her folks be upset if I wanted to buy her piano? I don't think they would, but I feel odd asking. It would mean so much. See what you think. I'll be down to visit in a few days."

"Elsie, you know they love you like you're a daughter."

"I can't even play it, you know. Just...it was so much a part of her."

"And Red would have wanted you to have it. C'mon," he gave me a pat, "this place is for sick people. I'll find the doc—

you get ready. Be right back, Blondie."

"On the drive to Skip's, Charlie made me promise to see the psychologist the hospital had recommended." I grinned at Lorenzo. "That would be you, sir."

Lorenzo nodded me on.

"Skip's apartment was in a duplex on 27th Street across from the Honeywell plant. Honeywell's hidden surveillance cameras watched the street in front of the house; it seemed like a safe place even though the neighborhood isn't the best."

Georgia squeezed Elsie's hand, her eyebrows raised in question.

Elsie knew what the question was. She'd never mentioned Skip to Georgia. They'd talked about Lynn, about Momma, Daddy, Jimmy, even Dr. Jack. But not Skip. Elsie took a deep breath.

"Skip wasn't there. Charlie was sure that he'd gone to the store and would be back any second, so I said I'd unpack and he should get going, get himself to Northfield. He did that, and I wandered the apartment for a long while, anxious to feel Skip's arms around me. At times you need that comfort."

I looked around the room. I was dragging this out and I knew it, but I felt emotionally drained and I wanted to stop.

"It was the start of winter, when the sun sets early in Minnesota. I remember how gray the rooms seemed. Cold too. I lay on Skip's bed and I could hear cars leave the Honeywell ramp around the early dinner hour and small children run and scream playing in the snow, waiting, no doubt, for a hot meal to warm them. The duplex Skip rented was old. I could hear mice scratch and run inside the walls. Then I thought of *Strawberry Fields*. Skip reminded me of *Strawberry Fields* and *Strawberry Fields* would always remind me of Lynn.

My wife has always been an early riser. Goodie for me.

Mildred, the servile bitch, dragged her ass out of bed hours ago, then left the house with my oldest daughter in tow. Off to church.

Say a little prayer for me.

Although communication can be easy, it's not in every case. And I felt antagonistic. Why should I have to put on a cheerful face for family? I duped them into believing I was asleep. It took the two twats hours to get ready. My oldest is a sniveling seven. Today, she was sniveling that she couldn't find her favorite sock. A Girlie doll sock. Mildred did the shopping for herself and the girls. I thought Girlie dolls were the ones with the big boobs and tiny feet. This was the first I knew they made socks for the *owners* of the Girlie dolls that would match what the dolls wore. Christ. I bet they cost me plenty.

Missy deserved to have the damn sock gone—she never put things away. I tried to teach her the right way to do things, to take care of her things, but she ignored me. I should have brought the little sock home with me. I could have slipped it inside her drawer and she'd be wearing it right at this very moment. I could visualize it on her small foot. Damn! That would have been a fantastic–orgasmic secret that only I knew. Mr. Big would get hard every time he saw the little shit–head wearing it. Details. They were so important.

Oh well, it was something to remember for next time. Ooops. Not going to be a next time. No next time.

I'll stay away from the Chit–Chat for a *long* time. Much as I like it there. Going back to the scene is dangerous. It was tricky. I found that out. No, all I had to do was stay away for awhile. There's no way they'll catch me. How? Trace Missy's sock?

Mildred, the whiner, had left the four–year–old home with Daddy and she'd gone running to the door screaming as soon as her Momma drove off. I pretended to be asleep until she fell on the floor exhausted. I didn't want to wake the brat, so

I stayed right in bed. I didn't mind. My early morning feelings of antagonism left with Mildred. Now, the replay of last night was like a drug. I felt that raw power bathe me. I'd ridden the bitch like the master jock I am. "Ride 'em Cowboy!" She was a wild horse that had to be broken. I was the only cowboy who could stay on for the ride.

I grabbed my white handkerchief and threw it over the swollen Mr. Big just in the nick of time. I shot into my hankie and it took off in flight, propelled.

It looked exactly like *Casper* the friendly ghost. This sight was one of my favorite optical illusions. I, a grown and powerful man, giggled, because I knew that while I lay here and watched friendly Casper fly, the redhead was once again being violated, this time by the pathologist for her autopsy.

Let's talk socks, Ma. Sox–box–fox.
Oh, Ma, what a paradox.

Chapter Twenty–Eight

"You didn't mention Skip." Georgia's voice was concerned yet still sent out its rays of calm to caress the group.
"No. I never talk about Skip."

This time no one said a word. The silence in the room was suffocating.

"Skip didn't return." I started, and then I broke down. *"Ever!"*
"He was dead!" I lost control completely. The words came out as a wail, an announcement dirge of death. *"He was deeeeead. Like them all!"*

My wail continued, bouncing from wall to wall. I felt the evil from this dirge yank at the group. It yanked and then pulled them upward by the hair on their heads, and while they hung there, helpless, it crawled over them and inspected their openings, their pores, looking for a way to gain entry into their bodies.

I stood and faced them and screamed at them as if it had been them who'd killed him. *"His throat was sliced, ear to ear."*

They hadn't killed him but they made me remember it, made me live it again, *now!*

I fell backwards onto the couch again. My arms wrapped myself; my body rocked fast. As I started it was as if I were a rocking chair left on an old porch to wile away warm summer nights and instead, suddenly the rocker is caught in a gale and whipped with sixty mile an hour winds until it speeds out of control and flies off into the eye of the storm. It's gone from the porch, forever more.

I seldom cried and never screamed these days until today. Some cried with me. Others were too stunned to move.

Georgia's eyes were closed. She held her hands, arms outstretched, fingers spread and flat, as if she were levitating—in the air in front of her—tuning forks, to call on spirits to protect, to keep evil away from the room.

Elsie looked around the room at the drained faces of her friends. This tale seemed to be the frosting on the devil's devils–food cake.

"How did you find out?" asked Lorenzo.

My tears stopped. I felt guilty. I hadn't ever mentioned to Lorenzo that Skip was dead. I tried not to think of Skip.

Sometimes, I'd be walking down the street, I'd hear the snap–crack a gum chewer makes as they passed me by, and the smell of Juicy Fruit would grab me, saying, Alvin! He'd live in my head then for days. At times like that his features were faded, but he was happy, a famous actor. He'd gone on to a life without me, but he was a happy man.

"What?" I asked Lorenzo. I'd forgotten the question.

"I was asking how you found out he was dead. Can you give us more specifics?"

"Um. It was a day later. Law, the detective, came by to talk to me about Lynn's case. It was mid–afternoon and I was asleep and he woke me. Law met Skip when he questioned him after the murder. And he saw him again when he got the okay for Skip to pick up some of my things. When I said Skip never showed up he called a car out right then, never even waited to talk about where Skip might have gone, just took out his phone and sent a car to our old address."

"And then?" Tony asked.

"Then we sat and talked about Lynn until his phone rang.

They found a body behind our place, what had been our place, under a pile of lumber the landlord was using for some repairs on the garage. It was a body that had no identification on it, a male that matched Skip's vague description, and his throat had been slit." Elsie started sobbing again. "Law took me to the morgue to identify the body."

"Oh dear God," said Judy.

"Why didn't you talk to anyone about this, Elsie?" Lorenzo's concern was evident.

"I didn't want to think about it."

"And the body. It was Skip?" asked Tony.

"It was Skip." I was drained and not going to say much more regardless of how they pressured me. "Law put a handkerchief over his nose and mouth when they pulled out the body. Everyone did. But all I could smell were bananas with a hint of strawberries."

I studied her file:

Address: PO Box 55, no street address given. I grimaced.

Call in emergency: Blank.

Previous employer: Blank.

Referred by: Blank.

Next of kin: Blank.

References: Blank.

I sat for a full minute and thought. How the fuck did El get hired? Of course I knew the answer. My office manager was not a man interested in references when faced with an ass like hers. It would have been almost too easy for this pro.

The mystery fucking woman.

Then it dawned on me.

I'll have her license plate checked out! Motor Vehicles

has to have her street address. Why the fuck didn't I think of this sooner?

I knew why.

She had my fucking brain scrambled is what she had. I didn't know what end my ass was attached to anymore. Any other cunt would have been history by now, but she was special. I had to have more of her. If I could once get enough of her I'd be done with her.

I dialed the Minnesota Motor Vehicle Department.

"*Yes, I would like some data on this name and plate number. My dealer ID number is 544-690173. Yes, Minnesota plate number CCS 669, name El Sanders. No, I do not have a middle initial. Yes, I'll hold.*"

I could feel my lip curl into a twisted smile–snarl.

Cunt. Time for her to learn who called the shots.

Wouldn't El be surprised to see me at her door?

Chapter Twenty-Nine

This bite–it investigation was making him old before his time.

Whatever his time was. They say you're only as old as you feel. What crap. He personally felt ninety–six. Anyway, it *was* a bite. Now he had to find time to personally interview the herbalist he had spoken to on the phone.

The pathologist had given him her name; she came very highly recommended. It was Georgia Fairbanks. He was sure they'd met before.

Harry'd said, "You gotta meet her, Law. I gotta feeling about this one."

"Eh, heh."

"What your thinkin' isn't true."

"I believe you Harry. Describe her. Close your eyes and tell me what you see of her."

"Okay. She's a striking caramel–skinned Native American with the moon–face of a cherub and sphinx–like eyes that could see clear into your soul."

That pretty much did it for Law. At the time he didn't think he could handle someone seeing clear to his anything, much less his soul. He figured that Harry, the pathologist, was trying to fix him up—kind of a, I owe you one favor, and Harry owe'd someone this. Besides, a man who said gotta as often as Harry was not to be trusted in matters of taste.

Law spoke to moon–face on the phone. Man alive. He might want to fix *himself* up with Ms. Fairbanks. But as soon as he heard her speak he remembered where they met.

He was going to the hospital to see Elsie after the murder and Ms. Fairbanks was standing right outside the room.

"Don't go in," she said, without knowing who he was or caring.

"I have official business. Police." He tried to walk around her, holding the flowers behind his back.

"I don't care *who* you are. She needs rest and time alone."

"And *you* would be—?" He knew when he asked that she was not an official staff person. And so the conversation went, well, it didn't go well. He was determined to see Elsie and knew that he could help her. This *woman* was determined to keep him out, believing that she was the help that Elsie needed. And when she saw the flowers he was attempting to hide she became suspicious of his intentions and that made him angry.

Still, her voice, and her take charge attitude turned him on. He felt himself drawn to her and would have pursued her if *she* hadn't been so angry with *him*.

She had no right to keep him out and eventually he won the argument, but lost the war.

It was her voice that got to him. So melodious. It played to him for weeks after the incident—a version of the Pied Piper's flute, with Law one of the city's rats ready to follow. She did not speak to him so much as she crooned.

Law shook his head.

He was losing what marbles he had left. It must be those new coffee beans Sara brought in last Monday. She said they were strong, had to be damn strong. The detective was in a mood to daydream. If only this filthy snow would melt. He had an itch to get on his bike and ride like the wind. And if he did that this native woman who was stuck in his brain would be his euphoric euphony.

His ex' used to say he loved to ride because it made him feel young. He was never going to grow up, she would say.

Law couldn't fault her opinion; it was right on the money. He didn't want to grow up.

For instance, he caught his reflection in the stainless coffee pot, he did not want to wear a blankin' mop on his head. He preferred his hair. So sue me, he thought. He wished his ex had gotten into motorcycles. Imagine having a woman to ride through life with, side by side. What she was into was the green stuff. And what she liked, she liked a lot. It consumed her. She had been sure she'd eventually wear him down, make him quit the force, take a high paying job with her Daddy. She didn't care a thing for him or his life. Probably married him because it was a challenge, thinking she could change him. Control him with her you–know–what.

Oh no. Law rubbed his eyes with fists. He couldn't face being a "*my wife never understood me*" kind of guy. A wifer–whiner. Nuts. Tell me it ain't so, Rosco.

A lot of things in this damn life were about control. Who had it. Who didn't.

He thought about Georgia's voice and sighed. He hadn't had a date in a long time, just because he preferred to take the easy way out. The safe way out.

He could have fallen for Elsie. Almost did. Did.

She was so damn young he'd have felt like a dirty old man if he had not backed off. Did he back off, or did she disappear? As he remembered, she disappeared. He'd heard rumors she'd gotten into drugs—didn't believe them at the time. He had his mind on other things. He worked day and night back then. Hadn't had his shield long and didn't want to lose it. Now that he thought about it, she was exactly the type to get caught up in drugs. What was she going to do to make herself feel good?

Meet some nice guy—trust him enough to settle down with him?

Spend time making friends without worrying about what would happen to them if she started to care?

Naw. She would a' been looking for a Band–Aid. And *he* should have known.

The question was, why was he kicking himself over this now? Timing's everything. Once he took her pooch back, he only saw her a few more times. Law sighed. He missed Pip. And he hoped to hell it wasn't drugs that made her disappear. Maybe that was why he kept mind strolling back to her—did she need him?

They'd gone on a few motorcycle rides—she was wild about riding—a potential wild bikin' woman. One of their last times together they went for a long ride and afterwards stopped off at Lyle's for a burger and a drink. Not the kind a joint he could have taken the ex' to, but Elsie took to it right away. She fit in. He never forgot some of the things she told him about riding and about what she thought while they rode.

He poured another cup of coffee. Why not feed the acid bubble inside? Thinking back, he could almost smell her she was so real to him. It was the smell of a warm spring night.

Lyle's was packing them in that night. You had to talk up to be heard. Sometimes you go to a bar—anywhere with a room full of animated people—you sit with someone and feel out of place. You can't hear exactly what the person with you is saying. If you talk loud enough to be heard it feels strained, or you're sure everyone can hear what you say. Then again, you can get lucky. When that happens it's as if you are the only two people in the place. People yell and carry on around you and there's just you two. Made a guy feel like Bogart.

He could hear her. See her.

One slender leg tucked under her butt, she leaned across the table to get closer to him—goldilocks falling over her eyes. Her eyes were violet—he'd never seen violet eyes. In the bar's candle–smoky light they took on the reflection of her china blue T–shirt.

Bogart and Goldi.

"When I'm riding in a car, it's as if I were inside this hermetically sealed bubble looking out at life around me. On the bike, I'm part of what's out there. Like the difference in being inside your house looking out the window, if you walk outside it becomes real, not just a picture. I'm not necessarily as comfortable—physically, you know—but my spirit is intertwined with nature."

Chin in hand, elbow on the table, he listened.

"It sounds sophomoric, Law, as I hear myself say all this. But it's how I feel. In an odd way I feel superior to those people who ride along side the bike in their cars. I'm transparent—from another dimension!"

He grinned and interrupted, "I wish you were older but, okay, what the hell. Wanna marry me? I'm in love with your ditzy mind—we could ride together, one with the wind, into the sunset. How's *that* for cornball?"

"Lynn used to call me ditzy." Elsie continued to talk but gave him a look that asked if he was making fun of her. "Maybe it's not the same for the driver—I'm sure there are more distractions. What do you think?"

As he looked back on this idyllic conversation he didn't remember giving her an answer—he sat like a nerd, mouth agape and admiration on his face. There had been no talk of Skip. He knew from the sad puppy look that often crossed her face that these rides were of some help.

"I only know what it's like from the passenger's view. Tonight as we rode," her eyes gleamed with fervor, "here's what I was thinking. You know the way all motorcyclists wave at one another as you pass by? No matter that they're from vastly different backgrounds—you know they must be—different in age, rich, poor, middle–class, different race, sex, sexual preference. But you don't know or care about that. If you're on a cycle you are all *kindred spirits*.

Kindred spirits.

Just think. You're part of some gigantic family. I mean,

Law, do you get it?"

Of course he got it. It made him feel ancient that he knew what an idealist she was. He would not be the one to shoot down her dream. He smiled encouragement, and kept such grim thoughts to himself. Plenty of time for her to learn about reality. Sure it was something like listening to a daughter who'd just started college, but he knew that thinking about these things was probably all that kept her mind from a visit back to hell.

"If you're on a ride and you need something—or you had trouble, you'd call on another biker—another member of the family."

"You mean like in a gang?"

"No." She was unfazed. "I don't mean like in a gang. I mean like in a *human* way."

He was tongue–tied, bemused, and taken. He took a long pull on his rum and cola. It was never quite this simple—at least not in his world. If more people thought this way, it couldn't be a bad thing. Was this a front? Did she believe what she was saying? Few got to see the side of human nature that he did. She'd had her share of wretchedness; why try to convince her there was more on the way? She needed a break. Maybe she found it on a bike. It worked for him. She was too revved to notice he wasn't saying much. Her first drink was only half gone—she was busy flipping back the side of her hair—and erupting with this voracious energy.

"It's like this," she was unstoppable. "When I drive down Lake Street there's a certain stretch where most of the people you see are black. A lot of them don't look all that happy. They have their reasons for that—after all, they live in the same world as me and it can be pretty damn shitty. Anyway, they don't look pleased, and maybe I hear on TV about the number of blacks involved in crimes in that area. I don't *know* hardly any blacks. Northfield was snow–white. There were no blacks in the history books in school, either. When I came to Minneapolis it was as if someone had skydropped a bundle of black people into this city. So, as I drive down the street—I feel nervous. It's not an act. I react to what I see. Dark unfamiliar faces. Some that are gloomy or even surly, and that feels threatening. How much of what I feel comes from what I see? Or is it a residue from last night's news or TV show? Well, Law, this is the exciting part.

Are you *listening?* Listen!

I know this works, 'cause I've done it many times. I'll be at the intersection, waiting for the light to change. I pick a person who looks particularly snarly and I make eye contact. And then I give them a big smile, right from the heart." She took a sip of wine. "So...what do you think happens?"

He shook his head—wanting to hear what she had to say and entranced by the china–blues that glistened over the french fries. From violet to china–blue.

She couldn't wait for him to answer. "They smile back. Always." She looked like she had discovered a cure for MS. "And, Law, with that smile—their face is transformed into a glowing friendly face. The face of a *kindred spirit*. It's the biker wave!"

If one person could start the world in the right direction. She'd be the one.

"Many of us are kindred spirits," her motor was revved, the wheels rotating, her imagination accelerating. "We just don't know it. If we could have a universal sign of some kind, like when we wave, that says, 'Hey, I'm one of you—I'm on your side.' Wouldn't that be great? We could pick one another out—help one another without being afraid. People are afraid to help one another now days, aren't they?"

Luckily the waitress was right at the table and he could order another round of drinks and avoid a straight answer. What do you say to someone so naive? He was about to try when she switched gears again.

"Law, tell me the truth." She sat back, his swizzle stick

between her teeth. On her it looked cute. Her expression turned like a faucet—melancholic. She held his eyes with hers.

"You're not going to be able to find him, are you?"

He surveyed his drink as if he expected some spectacular event to leap from it. When he looked up his eyes were weary. His voice portrayed a man dispirited, "I can't answer that, Elsie. You know yourself how little we have to go on. We haven't had one break. I can't go into the specifics of the case with you, but honey, I've tried everything I can think of and then some."

It was getting harder to meet her eye. He fell back into his murky drink, his voice low. "Right now, every way I turn it's a dead end. It's possible he'll do it again. If he does, maybe he'll give us more to go on."

"*Again?* You can't be serious! Do it *again?*" She began to fidget with her hair, this time twirling one strand round and round her finger. He could almost see the wheels of her mind churn. Then just as fast her face went blank—

"I must get Pip home. I'm so grateful to you for helping me out when I needed it; what would I have done?"

It looked like she was going to get right up and leave, but she settled back down.

"I can't believe she's gone. Why is it good people like Lynn have despicable things happen to them? Shouldn't someone do something to the monsters out there?"

This time she wanted an answer. Her clear eyes stared at his and he could feel the fire.

"That's what I do, Elsie. That's what I try to do. Punish the monsters."

She got up then, sat on his side of the booth, slid over to him and kissed him.

Today, as he brought himself back from that place in time, he still remembered the ache in his heart, the pain in his gut. Her words cut sharp. *"Shouldn't someone do something equally horrible to the monsters?"*

Law straightened. He looked at his watch. Even standing took too much effort for his lethargic butt. All of this thinking about opportunities long gone made him more tired than usual. His stomach rumbled; the thought of a Hungry-Man TV dinner in front of the tube got him moving towards the door. His head and his stomach were taking him home, but his poor tired feet were transporting him toward the evidence room.

Suddenly he realized where he was.

Ah well, he thought, it wouldn't hurt to take one last peek in the nostalgia room.

There was a cop on duty. "Clarence my man, let me have at that box from the Lynn Fahey murder."

Clarence looked at him like he'd asked for an extra ticket to Woodstock.

"It was, oh, three years ago. November—yeah November. That would be 1979. Oh, and by the way, may I say I love what you've done with your tie. The colors look like Pablo Picasso flung them on with his very own hand, and a great deal of his soul. Plus, I'm betting that if you were to steep it in a cup of hot water for, oh, twenty minutes tops, it'll make a delicious and quite hearty soup."

"Aw Law, you dicklicker you. You're so friggin' good to me. . .and, speaking of bein' good to me, and, speakin' of dicklickers, how's the wife?"

"*Ex*–wife. Fuck her." Law knew his lines—he and Clarence had been doing this routine, or a similar one, for years. Both had it down.

"Oh, I already have, thanks. Fucked her, that is."

"Very humor–*ass*. Give it to me. The box."

Technically, he should have said, *blank* her. But Clarence would ask what he was talking about and the old goat was too old to argue with, and anyway there were no small kids hanging out in the evidence room.

His tired body melted into the hard chair by the old rickety table.

And he felt what lay on the table ahead of him sock him in the groin. This was evil. Clarence was crazy to work down here. Law poked through the contents for what seemed to him the be*gillio*nth time. It was always eerie to go over these old case boxes. You knew they held secrets—you wished they'd speak—cry, no scream, out to you.

Same old, same old. Horror Incorporated.

Let's see. . .pieces of broken glass—that got Law's old motor running at full throttle. Brown glass from the Old Style beer bottle. At first that bottle had them excited; there were partial prints. How in the hell they were still there under all that blood was a real mystery. But in this business you take help where you can get it. The prints turned out to be nothing—they found a couple more bottles with the full set of prints out back in the trash. So, had he worn gloves? Law rubbed his red eyes. He couldn't get a bust in this case sitting in the middle of the Smithsonian.

His stomach grumbled. That frozen turkey dinner was calling his name. *Wife–in–a–freezer.*

Ah yes, the matchbook. From that Improv—the guy who left it got his throat slit. Skip. Name was Alvin Victory. The matches belonged to Alvin. He might have used them to light a joint, or not. But Skip and Elsie had been lovers. Recent lovers. And he'd gone back for her things, and it'd cost him his life. The question here was, why had the killer gone back to the scene so soon after the crime? Law reached behind and tried to rub the lower part of his back.

What else we got?

Broken ankle bracelet. That was a gold chain bracelet; it'd been a recent gift from Lynn's new, at that time, love, Charlie. What a mess this'd made of *his* life. Nothing fishy there. Poor joker. He was crazy in love with the redhead. Wonder how he's made out? Law yawned and his stomach gave a cry. Concentrate and get home and feed me it said.

Okay. *Okay*. His self talked and answered his self.

One gold earring. It was Lynn's and it had been ripped from her ear. The mate to it had vanished. The earring had a tiny gold musical note that hung from a chain. Classy. Like the woman who wore them.

Hair, broken fingernails—all belonged to the girl. Torn pieces of paper—meaningless...parts of clothing—same. He stretched his neck, rubbed it and sighed—then stared at the pile. Why the blank was he doing this—putting himself through this? Must have felt too good today. Needed a little *pull–me–down*, as opposed to the usual pick–me–up, at the close of a hard day.

And then Law sat straighter.

He stared at a Bic pen. He'd looked at that pen numerous times—never felt this...drawn. It was a cheap ballpoint. Could belong to anyone. He remembered that they'd found it in the back yard. Along the side was stamped Joyce Bryan Mazda. Followed by the address and phone number. He'd called the joint at the time. Sent someone out with a photo of Lynn, but no one there had ever seen her. One more dead-end. A discarded Bic.

Still, he had this feeling...

Then, wham, his eyes opened wide, as if to say—hey, dummy, you're on the scent! The memory was a hard punch in the goozle. And oh, he saw it clearly. There was an article in the paper, maybe six months ago, about women in the automobile business. This Joyce Bryan had been quite the tycoon.

The key word was *had*.

Had been.

She was dead. She'd been dead a couple years—maybe longer. Before she died she'd built an empire. The details of the article were hazy, but one thing was clear. Law'd read that her one and only son had taken over the business.

Her only son.

And his name was *Peter* Bryan.

Peter. Lot's of Peter's. But what about the logistics of that pen? Might pay them a visit himself. He looked at the box as he shoved an antacid in his mouth. Law believed in intuition. He did not believe in coincidence.

"Thanks for speaking up," he said out loud. "Better late than never."

Clarence watched the tired detective drag himself up the stairs, hat and coat in hand, and heard him mumble to himself. "Ah Peter, have we come full circle, then, have we?"

Chapter Thirty

"Do any of you do drugs?" Lorenzo's voice was hard. "How about what you might term *social* drugs?" His eyes inspected the room—they did not skim over her—they stopped and seemed to bore right through.

Elsie squirmed, not daring to look at Tony.

Willie Dixon sang, his voice deep and dark, "*I am the Blues.*" Lorenzo's mood music.

"Yeah, well," he cleared his throat.

"Let me give you pups something to think on. You're angry at someone for taking away your power. You might be searching for *escape* from that anger and from your feelings of helplessness. So. Here's what *could* happen. I don't say that it is, but it might. But what if you got your grubby mitts on some drugs. You think maybe you'll just try them once. Only this one time, right? And, when you do, well, it seems to fill the bill.

"Well, here's the real guts of it kids. You think you're pretty damn smart. You feel on top of the world. But, after that one time, or however many times, because there *will* be more than 'just once,' the day arrives—*I promise you it will*—when you *need* to have the drugs. Oh you don't need them to feel good! Oh no. Not good, just okay. And, after awhile those drugs will have the power over you; without them you can never again feel just okay. Not at all."

In his usual manner he pushed his large body up and paced. The power from Lorenzo whirled, circulatory, controlling them. If one had wanted to rise up and run out, well, no chance.

No chance in hell.

"Okay. Now the drugs have the *power*. They can treat you like everyone does who has power over you; they *stopped* making you feel good right away. Then they stop making you feel just okay. Why?"

None were dumb enough to try to answer.

"My guess is, they do it cuz they can. *Because they can*; that's how it is with power.

You *have* to take them—*you need them now*.

"Here is my question to you. Did those bad assed drugs take your power, like the people who abused you took it?"

He did not wait for them to answer.

"No damn way!" Lorenzo boomed. "*You gave it away.* Somethin' so screechin' hard for you to get. And *you* went and *you* gave it away."

He glared. White eyes hot with the fire in his soul. "That's it for today." His large body made the room tremble as he stormed out.

As with everything Lorenzo said, Elsie gave this talk about drugs a lot of thought.

Finally, she decided it did not apply to her. She didn't need to do drugs. Anytime she wanted to stop she could stop. She just did not want to stop quite yet. Besides, cocaine was an herb—kind of. And it was likely not what Lorenzo was talking about. Not a bad drug. An herb.

Tony slept over frequently these days. He was between lovers, and he thought Elsie was fabulous. Fabulous was Tony's favorite word—next to blow. Blow was by far number–one on his hit parade. Her stories about strawberries, bananas, dog food burgers, and even good ol' Jimmy, delighted him. But the R-E-V-E-N-G-E song was best. He changed some of the words to fit himself, and they each sang their own version-singing together on the chorus:

"I'm glad that we could have our R-E-V-E-N-G-E!" Together they were conspirators.

She listened to Tony's stories, too. "You said people look at you funny when they know you're gay. Do you think they are imagining what you do in bed or what?"

Just like the days with Lynn, she loved to talk about the things polite society considered taboo. "Tone, there must be some people that don't consider your sexcapades relevant to their lives."

He looked frail when he spoke. "You know," he confided, "I told my parents I was gay about the same time they found out about Father Barker. My Mom was cool. But Dad was like his son died and I was what survived him. He could not begin to figure out how to deal with me. I mean, after all, what was I? Dad was more upset about my being a 'homo'—his words—than he ever was about Father Barker. He made it seem as if maybe I led the poor priest astray." He paused. "He was disappointed in me. I was never a jock, and I liked girlie stuff. You know, art and music and fashion. I sicken him. He'll never forgive me for tainting the family name. Every time he calls me his fag–boy, I shrink some more. That's why I don't want to talk to him; soon there will be nothing left of me."

Elsie gave him a squeeze. "He's an ignorant oinker. We could win him over, Tony, but we'll worry about that later after I take care of some unfinished business."

Tony opened his mouth to ask what was unfinished—then stopped. His Mom used to say, "Do not ask the question if you don't want to hear the answer."

He went on, "Anyway, when I worked at K–Mart there was a lady—her name was Paula. She was a flamboyant character, a big beautiful woman who'd always been nice. It was in the summer, and the Minneapolis Police Federation had this promo to build better police relations with the gay community. A homo–promo! So they had a softball game with a group of us, and some of the news stations carried it on the 10 PM news. I came to work the next day and Paula walked up to me. She said, "Tony, I saw you on TV last night!"

"Man, was I speechless. I'd never dreamed that I was on the tube. As far as I knew, no one at work knew my secret. I managed to stutter and sputter out, 'What do you mean you saw me?'"

"The softball game," she said, "for the gays and the cops."

I bit my lip and nearly swallowed my tongue.

"I had no idea you were a cop!" she finished.

"Wow, the way we laughed together made me realize that there are good people who like me for me. After that I never tried to hide my being a fag–boy again."

Elsie gave him a parental look—one he'd seen on Lorenzo's face dozens of times. "Tone. Don't call yourself that. Okay? I don't have to tell you why. Lorenzo already gave the lecture and you know he's right. So don't do it. I won't have it."

Tony was seated at the kitchen table as she nagged at him. The conviction in her tone held so much power that he began to slip down in his chair, down until you could barely see the top of his black curly hair. He was about to disappear under the table. She grabbed his feet and pulled him the rest of the way down. They rolled on the floor and giggled, transformed back to childhood.

Then together they sighed, spent.

"You're my sis." said Tony. He kept his arm around her shoulder.

Propped against the wall they talked of lighter things. Like the fact that they both enjoyed sucking the weenie but for different reasons. That was a surprise to her. It was stretching it for Elsie to say she enjoyed it with only her one experience, but what an experience it had been.

Earlier that day they'd gone together and bought a half–ounce of cocaine. Now they decided to divide it into the small gram packets. It was fun doing this together. Something they were not supposed to do, yet it felt like a homey thing too, weighing it out, and playing in it...baking a cake. Almost.

Of course they sampled some of the goods—you do that with cake batter. Tony was right about the way it loosened all your inhibitions.

They had their greatest talks while doing lines together. It made for loose tongues.

Elsie realized that she and Lynn had never needed drugs to have these same close talks. She put it out of her mind. Tony and she wouldn't need them either, but for now, well, they helped. Helped her keep Lynn with her and still keep her sanity. Kind of a compromise with the gods.

Today they talked about the strawberry fields. He could not relate to it in the way that Elsie did.

"Els, maybe if I were really in love. That sounds like a *love* thing to me." The end of his nose had white powder on it—she leaned over and licked it off. He ignored her and continued. "Your description is not how I feel. It's not that it tastes so good or feels fabulous shooting in your mouth, like you say it was with you and Skip.

"For me it's the *power* of it. The *control*. The in–fucking–credible *control!*" This was a mighty high level of excitement from Tony. He didn't get this excited about anything, except the other kind of blow, cocaine. Maybe the fact that they were playing in their coke had him more revved.

She considered what he said about love. Could she have been in love with Skip?

It hurt to hear his name. It made her want to cry and scream.

Well, Skip was gone. Gone and never coming back.

It didn't matter if she'd *been* in love. She didn't have time for love stuff any more. She was going to be busy. And when she got really busy what would happen to Tony? It bothered her that this sweet kid did not have close friends.

Tony's lovers were ships that poke in the night. She wished she knew a nice guy for him. She decided the reason he had a difficult time with love had more to do with his being abused than he would ever imagine. It was the loss of control over his life.

If you fall in love, you give up your control. Don't you?

She wasn't sure. This control thing was screwed; it all began with the man–beasts who needed to show how tough they were with children.

At least that was how she saw it.

She had begun to form her plan.

Elsie was going to do something to help Tony.

Chapter Thirty-One

I have her address!
What happens next is up to me. *Me!*
I don't mind admitting that this is a feeling I enjoy as much as sex. Maybe more. Anticipation is about to make my veins pop.
 A soft knock on my office door interrupts my delicious schemes. I decide that I don't care to expose my cards quite yet. I wipe the smirk from my face, but the door doesn't open. Is she getting shy? After all the times I'd expected her to wait for my command to enter, I wasn't about to speak now only to find her in front of me ignoring my position of authority.
 There was the knock again.
 I cleared my voice, "Come in." I made some pretense of a study of the papers quickly spread before me.
 I kept my eyes on the papers, didn't allow them to lift, to drink in the bloom of her. Even though the footsteps moved with an odd shuffle, I still fully expected to see that form that could so easily inflame me until I exploded in rapture.

 Christ.
 It was Janet—one of the old bags in accounting.
 "Some payroll checks for you to sign, Sir."
 "Where's El?" I knew I'd asked the question too quickly and with too much intensity—I gave the documents my signature with no idea what they were.
 "She had to take her dog to the vet, Sir. She'll be a little late today."

"Her dog?"

"Yes, Sir. Pip, Sir." She took the papers from me, closed the door as her ample behind bustled out.

I sat. Not moving. Something about the name. *Where had I heard that name?* Pip. I tried to remember.

My mind played grab and gone.

Slippery.

A guppy that I was trying to snare with bare hands. For now—it eluded me. Well, what did it matter? It would come to me. And, in any case, it would soon be over.

I have her address!

I couldn't stop my mind from obsessing on the evening. I felt like a kid about to have his first fuck or a first trip around the world, or a poor man who'd just won the lotto! This night, tonight, will be the best, the wildest fucking night of my life. Mr. Big stood hard. I unzipped and pulled him out. Then, while I pictured the last time I had done what I planned to do today, what I had done to that redheaded spitfire, I jacked Mr. Big off all the way to Kalamazoo.

*Splat. . .splat. . .splat . . .*it hit the back of the inside of my desk.

Temporary relief.

There was no doubt I needed this to happen today—I was out of control and I knew it. When you're out of control you do stupid things, you make mistakes. I should know. The last one almost got me caught.

I'd been flying so high after the redhead that I thought, no, I *knew* that I was invincible. I'd given in to my weakness and curiosity and returned to see the place one last time. There were cops everywhere at first, then just the one car. And while they sat eating sandwiches and drinking coffee, I was going to find some way to slip inside to see the bloody bed.

I flashed on the bloody bed and forced myself to stop—so excited now that I could barely wait to face dear little El. I'll remember to bring the riding crop. This time I will remem-

ber. *I have her address!*
    El will be the wildest ride ever.
    Ride 'em, cowboy.
    Giddy–up...giddy–up...giddy–up, up, up.

    The room where the group held their meetings was without natural light. Few windows let fewer still rays of light in on the proceedings. The walls were painted yellow in an effort to brighten attitudes, but the paint that had been slapped on years ago was tinged, tobacco stained, chipped here and there to show school–house–brown enamel underneath.
    It was a cheerless room, but here in this room, they managed to make things happen. And there was always the music.
    The blues were not so blue. They portrayed freedom of spirit.
    Being abused is an ego destroying experience of varying degrees. Making you docile, wary, and listless. After the trauma, it's just as bad. You walk the streets alone; no one knows how much you hurt.
    Mean streets.
    They still expect you to pay for your milk at the local market with a smile.
    The bus driver doesn't say, "Oh, this one's on me, you poor dear."
    The mailman complains because your name fell off the mailbox; either take care of it, or tomorrow, no mail delivery.
    Bill collectors harass you about bills from your previous life. BTA. Before the attack/abuse. And then one day, you walk down the street and see someone you know from the neighborhood, and they say "beautiful day!"
    The register bell goes ding, and *you know.*
    You are all alone.
    So, the tobacco stained walls are not of much concern. It is the people who come here, who understand your pain like

no one ever will. These people are your only concern.

If you ran into Jane on the street you would think she was someone's mother or grandmother. Very ladylike, even proper. Her hair had recently begun to fade. She wore it straight back in a clasp off her face. The effect was soft rather than severe. Her face was lined, a map that showed her effort, her pain, her years of caring for many. With her roly–poly body, she would float well in the backyard pool. Then you hit on her eyes. Large and beautiful and blank. *Anybody there?* A thick glaze covered what lay beneath the surface.

Jane first came to group when she was recovering from cancer surgery. She appeared as lifeless as a raggedy stuffed doll. She was disinterested and withdrawn. Elsie worried that Jane might kill herself. Although cancer was certainly taken to be serious, it was more a reason to want to live in Elsie's mind. The truth came gradually.

Jane's husband had left her for his secretary. She still loved the man—you could tell. They'd been childhood sweethearts. If you could die of a broken heart she would be lying dead now, worm–food. That would have been the easy way for Jane.

No one in the group could get her to talk much until the day her daughter came to drive her home after their session. The daughter was proud that she could drive—just turned sweet sixteen and had gotten her driver's license. The group fussed over her, going on about how much the daughter resembled the mother. She looked like a very young Jane. Very special women, both of them.

The film disappeared from Jane's eyes as life returned. But what happened was not what they'd hoped. Jane began to sob. Her voice, an injured animal as she yowled out her pain.

Elsie hurried Jane's daughter, Del, to the waiting room while they tried to quiet the storm. Jane flung herself about—

twisting and flailing, as if some devil trapped inside her wanted desperately to get out. Finally, she was exhausted.

"Talk to us, Jane. Please," Tony begged.

Her voice was soft and strained, "Del is going to have a baby. She's three months pregnant."

At sixteen, not the best of circumstance but not worthy of this violent scene.

"Do you know the father of her baby, Jane?" Elsie asked, trying to find a clue to the uproar.

Jane continued with a story shot in a blast from hell.

"Yes, we know him. It's Del's Daddy that's the father of this baby. He's molested Del since she was almost a baby herself. They've been having actual intercourse for over five years."

Jane's wet eyes begged them to understand. "I don't think he is a *bad* man."

What?

"It could have happened," Jane said, "because Del looks so much like me—the way I used to look—when I was young, in bloom. Couldn't that be why he did it?" Jane asked.

"It?" repeated Tony.

Elsie was glad they'd taken Del to the waiting area, so *she* didn't have to listen to this crap. Coming from her mother, no less.

"He loved me so much," Jane said, "but growing old was hard for him to accept. I was a constant reminder to him that life was racing by. He got upset with me on my birthdays. I was getting old. If I was, that meant he was, too. Perhaps it was his love for me that got him into this. Del is the image of a younger me. Of what used to be, and could never be again."

They were silent.

Lorenzo was away this week. They didn't know how to proceed without him.

"Jane, have you told these things to Del? Have you mentioned these feelings to her?" Tony's dark complexion was pallid.

"Yes, of course, we talk about it often. I don't want her to hate her father. He *is* her father. He had his reasons. I haven't been the best wife. I put on these pounds lately, and then, then I got cancer. He knew he might lose me when he took up with his secretary. Not many men would want a woman without breasts. Would they? At the very least, I would be half a woman."

No one knew what to say to this fragile bird. They wanted to yell at her, to talk sense into her, but if they did that, she could disappear again. They had to keep her talking and out of her shell until Lorenzo returned.

They managed to do one good thing. Without placing blame they nudged Jane into having Del join a group of her own that day. A group for incest victims. Whatever Daddy's motivation, Del needed help.

Even Jane could see that.

Elsie loved the people in her group, but she began to show up less and less. She had her plan. She was beginning to live for that plan. The nose–candy helped keep her focused, helped her to put her feelings aside. She could deal with them at some later day. The mind–numbing drug and what she was about to do were now the only things that mattered. She'd made up her mind.

Justice would be done.

The house Elsie was interested in came with ten acres.

She went to see the property and fell in love with the land outside the home before she ever crossed the threshold. There was an immense rock garden on the south side that surrounded a thirty by thirty foot flower and herb garden. A garden on the south side was a good thing in Elsie's opinion. The soil appeared to be rich...she ran black moist handfuls through her fingers. To the west was a wooded area that covered most of an acre of the land. And to Elsie, the woods were even more bewitching than the garden. Plant life that grows in the woods is unique and replete with folklore.

She surrounded herself in this thorny tangle of greenery, and saw deep shadows that appeared to be a Dresden–blue and felt the spirits call to her.

Without stepping a foot inside the door, she knew this was home.

Moving into the house was not work. It was coming home.

The best of it was that she'd picked up Pip earlier that day. His absence had left her hollow. Now they were together again. With Lynn and Skip gone she and Pip were the family.

And with Pip home where he belonged she was free to stop seeing Law. She had to make that break. She liked him way too much for her own good, and he had feelings for her and she knew it. She couldn't take a chance that he'd find her new home. And if the feelings grew much stronger it could be major trouble. He was too smart not to ask questions about her lifestyle changes.

But if she didn't consider her feelings for him, Law would be easy to separate herself from because he felt guilty about his attraction to someone her age. His ethical standards would hold him in check. Besides he worked all the time.

Tony was different.

Tony would eventually pry all this out of her. Already he took it personally that she was evasive about her new address. He even dropped hints about wanting to live with her! To consider that possibility filled her with longing. Oh, she would love to have him here! But it would be far too dangerous for anyone in the group to know her plan. Too dangerous for them to be a part of her life.

She did one more line and watched the images of her friends fade off to a distant but happy place.

Depending on the luck of the draw, or *claw*, this plan could mean her death.

She was prepared to die to see justice done.

Chapter Thirty-Two

"Let's see what we can put together here," Law began. "We have our thirty–one–year–old pedophile, the Twinkie-king. What did you call him, Sara?"

"Phallic–boy."

"Yeah. The gun–in–the–shorts trickster. Nary a soul will shed a tear for that bloated blanker.

"Okay, then, we got the thirty–eight–year–old, *also* a pedophile, and a priest to boot."

"A priest who uses his Roman collar to pimp for him. He *should* sizzle in hell." Tonetti was Catholic so it was appropriate that he should judge Father Barker.

"Right, a forty–five–year–old adulterer, no huge sin by today's standards, but he's another child molester, and the *twist of the wrist* is that it's his own kid he's violating."

"I vote we cut off their dicks." Mitchell gave her knee–jerk reaction. "Oh. Excuse me. Somebody already did that little thing, no pun intended, for us."

"Last, we got the thirty–six–year–old, repeat offender, rapist. He takes a girl, ties her up for a couple of weeks, and it changes her life forever." Law shook his head. "Got to get this case wrapped. The sleaze seeps in an' out your brain then crawls around inside you. I'm takin' two showers a day."

"I know what you mean, all this bathing dries out my skin. But Law, look at the sunny side." The smirk on Sara's face told him the punch line coming was a jab at him. "It's better than your once–a–month–whether–I–need–it–or–not routine, you hunk you. Maybe you'll even get a date."

Law gave her his look of stone. Today, he was not in the

mood for their towel–fanny–slapping atmosphere. He took a sip of his scalding hot coffee, and brushed a bagel crumb from his tie. "Not to bog your small mind down with the details of your job, Ms. Mitchell, but what's the dope on the gun shops?"

Always the one to avoid letting the "family" actually get into a squabble, Tonetti busted in, "Oddly enough all the area gun shops remember seeing one, or more, good–looking blonde women with large breasts. Although they could not remember any other detail. I wonder what it was that made *that* particular detail stick in their minds?"

"You mean *details* plural don't you?" asked Mitchell. "When you've got large breasts, no one seems to notice the color of your eyes."

Law and Vince stared at one another. She would know. Neither would touch that—they would take her word for it.

"Each of these guys was seen, prior to his death, with a hot looking blonde babe with large breasts. Not one witness could remember any other detail about her."

"Could be a clever disguise. Maybe she's flat chested but very intelligent, an' wears the falsies as a cover. Or, maybe it's a guy. Think of it, no wig or funny makeup necessary." It was never easy to dismiss Mitchell's opinion.

"Hey," Tonetti asked a somewhat more enlightened question, "how do we know these guys didn't all have girlfriends they'd pissed off. Why are we sure it was the same woman?"

"*Because*, all evidence aside," Mitchell was in his face, "if you were a good–looking blonde with big boobies, would you be caught dead with any one of these creeps, even for the fun of it?"

"Okay, okay, back to work." Law's forehead had the deep crease it got when he was ready to kick some ass. "I heard on KSTP talk radio this a.m. that some of the local and national women's organizations are doing some fundraising for the suspect's defense—should we be so fortunate as to apprehend her."

"And," said Mitchell, "they're probably lining up the celebrities for her award ceremony, too.

"Does anyone really deserve to have his schlanker chewed off?" mused Vince. He always did like theoretical subjects.

"I admit chewing is harsh—slicing with a rusty, jagged butter knife would be the more appropriate sentence," spat out Mitchell.

The men shuddered at that vivid visual.

"One thing's sure. This is a woman with an *attitude* we're searching for. I'm not that sure I don't like her attitude." Mitchell had begun to take this personal. It got her hot.

Law tried to get back to business. He stood, "Look, I want to go over the additional information that has not been made public. I informed you about how she bites and slices them. Using, remember, something like a barber's straightedge or a scalpel. That could be important—we'll get back to it later.

Now that you know she doesn't kill them by nipping off their dicks, don't you *investigators* want to ask me any further questions?"

They sat, mute.

"Anything at all come to mind?"

Sara broke the silence. "Does she shave them first? So's not to get hair in her teeth when she bites?"

Law gave his biggest sigh and coupled it with a "*you–dumb–blankers*" look that he reserved for special occasions, such as, apparently, this. "You are so wrapped up in the bite–bit that you do not think to ask *how did they die?*"

Come to think of it, no one had *ever* asked him that—not even the news media. They were also pretty blanking interested in the bite–bit, as he cleverly put it. And speaking of clever, maybe she *was* flat chested and wearing falsies. She seemed a master of disguise.

Tonetti, his voice humbled only slightly, "I've been meaning to ask you, sir, how did the victims actually die?"

"Why Thank you, Vince. That is a very good question.

"They were poisoned."

He waited a minute to let that information sink in. Saw dumb vacant looks on both faces. No jokes. They must be in shock, thought Law. This'll be a good time to cover some ground.

"They were all poisoned by a narcotic herb. While you are sitting there with your mouths open, I will give you the low down on this plant. It's called Atropha Belladonna. AKA Deadly Nightshade."

"It has an alias?" Mitchell's mouth could move after all.

"During the middle ages, people believed deadly nightshade was the favorite plant of the devil. Symbolism abounds here. Try to pay attention. It was used frequently to kill. Yet the word Belladonna is derived from the Italian words meaning..."

"*Beautiful lady*," interrupted Tonetti.

"Yeah, beautiful lady. And we all know what atrophy means, especially if we looked it up in our dictionary. Delightful to gaze on, but dangerous."

"Where in the hell does one find such a thing?"

"Let's see," reading his notes, Law continued, "It's native to Europe, Asia, and North Africa, but has been cultivated in central Europe, England, Northern India, and, more recently, and more important to us, the US of A. It can be grown in meadows, forests, and any wooded shady areas."

"Narrows it down."

"Clam up, listen and learn. Today medicine uses many isolated compounds of this little piece of greenery. Atropine, as an antidote for certain poisons. Atropine was the only antidote against a nerve gas that the Germans developed during WWII. Deadly. It is an important drug for ophthalmologists, of all things. Interesting, I think, is the fact that the law used another compound of this herb, Scopolamine, for a brief time."

"Well shame on you, Law."

God. These children. "I spoke to an herbologist that Harry highly recommended, Ms. Georgia Fairbanks. She's quite the lady. Very interesting."

"Oooh, do I detect a note of interest on your part?" asked Mitchell.

"Yeah. And she's just nuts about me, too; now, can we get on with it?" Law was certain he was blushing, because, in fact, there had been a certain chemistry between the two of them. He was strongly considering hot pursuit of this "woman with the voice that lingered in his mind." He cleared his throat. Back to business. "It was administered as a truth serum to suspected criminals."

"So let me get this straight," Mitchell exuded uncontrollable excitement. "This is *awesome*. First, she gives them this truth serum herb, and then, as they are dying she bites them hard, one last symbolic triumph for the victims' victims."

"What gets me is how she can stand to touch their dicks with her mouth." Sara shuddered.

"Hey some women think it's a treat to gobble the. . ."

Tonetti was about to get smacked for being a smart ass so Law as his savior butted in.

"I don't think she does, not exactly, anyway," answered Law.

"What're you sayin'?" They both asked him at once.

"I'm sayin' that I think she covers them first. Something like a sheet of plastic wrap."

"Yes! Oh Lordie, don't I love it!" Mitchell jumped out of her chair. "First she gives them their own little blankie of plastic, bites down hard, and then slices it off! Do we know if they are dead or alive when she slices it?"

"Dead. We know for sure they are dead for the slice."

Mitchell went on, "So. She does not want to torture them—she wants to what? Prove a point? No. Wait. I think I've got it!

"*She wants to remove the weapon they all used on their victims*, and destroy it, hence the disposal. Well? Waddaya' think? Am I right?"

They stared. It seemed likely she was right on the money with this harebrained theory.

"After reading today's paper, I can see why you wanted to keep some of these details off the street. People would go nuts. They're already going nuts." She handed Law the newspaper.

"Before I look at this, have we found any connection between the victims' victims?"

Mitchell piped up, "I am still checking on that one, sir, but I know at least two, and possibly three, belonged to the same group for victims of abuse."

Law's expression was a drape of vengeance. "What do you know about this group?" His heart mysteriously pumped harder, his hands began to sweat.

"Headed by a psychologist by the name of Lorenzo Larimo, and. . ."

"*What?*" Law cut her off. He grabbed the report out of her hand, "Give me that, Sara."

She stared. He'd never been intentionally rude and he didn't even seem to notice what he'd done.

He spoke into the paper, "Give me a couple of hours—off the record. We might be on to. . .never mind, I'll let you know what's going down later today. For now, you're excused, but stay close."

His plan had been to go to Bryan Mazda after this meeting.

As he read the report Law knew there was a damn good chance this was Elsie's old group. He would swing by Lorenzo's office ASAP before going to the car dealership.

He picked up the newspaper Sara had told him to read to glance at it before he left. He had a pretty good idea what the article would be about. He'd never seen anything like this in all his years on the force.

Women loved her. They looked at Blondie like she was some kind of vigilante angel.

Law thought of his old bible classes that Ma made him sit through. Mostly he slept, but he remembered the angel of annihilation. In the story about Esther and Ahaseurus.

The avenger angel—Hasmed.

He read on:

It was clear the women did not want her caught. They wanted her alive and well and able to continue her holy mission.

Women were coming in out of nowhere, by the dozens, to confess to these murders. They had expected something like this; that was why the original and subsequent news releases were incomplete. Law was relieved they'd handled it that way. Imagine if the truth came out.

He rubbed his eyes. Blankin' case.

He could be in the middle of the biggest mess of his life with no way to determine who the real killer was. He had no idea there would be so many women out there who *wished* they had the guts or the power or whatever it took, to bite off some guy's weenie.

The actual murders were more humane than they had led the public to believe and they *still* thought of her as a hero.

He thought over what Mitchell had said.

They hadn't had their manhood removed until after death and then it was sliced off with some type of straightedge.

Why did that ring his chime?

All the men were snapped in the weenie once real hard prior to death. First the poison. Just one big drink—followed by a big bite—then *nitey–nite.*

No one, it seemed, had a garbage disposal that worked worth a shit. Which meant, of course, he did have her teeth marks.

But again, no saliva.

That's why he felt sure they were covered with some kind of easy to use material like this plastic wrap he'd mentioned.

His mind slipped back to the straightedge. It interested him, but there were hundreds of barbers and hair–stylists in town. Not to mention surgeons, and all the people who work with and supply them.

He had her teeth marks—but, that was not the cause of death. It was the poison.

Not even a real poison.

A blankin' herb.

Back to the article—he would never get on the move at this rate. He shouldn't find humor in this, but he found himself grinning.

The headline was an eye catcher:

DEEP THROAT, A THING OF THE PAST?

Twin Cities' residents have gone bite-it crazy. Led by the mystery woman, women are "coming out" all over. Team Rage—a local T–shirt company, said to design T–shirts for the masses—has come out with a whole new line of apparel. Local retail outlets cannot fill their shelves fast enough. Order requests are coming in from all over the world. Some examples of the new line are; BITE THE BULLET, LOVE AT FIRST BITE, I BITE!, OVERBITE, PSYCHO BITER, I BITE ANYTHING, IF IT MOVES–BITE IT, ONCE BITTEN–TWICE SHY, BIG GIRLS DON'T CRY–THEY BITE. The biggest seller seems to be BITERS ANONYMOUS! Reports are that all major cosmetic firms have released a new line of bright, vibrant red lipstick, and they cannot produce it fast enough. Mary Ann Cosmetics, long known for their conservatism, as shown by one of their many slogans, "It's nice to be important, but it's more important to be nice!" has just released its new spring "glamour" color, BITE RED.

Law felt eyes on him and sure enough there was Mitchell standing in the doorway, watching him and smiling. "Hmmm, Sara, would you say you girls have a bit of animosity brewing?"

"Is that what you detect? About us *girls*."

"Umhmm. Sorry about the girls, Sara."

"Can I quote you on that, boss?" She girlishly demurred.

Chapter Thirty-Three

What can cure can kill.

Those five words had been on the prowl throughout my brain ever since I'd picked that basket of oh so juicy berries. My house smelled like a witchery today. The glass pot simmered on the stove and gave the entire area an exotic aroma. The aroma was Belladonna. Herbs or poison? Take your choice. To cure or to kill.
In your bed–chamber keep,
From evil spells, potions alive with demons
witcheries will guard you in your sleep
and then there was,
What can cure, can kill.
I did a line of powder up my nose—then took my wooden spoon and stirred the mixture once again. It is important to handle plants properly. Never stir them with a metal object unless it is a magic sword. That made me giggle—for I did have something close to a magic sword. Certainly it was as sharp as a sword and it had worked magic!
Thanks Dad.
Atropha Belladonna—I believe that I was led to you by fate. My fate to become the goddess Atrophos. This is my real Karma. To cut the thread of life.
My eyes went to the piano. *Lynn, I promise you that very soon I will avenge you.*
He will suffer as you suffered.
And if he killed you, Skip, as I know in my heart he did, you will be able to rest knowing that he has paid the

price for his unspeakable crimes.

I went over the plan one last time in my mind. I will play him like a piano.

Peter, Peter, Pumpkin Eater.

Law went first to Lorenzo Larimo's office. He flipped open his shield in front of the receptionist and asked for her help.

"I can't help you Detective. What you request is private." She flat out refused to give him any information.

"Really?" So, he gave her some.

"Patty," he read from his notebook in a monotone," Patricia Patricks. Thirteen years old. She'd been kidnapped, held for eighteen days, repeatedly raped, assaulted, and sodomized. All this by a pedophile who had recently been paroled. Paroled for the third time for the same crime. The very same crime. "Been there, done that, wearin' the T–shirt," was his motto. He took great care to keep his victims alive so the justice system could *never put him away for long.*" Law looked at her directly when he carefully said each of those last words. "*His* name was Roger Dove."

The receptionist didn't look up.

"Roger was one of the victims of the bite–it Blondie.

"Her *first* victim."

Now she looked up.

That last part, about Patty's rapist being murdered by the bite—it woman was not information this receptionist had been privy to. Law could tell. They had kept the names of the bite–it victims pretty well secret—the press had the profiles on them—not the names. There had been speculation but no real bona fide leaks.

He could see the wheels go *merry–go–round* in her head.

"Look, we have reason to believe that this female suspect is in grave danger, and I think it's possible she was in the abuse victims' group right here in this center."

The receptionist was a woman in her late forties Law guessed. No name tag. She could have been a poker player with that face. But he could tell she was thinking and that was a good sign. . .or a bad sign, some kind of sign. No doubt her thoughts were of Patricia Patricks. She was a seasoned employee of Lorenzo's. . .yet not impervious to the facts Law had just given her.

He knew the exact second she made her decision.

With deliberation she turned to face the file cabinet and removed a single manila folder.

"Would you excuse me, Detective," she placed the beige folder on her desk, "I am going to go to the washroom." She caught his eye—his face was solemn—hers expressionless. "I will only be a minute." She emphasized minute.

She placed the manila folder on top of her desk.

He watched her walk, her back straight and proud, away from the private folder.

"Well, I'll be," he said under his breath. She evidently understood that he had to check out every lead at this juncture. And if the woman suspect were in danger this receptionist was willing to break the rules to come to her aide.

So, she went to the can. To Law, it seemed admirable.

Was her action some further indication of how serious women were taking this thing? Law thought it was. It was a sisterhood operation.

What they felt powerless to do alone maybe they could do in numbers.

He hastened to pick up the file, and then he knew for certain. This was the reason she'd been on his mind! He did not want to believe what was smack in front of him. Elsie Sanders. Her name flashed at him like a strobe. Elsie, Elsie. He dropped the file back on her desk just as the woman returned to the room.

"Do you have a current address for Elsie Sanders?"

"No."

"A current employer?"

"No, I'm sorry."

"Do you have a record of how long since the last time she came to participate in her group?"

"Yes, Detective Lawrence."

His eyes followed her nose as it turned down to the file that was now in her hands. "It has been eleven months."

Law smiled his appreciation. "Would you mind telling me your name?"

"Not at all. My name is Carol Larson."

He was on his way out the door when he thought of something else. "Would you happen to know what kind of car she drives?"

"Well, yes. I do know. She gave me a ride home one afternoon. It was long after she stopped. . .coming to group. She'd brought in a book for Tony." Her words came slow; her face was a puzzle. She'd always wondered why Elsie had stopped coming to group. "I don't recall the model but it was a small white Mazda."

Bingo.

Chapter Thirty-Four

I knew. I *knew* I'd heard that name. Somewhere...

I'd gone to the club for lunch and a steam. Pip. Where have I heard the name, Pip? It was in the steam room that all of a sudden, I knew. Just like that it hit me.

The redhead!

I let out a laugh that coiled all the way up from my balls. Good old Red!

I *had* heard that name. I got out quickly, drying myself. *How many people have a dog named Pip?* What was her roommate's name?

It was Elsie!...sure, Elsie.

El, El, El...Well, well, well.

I blinked and there it was again, that bloody bed I'd returned to see. Red's red bed. I laughed aloud!

And there before me, eye to eye, was what I later learned to be Blondie's boyfriend, his arms filled with her goodies.

Imagine my surprise.

Imagine his!

Only his few seconds of doubt saved me, and took him on his journey to that dark cubby hole in the morgue. The morgue coffin.

I can see why he hesitated when a loud yell would have made me turn and run like a rabbit. I could have been a detective working on the case, trying to solve the killer of his beloved's best friend; but in that last instant before the knife sliced and the blood spewed, he knew!

Luck was with me that day!

I was lucky to get away, lucky my dear Mildred and our darling offspring were on an outing and not home to greet me in my blood–soaked outfit. And lucky enough to have had the opportunity to remove a trophy from the pile lover–boy carried of Blondie's belongings. (I always thought of her as Blondie in those days.) It would be a nice touch to take that trophy with me tonight.

I have her address!

She might not yet know that it was I who killed her beloved. It was reported as a mugging that ended in murder. The police were never sure.

Something else gnawed its way into my consciousness: That waitress who had disappeared so quickly—the one with the dark hair.

How *could* I have been so dense?

No matter. I knew now, actually, I knew *how*. But most importantly, she did not know that I knew! Now, that, was the beauty of that!

I knew, and she did not know that I knew. I'll pack my riding crop and nestled tight will be the trophy. I nearly gave up my freedom—that trophy is proof of my courage.

One step forward and wearing new shoes!

I knew I'd liked that goofy mutt.

"I pretended he was Captain Hook. You know, in Peter Pan?"

Patty's words slipped inside Elsie's thoughts at the oddest times. It was listening to Patty, the youngest in the group, that made Elsie realize she *really* had to do this for all of them—all the members of her group. It wouldn't be enough to get Lynn's murderer.

These men had to meet with justice. Each one of them.

It was a *huge* leap to go from her plan, from thoughts about justice for her friends, to the actual *deeds*. But Patty's story was the one that made her know that she had to carry through and do it.

At thirteen years of age, Patty already knew she would never be able to bear children. The room he'd kept her tied in was small. About 6' by 6'. Not much more than a bed. The windows had been boarded, there was one bare light bulb—way high on the ceiling. While she was on her back and he was doing it to her, Patty formed a tunnel in front of her field of vision, that bulb was at the end. She didn't want to see his face.

In Patty's mind he had no face.

She looked down this tunnel at the far away light and pretended she was on a ship. Captain Hook's ship in Peter Pan. There she was, sleeping aboard the ship, when the storm came.

The storm raged and her body got thrown around the ship. As it rocked back and forth on an enraged sea, Patty was smashed and hurled against the tables and chairs, whatever was in her path. The pain was intense, yet she was sure that Peter Pan would soon come to take her off the ship.

They would fly up and away.

She held on tight as the intense pounding rocked her small frame.

Finally the storm would subside.

Usually that was when the stink would overpower her. The stench of his breath, his body, was one thing that could bring her off the ship and back to what was real—what was happening. He reeked so bad she would vomit. Then she would have to lie there and swallow her own puke.

The times that he tied her on her stomach, the pain was much worse, and she could not see the tunnel light. If she tried to close her eyes he threatened to cut them out. She learned to keep them open—yet see nothing.

So her bed was a fetid ship and the best of times on the ship were when the storm raged and the pain took over, then she was allowed to forget.

The picture of Patty's ordeal was on Elsie's mind as she fell asleep many nights. Some days Patty would sit and bang her head against the wall. Elsie wondered if she really wanted to hurt herself, or if maybe she just wanted her brain to stop. The doctors said that mentally Patty was not quite thirteen. Would she get older, or continue to get younger, or stay the same? The doctors couldn't say.

On the nights that Elsie thought about Patty, Elsie would end her "vision" with her own, very real, memory of what she'd done. She was proud that she'd had the courage to do what was right with Roger Dove. Elsie had tied him to the bed as soon as she could so that he'd swallow plenty of his own vomit. She remembered the shock on his face when she bit him—bit him hard! That was when he knew. Up until that final second he'd thought he was having a bad trip. When he knew the truth about Elsie and his fate he lost all control and messed the sheet.

But now, he was dead. Patty had been avenged. Roger Dove and what he had done lived, but his body was dust. Dust to dust.

Peter, Peter, Pumpkin Eater.
Elsie's dreams were paved with savage colors—unworldly hues. Fetid eruptions swirled and played with her body, tossed it, held her captive. Then the chromatic groan–storm would change—she would begin her slide into the black. And the black was void of all but noxious, putrid horror.

She awoke feeling alienated from everything, most of all herself.

She was empty. And when she tried to crawl out of her emotional nothingness she felt powerless.

Elsie sat on the ridge of sanity.

Her dream was an existential message—of herself, to

herself.

It was time to listen to the message.

Law rolled into the precinct in time to catch a phone call from a gun shop in Hopkins, a western suburb of Minneapolis. Dove had worked at the gun shop part time a few hours a month. For fun. A good-looking blonde dolly had picked him up the last couple of times he worked. He had bragged to the boys about what a hot number she was. He'd had big plans for her. The gun shop owner knew more about her cup size than the color of her eyes, but he did recall Dove calling her something like Bell.

"Yeah," the gun man said, "it coulda' been El. Yeah, sure, it *was* El. I'd thought at the time it was her first initial. L. Wondered what it stood for. Linnea? She was a beaut—had to have a sensuous name."

Like Sara said, large breasts could take a woman far without many of the men she met along the way remembering her face or much else. Anyway, thought Law, it was an excellent disguise.

His instincts didn't fail him often. He didn't have to ask what could make Elsie want to nail a turd like Dove or any of the others. She was trying to settle a score. More than one score.

And doing it.

How did she change so fast? Her innocence was on the way out when he last saw her. Life had transformed her into a woman with balls.

It was time to pay a visit to the Mazda dealership. He had a feeling it was a road that would lead him to Elsie, and he wasn't in any hurry to have to arrest her. But what would he do if she needed his protection? He knew the answer.

Law had this peculiarity—the hair on the back of his neck would stand stiff—like a bloodhound's tail—when there was serious danger, or he was close to solving a case. Which is it now, he wondered, as he drove to the dealership?

Could be both.

Peter was not in.

The petulant woman who seemed to be handling the job of secretary and general busybody—Janet something—was reluctant to let him into Mr. Bryan's office, but Law could be persuasive when he wanted to.

Standing in the spacious room with the solid oak desk that was bigger than his own bed, Law felt more than a strong dislike for the man who occupied this span of opulence. Even though he couldn't be certain that he'd found Lynn's murderer, in his gut he *knew*.

The man who occupied this space had murdered in cold blood—Lynn and Skip and who knew how many others. It was difficult to think of this bestial asshole in terms of the word *man*.

He tried to focus. The scent of leather was heavy. It curled his lip and he wrinkled his nose. Maybe it was mixed with the memory of the redhead.

He paced through the room—it was large enough to pace. As he snooped, he flipped at things with his lucky pen. Inspecting, detecting and yes, snooping. Charming family photographs, he thought, observing the girls' grinning faces. Were they really happy? Doubtful. Might be his imagination was working overtime.

On the south wall was what appeared to be a closet. Covered an entire wall. Law pushed the sliding door with his pen. . .yeah. A closet.

Something struck him as strange.

He opened the door all the way, exposed most of the contents at once. The word weird stuck in his head—like bubble gum under the seat in an old flick theatre, you never can quite clean it all off. He retreated a step to survey the closet and his mind tripped him back a few years:

Elsie in the hospital.

Her voice was so clear, she was right here! They were in this office together now.

"I'm trying my best to remember anything Lynn might have said about him. Anything that might help you."

Fat chance, Law was thinking at the time, *fat–fucking–chance*. He wasn't *blanking* yet in those days.

"I can't remember it—what Lynn said, but it was something weird about shoes. Peter had said something to her like, 'aren't my shoes good enough for you?'. . .not exactly that."

Law brought himself back to the closet and today. Well let's see. Would you say it was weird if a guy had roughly, oh, fifty pair of shoes in his office closet? And three shirts, one sport jacket, one coat. . .two ties, one pair of slacks, one old sweater, and. . .yeah. Fifty–three pairs of shoes. He bent over and picked up a particularly fancy pair.

Crocodile.

He remembered watching a show once on croc's. *The adult crocodiles have no natural enemies—they weigh up to a ton and no animal on the earth is safe from them.*

The croc's had something crusty smeared on the tops—unlike the rest which were all perfectly groomed and shined. His mouth felt like his tongue was swollen fat and dust–dry. Tiny frozen antennas poked out on the back of his neck.

Blankin' Godalmighty.

He had to find Elsie *fast*.

Ms. Petulant was ready and waiting to do her duty outside the office door.

"Do you have an employee by the name of Elsie Sanders?" he asked.

"No."

"Are you certain?"

"We have an El Sanders."

"Can you get me her address? Please. *Now*."

Her lips pruned together, dried and wrinkled. "Of course, I can get it for you, but it won't do you any good." She turned to waddle toward the main office.

He followed her, "Would you wait!" He had to touch her arm to stop her forward progress. "Why not?"

She pulled her arm away with a jerk, as if he were strong–arming her. "It's a PO Box is why not."

"You mean that's all you have?"

"That is precisely what I mean."

"How about *Mr. Bryan.* Do you have an address for *him?*"

There was that prune–lip again. "Well of course I do, Sir."

"Then, *get it!* . . . .please." He left out the "get off your ass" that clung like a slab of raw liver to his tongue.

Chapter Thirty–Five

What can cure can kill.

The big date was scheduled for Thursday evening and it was now late Wednesday afternoon.

Elsie had just finished her preparation of the liquid. She used a funnel and poured it into an exquisite crystal decanter, wiped the bottle carefully, and placed it on the credenza.

Her mind jogged repeatedly to the piano. And she couldn't keep her eyes off it. She began to polish, giving it a glass top shine that allowed her to see her reflection. On top of the piano as a finishing touch she placed a vase of fresh cut flowers from her garden. The blossoms were fragrant; their sweet scent filled the room. On closer inspection you could see one twisted herbal branch in the center of the arrangement. An esoteric touch? The branch drooped, heavily weighted with its load of plump blackberries.

She went to search out something to set under the vase to protect the finish of the piano from the occasional drips that oozed from the berries. They were ripe, bursting and ready. As was she. She smiled as she worked unconsciously humming an old Tammy Wynette tune.

She couldn't get that dream out of her mind. Usually she slept with her arms around Pip, or at least a part of her touching him for comfort. But knowing what was about to come she'd arranged for Pip to stay the week with Tony.

She couldn't chance her pup's life.

Her dream last night had been a frightening thing and horribly lucid—for when she woke she could remember how strange it was.

The setting was in an ancient cathedral–like building. There were golden statues and a ceiling covered with pastel painted angels. But inexplicably, in the center of the altar was a staircase, leading, spiraling-down.
Down?
In her dream she was about to be punished for not carrying out a plan.
Elsie felt guilty but enormously threatened by this plan.
She reached the bottom of the staircase and saw an old woman with features much like her own might one day become with age. The woman had a commanding presence and was bending over something akin to a witch's cauldron.
Was she a witch?
She stirred, as she crooned, over and over in a croaking sing–song voice:
"Gobble, gobble, lick, smack
He lost his prick with one swift hack
Smack. . .slurp. . .burp. . . ."

The dream haunted her, and at odd moments made her *giddy* as she busied herself preparing the liquid for the decanter. Of late, she had been dreaming of the beautiful goddess Atrophos so often that she began to see herself as this goddess-almost evolving into Atrophos.
Perhaps she *had* to be Atrophos to do these deeds. For although, as she often rationalized, they did make a choice to drink the drink of death, she made it, she fixed the trap, bated the trap and set up the *sting of death*.
The old woman of last night's dream did not fit—she slid into Elsie's thoughts—a lurking aura of evil.
. . .*sting of death*. . .*hack, smack, smack.*

This had been a dazzling sunny day. One of those first

spring days that make you feel good all over. The fog in her mind from the dream finally passed.

There's nothing wrong with having a plan, she thought, a really good plan, then watching it bear fruit. A juicy plump berry oozed, plop, onto the piano.

In the Middle Ages Belladonna was an ingredient in the refreshment served at wild orgies. Elsie had told all four men that fact.

For those men a little bit of knowledge proved to be a very dangerous thing!

She opened the sunny windows facing her garden. This had been the first phase of her scheme-the garden. How she loved digging in the earth with her bare hands. At first she was afraid the bees would come and sting her but they never did. They were used to seeing her putter about, and no doubt felt grateful for the beautiful things she grew, just as she was grateful for their help, too.

This was what life was all about. Creating new life. Well, she hadn't created it in the usual sense, but she had reaped and sowed and nurtured.

As ye sow, so shall ye reap.

Elsie was now about to reap.

She thought of the ditty the old woman's chant in her dream. . ."*gobble, gobble, lick, smack.*"

Sometimes she felt very clever. . .*reap, rape, reap, rape*, same letters, and, in this case. . .

The sound of her doorbell gave her a jolt.

Who could that be? No one ever came to visit. No one knew where she lived. Well, except for Tony. The house was too far off the road for solicitors.

Tony!

Against her best judgment, Elsie had given him her address. But she knew when she did it that he didn't have a car. Right after she gave in to him he'd begged, said he couldn't live without wheels. And finally, she'd taken him to buy a new, used car. But the car dealer was supposed to be fixing the brakes right now. They must have gotten the parts they said they'd have to order from someplace in town.

Whatever, it would be wonderful to see Tony!

She went to open the door.

Time for the main event!

An energy so potent I felt I would burst pumped through my veins—it was electric—it almost had a mind of its own. No, I thought. It's my mind, my extraordinary mind, that's what's in the power seat now. This super–fucking–charged feeling is all due to me!

I scrubbed my genitals with extra care. The sound of the shower's blast as it hit my backside, the red–hot steam rising around me in a hot cocoon that sizzled, brought memories of my dear sainted mother. I heard her rasp come up from the swirling drain, "If you are not clean, I can not be proud." That voice was the epitome of the fingernails on blackboard cliché.

I would never want Ma to think less of me for not being Mr. Clean.

Mr. Clean for Mr. Big.

That brought a guffaw that barked out of my mouth as I rubbed and scrubbed to prepare myself for the "coming" event.

The main event.

Ma's nag was constant, "Peter, would you be able to pass Mr. Clean's inspection?" I would know then that there was nothing I could do, she was coming with the scrub brush that she dubbed Mr. Clean, to give me a good going over. And Mr. Clean was scrupulous.

I would plead, "Ma, it's not dirty." and she would say, "Oh, but it is. It is very dirty!" My pleading voice was a source of humiliation, both then and now.

But, no problemo, mommy dearest, you helped to make me the strong man I am today. If only you could have lived long enough to see what your handiwork produced. I'd have enjoyed showing you, Ma.

As I dried myself off, my thoughts turned to the woman. . .to El. In a way, it was too bad. I could have used her awhile longer. My lip curled. It was not a matter of significance. Her actions had forced me to use her enough, this one time, for the memory to sustain me over and over again.

Today I will use her till she is used up.

I was ready. Shit was I ready. This time I remembered the riding crop. Wasn't that a sign that I was in control? And of course, I had these nice new tennies. I had wanted so to use the crocodiles, but they were soiled. And as much as I wanted to cover that soiled area with her flowing red fluid, I could not make myself wear those filthy shoes ever again. Whatever would Ma think? She wouldn't be impressed. Besides, I liked tennies. White. Pure.

Red and white were my favorite colors.

I could not wait to see her expression when she opened her door and saw my face. This was going to be a day chock full of surprises for our smarty–pants–El.

I wiped the hot fog from the mirror and slicked back my hair. Yessiree.

Surpriiiiiise!

And that was not the only surprise I had for her. My souvenir, my treasure taken from the arms of her boyfriend, would be presented to her with flourish and panache.

As I laced my new shoes I felt Mr. Big rise. Get ready for the occasion. Rise to it. Yessiree. No need to attempt to cover my lap this time. No need for my warm jacket today, El baby. Soon I will bury this bone.

I pictured her perfectly proportioned fanny.

Yeah.

Well, here I come, ready or not my beautiful little dove.

You bitchcunt. A blondie to go with the redhead.

I am clean as a whistle an' ready to ride! *And just in time for the main event.*

Chapter Thirty–Six

Peter's address was on Upton Avenue, on Lake Calhoun.

Trying to make it around Lake Calhoun at this time of year was blanking impossible.

The minutes ticked by; second by precious second pounded in his head. Went well with the heartburn. These days Law lived on Zantac.

He reached out and slapped the red light on top of his unmarked car. He felt a cramp shoot up his right leg. Times like this he wished he was shorter, or at least his legs weren't so damn long.

Why are all these people going to the lake today?...Don't they have jobs? Don't they have homes?...lawns to mow, dogs to walk, something else to do? A motorcycle swerved around him, weaving in and out of the cars; wish I had time to give the dipshit a ticket, he fumed...it's people like that...ah, at last. He stomped on his brake and felt the curb graze his front tire. Nice parking, Law. *Tough*, he answered himself. He slammed the door and was about to bolt up the stairs to the house when he stopped. Whoa boy, slow 'er down, take a deep breath. Won't do her any damn good if you're dead.

With some caution this time he proceeded to check the place over. Quite the joint. A veritable blanking mansion. He rang the bell. No answer. What caused his gut to burn? He felt sure that he could roast marshmallows inside himself. His stomach in a knot he moved around to the back. No sign of intelligent life. Seemed to be locked up tight. Tighter than the brasses' tight asses. Used to use that expression a great deal, now he wondered if they were all, all that tight. Maybe they did get some use now and again. His sense of humor was what helped him make it through this cops' life.

It seemed he'd have to take the time, take another ride around the lake, to get his hands on the policeman's favorite—that ever popular search warrant. Law muttered to himself about how the laws protected criminals and tied his hands. He was about to leave when an old decrepit man poked his head around the side of the house. By the look on his face he must have heard Law complain to himself and wondered who was trespassing.

Law flashed him his badge and ID; he could almost see the old man's heartbeat return to normal.

A palsied hand shook up to his head and removed a baseball cap to reveal that the remnant of a once fine head of hair was now thin, white, and plastered with sweat to his damp dome. His other trembling hand brought out an old orange mechanic's work rag, covered with grease and holes, and wiped his wet brow.

Law gave the old guy a minute, although his own motor was accelerating and wanted movement at any cost.

Law fired questions at him and he answered in a voice that was both weary and bored.

"Yep. I am the gardener."

"Yep, Mr. Bryan lives here." and, "Nope, he ain't home now."

Law tried to be patient. "When did he leave, do you know?"

"Oh, I s'pose it was, say, twenty minutes ago."

"Did he mention where he was going?"

"Nope. Didn't say where, but then, he never does. Weren't his way to say that, not to the help." Now that he was calmed, and knew he had nothing to fear, the old man wanted to go about his business.

"What kind of a car does he drive?"

"Got several."

Law could tell that the man was getting tired of show and tell, but he didn't have time to humor the old goat and was feeling a might testy himself. "I didn't ask about the family. What does *he* drive most of the time?"

"One a' them little Mazdas."

"Color?" Man, now I know how a snail feels, thought Law.

"Black."

"Is it that sporty one? The RX-7?"

The man proceeded to unlock the storage shed. "Um, yup." He got out a rake and what Law would call a "hoe thing." Law hated to even look at lawn care shit. It had a way of jumping into his hand, and making him feel guilty if he didn't use it. But he decided to take a look–see around the shed.

Cobwebs hung in patterns that spiders could possibly consider works of art—gave him the shivers. Something about the place felt wrong. For one thing, there was almost nothing in it.

"What's this shed used for?" He asked.

"Seldom used," the old voice grunted and croaked. "Never seen the family use it at all—just a shack for his lawn supplies. Keeps it locked, so's that his small ones don't get hurt, I s'pose. On one a' them evil rakes like you're shyin' away from yerself."

Law ignored the old man's bait, but was irritated that it was obvious.

Hmm. What was this . . .this trendy ornate old trunk high on the rafters. . .folks usually kept things like this that might be worth some cash, inside. Law climbed on a pile of cement blocks and pulled it down. It was heavy for him and hit hard on one side.

The old head snooped around the corner to see what the noise was and gave him a withering glare. "Don't want ta' be responsible for no damage."

Law ignored that, too. What about the damage to his shoulder bone?

The latch was open; either it had popped open just now, or someone had recently been inside. A thick layer of grime covered the trunk; it covered him with dust. Dirty, except for the very top. Someone *had* recently been inside—or been out here dusting.

Law yanked up the lid.

He looked inside...expecting what?

His face fell.

Shoes. Nothing but shoes...tennis shoes...dirty shoes, at that. Most likely from gardening.

He was about to close it when he looked closer.

Hey, wait a minute...that's not dirt. Nope. And he had a good idea that he knew what it was. Blood. Using his trusty pen he picked up a blood dried shoe-something small and shiny fell to the ground. He got down on his haunches and poked at it until it dangled from his pen.

His heart felt a squeeze.

Ohmygod.

It was a tiny gold earring. It had some crusty substance around it.

A thin chain with a small musical note dangled to and fro.

Law closed his eyes for just a second and heard a piano play off in the distance. And then he heard a voice, Elsie's voice, "something weird about shoes, I don't remember exactly what it was, but it was weird."

Right.

Chapter Thirty-Seven

The doorbell insisted.

Elsie hurried, eager to see Tony. Because she knew what was in store for her tomorrow, Thursday, she needed to see Tony. To say goodbye? No!

Just in case.

It crossed her mind to wonder why Pip hadn't barked. Odd. Tony must have brought Pip along with him. "I'm coming! Patience, my dear one!" Elsie said it loud enough to be heard outside the door as she flung it open wide.

"Why, Peter! What a pleasant surprise!"

She appeared happy to see him, and her smile looked like the genuine thing.

That threw him. She was a cool one, she was. Had she ever called him Peter before? No. He was certain she'd always called him Pete—or Sailor. Oh yes, she had called him Peter. It was that first time. The day when she wore the dark wig in the restaurant. You're quite the little spider girl, Elsie, my dove.

"Don't just stand there in the doorway, Peter. My don't you smell fresh as the surf! Come in. . .make yourself at home. Here, let me set your package down."

He kept his face blank, "Dear one? Whom were you expecting?"

She continued to chat, ignoring his question, as she led him inside. "I see you already have a beverage. I didn't know you drank beer." She shook the bag slightly. "Hmm, this package seems interesting, Peter. I hope it's a present for *moi*. Is it?"

"A token housewarming gift." *You bet those gorgeous tits and ass it is*, he thought.

"*All* for you, El; we'll open it together later. This is the first time I've ever been here, it seemed appropriate to bring you a trinket or two to show my esteem. If nothing else, in my dear mother's memory, to show you that she did not raise a barbarian."

"Well, how nice, Peter. I'm so pleased you have finally come by."

"I don't recall that you extended an invitation to *come by*."

"Well, of course, I would have thought you'd consider yourself as having an open invitation." Elsie raised her brow, "But you've never mentioned your mother before. Has she passed on?"

He ignored the mother query, unable to go beyond her, "so pleased you finally," etcetera. *Pleased, my ass*, he thought.

"Why don't you give me *le grande* tour of the place." He scanned the rooms; it was all her, everything in sight had her print on it.

A fitting place for her to die.

The realization that this would be the last day she had to enjoy this shrine of hers pleased him. That's what it was—a shrine. Her color, texture, scent, filled the air. He hoped she appreciated the moment, wallowed in it, because for her—it was the final dance.

"Are you sure you wouldn't care to sit and have a cocktail first—something hard, rather than the beer?" Her voice was pleasant.

"In a minute. Right now, I want to see where things are. I'll be more comfortable if I know where everything is." *Like your best, sharpest knives, bitch.*

"Well, of course, we want you to be comfortable, don't

we? Let me take you through the layout."

He followed her down the hall to what he imagined to be the bedroom, and sure enough, she led him right to the best room, first. It was the same color as the living room, ivory.

He thrilled for a moment at the thought of how it would soon look.

This room was pallid; he would give it vivid color. He saw himself as a king turned painter, *he was about to create, to make a visual statement that would expose his despotic soul.* The idea did not upset him.

His eyes rolled over the room, taking in the mammoth poster–bed. How fortunate—poster–beds made it easier to tie them down—more erotic, too. It was as if he had chosen it himself. He noticed the crystal decanter on the credenza. "What's in the jug?"

"A love potion. Would you like a sip?" *She could have bit her tongue!* She had not meant to invite him to drink the nectar yet—if at all. But the words were out. She could not take them back.

She must be more nervous than she realized. Elsie knew her plan's success depended that she keep a clear head.

His next words were no surprise.

"No, thanks. Not now."

Whatever she offered, he would very likely refuse.

"Where do you keep the kitchen?"

"Follow me." Her voice shook. *This was not going according to plan. Forget that he had found her. Forget that he showed up a day early. She had to find a way to slow this down, get her bearings, get control—control of herself and more importantly, of him.*

The kitchen was enormous; the appliances were chrome, except for an unusual mirrored refrigerator. Peter bared his teeth at himself, taken in by this unexpected, yet, he thought, striking reflection. The center–island was draped in aromatic floral plants, all in bloom. They drew your eye skyward. In addition to foliage that cascaded down like multi–colored lace, he noticed the ceiling went to a steeple point, with huge skylights on all sides. With so much light in the room you would seldom need artificial lighting, except at night when the view of the stars would be breathtaking.

Had she had many candle and star light intimate dinners in this idyllic setting, he mused?

He recalled her no–man–comes–to–my–house speech.

He was here, wasn't he? And *he* was a man. Was he, then, the first? First and last. He liked the idea.

A fireplace that was a backdrop for a cozy table setting covered the north wall. The bitch was good to herself, no question about it. His eyes flicked here and there—on the counter was what he searched for.

She made it easy. All out in plain sight.

He hoped that they were sharp knives, but it was not paramount; he felt strong as a snorting bull. There was more to the house to see, but he'd seen what concerned him. "I'll have that drink now. Do you have something other than wine? I don't drink wine."

I don't drink wine. Her heart skipped a fraction. *I don't drink wine.* The words felt heavy. And his attitude was not the same. This was not the Peter she knew. She remembered suddenly what Lynn had said that day after the phone call from him.

Lynn said that he had changed. Once he was no longer trying to impress, he became himself.

That meant he had made his decision.

He was going to kill her today.

I don't drink wine. How could she have over looked something so obvious when she'd remembered virtually every detail. Or thought she had.

Elsie led him to the wet bar in the living room, she thought of the few times his hands had actually been on her. Hideous moments she had endured and they would only be worthwhile if she accomplished her mission.

If she died *first* and he lived, *it was all for nothing.*

Get a grip, and get it now, she told herself.

"So. You're pleased to see me, are you, Elsie?" *Two can play at this El-Elsie, Pete-Peter, name-game,* he thought, "Why don't you show how pleased you are." He set down his beer bottle, and made a swift grope for her tits. They were covered, just barely, in a short cut off T–shirt. Short and tight.

Without a doubt, her slum–around–the–house–alone clothes. He pulled the shirt and displayed sumptuous breasts with one motion. Then squeezed both nipples twisting them hard. He pinched harder, a cruel sneer on his face.

She bit her tongue, did not flinch, and kept her tone low and controlled, "My aren't we in a rush? Why don't I change into something more alluring? I have something that I purchased for *you* for just this occasion. It will be so much more interesting to have you rip it off of me."

Was that what she thought this was all about? A game of some kind? She was in for some big surprises. "Sure, baby, but hurry."

"I'm ready too, Peter. I've been able to think of nothing else, but let's be a bit civilized, shall we? After all, we don't need to rush today. Why not prolong the encounter?"

She was absolutely right of course, though she did not yet know why. Prolong, to use her word, the encounter was precisely what he wanted to do. This was the ultimate; why not slow down and enjoy? She would soon beg him to end it, to be quick and merciful.

Just as her friend Red had begged for her life.

Elsie would find he had no mercy.

His eyes walked the room again, "You know, I think this place could use a touch of color; maybe an accent color." He sank back deep into the sofa cushions. *Like sitting on a huge marshmallow*, he thought. The place suited her. It was as if she were the only one who ever entered it—just as he thought—a shrine. He looked out the window...secluded. What a perfect choice for his *romantic* interlude. Like the poster–bed, he could not have chosen it better himself. He breathed deeply, relaxing further into the cushions.

"Nice piano."

Yes. "Why thank you, Peter." *Nice piano, she thought, and how very good of you to mention it; help me remember why I need to be strong.* "It belonged to an old, and very dear friend."

"Really? You don't say?" His eyes were steel. "Elsie, my love. Why don't you hand me the bag I brought with me?" He watched her bend to lift it and carry it with a slow sensual walk toward him.

He took it from her and removed something from the top of the bag. "Here." he said. "This is one of the gifts I brought you, my dove."

"How lovely."

Was that a catch in her voice?

Elsie looked at the small cedar chest in her hand and with the other hand opened the top. Why did she expect to see it packed with Juicy Fruit gum? She saw her image in the mirror glued inside the cover and thought of her desire all those years to become an actress.

"It pleases you, then?"

"Oh, my yes," her voice was soft, a caress. "Very much." She hadn't thought of Skip much these past few days. *Now she knew for certain that he was Skip's killer, too. A double homicide solved.*

She turned and began to move toward the bedroom, "Shall I go ahead and change?"

"Yeah. Sure, why not?"

"Feel free to roam the house, and by all means help yourself to any refreshments you might desire. Are you sure you would not care for something hard?"

"Baby, I *have* something hard. I want something to drink."

Her laugh said "wasn't he just the little dickens?" *Was her laugh too loud, too merry?*

"There's a complete wet bar to your left. I recommend the champagne. You can pour me a glass, if you wouldn't mind. I'll be out in just minutes." She turned back, "You know, I don't think I have seen you wear tennis shoes before today." She caught a glimpse of the smug look that crossed his face as she left the room.

I hope you're watching this, my two angels, she said to herself.

A double homicide solved.

Chapter Thirty-Eight

Elsie took great care with her preparations.

She'd planned for this for a very long time. The moment of accountability had arrived. She would have justice.

The ability to avenge her friends was, for Elsie, an anodyne similar to the cocaine she used. After today she would not need either one, or so she believed.

He obviously knew who she was. *Lynn's roommate.* He'd called her Elsie for the first time. That was his signal to her. And, then he'd brought the cedar box. He couldn't know that it'd been a gift from Skip...Alvin. But he'd taken it the day that he slit Skip's throat and he wanted her to know that he was the one.

Did Peter know she was the woman the newspapers wrote about? Elsie paused. *No,* she thought it unlikely that he'd realized *she* was Bite–Woman.

Even this savage monster would show some respect to Bite–Woman!

And, if he knew, there would be some degree of detectable fear—he wasn't that good at poker. But what he *did* know made this game more dangerous than she'd planned.

Then again, it was not much of a game if both sides did not have a chance to win, was it?

Now *this* was the attitude she had to get back!

To win you must first be willing to risk the loss of it all.

As she dressed, she felt her old confidence return. What did it matter *how* he found her? It changed her plan, sure it did, but it was still the same *game*. She felt confident that whatever was about to happen to her, at long last, *he* was going to get *his*.

He was.

Lately, Elsie didn't understand her feelings. The desire to survive had become an ache that attempted to possess her soul. She had to shake that pang of longing before it blinded her to her mission.

A strong will to survive was *not* what she needed.

It took away her edge.

All along, she'd moved forward knowing in her heart that this was her karma. Along with that was the knowledge that her chance for survival was slim. In her dreams she was a modern-day version of a *kamikaze*—believing that self was unimportant.

The goal was all that was important.

For months, hatred for this murdering swine had burned throughout her body!

But lately hatred had been replaced by an even more powerful force. That force was what propelled her forward at this moment.

It was the determination to see justice done.

Don't screw it up now, she told herself. *You are not you.* This is a show, an act, she talked one last time to herself. She rose above her body and looked down from above.

Gobble, gobble, lick, smack! She grinned.

Let justice be done!

Elsie, the goddess, returned to the living room to once again greet her guest. This time she felt "the force" flow through her. She was exhilarated! *This was a moment that belonged to the victims of the world. This was for the powerless.*

What can cure can kill.

Let the curtain rise on the final act!

Peter had just settled in on the sofa, a flute of champagne

in his hand. He felt secure. He'd managed to procure a sharp knife from her kitchen and had tucked it into the bag he'd brought with him. The weapon was nestled alongside the riding crop. He liked the concept of slicing her with her own cutlery.

Upon her entrance he rose and extended his glass forward for a toast. He stopped when he saw her and his face changed: startled.

Astounded at the sight of the goddess, he could barely speak, "Wait. Stand there. Let me look."

Ah hah! She'd caught him off guard and she knew it! She knew exactly how she appeared in this foolish get–up. She'd shopped at *Frederick's of Hollywood*. Her bra was black lace—what there was of it. There were holes cut out for the nipples, so that her own protruded and she had rouged them with a blood–red tint. Fastened around her waist was a white–gold metal chastity belt with a small lock in front. It hung strategically between her legs. She slowly turned so that he could see the small metal band that ran down between the cheeks of her derriere. It was cleverly designed; you could clearly see her blonde bush, but could not have access to either of her love entrances. She'd combed and brushed and oiled herself; the small hairs curled and curved around the apparatus, full and inviting.

Hair or silk?

The spider's lair was fully prepared.

Encircling the tops of her arms were four inch wide bronze slave–cuffs; over it all she wore a transparent ivory silk robe that flowed and yet clung to her curves. Her feet stepped seductively toward him on six–inch spiked black satin heels.

Yes, Elsie knew exactly how she looked. Lips, *blood red*. Cheeks, pale ivory.

Like a china doll? In Peter's mind, that could only mean, *easy to break*.

She twirled. . .the robe flew open; she turned again, this

time slower. . .*mannequinesque*! Her back was to him. She stopped—bent at the waist, way, far over, so that he could see how the access to her derriere was locked tight.

He felt the blood pulsate in both heads. Mr. Big was hard and Peter did not bother with an attempt to hide it.

"Well, Sailor," she purred. "I know how much you like to control your world and those in it. I thought you might like to have your own personal slave girl tonight."

"Where is the key, little dove?" his voice soft, cunning.

Mona Lisa smiled as Elsie spoke, "Is there some reason to hurry? I would love to linger with champagne and you. We can drink a toast on what is to 'come' before I bring you the key, my master."

She stared directly at him—a challenge of his control over himself. She could tell by his expression that Peter was not much in the mood for a toast. If she did not keep the action moving he would regain the upper hand. Right now, it was hers.

She sat across from him, leaned to the side and spread herself out on the ivory sofa. The sofa was the shade of her flesh. She let her legs slowly spread apart, wide apart; she let some of the champagne drip on her breasts. Then with a tip of the glass, she poured the cool crystal ivory liquid between her legs on her tendrils of cream.

"Ooooh, that is chilled just right. If only my fingers could slip inside this belt, my master. This is agony. To see you so hard makes me want to touch myself. At least the champagne cools my hot pussy so it will not melt with my desire before your hard prick is able to get inside."

She had him going; he was interested in nothing but her.

"This is where I was lying the night I phoned you. I need something to stick inside me now, my master," she began to squirm, her hips moving, undulating as if ready to explode. He was clearly on the edge, ready to pounce. Elsie moved fast, her body rhythmic and fluid, she stepped to the top of the glass table in front of him. So close to him. She had his complete attention. "Love is a fire."

"Love?" He was a dog on a hunt and he would follow the scent.

She spread her legs wide. Moaning she began to dance. She told herself this was just one more act in the performance of her lifetime. She put everything she had into it.

She flicked her nipples with deep red nails that matched the red she had used to rouge herself. One finger in her mouth, she sucked and she began to simulate orgasm. She went wild, gyrating in a frenzy of movement, clawing at her chastity belt. "Oh, master, I must have you inside me, please my master, only you can give me what I want. . .please, take me. Please."

His glass fell to the floor and spilled over the carpet. He grabbed her roughly, lifted her in his arms, and carried her in the direction of the bedroom. God, he wanted to fuck her. He wanted to ram her and fuck her and listen to the music of her dying cries. He was so hard he knew that if he bumped himself on something equally hard he would break his dick right in two. He threw her onto the four-poster bed, watched her body bounce and readied himself to pounce.

Let the games begin, thought Peter.

She read the look in his eyes.

"Wait, master, please. . .I don't want this to go fast. I want it to last! Let me get us more champagne. While we catch our breath I'll get the key. Don't *you* want this to last? We want to linger over each moment, my master."

The fucking key. Peter let her step away. "Get the key." He lay back on the bed to watch her, hands behind his head, ankles crossed. Her flesh was cream that flowed. *It would mix well with red*.

She walked to the credenza. *The glasses. There were no glasses by the decanter.*

What if his cock had not yet taken control of his brain?

"I'll get the champagne and glasses, master, I'll only be a moment." She let her lashes fall demurely from the form on the bed

His voice stormed its evil the dirge of the devil. "Fuck the champagne. Bring the key."

She would have to do as he requested. Next to the decanter was a small ornate box. Elsie moved in a daze. *Was that music that screamed in the bedroom or just inside her head?* She placed the box on his stomach, taking in the cold cruel face that stared at her body. She felt exposed, vulnerable. This was not going according to plan. Not *her* plan.

He opened it, not taking his eyes off her body until the last second.

On a bed of red velvet lay the key.

She whispered coyly, praying he could not hear the thumps of her heart, "I believe this is what you are looking for, my master." She dropped the small gold key into his open hand.

"Ah, the key." *Amazing how it relaxed him to feel the key in his possession; his fingers ran over the smooth finish.* He sighed, "Okay. That's better. I think we can have that drink now, slave. You are quite the tease, aren't you bitch?"

She lowered her eyes, "Yes, my master."

"What's in the decanter?"

"Oh, no master, I do not think that it is something that would please you. Let me get you the champagne." *What can cure can kill.*

Chapter Thirty-Nine

Would he find Elsie in time?
Find her *where?*
Law returned to Lorenzo Larimo's office. He phoned on the way and got the receptionist he'd talked to earlier. "Carol?...Detective Lawrence. I've got to have her address. Now. I'm on the way."
Someone there had to know where in the blank she lived.

He arrived to find the receptionist's desk empty and a note on the door to the back conference room. *Have a seat*, the note said, *I'm on a phone conference and will be out in a few minutes*. Law saw the red light on the phone that told him someone in another room was on one of the lines. Okay. He needed their help. Reason enough not to piss them off if he didn't have to.

He sat and flicked his fingernail. Impatient. This was why Elsie'd been living in his gut these past days. So he could save her.

But to save her he had to *get to where she was.*

Lord how much time do we spend waiting? Law's eyes paced the room until he finally got up and joined them. The place was tacky. It struck him how little money Lorenzo must make. Either he hadn't as yet got the word there was money in this sick-beaner business, or he *was* what Elsie thought he was. Out to help the people no one else gave a crap about. The people with no insurance.

This was crazy. She could be dying now. She could be dead. *Where the hell was everybody?*

Now he heard voices in the back room.

Okay. Soon. They'd be out soon.

There was a clock over the desk. Reminding him.

He walked over and pulled on the door to the file cabinet. Locked. Law headed toward the conference room door thinking, *screw it*. His hand was on the door just as Lorenzo himself thundered into the room. A striking young man followed him.

"Detective Lawrence this is Tony. He and Elsie are close friends. Tony has reluctantly agreed to speak with you for a few minutes. I've assured him that you will afford him every courtesy. He will call me if he needs me, understood?"

Law nodded his agreement. Tony pulled out a chair and seated himself across the table from the detective.

Lorenzo's tremendous frame bumped the surroundings as he made his way to the door he'd just come through; he carefully closed the door behind him and left them alone.

The cop and the young man sat and stared at one another.

Right away Law knew this was someone Elsie would trust and confide in. He could see that for some reason Tony was tense. *Why?* Law didn't have time to establish "rapport." And he had to put him at ease, fast.

"Ah, look. . .Tony. We don't have much time. I don't think Elsie has *any* time. I have to get right to it. Every minute counts. Are you reading me? I need you to trust me, and I don't know how to get you to do that in the few minutes we have. I have to find her. I need to find out where she is—*her address*—I have to have it *now*. I believe she's in danger. Grave danger."

And Tony said nary a word.

"I know you're close to her Tony. Maybe she's mentioned me to you. I handled the investigation on Lynn."

Nothing.

Law felt like shaking some sense into the young man but

he knew he had to keep his control. Because Tony held the key. The only key.

"I have a motorcycle. I used to take Elsie riding with me."

Tony appeared more interested in a spot on the table.

"Awhile back Pip stayed with me for a couple of months."

Law saw a light in Tony's eyes. "I won't lie to you, Tony. She may have done some things that could get her in trouble. I've been trying to find her for just that reason...."

No answer again.

"I guess Patty's a friend of yours too, right?"

Tony nodded.

"Then you know who Roger Dove is. Correct?"

Tony's face broke into a wide grin. "Was."

Progress.

"I know who he *was*."

"Yeah, right, *was*. Look, the man she's after this time is the man who killed Lynn. Probably he's the man who cut Skip's throat. Alvin Victory. Did she tell you about him, too?"

Tony nodded, yes.

"I have good reason to believe this man has murdered at least six women. So, help me. I don't want Elsie to be number seven."

Law saw the wheels churn. Was he getting through at all? Then he remembered the rumors of drugs. "Look, I've heard Elsie may have gotten into drugs. And right now I don't give a good goddamn. That's not why I'm here. I don't intend to pry into what either of you could be doing that is not legal with regard to the dope scene."

Law sat...his cards were on the table face up. Time to shut up, pray and, listen.

"Pip's a real Pip, isn't he?"

It was Law's turn to nod.

"She's been doing too much coke. I've been real worried about her. I was the one who first turned her on. I feel crummy about that. Worse even. I went through treatment. Been clean four months. It's way hard. I've been trying to get Els to stop. I can see how it's changing her. She's different. I don't know if that's why she's withdrawn from me, or if it's because of the other."

"The other?"

Tammy Wynette would have been proud. Tony sang the chorus line of R-E-V-E-N-G-E. Then he stopped and sat so still it was hard to tell if he was breathing.

"Let's let *me* be the judge of that, my little pricktease," Peter snarled.

This was more like it. Now he *wanted* the wine. Push it at him, he would balk. Pull it away, he wanted it.

But, in addition to his personality and character quirks Elsie knew she had something, someone guiding, helping her.

Could it be her angels Lynn and Skip?

"I have changed my mind, master. Unlock me. I want to feel you hard inside me everywhere." She called him master but her voice was in control.

"I said, sit down, bitch. You'll wait to get laid until I'm good and ready. Right now I want a drink. Now. *What. . .is in. . .the fucking. . .decanter?*"

Elsie forced a disappointed expression on her face. "It is called Atropha Belladonna, master. Surely a man of the world like yourself, a man of the world, has heard of it. In ancient times. . .well, it was used at wild orgies. It is a narcotic that can prolong orgasm. But a person must be very careful when they use it. If they were to drink too much they could die, or it would surely poison their system and make them quite ill. Do not sample the potion, master."

"Oh just shut the fuck up, slavebitch. Come here; rub my shoulders and hang those tits of *mine* in my face—so I can bite them off."

She came to him with the knowledge that she could not

avoid physical contact. It had to be done.

With his mouth full of her, a trickle of her blood dribbled from his cruel teeth and smeared his chin. He asked, "Have you used this *potion*, as you call it, with *other* men, then?"

She looked down—as if in shame.

"Have you?"

She stammered. "There could be no other men but you, my master, only you!" She wanted to cry out and rip at his face, but she would not.

He took his open hand, and slapped her as hard as he could across the face. His hand printed red welts on her face instantly like he'd turned on a television.

He would give this bitch a taste of what was to come.

"Don't ever lie to me, bitch-slave." He was beginning to like the idea of prolonging this so-called *game*. "Now. You move your pretty little ass; get that bag I brought with me. Get it now." he ordered. He wasn't worried that she'd check the bag and find the knife; this twit was too stupid, too caught up in her little contest of wills. And if she did, so what? He knew he was the stronger. It was time to play.

Play at fillet.

She returned quickly with the bag, and laid it by his feet.

He stood and barked orders like a drill sergeant. "Bend over the chair. Now. Do it....I will teach you not to lie to me, whore."

She did as he ordered—her bare buttocks high in the air.

Peter removed the riding crop from the bag. He heard her sharp intake of breath. This was the moment he'd waited for. He was about to show this prick-tease exactly who was in charge.

Elsie saw the riding crop as he took it out; she came close to fainting.

Had she misjudged her power over him? Was it going to end like this? She pictured Lynn's bloody body and Skip lying in the morgue with his throat cut ear to ear. Would she fail them this easily? As her mind raced on she heard his bitter words.

"You are nothing. You are a prick–tease–whore and you are my slave. You are *really* my slave. I can do whatever I wish to you; you have no will of your own ever again. Do you hear me? You'll never lie to me again *as long as you live*." His voice came out a cackle. Her obedience would not have to last long.

He struck her backside with vigor and heard the riding crop crack in time with his cackle.

Red spiders crept down her legs and spread over her ivory skin.

Elsie remembered how to scream out loud and did it just for him, knowing that it was what he needed to hear.

With each scream that spewed forth from her, Peter felt Mr. Big jump and pulsate. The rhythm of the riding crop, the sound of her screams, the colors that he, the artist, was creating, the virulence of the entire scene drove him to a frenzy, until he could not stop.

He'd wanted this to be merely a sample, the appetizer! But he couldn't stop himself!

He was out of control!

Chapter Forty

It was a Mexican standoff.
Law heard his stomach growl. Neither he nor Tony said a word.
Tony knew what Law needed and he knew why. Now it was up to him.
What is it with these abused kids, thought Law? *They learn to make themselves invisible. Do a pretty damn good job of it, too.* If he hadn't been in such a painful hurry to find Elsie it might be an interesting exercise this kid was putting him through.
Carol, Lorenzo's receptionist, came into the room and went directly to Tony. She leaned to whisper something in his ear then turned and left. She never looked in Law's direction.
A tear appeared on Tony's cheek from nowhere.
"Pip's at my place this week. Elsie said he missed me and she wanted me to have him for a few days." The tears rolled faster. "She said it would be like a sleep–over for us."
Next, his hand shot out and grabbed for the paper and pen. He slid them in front of him and began to write. "I've never been to this house. I wanted. . .I mean, I want to live with her. She wouldn't tell me the address until a few days ago. My car has been in the shop. I was just going to pick it up now. She always came here, to town, to see me." His dark eyes were wide and wet. "Don't let her die. Detective? Please, don't let her die. . .here's her address."
Law took the paper. "Thanks, buddy." He was on his way out the door when he realized Tony was still talking to him.

"We're close, you know? So, I knew something was up."
Yeah, thought Law. Something is sure up.

He shot his venom all over her backside.

Elsie felt each of the hot spurts. They were scalding. And every bit of liquid that hit her became a stain, a brand, *his brand*, on her flesh. And she wanted to scream with the pain that seared her very soul. She preferred the lash of his riding crop to his body fluid on her body.

She was branded.

"Mygodmygod." This was all he had imagined it would be and much more. But now he had to get himself back in control. It felt so fucking good to beat her; he could go on for an eternity.

But no, he had his plan. He did not want it to end like this. . .beating her to death this soon when she had so much more suffering to endure!

He would soon be inside her, on top of her, listening to her screams, feeling her buck under him with her inadequate attempts to buck him off.

Would she be as good to ride as her redheaded friend? Better. His money was on *better* than the redhead. He would wait for just the right moment to tell her that. Timing was everything. This was true art and he, the true artist!

Time for her real terror to begin.

"Do you understand what I'm telling you, Elsie? *This is not a game!* This is for real—for life. For *your* life. You *are* my slave. Now, be a good little whore; pour me a drink from that jug."

"I can not, my master, for it could harm you."

She was too freaking–fucking much!

Didn't she realize he knew who she was? That he knew she was Lynn's little roommate? Knew she'd hunted him down? Knew she wanted to kill him, planned to kill him? How stupid did she think he was?

It really didn't matter now. Peter knew he was the stronger, he was twice her size, he could take her in any fight. And besides, the blood running down her legs made him want her so much. He wanted this to go on. To last.

"Look at me, bitch." *Fine*, he thought, *I'll play*. I can't wait till the moment she discovers this is my game we're playing here, not hers. Not even close.

"Tell me the truth. Have you used this drink with other men?" He held the bloody crop, ready to be used in case she dared lie again.

She saw it in his hand, lowered her eyes. "Yes, master," her voice was a whisper.

"Elsie, this is not a game any longer, we're not at play. At least it's not the game you think we are playing."

Christ, didn't she get it yet?

Chapter Forty-One

A thirty-minute drive. Would she be alive in thirty minutes? The heinous memory of Lynn's torn and mutilated body tormented him. Was he going to see something similar again?

Law knew it would be a thirty-minute drive under the best of circumstances. As he drove through the city traffic, cursing himself that he did not heed his instincts sooner, he called in for backup. Tonetti and Mitchell had waited for his call.

Should have done it sooner, he thought.

He felt sure he would be too late, maybe only seconds, but late. For a man who trusted his instincts this wasn't a good way to feel.

As he drove he thought back to the night at Lyle's. Thinking of her as she was then made him feel closer now and he had to be close to her now.

And he was; her voice was in the car with him:

"They smile back. Always."

At the sound of her voice he grinned at himself in the rearview mirror.

How could he ever forget the look on her face? She knew she had discovered the cure for what ails the world.

"And, Law, when they smile—their faces are transformed into glowing friendly faces. The faces of kindred spirits. It's like the biker wave!"

If only one person could start the world in the right direction. That was what he'd thought then. It still hit him the same way. Where were all those glowing friendly faces she saw?

"Many of us are kindred spirits," her motor was revved,

the wheels rotating, her imagination on accelerate. *"We just don't know it. If we could have a universal sign of some kind, like when we wave, that says, 'Hey, I'm one of you— I'm on your side.' Wouldn't that be great? We could pick one another out—help one another without being afraid.*

People are afraid to help one another now days, aren't they?"

Were they? Law didn't want her words to be true. *Dear Lord*, he had to save her. The desire was a sharp stab.

Had Elsie been on his mind because he needed to solve this case or was it more? He knew it was more.

Please, God, let her be okay.

He heard her shocked voice say, *"You think he'll do it again?"*

"Now, *whore*, how many men?"

"Four. Four men, master."

He reached for the decanter, and since there were no wineglasses beside it, lifted it to his lips and drank. . .and drank. He set the decanter down and almost missed the table.

"It's time for you to know the truth, dearest dove."

On to the real game.

He appraised her bleeding body.

Why the stupid bitch was beaming!

"What is it you want to tell me, *Peter*, my love?"

"What?" He felt behind him for the bed. He had to sit a minute. Right here on the edge. He felt so relaxed, so light, *almost as if he could fly*. He rolled back onto the bed and stared at the ceiling; it swayed, and he was in a hammock under a big oak tree.

He wasn't about to give himself over to lying in a hammock on a sunny day. He tried to sit. "Slave whore. Remove my pants." His voice sounded strange to his own ears. It was deep. It vibrated. "Got a treat in store for you." What *was* wrong with his voice? It was slow. . .low. Looow and sl*ooo*w.

The room started to rock.

He *had* ordered her to remove his pants, hadn't he? His words were an echo, but he could see that she hadn't moved. With great effort he turned his head to see her fully.

She simply stood there, her face the picture of complete and utter happiness.

Why, she was in love with him! He must have misunderstood. She didn't know that redhead after all!

Look at her, *this woman adored him!*

He attempted to speak, but his throat was so dry. "Water...please...water, my dear little dove." His cracked lips tried to form the words...his throat felt burned, scalded.

Forget about removing his pants for now, he had to have water!

That first sip relaxed them. They felt light, as if they were floating, gliding really. Then their throats would begin to burn their pupils dilate. They were thirsty, very thirsty.

What was she holding in her hand? He blinked. Her jar of fucking Carmex? He needed water... *not lip–shit.* Was she crazy? She was speaking...he tried hard to focus, why was she talking instead of getting his water! Her mouth is moving.
. . .

Elsie had to yell for her words to penetrate his mind. "You remember how wet you made me, Peter baby? How I came, over and over again, because you were such a *stud*, such a pipe? Look here, Peter, it's my little jar of come. *Old Home yogurt*. Mmmmmgood."

She took a glob from the Carmex jar. "Let me put some on those dry lips of yours," she smeared —slapping the yogurt over his mouth and face.

He began to cry, to blubber, "I beg of you, El, help me."

Yogurt sucked up into his nostrils as he snorted it and gasped for breath.

Then, for no reason, he giggled. He'd become a small child crying, and blubbering, and giggling all at once.

Next came double vision.

Here's where they all mentioned my four huge tits. Funny how each one of them experienced much the same reaction to the juice. The double vision would make them giggle. The expected giddiness was taking over. Very soon their stomachs began to burn, erupt back up, and sour vomit would literally belch, a loud bark, from their mouths.

As they continued to belch and spit vomit all over themselves, I would introduce myself as Atrophos the goddess.

"My, my, look at those nice titties you've got for me...three...four? Why four?" Were there four glorious huge titties? Could there be *two* of her, he wondered?

He giggled uncontrollably.

What is she doing? She is unzipping my pants, pulling out my dick. Peter blinked. *I can't move my eyes.*

Where is Mr. Big? Oh. There. He is so small, defenseless, soft...would not be able to get the job done with that teenie weenie. Need to get the job done; this will never do.

"Momma...*Momma*...what is she doing to me?"

My God, my stomach. He tried to clutch himself but couldn't move his arms. And he couldn't think clearly. Where was that knife? He needed to find the knife, her knife...slit the filthy bitch...she *is* filthy too, Momma, just like you said. Only not *me*, Momma. I'm not the filthy one. She's a filthy bitch. Bring Mr. Clean. Bring your *bête noir*, Momma; we'll take care of this filthy bitch.

The room spun and Peter began to vomit. His mind was a

tilt–a–whirl and the motion made him so dizzy!

"Peter, look at me. Do you know who the goddess Atrophos is? The goddess who's duty it is to cut the thread of life?"

He tried to move his head, but could not; he swallowed his own puke and lay there gagging.

Why didn't Elsie help him? Because she is a filthy bitch. What nonsense was she babbling? Why talk about goddesses and tell him fairy tales when he needed her help!

Ahha, the subservient bitch is at last bending over him....

No! This was not the time to blow him!

What *could* she be thinking? Couldn't she see that he was sick, that he needed time to rest? He felt something...it was her soft lips...they began to close around him...then she stopped...ah, good.

At last, she is beginning to realize that I am too tired to have sex right now!

I am a sick man.

Tired and sick.

"PETER. LISTEN TO ME, YOU BASTARD. YOU HAVE TO HEAR THIS. THIS IS FOR LYNN—DO YOU HEAR ME? LYNN—THE REDHEAD. YES, THAT'S RIGHT, LYNN. AND FOR SKIP. LYNN AND SKIP. I AM HERE TO GIVE YOU A MESSAGE THAT COMES FROM THE SPIRITS OF ALL THE PEOPLE YOU HAVE DESTROYED."

What was she saying about the redhead? Then, she did know. She isn't in love with me after all?

"ARE YOU LISTENING? DO YOU HEAR ME, PETER?"

On the way to putting my mouth on them it was always the same. I'd see a glimmer of hope in their miserable eyes, but that flicker would pass as soon as I bit down. I hated putting my mouth on such slime. Lucky for me, the potion blurred their vision and I could first "blanket" them with a small square of plastic wrap. Even then, it was difficult to get that close to something so vile. But, I kept my goal in the front of my brain, kept it there till it grew and pushed all else out of sight. I wanted the complete shock of this experience to overwhelm their feeble hearts.

Although Peter's crime was the one that made me the avenger, it was no worse than the others.

Suddenly, Elsie realized that she didn't have to yell. He heard her every word. The "united–spirits" would have it no other way. She continued to tell him what fate held for him.

"The Spirits of the Victims have formed a union with me and when we use our power to unite we are stronger than steel. You, and others like you will be crushed under the heels of those you considered weak and powerless.

Now, I am going to bite your worthless limp dick off and then you will lay here and bleed to death.

UNDERSTAND WHAT I TELL YOU PETER FOR AT THIS MOMENT I AM MOTHER JUSTICE AND I ACT ON BEHALF OF EACH OF YOUR VICTIMS.

LIVE BY THE SWORD, DIE BY THE SWORD. YOU WILL SUFFER THE PAIN THAT YOU CAUSED OTHERS TO SUFFER. YOU WILL FEEL THEIR PAIN FOR YOU WILL BE THEIR PAIN.

YOU WILL SUFFER, YOU WILL BLEED. IT WILL TAKE HOURS FOR YOU TO DIE BUT THE PAIN WILL BE ENDLESS, THE PAIN WILL NEVER DIE. THIS IS THE ONLY SATISFACTION THAT I EVER GOT FROM YOU PETER. YOU ARE A WORTHLESS SLIME AND YOU WILL BURN IN HELL FOREVER LIKE THE VILE

DESPICABLE DEMON YOU ARE."

Peter's mind was plugged; the water rose fast.
Doesn't she realize that I control *her*? Ohgod...her mouth is going down on me again, not sucking softly the way I'd dreamed she would, the way I liked, but like a vise. Her teeth are razors!
Her eyes roll up to meet mine.
And in that one second Peter thought, *Oh no, I am powerless to stop her.*

She bit as hard as she could bite.
The most excruciating pain hit his body like a bolt of lightening; she clamped down hard. She lifted her head and looked again into his clouded eyes; he saw the red blood smeared on her lips.
What had she said about spirits? Her hair changed color, seesawing from one image to another, her face was like the surf, in and out, she was more than one person.

I knew it! There is an army here fighting me. Well, no wonder I can't seem to win. . . .
What about my shoes? *I must have my red spotted shoes!*

But, he knew that he wouldn't be taking these shoes to add to his collection in the trunk...it would be *his* blood in this ivory room.
Peter's lower lip quivered. He wanted to ride her, see her pain as he stabbed her with Mr. Big and stabbed her with the knife. Couldn't he have just this last one, this last time? If he could have just this one last thrill–kill, he would quit.
I will. I promise I will! She will be the last.
No. He would be the accent color. He watched her. And he knew.

She was walking out the door. *No*, he pleaded with his eyes, *help me, don't leave.*

Had she bitten it off? He could not tell...so much blood. He smelled the stench of his own vomit, and knew terror. His eyes blurred...have mercy on me. His lips tried in desperation to form words, but was there any sound coming out?

"Get me a doctor, you cunt!" I screamed inside myself. I thought I'd said it. She would not dare ignore me! Slowly, as if in a dream, I watched as she turned back to me...it seemed that it took her minutes to turn...I heard her voice from far away...at the end of a long tunnel. The words were so familiar, but her tone was different....

"Was it as good for you Sailor, as it was for me?"

Now Peter knew that nothing could save him. He is the one who is feeling the pain. At the moment of that realization his body jerked—convulsing.

The bucking started. Ah! I ride her after all!

But, no. He realizes that he can't hold his body still! He flails, unable to stop the bucking.

United spirits? Oh no! It cannot be!

This is wrong; this is not the way Peter had planned for it to end. Not the way it had been before. No, no, no. Not according to plan.

"Nooooooo!" At last his lips form a word. He hears a mournful bloodcurdling scream and suddenly he is up above himself. He looks down. He sees his face, sees his own mouth form an "o."

I realize the scream I hear is my own.

Chapter Forty–Two

What can cure can kill.
And so, for the twenty minutes or thereabouts left of their despairing suffering lives I would sit at the kitchen table with the razor in my hand and wait, not wanting to watch, but needing to dispose of the "thing" that they all possessed, the thing that helped to make them such evil men. I never did tell any of them that they'd be dead before I sliced it off.
It gave them something to think about while they waited to die.

Peter was not much different than the others had been. Listening to his screams of terror from her spot at the kitchen table Elsie pulled the bloody plastic wrap from her face and mouth, crumbled it and tossed it aside. She knew that she should feel a sense of victory, of relief. Even triumph.

She'd done what the law could not do. She had punished those who needed more that anything to be punished.

But then her methods would scar her soul forever.

The bloodied plastic wrap made her think of the way she'd been stained. Her body began to burn.

She felt an enormous void. Her heart was empty beyond description. She began to weep.

The time passed—enough time so that she knew he'd be dead. She pushed her weary body to her feet. It was time for her to do what she'd done with the others, slice off their weapon of choice and try to grind it in the garbage disposal.

Her journey into the bedroom seemed to take forever, but by the time she got there she'd begun to step lighter. This was the last one. She stood beside him and stared down at his body. It was motionless. Forevermore. His penis was shriveled, tiny, not at all like the other four.

Pathetic.

Peter had gulped down more of the Belladonna than the others. Her eyes found the decanter. Why, it was half gone! He'd had even more than she'd imagined.

Nasty greedy vicious monster.

In the end...you couldn't even get it up, Peter. It wouldn't be necessary to cut it off and put it in the disposal. Somehow, it seemed even more appropriate—to leave him like this: lying in her bed, *his penis as flaccid in death as his conscience had been flaccid in life.*

Why dismember what had been the only spirit the man had, when it was clearly gone.

You can't remove what isn't there.

She knelt by the side of the bed and whispered a prayer.

". . .we who are kindred spirits have begun our triumph over evil. As they live, so shall they die. Amen."

It was time to leave. Her bags were packed. Just in case she made it. She carried them to the living room and surveyed all that she would leave behind...none of it mattered to her now.

Only the piano. Lynn's piano.

With every movement she grew stronger. Her strength was returning with her attitude of love for all.

It was easy to allow evil to creep inside your soul.

Elsie had decided long ago that if evil could creep inside so could good. The spirits of the good could help her if they only would. And they had. Hadn't they? She was leaving the filth behind.

She took the newspaper she'd saved from two days ago, the one with Law's photo on the front page, and laid it on the piano. She wrote a hasty letter and put it in an envelope on top of the paper.

Law would find it.

Why did she know that after all this time he would come? She just knew. Elsie and Law were kindred spirits.

She looked at his picture. How could you look at this man and the one in the other room and call them both men? It seemed to her they were part of a different species. No. That thing in the bedroom—that was not a man.

She thought of her baby, Pip. She'd planned to leave Pipper to live with Tony. He and Pip would take care of one another. She would go away and never return. Tony would read the story in the paper or see it on the news, and he would know. He would know it had been her. And he would know why. *". . .we who are kindred spirits have begun our triumph over evil."*

She felt chilled and alone; she hugged her arms around her shivering body.

She looked at Lynn's piano and she stood straighter.

She picked up the phone and dialed.

Chapter Forty-Three

Law was close.
The turn off the main road had come and gone with no sight of a house. He'd been driving in circles for at least twenty minutes.
He thought he heard music. *Piano music.* Something dark and classical that he couldn't put his finger on. But then he couldn't be sure he was really hearing it.
The noise of the car and the wind and even the pounding of his heart were enough to make him doubt his own ears. Still, he turned and followed the "dirge–like" music that might not really be music.

Law saw the house and the cars all at once. There were two cars in her driveway. A black RX7 and a sparkling white one. The sun hit the clean chrome momentarily blinding him.
He felt his gut twist.
He got Mitchell on the radio. "Both cars are here." He told her.
They were ten or twelve minutes behind him.
"Well, I'm goin' in alone. Move it." Law said. He heard her yap—upset at him as he clicked off and got out of the car. This was it. The lodestone that yanked on his mind all throughout this case had led him here on this day. And because it'd been Elsie who'd been the pivot of his journey and then *spanked* him down in front of this house on this street, well then there must be some reason. And whatever it was would fire square when he went inside. Was he about to face a demon?

The piano still played. What began as a sublime and flowing melody of remembered words...kindred spirits...the biker wave...you think he'll do it again!...exploded and hit him with force of the cruel melodic notes: This could be bad, he thought, as he walked to the house, real bad.

The front door was unlocked. Bad sign. Revolver drawn he proceeded inside. Except for the sound of his breath the house was still. Like no one was home. No one alive.

First thing he noticed was the piano. Lynn's piano. He went to it and saw that the cover was up and the bench pulled out. There was a piece of sheet music open. He looked, curious. *"Requiem" by Wolfgang Amadeus Mozart.*

Had someone been playing?

The newspaper was there. He was a blankin' celebrity. The envelope with his name on it could be an omen, a sign of good to come. He hoped she wrote the letter recently. Then maybe she is alive. He slid it into his pocket. Not the time or place to read. Not if you value your life.

The brown Old Style beer bottle sat half empty on the glass table. Seeing the bottle just sit there both heartened him and filled him with fury. He remembered the last time he'd found that same brand of beer bottle at a crime scene. Was this a crime scene?

He walked—arms and gun extended toward what turned out to be the kitchen. The trail of blood drops on the ivory carpet leapt to fill his field of vision like a war cry. His throat rasped—fluids gone, and the beat of his heart screamed over the sound of the dirge—one that he knew by now played only inside his head—and that grew louder with each step. Ivory—the color of the carpet was the same color of her pale skin. Had she cut off his dick in here?

The chair by the kitchen table was smeared with blood just as was the floor under it. Someone had sat at the table and bled. Had she cut off his dick in *here*? This was one hell of a twister he was riding. Whose blood? Who? Which of them? His heartbeat filled his ears.

He checked for a garbage disposal and she had one.

He looked inside the drain; it was clean. What did that mean? Not much. Not without a body. Why jump to conclusions? She could still be okay. She could.

He thought of Alice in Wonderland and the yellow brick road as he followed the red spots on the carpet to the bedroom. And there it was.

The body lay face up on the large bed.

Law let his arms fall to his sides; one finger was still on the trigger.

He stood by the bedside and took inventory.

So. Elsie'd been right years ago. Peter Bryan had been a nice looking man. He was tall. And, yeah, he was also white.

Right at the moment he looked damn foolish.

Peter was fully dressed; he wore brand spanking new out–of–the–box white tennis shoes. Law sniffed.

Vomit covered the dead man's face and neck. He reeked of puke and shit. Messed his drawers.

Only his penis was exposed. It was a tiny, shriveled, weak appendage.

The word flaccid came to mind.

Law mind tripped back to another time. The day he'd stood very much like this and looked at Lynn's tortured tormented body. That day he'd thought that the demon would never be brought down. What lay before him now would make the devils laugh. Could this be the same penis that had done so much harm? Did not seem possible. It looked out of place for such an iron man. There was a small amount of blood on it.

You could see deep teeth marks. The blood was not yet dry. Law hadn't missed Elsie by much. But he was sure that she was gone.

Again he considered the blood in the kitchen. It couldn't have been from the bite. . .then he saw the tangled snake of the riding crop at his feet...the tail of it was covered with blood.

Elsie's blood! He was sure of that, too.

He picked up the paper sack to look inside. Wrapped in a paper towel he found a knife. Would the knife have Peter's prints on it? Law would bet on it.

Did that mean self-defense for Elsie? If she made it alive.

He looked again at the body that lay before him. You bastard. You blanking, *fucking* ball-less bastard.

Why didn't she cut off his dick? He looked again at that flaccid midget prick and he knew exactly why. There was not a shred of chance that this figure had any of his once-evil spirit left. Nothing remained.

This vessel of *rakshasa* was empty.

Law heard the police sirens and sighed, eager to leave this place and go home. He had a lot of thinking to do. He started out and noticed the bottle. It was a fancy glass bottle on the credenza; it had the stopper off and a note beside it:

Do not drink!

This is the herb Atropha Belladonna. It can be narcotic and even, as you see, fatal—if taken in sufficient quantity. I do not wish to destroy your evidence, but I would not want to be responsible for an accident.

Elsie Sanders.

She even signed her name. He noticed again that the bottle was half empty. Must be the reason this one wasn't tied to the bed. He partook of so much of the juice of death all on his own, that in the end anyway, she, Bite-Woman, was completely in control.

No need to tie a man whose own hate ties him.

It was a perfect sting.

Chapter Forty–Four

Law poured himself a double Jack and sat in his most comfortable chair. He felt unsettled. Let down. Confused by his feelings.

He'd been damn anxious to see her. No surprise there. But what about her vanishing and how he felt about that.

He felt relieved.

Not okay of him. Was it?

How did she get away without her car? They'd probably find her. But he hoped not.

How the blank could he feel this way? It was *his* blanking case. He was a cop. Cops want to catch criminals. There was no doubt she was a criminal, was there? Only the degree was in doubt.

Then there was the public outcry—he could imagine it— if he *did* apprehend this dangerous woman.

It made his head hurt to think about this shit. And there *was* also his heart to consider. He opened the envelope that had been left for him at the crime scene and began to read:

My Dear Law,

I have a strong feeling that you are on your way. I've learned to trust my feelings just as I know you trust yours, so if it's true, I am very grateful for whatever it is that is driving you to find me.

I know it is more than simply wanting to solve a case or apprehend a criminal. When I saw in the paper that the bite–it case had been assigned to you, I knew you'd figure it out.

The law would find me guilty, right? It's important to me that you understand. You're the Law I care about.

I DID NOT KILL ANY OF THEM. You do understand that, don't you? It's important to me that you do. Well, not with my own hand. I did provide the means for them to die. Belladonna grows in my garden and I admit to you, I grew it only for the purpose that it was used.

To destroy human life? No. That's wrong.

To destroy life that was not human.

I begged them not to drink it, Law. I promise you. I begged every one of them not to drink it. I told them exactly what it was and what might happen if they had too much of the Belladonna juice. Of course, I knew what each of them would do. Of that I am guilty.

Of understanding, of knowing INhuman nature, I plead guilty.

There is no justice, Law.

No justice for the weaker ones, the softer ones. I just could not live with that. I used a great deal of drugs to numb my mind and my soul, but that's behind me now; for whatever happens, I am free. I know that it was wrong of me to use those drugs and I'll never touch them again. That, to me, is the worst of my sins and for that I am heartily sorry.

In the beginning, in fact all along this journey, I was sure that I wanted to die too, but now that it's over I feel so free. I want to live! I will not be needing anything to numb my mind or soul, because I feel satisfied. Content. For the first time in a long time, I feel contentment.

I want you to know that I know you tried to help me. You did everything you could do to help me survive because you knew that within the law there was absolutely nothing more to be done.

I love you Law. Another time I could have fallen in love with you, but just as you were busy with your work,

I was busy with my plan. Even when I did not consciously know it yet, I was moving toward my goal.
I wish things could have been different—maybe some day.
This last cliché I say to make you laugh because you really take life too seriously.
A good man is hard to find.
*A **hard** man is not that damn important.*

Love,
Bite–Woman

P.S. When you ride, smile at all those unhappy, snarly looking faces—and when they smile back at you, think of Elsie

The letter slipped out of his hand and fell into his lap and Law stared—he thought back over this long day.
"Requiem" by Wolfgang Amadeus Mozart.
Had someone played the piano? Elsie was gone.
Besides, Elsie couldn't play the piano.

Epilogue

I hope they think I've left the country.
I gave my Pip a hug and kissed him, too, as the wind blew wild through my hair. I like this little red VW bug convertible. How fortuitous that Tony decided to buy it last week. When I helped him pick it out, I'd no idea how important it would become to me, to us!

At that last moment today, as I stood with my arms around myself, I had a change of heart and mind. I'd felt so alone. Why not have Tony and Pip with me—at least for a while?

I watched Tony as he drove. He's as happy as I've ever seen him. Here he is with his two favorite "beings," myself and Pip, driving down the highway of life without a care in the world.

Maybe other women, women with "spirit," have done what I did, do you think? I wondered.

Or, maybe now, they will.

Take a nightmare, conquer it, and make it yours!

As we drove down the road we sang a merry song:
"Our R-E-V-E-N-G-E became final today!" The car sped along. The sun shone on our faces and we were bathed in the scent of the outdoors. I knew I could do anything and do it without drugs. I was happy and free. A fleeting thought hit me and I turned to yell over the wind at Tony.

"I wonder if the good Dr. Jack is still doing the Northfield high school girls' physicals?"